I0819873

THE PARATIME CHRONICLES
VOLUME I

PARATIME PARASITES

EDITED BY

JOHN F. CARR

Pequod Press

THE PARATIME CHRONICLES, Volume I
Paratime Parasites
A Pequod Press Anthology

First Edition

Printed in the United States of America
First Printing 2018

V 10 9 8 7 6 5 4 3 2 1

ISBN: 978-0-937912-74-4

Pequod Press
P.O. Box 80
Boalsburg, PA 16827
www.PequodPress.com

Paratime Books by H. Beam Piper

Paratime
Lord Kalvan of Otherwhen
The Complete Paratime

Paratime Books by John F. Carr

Time Crime (with H. Beam Piper)
Paratime Trouble
The Paratime Police Chronicles, Vol. I (with H. Beam Piper)

Lord Kalvan Novels by John F. Carr

Great Kings' War (with Roland Green)
Kalvan Kingmaker
The Hos-Blethan Affair (with Wolfgang Diehr)
Siege of Tarr-Hostigos
The Fireseed Wars
Gunpowder God
Down Styphon!

ACKNOWLEDGEMENTS

Special thanks go to Victoria Alexander for all her help going over the early drafts and her expertise as editor. And to the Copyediting Team: Dwight Decker, Larry Hopkins and Victoria Alexander.

To the Paratime Study Group, Jim Landau, Jevon Kasich and Eric Fisher.

A tip of the hat, to Sean Bodley, who came up with the cover design and executed it so well.

Finally, to H. Beam Piper who inspired this book!

TABLE OF CONTENTS

On Paratime:

A Beginner's Guide to the Mechanics of Crosstemporal travel

Dr. Regnol Krath, Dhergabar University

What exactly is Paratime, and what is a Paratime line? Paratime consists of the sum of all possible quantum energy states of the universe at a given moment over the entirety of time. A good way to visualize it would be as a river, a *very* wide, and *very* long river. The width of this river is defined by all the possible quantum energy states the universe can assume and its length by time. This, however, is not a placid, harmonious river. Whilc all quantum states are possible, not all are equal, or rather some are more equal than others.

Moving from one preferred state to another as time progresses moment by moment, flowing along the paths of least and lesser resistance there are currents within the stream of Paratime. These currents are what we call time-lines (in theory *every* path regardless of its probability could be said to constitute a time-line, but as they say: "In theory there is no difference between theory and practice, in practice there is." (More on that later). They are the signal to the random paths noise, characterized by their "intensity" and their "shift." Intensity refers to the strength of time-lines Paratime signature and is a measure for both its mean probability as well as an indicator of its potential for splitting off "viable" subcurrents/time-lines (i.e. a "weak" time-line with a borderline level signature would be unable to create any sub-time-lines, as these inevitably even weaker progeny would be swallowed up by the "background radiation" so to speak). By the same token a formerly strong time-line that suddenly starts to follow along a consistently low probability path eventually "peters out," when its signal weakens enough to fall below your G-H field generator's sensitivity threshold).

A time-line's shift is the dimensionless parameter used to describe its "coordinates." As there are no absolute positions within Paratime all time-lines' locations are relative and determined in relation, their shift, to a baseline (HTL) whose Ghaldron Hesthor field frequency is defined as 0.d KTL =3D 1012 * D F/ Fo =3D 1012 * (FKTL - FHTL) / Fo3D 1012 * (- 64,392 - 0) Ghd / 270 TGhd =3D - 0,23488 pptd KTL =3D Shift for the Kalvan time-line.

FKTL =3D Resonanz frequency for the Kalvan time-line

FHTL =3D Resonanz frequency for the HTL

F0 =3D Operating frequency of the G-H field generator

ppt =3D parts per trillion (as D F is usually very small in comparison to F0 the factor 1012 was introduced, and it has become common practice to note in ppt) Ghd =3D Ghaldron's. Unit used to measure the frequency of a Ghaldron Hesthor field (TGhd=3D 1012 Ghd)

+/- =3D a positive / negative d value signifies, whether a particular time-line lies "upfield" or "downfield" in relation to the HTL baseline

(+ =3D upfield, - 3D downfield)

There are three distinct classes of currents within the Paratime stream. All three differ both in scale, range and type of the changes between various members of a class, as well as in the magnitude and nature of the forces that are responsible for their respective formation.

1.) Meta-currents:

Immensely strong and "broad" meta-currents are driven and shaped by the basic forces of the universe itself. Divergent Meta-currents usually represent either significant differences in the laws of nature, or other discrepancies on a cosmic scale. The set of time-lines contained within a particular Meta-current all share the same universal ground rules (i.e., gravity, entropy, inertia...). Unless their name happens to be god the actions of sentients have no measurable influence on the development/creation of Meta-currents (i.e. while an ant can move a few handfuls of sand grain by grain and pile them up into a small hill, it can't carry the Sahara off to Outer Mongolia in order to build the Texas version of a sandcastle with it there). Each Meta-current has its own distinctive base potential, a "meta shift" so to speak. The vast differential in energy potentials between these makes traveling from a time-line in one Meta-current to a time-line belonging to another Meta-current not outright theoretically impossible, at the very least technologically "extremely challenging" as well as hideously expensive (and that's putting it mildly). It would be the Paratime equivalent of crossing the gulf between two galaxies.

2.) Currents:

The "normal" time-lines are all part of a particular meta-current, which not only sets its framework regarding the laws of nature and how they apply, but also their base energy potential for them (there may exist some "exotics"—singular time-lines so weird they are their own Meta-current, but those would be way out there flukes, along the line of a "single monkey with a typewriter producing the complete works of Shakespeare on his first try"—variety). They are generated and in their development governed by impersonal forces of a local scale (geologic, climatic, solar mechanics) on the one hand, and the actions of sentients on the other.

Of the two, the actions of sentients are *much* more effective at producing alternative time-lines. The reason for this is that, though usually weaker by several orders of magnitude in terms of raw, overall power, the actions of sentients poses a quality of "purposefulness." By concentrating the energy available on *selectively* boosting the probability of specific possible futures (as opposed to the diffuse, scattershot approach of the forces of nature) this purposefulness acts as a focus, a force multiplier like Archimedes' lever if you will, with which to lift the earth (or rather the time-line in this case) off its hinges.

3.) Micro-currents:

In many respects micro-currents are unto "normal" currents as "normal" currents are unto Meta-currents. It's true, that small actions can have large consequences, but let's face it, with every moment there are a lot of things going on where different outcomes would have little to no impact on a measurable scale. If the electron of a particular hydrogen atom in the Magellan Cloud flips its spin one way instead of the other at a certain moment in 1942 on a time-line of the Europo-American subsector it will not change the eventual outcome of their second global war. However, whether we macroscopic beings are able to appreciate it or not does not matter, our physiological and technological limitations are irrelevant to the laws of Paratime physics. *Any* change in the quantum state which does not reduce the overall probability to zero *will* result in a time-line.

If you just thought "Hold on there, that can't be right, or there would be a lot, I mean a LOT more time-lines than we know of. And for that matter, if what you say were true wouldn't that mean every time some grubby old prole in Old Town Dhergabar sneezes a gazillion alternate home time-lines should suddenly pop into existence?" I congratulate you, Citizen. You are obviously one of the 2.1% of the students who did *not* sleep through their mandatory introduction lecture on the basics of Paratime at Dhergabar University. There are many more time-lines (including alternate home time-lines) out there than we know of. The reason why they are unknown and will continue to stay that way in the foreseeable future is technological in nature. I will explain.

Every time-line has a *very* large number of these micro-currents attached to it like lampreys to a shark. Due to the miniscule nature of the changes in question (usually they come into existence because of variations on a very small, even subatomic or quantum scale like in the previously given example, where the two alternate universes only differed in the spin orientation of a single electron) the resulting time-lines are extremely close to each other both in terms of probability and quantum state/shift. So close in fact, that no one has yet been able to successfully isolate one from another. Like with the crossing from one meta-current to another it is theoretically possible to reach the various micro-currents of a given time-line. In practice, however, there are enormous technological hurdles to be overcome first, before a Ghaldron-Hesthor generator could be built whose field can be tuned in small enough increments to achieve the resolution necessary for separating the time-line's signal into its underlying hyper-structure. As long as no one constructs such a hyper-conveyer (and I for one am not holding my breath waiting for that to happen) these myriad of time-lines will remain "out of phase" and therefore might as well for practical purposes not exist at all.

<end of entry>

Thank you for choosing a Volthan Technologies Inc. Info booth, Citizen.

Volthan Technologies, serving your information needs since 3452 P.E.

Have a nice day.

PARATIME

I love "Paratime." It was the first time I encountered a book that concentrated on a race that moved between alternate Earths as opposed to books that were set only on one. I'm not sure if it's just me, but all of the 'classic' science fiction future worlds imagined in the 1940's and 1950's have always have come across as slightly creepy to me. The robots rolling about serving people's whims, the rocket ships, and general decadence that they seemed to have. That the Home Time Line culture is based on theft and slavery makes them hard to like. One sort of wants to see bad things happen to them.

Jason Kastich
Member of the Paratime Study Team

H. Beam Piper showed an early interest in precognition and time travel. Piper's first mention of time travel appears in the 1947-1948 issue of a small writers' publication, the *Amateur Spectator*, the official organ of the Spectator Club. In a piece titled, "Precognition and a Theory of Time," Piper writes about his ideas on time and General Semantics. Many of Piper's ideas were derived from J. W. Dunne's essay, "An Experiment with Time." A year later his first Paratime Police story, "Police Operation," appeared in the July, 1948, issue of *Astounding Science Fiction*.

Alternate history stories are an integral part of science fiction; the story, "Sideways in Time," by Murray Leinster was first published in the June 1934 issue of *Astounding Science Fiction*. Paratime was H. Beam Piper's own unique take on the time travel genre, postulating the existence of an entire civilization that could travel through alternate time-lines. Instead of going into the future or the past, Piper created a sideways in time traveling race, who used literally millions of selected time-lines, or alternate worlds, as resource supply bases for their Home Time Line.

While alternate world time travel is not wholly Piper's invention, he did put his own unique spin on parallel worlds with his Paratime Police. Piper's Paratime stories have influenced most modern time travel and alternate history science fiction works, including Poul Anderson's Time Traders books, Andre Norton's Time series, Keith Laumer's Imperium, as well as Harry Turtledove's Crosstime series which is dedicated to Piper.

In his Paratime series, H. Beam Piper postulated an almost infinite number of parallel earthly worlds or time-lines, where in each sector, subsector and belt of time-lines events occurred differently. Unknown to the inhabitants, some of these outtime time-lines are exploited by the parasitic inhabitants of the Home Time Line who have invented a way to travel from one time-line to another. The Paratimers use that secret technology to steal raw materials, finished goods, rare artworks, cultural artifacts and technological devices which their own exhausted and resource depleted earth can no longer provide. The Home Time Line culture also appears to be in an ideational, scientific and cultural stasis, and, as a result (although they would never admit it), they hijack not only physical objects but cultural ideas and scientific and technological innovations from the outtime worlds they prey upon.

Most First Level inhabitants view the outtime worlds they rob as objects for their own enrichment, cultures not worthy of consideration. They display no guilt about their depredations; in general they look upon the natives of the outtime worlds as barbarians, regardless of what cultural or scientific heights these cultures have reached. In fact, a few Second Level time-lines have achieved interstellar spaceflight, but they are still considered backward by the Home time-liners. The Home Time Line society has created the Paratime Police to keep the First Level time-line travelers in check and—most importantly—to protect the secret of Paratime travel.

Piper's Paratime series features the Paratime Police who are responsible for policing the almost infinite number of time-lines as well as ensuring that the secret of Paratime Transposition is not discovered by the inhabitants of any other time-line. The Paratime stories feature the adventures of the Paratime Police's top troubleshooter Verkan Vall and his wife, Dalla, who has a penchant for attracting trouble.

The Paratime series as written by H. Beam Piper consists of four stories: "Police Operation," "Last Enemy," "Temple Trouble," "Time Crime," and one novel, *Lord Kalvan of Otherwhen*, all of which involve Verkan Vall and the Paratime Police. There is internal evidence that both "He Walked Around the Horses" and "Genesis" could fall under the Paratime umbrella, although neither story involves the Paratime Police.

The idea of parallel worlds is an old one that appears in mythology and folk tales with roots in the accounts of mythical homes of the gods, fairy tales and astral planes. Mark Twain's *A Connecticut Yankee in King Arthur's Court* was one of the first books to bring the theme of alternate worlds to popular attention. The genre was further popularized for American audiences through L. Frank Baum's children's book, *The Wizard of Oz*, where Dorothy travels to an alternate "dream" world. This groundbreaking children's novel was so popular it spawned not only a successful movie, but also an entire series which continued long after Baum's death in 1919. Edgar Rice Burroughs, A. Merritt and Henry Kuttner were among the first writers to bring this theme into science fiction.

The usual treatment of the parallel worlds theme has been for the author to create a series of alternate worlds as part of a continuum of increasing historical variation from a template world, usually a present time, or future, version of our own earth. This method is primarily directed at speculations of the "What if" variety, such as in what if the Confederacy had won the

Civil War, or the Nazis had won World War II? The "What If" question has long been popular among professional and amateur historians; there are dozens of websites on the Internet dedicated to Alternate Worlds, many of which offer elaborate alternative histories for readers to enjoy.

Most of these "alternates" are based on a particular historical branch, that is, history taking a different path at some critical juncture of Western Civilization—usually a war or pivotal battle, such as Carthage winning the Punic Wars with Rome, or Napoleon defeating Wellington and so forth. The further in the past these branches occur, the more bizarre and unusual the alternative world appears to the travelers from the template world, i.e., our own world.

British SF author Kenneth Bulmer put a new spin on Paratime by creating alternate world portals or gates which have become standard fare for many alternate world yarns. His Keys to the Dimension series ran to seven novels: *The Key to Irunium*, *The Key To Venudine*, *The Wizards of Senchuria*, *The Ships of Durostorum*, *The Hunters of Jugandai*, *The Chariots of Ra* and *The Diamond Contessa*. Bulmer's first Keys to the Dimension novel didn't appear until 1967 and was heavily influenced by Piper.

Keith Laumer came up with his own sideways time travel slant in the Imperium. This series is a continuum of parallel worlds policed by the Imperium, a government based in an alternate Stockholm. *The Worlds of the Imperium* was published in 1962 and was undoubtedly influenced by Piper's Paratime. The Imperium and Paratime technologies describe an angled path across the lines because they move forward at a normal time rate while moving sideways. The Imperium is formed in an alternate history where the American Revolution did not occur, and the British Empire and Germany merged into a unified empire in 1900. The protagonist, an American diplomat, Bayard, is kidnapped by the Imperium because in a third parallel Earth he is waging war against his abductors. Further adventures follow after Bayard decides to remain in the service of the Imperium.

The Imperium has a different view of the time-lines, seeing them as a tangle rather than an infinite number of straight, parallel lines. The Imperium's technology has been developed on several time-lines but in many cases has caused damage and destruction to multiple time-lines, including the massive area called the Blight, consisting of lines where all life except on the Imperium line had been destroyed or massively mutated, yet two other untouched lines exist, one is Bayard's home line; the other one is the time-line where Bayard's enemies tried to strand him. There are also at least two other vastly divergent lines where the species that became sapient are not *Homo sapiens* and have developed time-line traveling technology similar to the Imperium, with one having developed a system that's a form-fitting suit.

Other Piper-influenced examples of sideways time travel include Richard Meredith's Time-liner Trilogy books, Robert Adam's Castaways in Time series, Leo Frankowski's Cross-Time Engineer series, Michael McCollum's A Greater Infinity and Harry Turtledove's Crosstime Traffic series, of which the first title is *Gunpowder Empire*, a nod to Piper's *Lord Kalvan of Otherwhen.*

Paratime has even reached other types of media such as the *Sliders* television show which was the most successful version. The television shows *Fringe, Spellbinder,* and *Parallax* were TV series that used this device quite successfully.

As most writers do, Piper freely used autobiographical incidents in his work. In *Murder in the Gunroom*, Piper gives us his view of science-fiction writing, when he has one of his characters—a science fiction writer—give the following answer as to what he's writing:

"Science fiction. I do a lot of stories for the pulps... Space Trails, *and* Other Worlds *and* Wonder Stories*: mags like that. Most of it's standardized formula-stuff; what's known in the trade as space-operas. My best stuff goes to* Astonishing [a barely disguised Astounding—jfc]. *Parenthetically, you mustn't judge any of these magazines by their names. It seems to be a convention to use hyperbolic names for science fiction magazine; a heritage from an earlier and ruder day. What I do for* Astonishing *is really hard work, and I enjoy it. I'm working now on one of them, based on J.W. Dunne's time-theories, if you know what they are."*

J. W. Dunne's essay, "An Experiment with Time," provided the basis for many of Piper's ideas concerning Paratime, although he did drop most of the pseudo-scientific trappings after his first Paratime Police story, "Police Operation." After noticing a strange mixture of past and future events in his dreams, J. W. Dunne—an Irish aeronautical engineer—began to systematically study them. He noted that there was a fifty-fifty split between the future and the past. This precognitive element of dreams led Dunne to speculate that there must exist a second-level "supertime" that measures the rate at which time passes. This of course implies the existence of other "supertimes," which led him to the idea of serial time—an infinite series of different "times." Dunne went on to create the "supermind" to explain how we could survive in an infinite number of "times."

In his first Paratime story, "Police Operation," Piper took Dunne's "supermind" and renamed it the extraphysical ego component. The sideways time device the Paratimers developed was based on the Ghaldron-Hesthor Transposition Field, which was a three-way collaboration between Ghaldron (who was working to develop a spacewarp drive), Hesthor (who was working on the theoretical basis for linear time travel) and Rhogom (who was studying precognition). Rhogom's Doctrine—which is based on Dunne's time theories—states "We exist perpetually in all moments within our lifespan; our extraphysical ego component (EPC) passes from the ego existing at one moment to the ego existing at the next. During unconsciousness, the EPC is 'time-free': it may detach, and connect at some other moment, with the ego existing at that time-point. That's how we pre-cog. We take an auto hypno and recover memories brought back from the future moment and are buried in the subconscious mind."

Using Dunne's time theories, Piper explains the concept of time-lines in this manner: "All time-lines are totally present, in perpetual co-existence. The EPC passes from one moment, on one time-line, to the next moment on the next time-line, so that the true passage of the EPC from moment to moment is a two-dimensional diagonal.... Now, what we do, in Paratime transposition, is to build up the hyper-temporal field to include the time-line we want to reach, and then shift over to it. Same point in the plenum; same point in primary time—plus primary time elapsed during mechanical and electronic lag in the relays—but a line of secondary time."

In "Police Operation," the first Paratime story, Piper postulates a near infinity of First Level Time-Lines with a Verkan Vall variant in each one; this is glossed over in later stories, probably because of the paradoxes it creates. Most importantly, if there is more than one First Level origin civilization there is no Paratime Secret. This also leaves us with an infinite number of Verkan Valls (our main protagonist); therefore, why should readers care if any single one of them dies since there's always another replacement Verkan on another nearby First Level time-line? This of course kills reader suspense as well as any identification with the main character, who is in effect—immortal.

Like Asimov with his Foundation series and Heinlein with his future history, Piper found himself with some elements in his Paratime creation that he had to either modify or eliminate. Therefore, Piper jettisons all this talk of the EPC and detached ego after his first Paratime Police yarn and it never appears again in any of the newer Paratime stories.

H. Beam Piper's origin point for Paratime is the Home Time Line (often referred to as First Level), which contains an advanced civilization based on the successful Martian colonization of Earth between 75,000 to 100,000 years ago. Home Time Line is not the most civilized time-line, but the only time-line that has uncovered the secret of Paratime transposition. The Home Time Line Paratimers have a very bad track record, starting with their home world, Mars. After having exhausted Mars of natural resources, the Martians (*homo-sapiens* or Cro-Magnon Man) launched five rickety ships to Earth whose arrival, or not, created the base levels of Paratime probability. Over the ensuing millennia the newcomers depleted the resources of Earth and the rest of the solar system as they had back on Mars.

Paratime as a whole includes parallel universes on the order of 10 to the 100,000 power lines of probability. This is an enormous number of time-lines. Piper divided the Paratime alternate worlds into levels, sectors, subsectors, belts and individual time-lines. There are five primary levels of Paratime, all of which are based on the different outcomes of the Martians' attempt to colonize earth (or Terra) over 75,000 to 100,000 years ago. Areas on different levels that show common cultural origins and characteristics are called sectors. Sectors are then somewhat arbitrarily divided into subsectors, which are further broken into belts—areas within subsectors that share common conditions resulting from a recent divarication, or break from the parent subsector. The individual worlds are called a time-line.

As Piper puts it: "Few, on First Level [the primary time-line], realized just how many of these uncountable time-lines had never seen man's imprint. Even after twelve thousand years of parasitism upon other Second, Third, and Fourth level time-lines. First Level Para-topographers had described less than one tenth of one percent of all the 'known' time-lines. In actuality it was an impossible job; few Paratime theorists still believed they would ever completely map this near infinity of diverging time-lines."

***

Piper's Paratimers travel inside mesh-covered conveyers, dome-shaped inter-dimensional time buses or trucks, which pass through alternate time-lines like frames in a film projector. These paratemporal conveyers are primarily used by the Home Time Line to loot precious metals, artifacts, new inventions, technology, cultural treasures, resources and *objects d' art* from a near infinity of alternate worlds. The Home time-liners are an admitted race of parasites, preying off other time-lines by stealing their goods and resources. It's the Paratime Police's job to make sure things don't get out of hand and the Paratime Secret is kept inviolate.

The transpositional conveyers—which are based on the Home Time Line (First Level)—shift through the levels, sectors, subsectors, belts and time-lines via the Ghaldron-Hesthor field generator. As Piper explains, "the Ghaldron-Hesthor field-generator is like every other mechanism; it can operate only in the area of primary time in which it exists. It can transpose to any other time-line, and carry with it anything inside its field, but it can't go outside its own temporal area of existence, any more than a bullet from that rifle can hit the target a week before it's fired. Anything inside the field is supposed to be unaffected by anything outside. Supposed to be is the way to put it; it doesn't always work. Once in a while, something pretty nasty gets picked up in transit."

Travel between time-lines is measured in parayears, each one consisting of ten thousand time-lines. The transposition from one time-line to another takes half an hour, which is the time required to build up and collapse the transpositional field. It is therefore impossible to make transtemporal jumps of less than ten parayears, or a hundred thousand time-lines. This creates some real difficulties for the Paratime Police in "Time Crime," when the Paratime cops have to chase down the Wizard Traders, a large gang of First Level time slavers, who have bases on several levels and sectors—many on nearby time-lines.

The transposition field is impenetrable except when two Paratime conveyers, going in opposite *directions*, interpenetrate. When this occurs—far more often than the Paratime Commission likes due to the high volume of conveyers traveling between time-lines—the field weakens and material objects and even lifeforms can enter the field. *Lord Kalvan of Otherwhen* is the story of what happens when a Pennsylvania State Police Officer is picked up by a cross-time conveyer and dropped off on a primitive time-line, on Aryan-Transpacific, Styphon's House Subsector.

FIRST LEVEL

After having depleted Mars of resources and faced with a dying world, losing water and oxygen, the Martians are forced to send jury-rigged spaceships to Earth in a desperate attempt at survival. On the First Level the Martian colony was a complete success and it begins with the remnants of Martian society and technology. First Level is four standard deviations left of mean and covers just one half of one percent of all lines of probability. On First Level the new colony was a complete success, so much so that the Martian colonists began to repeat the same mistakes they'd done on Mars, which had rendered that planet devoid of life.

As Verkan Vall puts it: "Our ancestors had pretty well exhausted the resources of this planet [Earth]. We had a world population of half a billion, and it was all they could do to stay alive. After we began Paratime transportation, our population climbed to ten billion, and there it stayed for the last eight thousand years.... We've tapped the resources of those other worlds on other time-lines, a little here, a little there, and not enough to really hurt anybody. We've left our mark in a few places—the Dakota Badlands, and the Gobi, on the Fourth Level, for instance...."

First Level civilization is the ultimate parasite culture, drawing secretly on the resources and populations of billions of other time-lines. It's no wonder that the Paratime Secret is sacrosanct and guarded so rigidly by the Paratime Police, who have only one inflexible law regarding outtime activities: "The secret of Paratime transposition must be kept inviolate, and any activity tending to endanger it is prohibited."

First Level society sees itself as a rational culture, based on the fundamental laws and rules of science. They have, in Piper's words, "forgotten all the taboos and terminologies of naturalistic religion and sex inhibition." The government is loosely patterned on the British parliamentary system, but without the monarchy. They have an Executive Council which passes laws and is powerful enough to censure the Paratime Police. They also have an hereditary nobility which commands respect, much like the British monarchy, but Piper never makes it clear whether or not they have any governing function.

One of the most powerful institutions on Home Time Line is the Bureau of Psychological Hygiene. The Bureaus' job is to ensure social and mental stability among the Home Time Line population. "We define people as criminals when they suffer from psychological aberrations of an antisocial character, usually paranoid—excessive egoism, disregard for the rights of others, inability to recognize the social necessity for mutual cooperation and confidence. On Home Time Line, we have universal psychological testing, for the purpose of detecting and eliminating...crime and/or anti-social behavior."

The Bureau of Psychological Hygiene is the major First Level institution for social control; it's effective, but—as shown in "Time Crime"—far from perfect. Of all the First Level's unsavory institutions the Bureau of Psycho-Hygiene is the worst. The idea behind such a bureau seems rooted in the (racial) hygiene movements of the 1930s and the communist re-education camps. The mental purity of a people is no more possible than racial purity. However, in their arrogance, the Home Time-liners believe that it proves they are more civilized than the various outtimers they scavenge from.

One of their cures for mental instability (which could mean anything from outright psychosis to criminal psychopathology) is psycho-rehabilitation, which is described as "a year of unremitting agony, physical and mental, worse than a Khiftan torture rack"—leaving the patient with a new personality. In some ways, the cure sounds worse than the ill. In "Time Crime" it's obvious that there are a number of citizens living on First Level who are emotionally unstable and outright criminal. And noises are made about investigating the Bureau to find out how "people with potentially criminal characteristics missed being spotted by psychotesting."

By the mid-fifties, when Piper wrote "Time Crime," First Level civilization was beginning to show its warts. Utopias are inherently dull—if the human condition is perfected, there's very little conflict for good stories—and Piper was first and foremost a great storyteller. Furthermore, Piper, as reflected in his letters and fiction, was growing increasingly cynical about the nature of the human beast and the future of democratic institutions. Despite all of the Bureau of Psychological Hygiene's testing and hypno-conditioning, we learn it has been infiltrated and compromised by a criminal conspiracy.

Along with psychological adjustment, most Home Time-liners have perfect recall, and access to memory dumps through hypno-mech via narco-hypnotic tapes. In "Time Crime," we see how it is used to learn outtime cultures and language: "'I'll need a hypno-mech for Kharanda, myself.' While he slept, the Kharand's language, with all its vocabulary and grammar, became part of his subconscious knowledge, needing only the mental pronunciation of a trigger-symbol to bring it into consciousness."

Not surprisingly, Home Time Line is supported by the labor and, in some cases, outright slavery of outtime peoples. On First Level there is a large subject population of indentured servants, who appear to be little more than slaves, with only token rights. "As far as that goes, what's the difference between that [what the outtime slave dealers are doing] and the way we drag those Fourth Level Primitive Sector-Complex people off to Fifth Level Service Sector to work for us?" The paratimers' rationale is: "We need a certain amount of human labor, for tasks requiring original thought and decision that are beyond the ability of robots, and most of it is work our Citizens simply wouldn't perform."

There's a great deal of prejudice against these Fourth Level servants and it takes many generations of service and an enlightened master before they can earn First Level Citizenship. The Proles, as they are called, have their own subculture and live in ghettos or in servant quarters in their masters' homes. By the end of "Time Crime," First Level society—far from being a utopia—looks like a funhouse mirror image of our own society.

Home Time Line may be a singularity, but it's not the only First Level society. We also have the Dwarma Sector and the Abzar Sector:

Dwarma Sector

The people of the First Level Dwarma Sector [mentioned in "Time Crime"] after having successfully colonized Terra had an overpopulation crash. They were reduced by starvation to a tiny handful, had abandoned their cities and renounced their technologies and created for themselves a farm-and-village culture without progress or change or curiosity or struggle or ambition, and a way of life in which every day was like every other day that had been or that would come. The Dwarma Sector is one where the Martian colonizers never developed transtemporal transposition and without the other time-lines to live off of became decivilized and reverted to primitive social forms.

Nor do they have any need for policing: "When somebody does something wrong, his neighbors all come and talk to him about it till he gets ashamed, then they all forgive him and have a feast. They're lovely people, so kind and gentle. But you'll get awfully tired of them in about a month. They have absolutely no respect for anybody's privacy. In fact, it seems slightly indecent to them for anybody to want privacy."

Abzar Sector

The Abzar people [mentioned in "Time Crime"] made the same mistakes as Dwarma Sector. "They had wasted their resources to the last, fighting bitterly over the ultimate crumbs, with fission bombs, and with muskets, and with swords, and with spears and clubs, and finally they had died out, leaving a planet of almost uniform desert dotted with vast empty cities which even twelve thousand years had hardly begun to obliterate."

On Home Time Line the Paratime Police are not only commissioned to protect the Paratime Secret, but to maintain order throughout all surveyed time-lines of Paratime. Paratime Police Chief's Special Investigator Verkan Vall and his on again, off again wife Hadron Dalla are the predominant viewpoint characters in all the Paratime stories. *Lord Kalvan of Otherwhen*, which features a hijacked Pennsylvania State Trooper, Calvin Morrison, is the lone exception. In this novel, Verkan Vall is a secondary character, but now soon to be Paratime police chief when Chief Tortha Karf retires. This is due to the fact that it is Morrison's story.

This is how the Paratime police view their outtime job: "Now, it's just not possible to frame any single code of laws applicable to conditions on all of these. The best we can do is prohibit certain flagrantly immoral types of activity, such as slave-trading, introduction of new types of narcotic drugs, or out-and-out piracy and brigandage. If you're in doubt as to the legality of anything you want to do outtime, go to the Judicial Section of the Paratime Commission and get an opinion on it. That's where you made your whole mistake. You didn't find out just how far it was allowable for you to go."

The Paratime Police Department is huge with over two million agents, one third of them on Home Time Line running the department while the other two-thirds are out in the field. The Paratime Police Chief is Tortha Karf, a competent though somewhat blustery chief reminiscent of Perry White in the *Superman* TV show. However, even with all these agents, the Paratime Police are hard-pressed to maintain order throughout Paratime. Tortha Karf's overview of the Paratime Police states: "We're jugglers, trying to keep our traders and sociological observers and tourists and plain idiots out of trouble; trying to prevent panics and disturbances and dislocations of local economy as a result of our operations; trying to keep out of outtime politics—and, at all times, at all costs and hazards, by all means, guard the secret of Paratime Transposition."

It's the Paratime Police's job to keep this immense ball of yarn from unravelling and, while they're doing their best, there are a lot of places where it's beginning to unravel—and that's where the fun is. This fascinating society of cross-time travelers makes for some great stories and it's no wonder this series was one of John W. Campbell's favorites.

SECOND LEVEL

Second Level is where the Martian colonization attempt on Earth had been almost as successful as it had been on First Level. "Its time-lines descend from the probability of one or more shiploads of colonists having come to Terra from Mars about seventy-five to a hundred thousand years ago, and then having been cut off from the home planet and forced to develop a civilization of their own here. The difference was there had been wars and catastrophes that had created dark-age intervals. Still, some Second Level civilizations had developed over-light-speed drives for interstellar ships, which First Level had yet to do. Other than the Ghaldron-Hesthor Transposition-Field, most of its sectors were as civilized as First Level." As on First Level, there is contact and colonies on Mars and Venus.

First Level has learned a great deal from viewing the experiences on Second Level: "During the Crisis, after the Fourth Interplanetary War, we might have adopted Palnar Sarn's 'Dictatorship of the Chosen' scheme, if we hadn't seen what an exactly similar scheme had done to the Jak-Hakka Civilization, on the Second Level. When Palnar Sarn was told about that, he went into Paratime to see for himself, and when he returned, he renounced his proposal in horror."

Most of the Paratime stories, except for "Last Enemy," focus on either the First Level or the Fourth level, although there are references to really sophisticated time-lines such as Second Level Triplanetary.

Akor-Neb Sector

The Akor-Neb civilization on Earth is almost the equal of First Level. "Like all the Second Level, Akor-Neb civilization is of a fairly high culture-order, even for Second Level. An atomic-power, interplanetary culture; gravity-counteraction, direct conversion of nuclear energy to electrical power, that sort of thing. We buy fine synthetic plastics and fabrics from them."

From "Last Enemy" we learn from Verkan Vall more about the Akor-Neb: "They have a single System-wide government, a single race, and a universal language. They're a dark-brown race, which evolved in its present form about fifty thousand years ago; the present civilization is about ten thousand years old, developed out of the wreckage of several earlier civilizations which decayed or fell through wars, exhaustion of resources, et cetera. They have legends, maybe historical records, of their extraterrestrial origin."

Khiftan Sector

The Khiftan Sector is one of the Second Level societies that didn't recover from its dark age. The Sector is ruled by a theocracy called the Khiftan priesthood. It's used throughout the Paratime stories as a particularly heinous place to be. The priests dress in fringed robes and cloth-of-gold sashes and conical caps. They specialize in instruments of torture: "the whip showed a cylindrical handle, indicated as twelve inches in length and one in diameter, fitted with a thumb-switch. 'That's definitely Second Level Khiftan,' Vall said, handing it back. 'Made of braided copper or silver wire and powered with a little nuclear-conversion battery in the grip. They heat up to about two hundred centigrade; produce really painful burns.' 'Why, that's beastly!' Dalla exclaimed. 'Anything on the Khiftan Sector is.'"

The Khiftan gods are often used as First Level curse words: "He mentioned Fasif, Great God of Khift, in a manner which would have gotten him an acid-bath if the Khiftan priests had heard him." The Khiftans are slave holders and all in all it's a terrible place to get stranded, but a nice place to exile troublesome First Level enemies.

THIRD LEVEL

Third Level is the probability of an abortive attempt to colonize Earth from Mars about a hundred thousand years ago. In "Time Crime" Verkan describes it thusly: "A few survivors—a shipload or so—were left to shift for themselves while the parent civilization on Mars died out. They lost all vestiges of their original Martian culture, even memory of their extraterrestrial origin. About fifteen hundred to two thousand years ago, a reasonably high electrochemical civilization developed and they began working with nuclear energy and developed reaction-drive spaceships. But they'd concentrated so on the inorganic sciences, and so far neglected the bio-sciences, that when they launched their first ship for Venus they hadn't yet developed a germ theory of disease."

"What happened when they ran into the green-vomit fever?" Dalla asked.

"About what you could expect. The first—and only—ship to return brought it back to Terra. Of course, nobody knew what it was, and before the epidemic ended, it had almost depopulated this planet.

"Since the survivors knew nothing about germs, they blamed it on the anger of the gods—the old story of recourse to supernaturalism in the absence of a known explanation—and a fanatically anti-scientific cult got control. Of course, space travel was taboo; so was nuclear and even electric power. For some reason, steam power and gunpowder weren't offensive to the gods. They went back to a low-order steam-power, black-powder, culture, and haven't gotten beyond that to this day. The relatively civilized regions are on the east coast of Asia and the west coast of North America; civilized race more or less Caucasian. Political organization just barely above the tribal level—thousands of petty kingdoms and republics and principalities and feudal holdings and robbers' roosts."

Most of Third Level is proscribed for Home Time Line exploitation and infiltration due to too many thermo-nuclear weapons and too many competing national sovereignties, always a disaster-fraught combination. The colonists have lost all traces of Martian civilization and culture, even memories of their mother world, while on Mars civilization withered away.

There are whole Sectors on Second and Third Levels that are off-limits to Paratimers due to biological and chemical poisoning.

Esaron Sector

In "Time Crime," the Wizard Traders (a First Level criminal syndicate specializing in outtime slavery and theft) have a base in the Esaron Sector, which Verkan describes thusly: "The principal industries are brigandage, piracy, slave-raiding, cattle-rustling and inter-communal warfare. They have a few ramshackle steam railways, and some steamboats on the rivers. We sell them coal and manufactured goods, mostly in exchange for foodstuffs and tobacco. Consolidated Outtime Foodstuffs has the sector franchise...."

Other than the names of a few other sectors, such as Third Level Luvarian Empire Sector which is pretty advanced, the Third Level Khanga pirates of the Caribbean Islands and the Third-Level Illyalla people, Piper has little to say about the Third Level.

FOURTH LEVEL

Fourth Level is the largest of all the levels and the level where we find our own time-line (or should I say Piper's time-line) on the Europo-American Sector. On Fourth Level a disaster occurred to the original colonists and the result was all civilization and technology were lost. Therefore, the inhabitants believe they are an indigenous race with a long history of savagery. The other levels devolved from low-probability accidents; Fourth Level is the maximum probability. It was divided into many sectors and subsectors in which civilization had first appeared in the Fertile Crescent and Nile River Valley, and on the Indus and Yangtze Rivers. Europo-American Sector is the big one where the Paratimers obtain most of their resources, although it's dangerous, too, with too many thermonuclear weapons and competing nations.

Fourth Level is divided into three basic sector groups:

Nilo-Mesopotamian Basic Sector-Group

As Piper describes in *Lord Kalvan of Otherwhen*: "On most Nilo-Mesopotamian sectors, like the Macedonian Empire Sector, or the Alexandrian-Roman or Alexandrian-Punic or Indo-Turanian or Europo-American, there was an Aryan invasion of Eastern Europe and Asia Minor about four thousand elapsed years ago. On this sector, the ancestors of the Aryans came in about fifteen centuries earlier, as Neolithic savages, about the time that the Sumerian and Egyptian civilizations were first developing, and overran all southeast Europe, Asia Minor and the Nile Valley. They developed to the bronze-age culture of the civilizations they overthrew, and then, more slowly, to an iron-age culture. About two thousand years ago, they were using hardened steel and building large stone cities, just as they do now. At that time, they reached cultural stasis. But as for their religious beliefs, you've described them quite accurately. A god is only worshiped as long as the people think him powerful enough to aid and protect them; when they lose that confidence, he is discarded and the god of some neighboring people is adopted instead." This level is the most fertile ground for First Level exploitation and resource theft, especially in regards to art, cultural innovations and technology.

Indus-Ganges-Irrawaddy Basic Sector-Group

The Indus-Ganges-Irrawaddy Basic Sector-Grouping was derived from the probability of civilization having developed late on the Indian subcontinent, with the rest of the world, including Europe, in Stone Age savagery or early Bronze Age barbarism. Most of the civilizations in this Sector have a pre-mechanical, animal-power, handcraft, edged-weapon culture.

Yangtze Basic Sector Group

Piper never describes this Sector in any of the Paratime stories but it may be another backward sector, another Oriental Hydraulic Despotism where the government maintains social control through the dispensation of water resources. These governments were typical throughout most of the Orient with centralized governments maintaining power through their control of water resources.

In his Paratime series Piper mentions enough combinations of cultures and historical analogs to tantalize any history buff as well as keep him anxious for more stories. With ten to the hundred thousandth possible timelines, Piper could justify almost any historical possibility: such as Aryan-Transpacific Sector where he turned the Indo-Aryan migrations around, provided them with ships and sent them to the coast of North America where they slaughtered the American Indians and began a new civilization that would not change for several thousand years—until the arrival of an unwitting transtemporal conveyer hitchhiker, Pennsylvania State Trooper, Calvin Morrison.

FIFTH LEVEL

The Fifth Level is the probability of the complete failure of Martian colonization. No human population was established and only indigenous quasi-human life evolved on Earth; nature not man was triumphant. In *Lord Kalvan of Otherwhen*, Piper described it: "And Fifth Level on a few sectors, subhuman brutes, speechless and fireless, were cracking nuts and each other's heads with stones, and on most of it nothing even vaguely humanoid had appeared."

Fifth Level is also home to the Paratime Police Terminal, where a duplicate of Paratime Police Headquarters had been built. Pol-Term, as it's often referred to, is much more secure than First Level Police Headquarters. Only Paratime personnel or authorized persons may visit: as stated in "Time Crime:" "Dalla had never been on Police Terminal Time Line; very few people, outside the Paratime Police, ever had." Police Terminal is also covered with transposition depots at the site of every major city, town and important junction that exists on every major Level and Sector within Paratime, which enables the Paratime Police to transpose to any place where they were needed.

The majority of humans on Fifth Level are Proles who are sent there to work in the Service and Industrial Sector worlds with First Level overseers. They labor there to keep heavy and light industrial installations off Home Time Line. "The Service Sector Proles were not indigenous to the Fifth Level, but were brought from time-lines of near savagery, which they voluntarily left for a better life. The Paratime Transpositional Code limited the colonization of Service Sector time-lines to natives below second-order barbarism. The Serv-Sec Proles were the ones who did most of the administrative and record keeping for Home Time-Line. The proles who were dumped in the Fifth Level, Industrial Sectors, where the machines and robots of First Level were manufactured, were at the bottom rung of the Service Sector. Here were the survivors of Paratime screw-ups, when policy or criminal mistakes had made it necessary to transplant entire tribes and sometimes nations to protect them from their hostile neighbors, or to protect the Paratime secret. No matter—it seemed—how diligently the undermanned and overworked Paratime Police worked, there were always new bodies to fill another industrial time-line on Fifth Level."

In "Time Crime" Javrath Brend states: "We recruit those Fourth Level Primitives out of probability worlds of Stone Age savagery, and transpose them to our own Fifth Level time lines, practically outtime extensions of the Home Time Line. There's absolutely no question of the Paratime Secret being compromised."

"Beside, we need a certain amount of human labor, for tasks requiring original thought and decision that are beyond the ability of robots, and most of it is work our Citizens simply wouldn't perform," Thalvan Dras added.

"Well, from a moral standpoint, wouldn't these Esaron Sector people who buy the slaves justify slavery in the same terms?" a woman whom Vall had identified as a Left Moderate Council Member asked.

"There's still a big difference," Dalla told her. "The ServSec Proles aren't beaten or tortured or chained; we don't break up families or separate friends. When we recruit Fourth Level Primitives, we take whole tribes, and they come willingly...."

The Proles are the other dirty secret of Paratime. The Paratimers depend upon their proles to do the jobs they no longer want to do. On the other hand, Proles are also Home Time Line's greatest fear. Like Rome and the Deep South, one of their biggest bugaboos is a Prole insurrection. Here Ranthar Jard speaking with Verkan Vall says: "Where in blazes did he get them all?" Ranthar Jard demanded. Verkan replies: "They're guard troops, from Service Sector and Industrial Sector. We'll get you the same sort of a force. I only hope we don't have another Prole insurrection while they're away—"

Fifth Level is also where many Home Time-liners have outtime villas and mansions, on uninhabited time-lines. Some choose to relax surrounded by robot servers, or impress visitors by surrounding themselves with big clans or groups of outtimers who were on the wrong side of someone's war or were survivors of disasters. Chief Tortha has his own tribe of servants on his private hideaway, a Fifth Level equivalent of Sicily.

Piper's last novel was a Paratime story, *Lord Kalvan of Otherwhen*, and remains one of his most beloved novels.

H. Beam Piper was quite aware of how important his Paratime series was. In a conversation about time travel with Mike Knerr, who was Piper's protégé during the last few years of his life, Piper said: "'Yes, anyone can write about time travel.'

"But not about parallel time and a police force?" Knerr asked.

"No. I own the copyright to that.'"

H. Beam Piper's third story sale was to John W. Campbell, Editor of *Astounding Science Fiction*; it was his first Paratime story, "Police Operation." According to Piper's Story Log, Piper mailed it on January 2nd, 1948 and it was accepted by Campbell on the 16th. It was published in the April edition of *Astounding*. Little did Piper know that the Paratime concept would be one of his most important contributions to SF field.

In "Police Operation" Piper introduces the Paratime Police, whose primary mission is to protect the secret of Paratime travel. This first story is a police procedural wherein Verkan Vall (the Paratime Police Special Chief's Assistant) is charged with investigating the death of a First Level noble who was killed in an auto accident on a time-line very similar to our own time-line. Normally, nothing would have happened, but the Paratimer had brought a Venusian Nighthound with him—a vicious beast which was killing farm animals in the vicinity. It is against Paratime regulations for Paratimers to introduce non-native species to time-lines they visit because the appearance might raise suspicion that "outsiders" are doing mischief. When the local game wardens and State Police are called in to track the Nighthound, Verkan Vall gets involved to protect the Paratime secret.

For this first story, Piper did a lot of speculating on both alternate worlds travel and the nature of the extraphysical ego component. He also has multiple First Level alternate worlds, which results in uncountable duplicates of Verkan Vall and the rest of the Paratime Police crew. I've taken the liberty to remove this section from this first Paratime story so that it fits in seamlessly with Piper's later Paratime stories.

POLICE OPERATION

H. Beam Piper

There may be something in the nature of an occult police force, which operates to divert human suspicions, and to supply explanations that are good enough for whatever, somewhat in the nature of minds, human beings have—or that, if there be occult mischief makers and occult ravagers, they may be of a world also of other beings that are acting to check them, and to explain them, not benevolently, but to divert suspicion from themselves, because they, too, may be exploiting life upon this earth, but in ways more subtle, and in orderly, or organized, fashion.

Charles Fort
LO!

I

1948 A.D.

John Strawmyer stood, an irate figure in faded overalls and sweat-whitened black shirt, apart from the others, his back to the weathered farm-buildings and the line of yellowing woods and the cirrus-streaked blue October sky. He thrust out a work-gnarled hand accusingly. "That there heifer was worth two hund'rd, two hund'rd an' fifty dollars!" he clamored. "An' that there dog was just like one uh the fam'ly; An' now look at'm! I don't like t' use profane language, but you'ns gotta *do* some'n about this!"

Steve Parker, the district game protector, aimed his Leica at the carcass of the dog and snapped the shutter. "We're doing something about it," he said shortly. Then he stepped ten feet to the left and edged around the mangled heifer, choosing an angle for his camera shot.

The two men in the gray whipcords of the State police, seeing that Parker was through with the dog, moved in and squatted to examine it. The one with the triple chevrons on his sleeves took it by both forefeet and flipped it over on its back. It had been a big brute, of nondescript breed, with a rough black-and-brown coat. Something had clawed it deeply about the head, its throat was slashed transversely several times, and it had been disemboweled by a single slash that had opened its belly from breastbone to tail. They looked at it carefully, and then went to stand beside Parker while he photographed the dead heifer.

Like the dog, it had been talon-raked on either side of the head, and its throat had been slashed deeply several times. In addition, flesh had been torn from one flank in great strips.

"I can't kill a bear outa season, no!" Strawmyer continued his complaint. "But a bear comes an' kills my stock an' my dog; that there's all right! That's the kinda deal a farmer always gits, in this state! I don't like t' use profane language—"

"Then don't!" Parker barked at him, impatiently. "Don't use any kind of language. Just put in your claim and shut up!" He turned to the men in whipcords and gray Stetsons. "You boys seen everything?" he asked. "Then let's go."

They walked briskly back to the barnyard, Strawmyer following them, still vociferating about the wrongs of the farmer at the hands of a cynical and corrupt State government. They climbed into the State police car, the sergeant and the private in front and Parker into the rear, laying his camera on the seat beside a Winchester carbine.

"Weren't you pretty short with that fellow, back there, Steve?" the Sergeant asked as the private started the car.

"Not too short. 'I don't like t' use profane language,'" Parker mimicked the bereaved heifer owner, and then he went on to specify: "I'm morally certain that he's shot at least four illegal deer in the last year. When and if I ever get anything on him, he's going to be sorrier for himself then he is now."

"They're the characters that always beef their heads off," the Sergeant agreed. "You think that whatever did this was the same as the others?"

"Yes. The dog must have jumped it while it was eating at the heifer. Same superficial scratches about the head, and deep cuts on the throat or belly. The bigger the animal, the farther front the big slashes occur. Evidently something grabs them by the head with front claws, and slashes with hind claws; that's why I think it's a bobcat."

""You know," the private said, "I saw a lot of wounds like that during the war. My outfit landed on Mindanao, where the guerrillas had been active. And this looks like bolo-work to me."

"The surplus-stores are full of machetes and jungle knives," the Sergeant considered. "I think I'll call up Doc Winters, at the County Hospital, and see if all his squirrel-fodder is present and accounted for."

"But most of the livestock was eaten at, like the heifer," Parker objected.

"By definition, nuts have abnormal tastes," the Sergeant replied. "Or the eating might have been done later, by foxes."

"I hope so; that'd let me out," Parker said.

"Ha, listen to the man!" the private howled, stopping the car at the end of the lane. "He thinks a nut with a machete and a Tarzan complex is just good clean fun. Which way, now?"

"Well, let's see." The Sergeant had unfolded a quadrangle sheet; the game protector leaned forward to look at it over his shoulder. He ran a finger from one to another of a series of variously colored crosses which had been marked on the map. "Monday night, over here on Copperhead Mountain, that cow was killed," he said. "The next night, about ten o'clock, that sheep flock was hit, on this side of Copperhead, right about here. Early Wednesday night, that mule got slashed up in the woods back of the Weston farm. It was only slightly injured; must have kicked the whatzit and got away, but the whatzit wasn't too badly hurt, because a few hours later, it hit that turkey-flock on the Rhymer farm. And last night, it did that."

He jerked a thumb over his shoulder at the Strawmyer farm. "See, following the ridges, working toward the southeast, avoiding open ground, killing only at night. Could be a bobcat, at that."

"Or Jink's maniac with the machete," Parker agreed. "Let's go up by Hindman's gap and see if we can see anything."

II

They turned, after a while, into a rutted dirt road, which deteriorated steadily into a grass-grown track through the woods. Finally, they stopped, and the private backed off the road. The three men got out; Parker with his Winchester, the sergeant checking the drum of a Thompson, and the private pumping a buckshot shell into the chamber of a riot gun. For half an hour, they followed the brush-grown trail beside the little stream; once, they passed a dark gray commercial-model jeep, backed to one side.

Then they came to the head of the gap. A man, wearing a tweed coat, tan field boots, and khaki breeches, was sitting on a log, smoking a pipe; he had a bolt-action rifle across his knees, and a pair of binoculars hung from his neck. He seemed about thirty years old, and any bobby-soxer's idol of the screen would have envied him the handsome regularity of his strangely immobile features.

As Parker and the two State policemen approached, he rose, slinging his rifle, and greeted them.

"Sergeant Haines, isn't it?" he asked pleasantly. "Are you gentlemen out hunting the critter, too?"

"Good afternoon, Mr. Lee. I thought that was your jeep I saw, down the road a little."

The Sergeant turned to the others. "Mr. Richard Lee; staying at the old Kinchwalter place, the other side of Rutter's Fort. This is Mr. Parker, the district game protector. And Private Zinkowski." He glanced at the rifle. "Are you out hunting for it, too?"

"Yes, I thought I might find something, up here. What do you think it is?"

"I don't know," the Sergeant admitted. "It could be a bobcat. Canada lynx. Jink, here, has a theory that it's some escapee from the paper-doll factory, with a machete. Me, I hope not, but I'm not ignoring the possibility."

The man with the matinee-idol's face nodded. "It could be a lynx. I understand they're not unknown, in this section."

"We paid bounties on two in this county, in the last year," Parker said. "Odd rifle you have, there; mind if I look at it?"

"Not at all." The man who had been introduced as Richard Lee unslung and handed it over. "The chamber's loaded," he cautioned.

"I never saw one like this," Parker said.

"Foreign?"

"I think so. I don't know anything about it; it belongs to a friend of mine, who loaned it to me. I think the action's German, or Czech; the rest of it's a custom job, by some west coast gunmaker. It's chambered for some ultra-velocity wildcat load."

The rifle passed from hand to hand; the three men examined it in turn, commenting admiringly.

"You find anything, Mr. Lee?" the Sergeant asked, handing it back.

"Not a trace." The man called Lee slung the rifle and began to dump the ashes from his pipe. "I was along the top of this ridge for about a mile on either side of the gap, and down the other side as far as Hindman's Run; I didn't find any tracks, or any indication of where it had made a kill."

The game protector nodded, turning to Sergeant Haines. "There's no use us going any farther," he said. "Ten to one, it followed that line of woods back of Strawmyer's, and crossed over to the other ridge. I think our best bet would be the hollow at the head of Lowrie's Run. What do you think?"

The Sergeant agreed.

The man called Richard Lee began to refill his pipe methodically. "I think I shall stay here for a while, but I believe you're right. Lowrie's Run, or across Lowrie's Gap into Coon Valley," he said.

III

After Parker and the State policemen had gone, the man whom they had addressed as Richard Lee returned to his log and sat smoking, his rifle across his knees. From time to time, he glanced at his wristwatch and raised his head to listen. At length, faint in the distance, he heard the sound of a motor starting.

Instantly, he was on his feet. From the end of the hollow log on which he had been sitting, he produced a canvas musette-bag. Walking briskly to a patch of damp ground beside the little stream, he leaned the rifle against a tree and opened the bag. First, he took out a pair of gloves of some greenish, rubber-like substance, and put them on, drawing the long gauntlets up over his coat sleeves. Then he produced a bottle and unscrewed the cap. Being careful to avoid splashing his clothes, he went about, pouring a clear liquid upon the ground in several places. Where he poured, white vapors rose, and twigs and grass grumbled into brownish dust.

After he had replaced the cap and returned the bottle to the bag, he waited for a few minutes, then took a spatula from the musette and dug where he had poured the fluid, prying loose four black, irregular-shaped lumps of matter, which he carried to the running water and washed carefully, before wrapping them and putting them in the bag, along with the gloves. Then he slung bag and rifle and started down the trail to where he had parked the jeep.

Half an hour later, after driving through the little farming village of Rutter's Fort, he pulled into the barnyard of a rundown farm and backed through the open doors of the barn. He closed the double doors behind him, and barred them from within. Then he went to the rear wall of the barn, which was much closer to the front than the outside dimensions of the barn would have indicated.

He took from his pocket a black object like an automatic pencil. Hunting over the rough plank wall, he found a small hole and inserted the pointed end of the pseudo-pencil, pressing on the other end. For an instant, nothing happened. Then a ten-foot-square section of the wall receded two feet and slid noiselessly to one side. The section which had slid inward had been built of three-inch steel, masked by a thin covering of boards; the wall around it was two-foot concrete, similarly camouflaged. He stepped quickly inside.

Fumbling at the right side of the opening, he found a switch and flicked it. Instantly, the massive steel plate slid back into place with a soft, oily click. As it did, lights came on within the hidden room, disclosing a great semiglobe of some fine metallic mesh, thirty feet in diameter and fifteen in height. There was a sliding door at one side of this; the man called Richard Lee opened and entered through it, closing it behind him. Then he turned to the center of the hollow dome, where an armchair was placed in front of a small desk below a large instrument panel. The gauges and dials on the panel, and the levers and switches and buttons on the desk control board, were all lettered and numbered with characters not of the Roman alphabet or the Arabic notation, and, within instant reach of the occupant of the chair, a pistol-like weapon lay on the desk. It had a conventional index-finger trigger and a hand-fit grip, but, instead of a tubular barrel, two slender parallel metal rods extended about four inches forward of the receiver, joined together at what would correspond to the muzzle by a streamlined knob of some light blue ceramic or plastic substance.

The man with the handsome immobile face deposited his rifle and musette on the floor beside the chair and sat down. First, he picked up the pistol-like weapon and checked it, and then he examined the many instruments on the panel in front of him. Finally, he flicked a switch on the control board.

At once, a small humming began, from some point overhead. It wavered and shrilled and mounted in intensity, and then fell to a steady monotone. The dome about him flickered with a queer, cold iridescence, and slowly vanished. The hidden room vanished, and he was looking into the shadowy interior of a deserted barn. The barn vanished; blue sky appeared above, streaked with wisps of high cirrus cloud. The autumn landscape flickered unreally. Buildings appeared and vanished, and other buildings came and went in a twinkling. All around him, half-seen shapes moved briefly and disappeared.

Once, the figure of a man appeared, inside the circle of the dome. He had an angry, brutal face, and he wore a black tunic piped with silver, and black breeches, and polished black boots, and there was an insignia, composed of a cross and thunderbolt, on his cap. He held an automatic pistol in his hand. Instantly, the man at the desk snatched up his own weapon and thumbed off the safety, but before he could lift and aim it, the intruder stumbled and passed outside the force-field which surrounded the chair and instruments.

For a while, there were fires raging outside, and for a while, the man at the desk was surrounded by a great hall, with a high, vaulted ceiling, through which figures flitted and vanished. For a while, there were vistas of deep forests, always set in the same background of mountains and always under the same blue cirrus-laced sky. There was an interval of flickering blue-white light, of unbearable intensity. Then the man at the desk was surrounded by the interior of vast industrial works.

The moving figures around him slowed, and became more distinct. For an instant, the man in the chair grinned as he found himself looking into a big washroom, where a tall blonde girl was taking a shower bath, and a pert little redhead was vigorously drying herself with a towel. The dome grew visible, coruscating with many-colored lights and then the humming died and the dome became a cold and inert mesh of fine white metal. A green light above flashed on and off slowly. He stabbed a button and flipped a switch, then got to his feet, picking up his rifle and musette and fumbling under his shirt for a small mesh bag, from which he took an inch-wide disk of blue plastic. Unlocking a container on the instrument panel, he removed a small roll of solidograph-film, which he stowed in his bag. Then he slid open the door and emerged into his own dimension of space-time.

Outside was a wide hallway, with a pale green floor, paler green walls, and a ceiling of greenish off-white. A big hole had been cut to accommodate the dome, and across the hallway a desk had been set up, and at it sat a clerk in a pale blue tunic, who was just taking the audio-plugs of a music-box out of his ears. A couple of policemen in green uniforms, with ultrasonic paralyzers dangling by thongs from their left wrists and holstered sigma-ray needlers like the one on the desk inside the dome, were kidding with some girls in vivid orange and scarlet and green smocks. One of these, in bright green, was a duplicate of the one he had seen rubbing herself down with a towel.

"Here comes your boss-man," one of the girls told the cops, as he approached. They both turned and saluted casually. The man who had lately been using the name of Richard Lee responded to their greeting and went to the desk. The policemen grasped their paralyzers, drew their needlers, and hurried into the dome.

Taking the disk of blue plastic from his packet, he handed it to the clerk at the desk, who dropped it into a slot in the voder in front of him. Instantly, a mechanical voice responded:

"Verkan Vall, blue-seal noble, hereditary Mavrad of Nerros. Special Chief's Assistant, Paratime Police, special assignment. Subject to no orders below those of Tortha Karf, Chief of Paratime Police. To be given all courtesies and co-operation within the Paratime Transposition Code and the Police Powers Code. Further particulars?"

The clerk pressed the 'no'-button. The blue sigil fell out the release-slot and was handed back to its bearer.

The two policemen came out of the dome, their needlers holstered and their vigilance relaxed. They were lighting cigarettes as they emerged. "It's all right, sir," one of them said. "You didn't bring anything in with you, this trip."

The other cop chuckled. "Remember that Fifth Level wild-man who came in on the freight conveyer at Jandar, last month?" he asked.

If he was hoping that some of the girls would want to know, what wild-man, it was a vain hope. With a blue-seal Mavrad around, what chance did a couple of ordinary coppers have? The girls were already converging on Verkan Vall.

"When are you going to get that monstrosity out of our restroom," the little redhead in green coveralls was demanding. "If it wasn't for that thing, I'd be taking a shower, right now."

"You were just finishing one, about fifty paraseconds off, when I came through," Verkan Vall told her.

The girl looked at him in obviously feigned indignation. "Why, you— You *parapeeper!*"

Verkan Vall chuckled and turned to the clerk. "I want a strato-rocket and pilot, for Dhergabar, right away. Call Dhergabar Paratime Police Field and give them my ETA; have an air-taxi meet me, and have the chief notified that I'm coming in. Extraordinary report. Keep a guard over the conveyer; I think I'm going to need it, again, soon." He turned to the little redhead. "Want to show me the way out of here, to the rocket field?" he asked.

Outside, on the open landing field, Verkan Vall glanced up at the sky, then looked at his watch. It had been twenty minutes since he had backed the jeep into the barn, on that distant other time-line; the same delicate lines of white cirrus were etched across the blue above. The constancy of the weather, even across two hundred thousand parayears of perpendicular time, never failed to impress him. The long curve of the mountains was the same, and they were mottled with the same autumn colors, but where the little village of Rutter's Fort stood on that other line of probability, the white towers of an apartment-city rose—the living quarters of the plant personnel. The rocket that was to take him to headquarters was being hoisted with a crane and lowered into the firing-stand, and he walked briskly toward it, his rifle and musette slung. A boyish-looking pilot was on the platform, opening the door of the rocket; he stood aside for Verkan Vall to enter, then followed and closed it, dogging it shut while his passenger stowed his bag and rifle and strapped himself into a seat.

"Dhergabar Commercial Terminal, sir?" the pilot asked, taking the adjoining seat at the controls.

"Paratime Police Field, back of the Paratime Administration Building."

"Right, sir. Twenty seconds to blast, when you're ready."

"Ready now." Verkan Vall relaxed, counting seconds subconsciously.

The rocket trembled, and Verkan Vall felt himself being pushed gently back against the upholstery. The seats, and the pilot's instrument panel in front of them, swung on gimbals, and the finger of the indicator swept slowly over a ninety-degree arc as the rocket rose and leveled. By then, the high cirrus clouds Verkan Vall had watched from the field were far below; they were well into the stratosphere.

There would be nothing to do, now, for the three hours in which the rocket sped northward across the pole and southward to Dhergabar; the navigation was entirely in the electronic hands of the robot controls. Verkan Vall got out his pipe and lit it; the pilot lit a cigarette.

"That's an odd pipe, sir," the pilot said. "Outtime item?"

"Yes, Fourth Probability Level; typical of the whole Paratime belt I was working in." Verkan Vall handed it over for inspection. "The bowl's natural brier-root; the stem's a sort of plastic made from the sap of certain tropical trees. The little white dot is the maker's trademark; it's made of elephant tusk."

"Sounds pretty crude to me, sir." The pilot handed it back. "Nice workmanship, though. Looks like good machine production."

"Yes. The sector I was on is really quite advanced, for an electro-chemical civilization. That weapon I brought back with me—that solid-missile projector—is typical of most Fourth Level culture. Moving parts machined to the closest tolerances, and interchangeable with similar parts of all similar weapons. The missile is a small bolt of cupro-alloy coated lead, propelled by expanding gases from the ignition of some nitro-cellulose compound. Most of their scientific advance occurred within the past century, and most of that in the past forty years. Of course, the life-expectancy on that level is only about seventy years."

"Humph! I'm seventy-eight, last birthday," the boyish-looking pilot snorted. "Their medical science must be mostly witchcraft!"

"Until quite recently, it was," Verkan Vall agreed. "Same story there as in everything else—rapid advancement in the past few decades, after thousands of years of cultural inertia."

"You know, sir, I don't really understand this Paratime stuff," the pilot confessed. "I know that all time is totally present, and that every moment has its own past-future line of event-sequence, and that all events in space-time occur according to maximum probability, but I just don't get this alternate probability stuff, at all. If something exists, it's because it's the maximum-probability effect of prior causes; why does anything else exist on any other time-line?"

Verkan Vall blew smoke at the air-renovator. A lecture on Paratime theory would nicely fill in the three-hour interval until the landing at Dhergabar. At least, this kid was asking intelligent questions.

"Well, you know the principal of time-passage, I suppose?" he began.

"Yes, of course; Rhogom's Doctrine. The basis of most of our psychical science. We exist perpetually at all moments within our life-span; our extraphysical ego component passes from the ego existing at one moment to the ego existing at the next. During unconsciousness, the EPC is 'time-free;' it may detach, and connect at some other moment, with the ego existing at that time-point. That's how we precog. We take an autohypno and recover memories brought back from the future moment and buried in the subconscious mind."

"That's right," Verkan Vall told him. "And even without the autohypno, a lot of precognitive matter leaks out of the subconscious and into the conscious mind, usually in distorted forms, or else inspires 'instinctive' acts, the motivation for which is not brought to the level of consciousness. For instance, suppose, you're walking along North Promenade, in Dhergabar, and you come to the Martian Palace Café, and you go in for a drink, and meet some girl, and strike up an acquaintance with her. This chance acquaintance develops into a love affair, and a year later, out of jealousy, she rays you half a dozen times with a needler."

"Just about that happened to a friend of mine, not long ago," the pilot said. "Go on, sir."

"Well, in the microsecond or so before you die—or afterward, for that matter, because we know that the extraphysical component survives physical destruction—your EPC slips back a couple of years, and re-connects at some point pastward of your first meeting with this girl, and carries with it memories of everything up to the moment of detachment, all of which are indelibly recorded in your subconscious mind. So, when you re-experience the event of standing outside the Martian Palace with a thirst, you go on to the Starway, or Nhergal's, or some other bar. In both cases, on both time-lines, you follow the line of maximum probability; in the second case, your subconscious future memories are an added causal factor."

"And when I back-slip, after I've been needled, I generate a new time-line? Is that it?"

Verkan Vall made a small sound of impatience. "No such thing!" he exclaimed. "It's semantically inadmissible to talk about the total presence of time with one breath and about generating new time-lines with the next. *All* time-lines are totally present, in perpetual co-existence. The theory is that the EPC passes from one moment, on one time-line, to the next moment on the next line, so that the true passage of the EPC from moment to moment is a two-dimensional diagonal. So, in the case we're using, the event of your going into the Martian Palace exists on one time-line, and the event of your passing along to the Starway exists on another, but both are events in real existence.

"Now, what we do, in paratime transposition, is to build up a hypertemporal field to include the time-line we want to reach, and then shift over to it. Same point in the plenum; same point in primary time—plus primary time elapsed during mechanical and electronic lag in the relays—but a different line of secondary time."

"Then why don't we have past-future time travel on our own time-line?" the pilot wanted to know.

That was a question every Paratimer has to answer, every time he talks paratime to the laity. Verkan Vall had been expecting it; he answered patiently.

"The Ghaldron-Hesthor field-generator is like every other mechanism; it can operate only in the area of primary time in which it exists. It can transpose to any other time-line, and carry with it anything inside its field, but it can't go outside its own temporal area of existence, any more than a bullet from that rifle can hit the target a week before it's fired," Verkan Vall pointed out. "Anything inside the field is supposed to be unaffected by anything outside. *Supposed to be* is the way to put it; it doesn't always work. Once in a while, something pretty nasty gets picked up in transit."

He thought, briefly, of the man in the black tunic. "That's why we have armed guards at terminals."

"Suppose you pick up a blast from a nucleonic bomb," the pilot asked, "or something red-hot, or radioactive?"

"We have a monument, at Paratime Police Headquarters, in Dhergabar, bearing the names of our own personnel who didn't make it back. It's a large monument; over the past ten thousand years, it's been inscribed with quite a few names."

"You can have it; I'll stick to rockets!" the pilot replied. "Tell me another thing, though: What's all this about levels, and sectors, and belts? What's the difference?"

"Purely arbitrary terms. There are five main probability levels, derived from the five possible outcomes of the attempt to colonize this planet, seventy-five thousand years ago. We're on the First Level—complete success, and colony fully established. The Fifth Level is the probability of complete failure—no human population established on this planet, and indigenous quasi-human life evolved indigenously. On the Fourth Level, the colonists evidently met with some disaster and lost all memory of their extraterrestrial origin, as well as all extraterrestrial culture. As far as they know, they are an indigenous race; they have a long pre-history of stone age savagery.

"Sectors are areas of paratime on any level in which the prevalent culture has a common origin and common characteristics. They are divided more or less arbitrarily into sub-sectors. Belts are areas within sub-sectors where conditions are the result of recent alternate probabilities. For instance, I've just come from the Europo-American Sector of the Fourth Level, an area of about ten thousand parayears in depth, in which the dominant civilization developed on the North-West Continent of the Major Land Mass, and spread from there to the Minor Land Mass.

"The line on which I was operating is also part of a subsector of about three thousand parayears' depth, and a belt developing from one of several probable outcomes of a war concluded about three elapsed years ago. On that time-line, the field at the Hagraban Synthetics Works, where we took off, is part of an abandoned farm; on the site of Hagraban City is a little farming village. Those things are there, right now, both in primary time and in the plenum. They are about two hundred and fifty thousand parayears perpendicular to each other, and each is of the same general order of reality."

The red light overhead flashed on. The pilot looked into his visor and put his hands to the manual controls, in case of failure of the robot controls. The rocket landed smoothly, however; there was a slight jar as it was grappled by the crane and hoisted upright, the seats turning in their gimbals. Pilot and passenger unstrapped themselves and hurried through the refrigerated outlet and away from the glowing-hot rocket.

IV

An air-taxi, emblazoned with the device of the Paratime Police, was waiting. Verkan Vall said good-bye to the rocket-pilot and took his seat beside the pilot of the aircab; the latter lifted his vehicle above the building level and then set it down on the landing-stage of the Paratime Police Building in a long, side-swooping glide. An express elevator took Verkan Vall down to one of the middle stages, where he showed his sigil to the guard outside the door of Tortha Karf's office and was admitted at once.

The Paratime Police chief rose from behind his semicircular desk, with its array of keyboards and viewing-screens and communicators. He was a big man, well past his four hundredth year; his hair was iron-gray and thinning in front, he had begun to grow thick at the waist, and his calm features bore the lines of middle age. He wore the dark-green uniform of the Paratime Police.

"Well, Vall," he greeted. "Everything secure?"

"Not exactly, sir." Verkan Vall came around the desk, deposited his rifle and bag on the floor, and sat down in one of the spare chairs. "I'll have to go back again."

"So?" His chief lit a cigarette and waited.

"I traced Gavran Sarn."

Verkan Vall got out his pipe and began to fill it. "But that's only the beginning. I have to trace something else. Gavran Sarn exceeded his Paratime permit, and took one of his pets along. A Venusian nighthound."

Tortha Karf's expression did not alter; it merely grew more intense. He used one of the short, semantically ugly terms which serve, in place of profanity, as the emotional release of a race that has forgotten all the taboos and terminologies of supernaturalistic religion and sex-inhibition.

"You're sure of this, of course." It was less a question than a statement.

Verkan Vall bent and took cloth-wrapped objects from his bag, unwrapping them and laying them on the desk. They were casts, in hard black plastic, of the footprints of some large three-toed animal.

"What do these look like, sir?" he asked.

Tortha Karf fingered them and nodded. Then he became as visibly angry as a man of his civilization and culture-level ever permitted himself.

"What does that fool think we have a Paratime Code for?" he demanded. "It's entirely illegal to transpose any extraterrestrial animal or object to any time-line on which space-travel is unknown. I don't care if he is a green-seal Thavrad; he'll face charges, when he gets back, for this!"

"He *was* a green-seal Thavrad," Verkan Vall corrected. "And he won't be coming back."

"I hope you didn't have to deal summarily with him," Tortha Karf said. "With his title, and social position, and his family's political importance, that might make difficulties. Not that it wouldn't be all right with me, of course, but we never seem to be able to make either the Management or the public realize the extremities to which we are forced, at times." He sighed. "We probably never shall."

Verkan Vall smiled faintly. "Oh, no, sir; nothing like that. He was dead before I transposed to that time-line. He was killed when he wrecked a self-propelled vehicle he was using. One of those Fourth Level automobiles. I posed as a relative and tried to claim his body for the burial-ceremony observed on that cultural level, but was told that it had been completely destroyed by fire when the fuel tank of this automobile burned. I was given certain of his effects which had passed through the fire; I found his sigil concealed inside what appeared to be a cigarette case."

He took a green disk from the bag and laid it on the desk. "There's no question; Gavran Sarn died in the wreck of that automobile."

"And the nighthound?"

"It was in the car with him, but it escaped. You know how fast those things are. I found that track"—he indicated one of the black casts—"in some dried mud near the scene of the wreck. As you see, the cast is slightly defective. The others were fresh this morning, when I made them."

"And what have you done so far."

"I rented an old farm near the scene of the wreck, and installed my field-generator there. It runs through to the Hagraban Synthetics Works, about a hundred miles east of Thalna-Jarvizar. I have my this-line terminal in the girls' restroom at the durable plastics factory; handled that on a local police-power writ. Since then, I've been hunting for the nighthound. I think I can find it, but I'll need some special equipment, and hypno-mech indoctrination. That's why I came back."

"Has it been attracting any attention?" Tortha Karf asked anxiously.

"Killing cattle in the locality; causing considerable excitement. Fortunately, it's a locality of forested mountains and valley farms, rather than a built-up industrial district. Local police and wild-game protection officers are concerned; all the farmers excited, and going armed. The theory is that it's either a wildcat of some sort, or a maniac armed with a cutlass. Either theory would conform, more or less, to the nature of its depredations. Nobody has actually seen it."

"That's good!" Tortha Karf was relieved. "Well, you'll have to go and bring it out, or kill it and obliterate the body. You know why, as well as I do."

"Certainly, sir," Verkan Vall replied. "In a primitive culture, things like this would be assigned supernatural explanations, and imbedded in the locally accepted religion. But this culture, while nominally religious, is highly rationalistic in practice. Typical lag-effect, characteristic of all expanding cultures. And this Europo-American Sector really has an expanding culture. A hundred and fifty years ago, the inhabitants of this particular time-line didn't even know how to apply steam power; now they've begun to release nuclear energy, in a few crude forms."

Tortha Karf whistled, softly. "That's quite a jump. There's a sector that'll be in for trouble, in the next few centuries."

"That is realized, locally, sir." Verkan Vall concentrated on relighting his pipe, for a moment, then continued: "I would predict space-travel on that sector within the next century. Maybe the next half-century, at least to the Moon. And the art of taxidermy is very highly developed. Now, suppose some farmer shoots that thing; what would he do with it, sir?"

Tortha Karf grunted. "Nice logic, Vall. On a most uncomfortable possibility. He'd have it mounted, and it'd be put in a museum, somewhere. And as soon as the first spaceship reaches Venus, and they find those things in a wild state, they'll have the mounted specimen identified."

"Exactly. And then, instead of beating their brains about *where* their specimen came from, they'll begin asking *when* it came from. They're quite capable of such reasoning, even now."

"A hundred years isn't a particularly long time," Tortha Karf considered. "I'll be retired, then, but you'll have my job, and it'll be your headache. You'd better get this cleaned up, now, while it can be handled. What are you going to do?"

"I'm not sure, now, sir. I want hypno-mech indoctrination, first." Verkan Vall gestured toward the communicator on the desk. "May I?" he asked.

"Certainly." Tortha Karf slid the instrument across the desk. "Anything you want."

"Thank you, sir." Verkan Vall snapped on the code-index, found the symbol he wanted, and then punched it on the keyboard. "Special Chief's Assistant, Verkan Vall," he identified himself. "Speaking from office of Tortha Karf, Chief Paratime Police. I want a complete hypno-mech on Venusian nighthounds, emphasis on wild state, special emphasis domesticated nighthounds reverted to wild state in terrestrial surroundings, extra-special emphasis hunting techniques applicable to same. The word 'nighthound' will do for trigger-symbol."

He turned to Tortha Karf. "Can I take it here?"

Tortha Karf nodded, pointing to a row of booths along the far wall of the office.

"Make set-up for wired transmission; I'll take it here."

"Very well, sir; in fifteen minutes," a voice replied out of the communicator.

Verkan Vall slid the communicator back. "By the way, sir; I had a hitchhiker, on the way back. Carried him about a hundred or so parayears; picked him up about three hundred parayears after leaving my other-line terminal. Nasty-looking fellow, in a black uniform; looked like one of these private-army storm troopers you find all through that sector. Armed, and hostile. I thought I'd have to ray him, but he blundered outside the field almost at once. I have a record, if you'd care to see it."

"Yes, put it on," Tortha Karf gestured toward the solidograph-projector. "It's set for miniature reproduction here on the desk; that be all right?"

Verkan Vall nodded, getting out the film and loading it into the projector. When he pressed a button, a dome of radiance appeared on the desk top; two feet in width and a foot in height. In the middle of this appeared a small solidograph image of the interior of the conveyer, showing the desk, and the control board, and the figure of Verkan Vall seated at it. The little figure of the storm trooper appeared, pistol in hand. The little Verkan Vall snatched up his tiny needler; the storm trooper moved into one side of the dome and vanished.

Verkan Vall flipped a switch and cut out the image.

"Yes. I don't know what causes that, but it happens, now and then," Tortha Karf said. "Usually at the beginning of a transposition. I remember, when I was just a kid, about a hundred and fifty years ago—a hundred and fifty-nine, to be exact—I picked up a fellow on the Fourth Level, just about where you're operating, and dragged him a couple of hundred parayears. I went back to find him and return him to his own time-line, but before I could locate him, he'd been arrested by the local authorities as a suspicious character, and got himself shot trying to escape.

"I felt badly about that, but—" Tortha Karf shrugged. "Anything else happen on the trip?"

"I ran through a belt of intermittent nucleonic bombing on the Second Level." Verkan Vall mentioned an approximate paratime location.

"Aargh! That Khiftan civilization—by courtesy so called!" Tortha Karf pulled a wry face—"I suppose the intra-family enmities of the Hvadka Dynasty have reached critical mass again. They'll fool around till they blast themselves back to the stone age.

"Intellectually, they're about there, now. I had to operate in that sector, once—"

"Oh, yes, another thing, sir. This rifle." Verkan Vall picked it up, emptied the magazine, and handed it to his superior. "The supplies office slipped up on this; it's not appropriate to my line of operation. It's a lovely rifle, but it's about two hundred percent in advance of existing arms design on my line. It excited the curiosity of a couple of police officers and a game-protector, who should be familiar with the weapons of their own time-line. I evaded by disclaiming ownership or intimate knowledge, and they seemed satisfied, but it worried me."

"Yes. That was made in our duplicating shops, here in Dhergabar." Tortha Karf carried it to a photographic bench, behind his desk. "I'll have it checked, while you're taking your hypno-mech. Want to exchange it for something authentic?"

"Why, no, sir. It's been identified to me, and I'd excite less suspicion with it than I would if I abandoned it and mysteriously acquired another rifle. I just wanted a check, and Supplies warned to be more careful in future."

Tortha Karf nodded approvingly. The young Mavrad of Nerros was thinking as a Paratimer should. "What's the designation of your line, again?"

Verkan Vall told him. It was a short numerical term of six places, but it expressed a number of the order of ten to the fortieth power, exact to the last digit. Tortha Karf repeated it into his stenomemograph, with explanatory comment.

"There seems to be quite a few things going wrong, in that area," he said. "Let's see, now." He punched the designation on a keyboard; instantly, it appeared on a translucent screen in front of him. He punched another combination, and, at the top of the screen, under the number, there appeared:

EVENTS, PAST ELAPSED FIVE YEARS.

He punched again; below this line appeared the sub-heading:

EVENTS INVOLVING PARATIME TRANSPOSITION.

Another code-combination added a third line:

(ATTRACTING PUBLIC NOTICE AMONG INHABITANTS.)

He pressed the start-button; the headings vanished, to be replaced by page after page of print, succeeding one another on the screen as the two men read. They told strange and apparently disconnected stories—of unexplained fires and explosions; of people vanishing without trace; of unaccountable disasters to aircraft. There were many stories of an epidemic of mysterious disk-shaped objects seen in the sky, singly or in numbers. To each account was appended one or more reference-numbers.

Sometimes Tortha Karf or Verkan Vall would punch one of these, and read, on an adjoining screen, the explanatory matter referred to. Finally Tortha Karf leaned back and lit a fresh cigarette.

"Yes, indeed, Vall; very definitely we will have to take action in the matter of the runaway nighthound of the late Gavran Sarn," he said. "I'd forgotten that that was the time-line onto which the *Ardrath* expedition launched those antigrav disks. If this extraterrestrial monstrosity turns up, on the heels of that 'Flying Saucer' business, everybody above the order of intelligence of a cretin will suspect some connection."

"What really happened, in the *Ardrath* matter?" Verkan Vall inquired. "I was on the Third Level, on that Luvarian Empire operation, at the time."

"That's right; you missed that. Well, it was one of these joint-operation things. The Paratime Commission and the Space Patrol were experimenting with a new technique for throwing a spaceship into paratime. They used the cruiser *Ardrath*, Kalzarn Jann commanding. Went into space about halfway to the Moon and took up orbit, keeping on the sunlit side of the planet to avoid being observed. That was all right. But then, Captain Kalzarn ordered away a flight of antigrav disks, fully manned, to take pictures, and finally authorized a landing in the western mountain range, Northern Continent, Minor Land-Mass. That's when the trouble started."

He flipped the run-back switch, till he had recovered the page he wanted. Verkan Vall read of a Fourth Level aviator, in his little airscrew-drive craft, sighting nine high-flying saucerlike objects.

"That was how it began," Tortha Karf told him. "Before long, as other incidents of the same sort occurred, our people on that line began sending back to know what was going on. Naturally, from the different descriptions of these *saucers*, they recognized the objects as antigrav landing-disks from a spaceship. So I went to the Commission and raised atomic blazes about it, and the *Ardrath* was ordered to confine operations to the lower areas of the Fifth Level. Then our people on that time-line went to work with corrective action. Here."

He wiped the screen and then began punching combinations. Page after page appeared, bearing accounts of people who had claimed to have seen the mysterious disks, and each report was more fantastic than the last.

"The standard smother-out technique," Verkan Vall grinned. "I only heard a little talk about the 'Flying Saucers,' and all of that was in joke. In that order of culture, you can always discredit one true story by setting up ten others, palpably false, parallel to it— Wasn't that the time-line the Tharmax Trading Corporation almost lost their paratime license on?"

"That's right; it was! They bought up all the cigarettes, and caused a conspicuous shortage, after Fourth Level cigarettes had been introduced on this line and had become popular. They should have spread their purchases over a number of lines, and kept them within the local supply-demand frame. And they also got into trouble with the local government for selling unrationed petrol and automobile tires. We had to send in a special-operations group, and they came closer to having to engage in outtime local politics than I care to think of."

Tortha Karf quoted a line from a currently popular song about the sorrows of a policeman's life. "We're jugglers, Vall; trying to keep our traders and sociological observers and tourists and plain idiots like the late Gavran Sarn out of trouble; trying to prevent panics and disturbances and dislocations of local economy as a result of our operations; trying to keep out of outtime politics—and, at all times, at all costs and hazards, by all means, guarding the secret of Paratime Transposition. Sometimes I wish Ghaldron Karf and Hesthor Ghrom had strangled in their cradles!"

Verkan Vall shook his head. "No, Chief," he said. "You don't mean that; not really. We've been Paratiming for the past ten thousand years. When the Ghaldron-Hesthor Transtemporal Field was discovered, our ancestors had pretty well exhausted the resources of this planet. We had a world population of half a billion, and it was all they could do to keep alive. After we began Paratime Transposition, our population climbed to ten billion, and there it stayed for the last eight thousand years. Just enough of us to enjoy our planet and the other planets of the system to the fullest; enough of everything for everybody that nobody needs fight anybody for anything.

"We've tapped the resources of those other worlds on other time-lines, a little here, a little there, and not enough to really hurt anybody. We've left our mark in a few places—the Dakota Badlands, and the Gobi, on the Fourth Level, for instance—but we've done no great damage to any of them."

"Except the time they blew up half the Southern Island Continent, over about five hundred parayears on the Third Level," Tortha Karf mentioned.

"Regrettable accident, to be sure," Verkan Vall conceded. "And look how much we've learned from the experiences of those other time-lines. During the Crisis, after the Fourth Interplanetary War, we might have adopted Palnar Sarn's 'Dictatorship of the Chosen' scheme, if we hadn't seen what an exactly similar scheme had done to the Jak-Hakka Civilization, on the Second Level. When Palnar Sarn was told about that, he went into Paratime to see for himself, and when he returned, he renounced his proposal in horror."

Tortha Karf nodded. He wouldn't be making any mistake in turning his post over to the Mavrad of Nerros on his retirement.

"Yes, Vall; I know," he said. "But when you've been at this desk as long as I have, you'll have a sour moment or two, now and then, too."

A blue light flashed over one of the booths across the room. Verkan Vall got to his feet, removing his coat and hanging it on the back of his chair, and crossed the room, rolling up his left shirt sleeve. There was a relaxer-chair in the booth, with a blue plastic helmet above it. He glanced at the indicator-screen to make sure he was getting the indoctrination he called for, and then sat down in the chair and lowered the helmet over his head, inserting the ear plugs and fastening the chin strap. Then he touched his left arm with an injector which was lying on the arm of the chair, and at the same time flipped the starter switch.

Soft, slow music began to chant out of the earphones. The insidious fingers of the drug blocked off his senses, one by one. The music diminished, and the words of the hypnotic formula lulled him to sleep.

He woke, hearing the lively strains of dance music. For a while, he lay relaxed. Then he snapped off the switch, took out the ear plugs, removed the helmet and rose to his feet. Deep in his subconscious mind was the entire body of knowledge about the Venusian nighthound. He mentally pronounced the word, and at once it began flooding into his conscious mind. He knew the animal's evolutionary history, its anatomy, its characteristics, its dietary and reproductive habits, how it hunted, how it fought its enemies, how it eluded pursuit, and how best it could be tracked down and killed.

He nodded. Already, a plan for dealing with Gavran Sarn's renegade pet was taking shape in his mind.

He picked a plastic cup from the dispenser, filled it from a cooler-tap with amber-colored spiced wine, and drank, tossing the cup into the disposal-bin. He placed a fresh injector on the arm of the chair, ready for the next user of the booth. Then he emerged, glancing at his Fourth Level wristwatch and mentally translating to the First Level time-scale. Three hours had passed; there had been more to learn about his quarry than he had expected.

V

Tortha Karf was sitting behind his desk, smoking a cigarette. It seemed as though he had not moved since Verkan Vall had left him, though the special agent knew that he had dined, attended several conferences, and done many other things.

"I checked up on your hitchhiker, Vall," the chief said. "We won't bother about him. He's a member of something called the Christian Avengers—one of those typical Europo-American race-and-religious hate groups. He belongs in a belt that is the outcome of the Hitler victory of 1940, whatever that was. Something unpleasant, I daresay. We don't owe him anything; people of that sort should be stepped on, like cockroaches. And he won't make any more trouble on the line where you dropped him than they have there already. It's in a belt of complete social and political anarchy; somebody probably shot him as soon as he emerged, because he wasn't wearing the right sort of a uniform. Nineteen-forty what, by the way?"

"Elapsed years since the birth of some religious leader," Verkan Vall explained. "And did you find out about my rifle?"

"Oh, yes. It's reproduction of something that's called a Sharp's Model '37.235 Ultraspeed-Express. Made on an adjoining Paratime belt by a company that went out of business sixty-seven years ago, elapsed time, on your line of operation. What made the difference was the Second War Between The States. I don't know what that was, either—I'm not too well up on Fourth Level history—but whatever, your line of operation didn't have it. Probably just as well for them, though they very likely had something else, as bad or worse. I put in a complaint to Supplies about it, and got you some more ammunition and reloading tools. Now, tell me what you're going to do about this nighthound business."

Tortha Karf was silent for a while, after Verkan Vall had finished. "You're taking some awful chances, Vall," he said, at length. "The way you plan doing it, the advantages will all be with the nighthound. Those things can see as well at night as you can in daylight. I suppose you know that, though; you're the nighthound specialist, now."

"Yes. But they're accustomed to the Venus hotland marshes; it's been dry weather for the last two weeks, all over the northeastern section of the Northern Continent. I'll be able to hear it, long before it gets close to me. And I'll be wearing an electric headlamp. When I snap that on, it'll be dazzled, for a moment."

"Well, as I said, you're the nighthound specialist. There's the communicator; order anything you need." He lit a fresh cigarette from the end of the old one before crushing it out. "But be careful, Vall. It took me close to forty years to make a Paratimer out of you; I don't want to have to repeat the process with somebody else before I can retire."

VI

The grass was wet as Verkan Vall—who reminded himself that here he was called Richard Lee—crossed the yard from the farmhouse to the ramshackle barn, in the early autumn darkness. It had been raining that morning when the strato-rocket from Dhergabar had landed him at the Hagraban Synthetics Works, on the First Level; unaffected by the probabilities of human history, the same rain had been coming down on the old Kinchwalter farm, near Rutter's Fort, on the Fourth Level. And it had persisted all day, in a slow, deliberate drizzle.

He didn't like that. The woods would be wet, muffling his quarry's footsteps, and canceling his only advantage over the night-prowler he hunted. He had no idea, however, of postponing the hunt. If anything, the rain had made it all the more imperative that the nighthound be killed at once.

At this season, a falling temperature would speedily follow. The nighthound, a creature of the hot Venus marshes, would suffer from the cold, and, taught by years of domestication to find warmth among human habitations, it would invade some isolated farmhouse, or, worse, one of the little valley villages. If it were not killed tonight, the incident he had come to prevent would certainly occur.

Going to the barn, he spread an old horse blanket on the seat of the jeep, laid his rifle on it, and then backed the jeep outside. Then he took off his coat, removing his pipe and tobacco from the pockets, and spread it on the wet grass. He unwrapped a package and took out a small plastic spray-gun he had brought with him from the First Level, aiming it at the coat and pressing the trigger until it blew itself empty.

A sickening, rancid fetor tainted the air—the scent of the giant poison-roach of Venus, the one creature for which the nighthound bore an inborn, implacable hatred. It was because of this compulsive urge to attack and kill the deadly poison-roach that the first human settlers on Venus, long millennia ago, had domesticated the ugly and savage nighthound. He remembered that the Gavran family derived their title from their vast Venus hotlands estates; that Gavran Sarn, the man who had brought this thing to the Fourth Level, had been born on the inner planet.

When Verkan Vall donned that coat, he would become his own living bait for the murderous fury of the creature he sought. At the moment, mastering his queasiness and putting on the coat, he objected less to that danger than to the hideous stench of the scent, which had been obtained when a valuable specimen had been sacrificed at the Dhergabar Museum of Extraterrestrial Zoology, the evening before. Carrying the wrapper and the spray-gun to an outside fireplace, he snapped his lighter to them and tossed them in. They were highly inflammable, blazing up and vanishing in a moment.

He tested the electric headlamp on the front of his cap; checked his rifle; drew the heavy revolver, an authentic product of this line of operation, and flipped the cylinder out and in again. Then he got into the jeep and drove away. For half an hour, he drove quickly along the valley roads. Now and then, he passed farmhouses, and dogs, puzzled and angered by the alien scent his coat bore, barked furiously. At length, he turned into a back road, and from this to the barely discernible trace of an old log road.

The rain had stopped, and, in order to be ready to fire in any direction at any time, he had removed the top of the jeep. Now he had to crouch below the windshield to avoid overhanging branches. Once three deer—a buck and two does—stopped in front of him and stared for a moment, then bounded away with a flutter of white tails. He was driving slowly, now; laying behind him a reeking trail of scent.

There had been another stock-killing, the night before, while he had been on the First Level. The locality of this latest depredation had confirmed his estimate of the beast's probable movements, and indicated where it might be prowling, tonight. He was certain that it was somewhere near; sooner or later, it would pick up the scent.

Finally, he stopped, snapping out his lights. He had chosen this spot carefully, while studying the Geological Survey map, that afternoon; he was on the grade of an old railroad line, now abandoned and its track long removed, which had served the logging operations of fifty years ago.

On one side, the mountain slanted sharply upward; on the other, it fell away sharply. If the nighthound were below him, it would have to climb that forty-five degree slope, and could not avoid dislodging loose stones, or otherwise making a noise. He would get out on that side; if the nighthound were above him, the jeep would protect him when it charged.

He got to the ground, thumbing off the safety of his rifle, and an instant later he knew that he had made a mistake which could easily cost him his life; a mistake from which neither his comprehensive logic nor his hypnotically acquired knowledge of the beast's habits had saved him. As he stepped to the ground, facing toward the front of the jeep, he heard a low, whining cry behind him, and a rush of padded feet. He whirled, snapping on the headlamp with his left hand and thrusting out his rifle pistol-wise in his right.

For a split second, he saw the charging animal, its long, lizard-like head split in a toothy grin, its talon-tipped fore-paws extended. He fired, and the bullet went wild. The next instant, the rifle was knocked from his hand. Instinctively, he flung up his left arm to shield his eyes. Claws raked his left arm and shoulder, something struck him heavily along the left side, and his cap-light went out as he dropped and rolled under the jeep, drawing in his legs and fumbling under his coat for the revolver.

In that instant, he knew what had gone wrong. His plan had been entirely too much of a success. The nighthound had winded him as he had driven up the old railroad-grade, and had followed. Its best running speed had been just good enough to keep it a hundred or so feet behind the jeep, and the motor-noise had covered the padding of its feet. In the few moments between stopping the little car and getting out, the nighthound had been able to close the distance and spring upon him.

It was characteristic of First-Level mentality that Verkan Vall wasted no moments on self-reproach or panic. While he was still rolling under his jeep, his mind had been busy with plans to retrieve the situation. Something touched the heel of one boot, and he froze his leg into immobility, at the same time trying to get the big Smith & Wesson free.

The shoulder-holster, he found, was badly torn, though made of the heaviest skirting-leather, and the spring which retained the weapon in place had been wrenched and bent until he needed both hands to draw. The eight-inch slashing-claw of the nighthound's right intermediary limb had raked him; only the instinctive motion of throwing up his arm, and the fact that he wore the revolver in a shoulder-holster, had saved his life.

The nighthound was prowling around the jeep, whining frantically. It was badly confused. It could see quite well, even in the close darkness of the starless night; its eyes were of a nature capable of perceiving infrared radiations as light. There were plenty of these; the jeep's engine, lately running on four-wheel drive, was quite hot. Had he been standing alone, especially on this raw, chilly night, Verkan Vall's own body heat would have lighted him up like a jack-o'-lantern.

Now, however, the hot engine above him masked his own radiations. Moreover, the poison-roach scent on his coat was coming up through the floor board and mingling with the scent on the seat, yet the nighthound couldn't find the two-and-a-half foot insectlike thing that should have been producing it. Verkan Vall lay motionless, wondering how long the next move would be in coming. Then he heard a thud above him, followed by a furious tearing as the nighthound ripped the blanket and began rending at the seat cushion.

"Hope it gets a paw-full of seat-springs," Verkan Vall commented mentally. He had already found a stone about the size of his two fists, and another slightly smaller, and had put one in each of the side pockets of the coat. Now he slipped his revolver into his waist-belt and writhed out of the coat, shedding the ruined shoulder-holster at the same time. Wriggling on the flat of his back, he squirmed between the rear wheels, until he was able to sit up, behind the jeep. Then, swinging the weighted coat, he flung it forward, over the nighthound and the jeep itself, at the same time drawing his revolver.

Immediately, the nighthound, lured by the sudden movement of the principal source of the scent, jumped out of the jeep and bounded after the coat, and there was considerable noise in the brush on the lower side of the railroad grade. At once, Verkan Vall swarmed into the jeep and snapped on the lights. His stratagem had succeeded beautifully. The stinking coat had landed on the top of a small bush, about ten feet in front of the jeep and ten feet from the ground.

The nighthound, erect on its haunches, was reaching out with its front paws to drag it down, and slashing angrily at it with its single-clawed intermediary limbs. Its back was to Verkan Vall. His sights clearly defined by the lights in front of him, the Paratimer centered them on the base of the creature's spine, just above its secondary shoulders, and carefully squeezed the trigger. The big .357 Magnum bucked in his hand and belched flame and sound—if only these Fourth Level weapons weren't so confoundedly boisterous!—and the nighthound screamed and fell.

Re-cocking the revolver, Verkan Vall waited for an instant, then nodded in satisfaction. The beast's spine had been smashed, and its hind quarters, and even its intermediary fighting limbs had been paralyzed. He aimed carefully for a second shot and fired into the base of the thing's skull. It quivered and died.

Getting a flashlight, he found his rifle, sticking muzzle-down in the mud a little behind and to the right of the jeep, and swore briefly in the local Fourth Level idiom, for Verkan Vall was a man who loved good weapons, be they sigma-ray needlers, neutron-disruption blasters or the solid-missile projectors of the lower levels. By this time, he was feeling considerable pain from the claw-wounds he had received.

He peeled off his shirt and tossed it over the hood of the jeep. Tortha Karf had advised him to carry a needler, or a blaster or a neurostat-gun, but Verkan Vall had been unwilling to take such arms onto the Fourth Level. In event of mishap to himself, it would be all too easy for such a weapon to fall into the hands of someone able to deduce from it scientific principles too far in advance of the general Fourth Level culture.

But there had been one First Level item which he had permitted himself, mainly because, suitably packaged, it was not readily identifiable as such. Digging a respectable Fourth-Level leatherette case from under the seat, he opened it and took out a pint bottle with a red poison-label and a towel. Saturating the towel with the contents of the bottle, he rubbed every inch of his torso with it, so as not to miss even the smallest break made in his skin by the septic claws of the nighthound.

Whenever the lotion-soaked towel touched raw skin, a pain like the burn of a hot iron shot through him; before he was through, he was in agony. Satisfied that he had disinfected every wound, he dropped the towel and clung weakly to the side of the jeep.

He grunted out a string of English oaths, and capped them with an obscene Spanish blasphemy he had picked up among the Fourth Level inhabitants of his island home of Nerros, to the south, and a thundering curse in the name of Mogga, Fire-God of Dool, in a Third-Level tongue. He mentioned Fasif, Great God of Khift, in a manner which would have got him an acid-bath if the Khiftan priests had heard him. He alluded to the baroque amatory practices of the Third-Level Illyalla people, and soothed himself, in the classical Dar-Halma tongue, with one of those rambling genealogical insults favored in the Indo-Turanian Sector of the Fourth Level. By this time, the pain had subsided to an over-all smarting itch.

He'd have to bear with that until his work was finished and he could enjoy a hot bath. He got another bottle out of the first-aid kit—a flat pint, labeled "Old Overholt," containing a locally-manufactured specific for inward and subjective wounds—and medicated himself copiously from it, corking it and slipping it into his hip pocket against future need.

He gathered up the ruined shoulder-holster and threw it under the back seat. He put on his shirt. Then he went and dragged the dead nighthound onto the grade by its stumpy tail. It was an ugly thing, weighing close to two hundred pounds, with powerfully muscled hind legs which furnished the bulk of its motive power, and sturdy three-clawed front legs. Its secondary limbs, about a third of the way back from its front shoulders, were long and slender; normally, they were carried folded closely against the body, and each was armed with a single curving claw.

The revolver bullet had gone in at the base of the skull and emerged under the jaw; the head was relatively undamaged. Verkan Vall was glad of that; he wanted that head for the trophy-room of his home on Nerros. Grunting and straining, he got the thing into the back of the jeep, and flung his almost shredded tweed coat over it.

A last look around assured him that he had left nothing unaccountable or suspicious. The brush was broken where the nighthound had been tearing at the coat; a bear might have done that. There were splashes of the viscid stuff the thing had used for blood, but they wouldn't be there long. Terrestrial rodents liked nighthound blood, and the woods were full of mice. He climbed in under the wheel, backed, turned, and drove away.

VII

Inside the Paratime-Transposition dome, Verkan Vall turned from the body of the nighthound, which he had just dragged in, and considered the inert form of another animal—a stump-tailed, tuft-eared, tawny Canada lynx. That particular animal had already made two Paratime transpositions; captured in the vast wilderness of Fifth-Level North America, it had been taken to the First Level and placed in the Dhergabar Zoological Gardens, and then, requisitioned on the authority of Tortha Karf, it had been brought to the Fourth Level by Verkan Vall. It was almost at the end of all its travels.

Verkan Vall prodded the supine animal with the toe of his boot; it twitched slightly. Its feet were cross-bound with straps, but when he saw that the narcotic was wearing off, Verkan Vall snatched a syringe, parted the fur at the base of its neck, and gave it an injection. After a moment, he picked it up in his arms and carried it out to the jeep.

"All right, pussycat," he said, placing it under the rear seat, "this is the one-way ride. The way you're doped up, it won't hurt a bit."

He went back and rummaged in the debris of the long-deserted barn. He picked up a hoe, and discarded it as too light. An old plowshare was too unhandy. He considered a grate-bar from a heating furnace, and then he found the poleaxe, lying among a pile of worm-eaten boards. Its handle had been shortened, at some time, to about twelve inches, converting it into a heavy hatchet. He weighed it, and tried it on a block of wood, and then, making sure that the secret door was closed, he went out again and drove off.

An hour later, he returned. Opening the secret door, he carried the ruined shoulder holster, and the straps that had bound the bobcat's feet, and the ax, now splotched with blood and tawny cat-hairs, into the dome. Then he closed the secret room, and took a long drink from the bottle on his hip.

Thc job was done. He would take a hot bath, and sleep in the farmhouse till noon, and then he would return to the First Level. Maybe Tortha Karf would want him to come back here for a while. The situation on this time-line was far from satisfactory, even if the crisis threatened by Gavran Sarn's renegade pet had been averted. The presence of a chief's assistant might be desirable. At least, he had a right to expect a short vacation.

He thought of the little redhead at the Hagraban Synthetics Works. What was her name? Something Kara—Morvan Kara; that was it. She'd be coming off shift about the time he'd make First Level, tomorrow afternoon. The claw-wounds were still smarting vexatiously—a hot bath, and a night's sleep. He took another drink, lit his pipe, picked up his rifle and started across the yard to the house.

Private Zinkowski cradled the telephone and got up from the desk, stretching. He left the orderly-room and walked across the hall to the recreation room, where the rest of the boys were loafing. Sergeant Haines, in a languid gin-rummy game with Corporal Conner, a sheriff's deputy, and a mechanic from the service station down the road, looked up.

"Well, Sarge, I think we can write off those stock-killings," the private said.

"Yeah?" The sergeant's interest quickened.

"Yeah. I think the whatzit's had it. I just got a buzz from the railroad cops at Logansport. It seems a track-walker found a dead bobcat on the Logan River branch, about a mile or so below MMY signal tower. Looks like it tangled with that night freight up-river, and came off second best. It was near chopped to hamburger."

"MMY signal tower; that's right below Yoder's Crossing," the Sergeant considered. "The Strawmyer farm night-before-last, the Amrine farm last night— Yeah, that would be about right."

"That'll suit Steve Parker; bobcats aren't protected, so it's not his trouble. And they're not a violation of state law, so it's none of our worry," Conner said. "Your deal, isn't it, Sarge?"

"Yeah. Wait a minute." The Sergeant got to his feet. "I promised Sam Kane, the AP man at Logansport, that I'd let him in on anything new." He got up and started for the phone. "Phantom Killer!" He blew an impolite noise.

"Well, it was a lot of excitement, while it lasted," the deputy sheriff said. "Just like that Flying Saucer thing."

LAST ENEMY

H. Beam Piper

I

1950 A.D.

Along the U-shaped table, the subdued clatter of dinnerware and the buzz of conversation was dying out; the soft music that drifted down from the overhead sound outlets seemed louder as the competing noises diminished. The feast was drawing to a close, and Dallona of Hadron fidgeted nervously with the stem of her wineglass as last-moment doubts assailed her. The old man at whose right she sat noticed, and reached out to lay his hand on hers.

"My dear, you're worried," he said softly. "You, of all people, shouldn't be, you know."

"The theory isn't complete," she replied. "And I could wish for more positive verification. I'd hate to think I'd got you into this—"

Garnon of Roxor laughed. "No, no!" he assured her. "I'd decided upon this long before you announced the results of your experiments. Ask Girzon; he'll bear me out."

"That's true," the young man who sat at Garnon's left said, leaning forward. "Father has meant to take this step for a long time. He was waiting until after the election, and then he decided to do it now, to give you an opportunity to make experimental use of it."

The man on Dallona's right added his voice. Like the others at the table, he was of medium stature, brown-skinned and dark-eyed, with a wide mouth, prominent cheekbones and a short, square jaw. Unlike the others, he was armed, with a knife and pistol on his belt, and on the breast of his black tunic he wore a scarlet oval patch on which a pair of black wings, with a tapering silver object between them had been superimposed.

"Yes, Lady Dallona; the Lord Garnon and I discussed this, oh, two years ago at the least. Really, I'm surprised that you seem to shrink from it, now. Of course, you're Venus-born, and customs there may be different, but with your scientific knowledge—"

"That may be the trouble, Dirzed," Dallona told him. "A scientist gets in the way of doubting, and one doubts one's own theories most of all."

"That's the scientific attitude, I'm told," Dirzed replied, smiling. "But somehow, I cannot think of you as a scientist." His eyes traveled over her in a way that would have made most women, scientists or otherwise, blush.

It gave Dallona of Hadron a feeling of pleasure. Men often looked at her that way, especially here at Darsh. Novelty had something to do with it—her skin was considerably lighter than usual, and there was a pleasing oddness about the structure of her face. Her alleged Venusian origin was probably accepted as the explanation of that, as of so many other things.

As she was about to reply, a man in dark gray, one of the upper-servants who were accepted as social equals by the Akor-Neb nobles, approached the table. He nodded respectfully to Garnon of Roxor.

"I hate to seem to hurry things, sir, but the boy's ready. He's in a trance-state now," he reported, pointing to the pair of visiplates at the end of the room. Both of the ten-foot-square plates were activated. One was a solid luminous white; on the other was the image of a boy of twelve or fourteen, seated at a big writing machine. Even allowing for the fact that the boy was in a hypnotic trance, there was an expression of idiocy on his loose-lipped, slack-jawed face, a pervading dullness.

"One of our best sensitives," said a man with a beard, several places down the table on Dallona's right. "You remember him, Dallona; he produced that communication from the discarnate Assassin, Sirzim. Normally, he's a low-grade imbecile, but in trance-state he's wonderful. And there can be no argument that the communications he produces originate in his own mind; he doesn't have mind enough, of his own, to operate that machine."

Garnon of Roxor rose to his feet, the others rising with him. He unfastened a jewel from the front of his tunic and handed it to Dallona. "Here, my dear Lady Dallona; I want you to have this," he said. "It's been in the family of Roxor for six generations, but I know that you will appreciate and cherish it."

He twisted a heavy ring from his left hand and gave it to his son. He unstrapped his wristwatch and passed it across the table to the gray-clad upper-servant. He gave a pocket case, containing writing tools, slide rule and magnifier, to the bearded man on the other side of Dallona.

"Something you can use, Dr. Harnosh," he said. Then he took a belt, with a knife and holstered pistol, from a servant who had brought it to him, and gave it to the man with the red badge.

"And something for you, Dirzed. The pistol's by Farnor of Yand, and the knife was forged and tempered on Luna."

The man with the winged-bullet badge took the weapons, exclaiming in appreciation. Then he removed his own belt and buckled on the gift.

"The pistol's fully loaded," Garnon told him.

Dirzed drew it and checked—a man of his craft took no statement about weapons without verification—then slipped it back into the holster.

"Shall I use it?" he asked.

"By all means; I'd had that in mind when I selected it for you."

Another man, to the left of Girzon, received a cigarette case and lighter. He and Garnon hooked fingers and clapped shoulders. "Our views haven't been the same, Garnon," he said, "but I've always valued your friendship. I'm sorry you're doing this, now; I believe you'll be disappointed."

Garnon chuckled. "Would you care to make a small wager on that, Nirzav?" he asked. "You know what I'm putting up. If I'm proven right, will you accept the Volitionalist theory as verified?"

Nirzav chewed his mustache for a moment. "Yes, Garnon, I will." He pointed toward the blankly white screen. "If we get anything conclusive on that, I'll have no other choice."

"All right, friends," Garnon said to those around him. "Will you walk with me to the end of the room?"

Servants removed a section from the table in front of him, to allow him and a few others to pass through; the rest of the guests remained standing at the table, facing toward the inside of the room. Garnon's son, Girzon, and the gray-mustached Nirzav of Shonna, walked on his left; Dallona of Hadron and Dr. Harnosh of Hosh on his right. The gray-clad upper-servant, and two or three ladies, and a nobleman with a small chin-beard, and several others, joined them; of those who had sat close to Garnon, only the man in the black tunic with the scarlet badge hung back. He stood still, by the break in the table, watching Garnon of Roxor walk away from him.

Then Dirzed the Assassin drew the pistol he had lately received as a gift, hefted it in his hand, thumbed off the safety, and aimed at the back of Garnon's head. They had nearly reached the end of the room when the pistol cracked.

Dallona of Hadron started, almost as though the bullet had crashed into her own body, then caught herself and kept on walking. She closed her eyes and laid a hand on Dr. Harnosh's arm for guidance, concentrating her mind upon a single question. The others went on as though Garnon of Roxor were still walking among them.

"Look!" Harnosh of Hosh cried, pointing to the image in the visiplate ahead. "He's under control!"

They all stopped short, and Dirzed, holstering his pistol, hurried forward to join them. Behind, a couple of servants had approached with a stretcher and were gathering up the crumpled figure that had, a moment ago, been Garnon.

A change had come over the boy at the writing machine. His eyes were still glazed with the stupor of the hypnotic trance, but the slack jaw had stiffened, and the loose mouth was compressed in a purposeful line. As they watched, his hands went out to the keyboard in front of him and began to move over it, and as they did, letters appeared on the white screen on the left.

Garnon of Roxor, discarnate, communicating, they read. The machine stopped for a moment, then began again. *To Dallona of Hadron: The question you asked, after I discarnated, was: What was the last book I read, before the feast? While waiting for my valet to prepare my bath, I read the first ten verses of the fourth Canto of* Splendor of Space, *by Larnov of Horka, in my bedroom. When the bath was ready, I marked the page with a strip of message tape, containing a message from the bailiff of my estate on the Shevva River, concerning a breakdown at the power plant, and laid the book on the ivory-inlaid table beside the big red chair.*

Harnosh of Hosh looked at Dallona inquiringly; she nodded. "I rejected the question I had in my mind, and substituted that one, after the shot," she said.

He turned quickly to the upper-servant. "Check on that, right away, Kirzon," he directed.

As the upper-servant hurried out, the writing machine started again. *And to my son, Girzon: I will not use your son, Garnon, as a reincarnation-vehicle; I will remain discarnate until he is grown and has a son of his own; if he has no male child, I will reincarnate in the first available male child of the family of Roxor, or of some family allied to us by marriage. In any case, I will communicate before reincarnating.*

To Nirzav of Shonna: Ten days ago, when I dined at your home, I took a small knife and cut three notches, two close together and one a little apart from the others, on the underside of the table. As I remember, I sat two places down on the left. If you find them, you will know that I have won that wager that I spoke of a few minutes ago.

"I'll have my butler check on that, right away," Nirzav said. His eyes were wide with amazement, and he had begun to sweat; a man does not casually watch the beliefs of a lifetime invalidated in a few moments.

To Dirzed the Assassin: the machine continued. *You have served me faithfully, in the last ten years, never more so than with the last shot you fired in my service. After you fired, the thought was in your mind that you would like to take service with the Lady Dallona of Hadron, whom you believe will need the protection of a member of the Society of Assassins. I advise you to do so, and I advise her to accept your offer. Her work, since she has come to Darsh, has not made her popular in some quarters. No doubt Nirzav of Shonna can bear me out on that.*

"I won't betray things told me in confidence, or said at the Councils of the Statisticalists, but he's right," Nirzav said. "You need a good Assassin, and there are few better than Dirzed."

I see that this sensitive is growing weary, the letters on the screen spelled out. *His body is not strong enough for prolonged communication. I bid you all farewell, for the time; I will communicate again. Good evening, my friends, and I thank you for your presence at the feast.*

The boy, on the other screen, slumped back in his chair, his face relaxing into its customary expression of vacancy.

"Will you accept my offer of service, Lady Dallona?" Dirzed asked. "It's as Garnon said; you've made enemies."

Dallona smiled at him. "I've not been too deep in my work to know that. I'm glad to accept your offer, Dirzed."

II

Nirzav of Shonna had already turned away from the group and was hurrying from the room, to call his home for confirmation on the notches made on the underside of his dining table. As he went out the door, he almost collided with the upper-servant, who was rushing in with a book in his hand.

"Here it is," the latter exclaimed, holding up the book. "Larnov's *Splendor of Space*, just where he said it would be. I had a couple of servants with me as witnesses; I can call them in now, if you wish."

He handed the book to Harnosh of Hosh. "See, a strip of message tape in it, at the tenth verse of the Fourth Canto."

Nirzav of Shonna re-entered the room; he was chewing his mustache and muttering to himself. As he rejoined the group in front of the now dark visiplates, he raised his voice, addressing them all generally. "My butler found the notches, just as the communication described," he said.

"This settles it! Garnon, if you're where you can hear me, you've won. I can't believe in the Statisticalist doctrines after this, or in the political program based upon them. I'll announce my change of attitude at the next meeting of the Executive Council, and resign my seat. I was elected by Statisticalist votes, and I cannot hold office as a Volitionalist."

"You'll need a couple of Assassins, too," the nobleman with the chin-beard told him. "Your former colleagues and fellow-party-members are regrettably given to the forcible discarnation of those who differ with them."

"I've never employed personal Assassins before," Nirzav replied, "but I think you're right. As soon as I get home, I'll call Assassins' Hall and make the necessary arrangements."

"Better do it now," Girzon of Roxor told him, lowering his voice. "There are over a hundred guests here, and I can't vouch for all of them. The Statisticalists would be sure to have a spy planted among them. My father was one of their most dangerous opponents, when he was on the Council; they've always been afraid he'd come out of retirement and stand for re-election. They'd want to make sure he was really discarnate. And if that's the case, you can be sure your change of attitude is known to old Mirzark of Bashad by this time. He won't dare allow you to make a public renunciation of Statisticalism."

He turned to the other nobleman. "Prince Jirzyn, why don't you call the Volitionist headquarters and have a couple of our Assassins sent here to escort Lord Nirzav home?"

"I'll do that immediately," Jirzyn of Starpha said. "It's as Lord Girzon says; we can be pretty sure there was a spy among the guests, and now that you've come over to our way of thinking, we're responsible for your safety."

He left the room to make the necessary visiphone call. Dallona, accompanied by Dirzed, returned to her place at the table, where she was joined by Harnosh of Hosh and some of the others.

"There's no question about the results," Harnosh was exulting. "I'll grant that the boy might have picked up some of that stuff telepathically from the carnate minds present here; even from the mind of Garnon, before he was discarnated. But he could not have picked up enough data, in that way, to make a connected and coherent communication. It takes a sensitive with a powerful mind of his own to practice telesthesia, and that boy's almost an idiot."

He turned to Dallona. "You asked a question, mentally, after Garnon was discarnate, and got an answer that could have been contained only in Garnon's mind. I think it's conclusive proof that the discarnate Garnon was fully conscious and communicating."

"Dirzed also asked a question, mentally, after the discarnation, and got an answer. Dr. Harnosh, we can state positively that the surviving individuality is fully conscious in the discarnate state, is telepathically sensitive, and is capable of telepathic communication with other minds," Dallona agreed. "And in view of our earlier work with memory-recalls, we're justified in stating positively that the individual is capable of exercising choice in reincarnation vehicles."

"My father had been considering voluntary discarnation for a long time," Girzon of Roxor said. "Ever since the discarnation of my mother. He deferred that step because he was unwilling to deprive the Volitionalist Party of his support. Now it would seem that he has done more to combat Statisticalism by discarnating than he ever did in his carnate existence."

"I don't know, Girzon," Jirzyn of Starpha said, as he joined the group. "The Statisticalists will denounce the whole thing as a prearranged fraud. And if they can discarnate the Lady Dallona before she can record her testimony under truth hypnosis or on a lie detector, we're no better off than we were before. Dirzed, you have a great responsibility in guarding the Lady Dallona; some extraordinary security precautions will be needed."

III

In his office, in the First Level city of Dhergabar, Tortha Karf, Chief of Paratime Police, leaned forward in his chair to hold his lighter for his special assistant, Verkan Vall, then lit his own cigarette. He was a man of middle age—his three hundredth birthday was only a decade or so off—and he had begun to acquire a double chin and a bulge at his waistline. His hair, once black, had turned a uniform iron-gray and was beginning to thin in front.

"What do you know about the Second Level Akor-Neb Sector, Vall?" he inquired. "Ever work in that Paratime-area?"

Verkan Vall's handsome features became even more immobile than usual as he mentally pronounced the verbal trigger symbols which should bring hypnotically-acquired knowledge into his conscious mind. Then he shook his head. "Must be a singularly well-behaved sector, sir," he said. "Or else we've been lucky, so far. I never was on an Akor-Neb operation; don't even have a hypno-mech for that sector. All I know is from general reading.

"Like all the Second Level, its time-lines descend from the probability of one or more shiploads of colonists having come to Terra from Mars about seventy-five to a hundred thousand years ago, and then having been cut off from the home planet and forced to develop a civilization of their own here. The Akor-Neb civilization is of a fairly high culture-order, even for Second Level. An atomic-power, interplanetary culture; gravity-counteraction, direct conversion of nuclear energy to electrical power, that sort of thing. We buy fine synthetic plastics and fabrics from them."

He fingered the material of his smartly-cut green police uniform. "I think this cloth is Akor-Neb. We sell a lot of Venusian *zerfa*-leaf; they smoke it, straight and mixed with tobacco. They have a single System-wide government, a single race and a universal language. They're a dark-brown race, which evolved in its present form about fifty thousand years ago; the present civilization is about ten thousand years old, developed out of the wreckage of several earlier civilizations which decayed or fell through wars, exhaustion of resources, et cetera. They have legends, maybe historical records, of their extraterrestrial origin."

Tortha Karf nodded. "Pretty good, for consciously acquired knowledge," he commented. "Well, our luck's run out, on that sector; we have troubles there, now. I want you to go iron them out. I know, you've been going pretty hard, lately—that nighthound business, on the Fourth Level Europo-American Sector, wasn't any picnic. But the fact is that a lot of my ordinary and deputy assistants have a little too much regard for the alleged sanctity of human life, and this is something that may need some pretty drastic action."

"Some of our people getting out of line?" Verkan Vall asked.

"Well, the data isn't too complete, but one of our people has run into trouble on that sector, and needs rescuing—a psychic-science researcher, a young lady named Hadron Dalla. I believe you know her, don't you?" Tortha Karf asked innocently.

"Slightly," Verkan Vall deadpanned. "I enjoyed a brief but rather hectic companionate-marriage with her, about twenty years ago. What sort of a jam's little Dalla got herself into, now?"

"Well, frankly, we don't know. I hope she's still alive, but I'm not unduly optimistic. It seems that about a year ago, Dr. Hadron transposed to the Second Level, to study alleged proof of reincarnation which the Akor-Neb people were reported to possess. She went to Gindrabar, on Venus, and transposed to the Second Paratime Level, to a station maintained by Outtime Import & Export Trading Corporation—a *zerfa* plantation just east of the High Ridge country. There she assumed an identity as the daughter of a planter, and took the name of Dallona of Hadron.

"Parenthetically, all Akor-Neb family-names are prepositional; family-names were originally place names. I believe that ancient Akor-Neb marital relations were too complicated to permit exact establishment of paternity. And all Akor-Neb men's personal names have *-irz-* or *-arn-* inserted in the middle, and women's names end in *-itra-* or *-ona*. You could call yourself Virzal of Verkan, for instance.

"Anyhow, she made the Second Level Venus-Terra trip on a regular passenger liner, and landed at the Akor-Neb city of Ghamma, on the upper Nile. There she established contact with the Outtime Trading Corporation representative, Zortan Brend, locally known as Brarnend of Zorda. He couldn't call himself Brarnend of Zortan—in the Akor-Neb language, *zortan* is a particularly nasty dirty-word.

"Hadron Dalla spent a few weeks at his residence, briefing herself on local conditions. Then she went to the capital city, Darsh, in eastern Europe, and enrolled as a student at something called the Independent Institute for Reincarnation Research, having secured a letter of introduction to its director, a Dr. Harnosh of Hosh.

"Almost at once, she began sending in reports to her home organization, the Rhogom Memorial Foundation of Psychic Science, here at Dhergabar, through Zortan Brend. The people there were wildly enthusiastic. I don't have more than the average intelligent—I hope—layman's knowledge of psychics, but Dr. Volzar Darv, the Director of Rhogom Foundation, tells me that even in the present incomplete form, her reports have opened whole new horizons in the science. It seems that these Akor-Neb people have actually demonstrated, as a scientific fact, that the human individuality reincarnates after physical death—that your personality, and mine, have existed, as such, for ages, and will exist for ages to come. More, they have means of recovering, from almost anybody, memories of past reincarnations.

"Well, after about a month, the people at this Reincarnation Institute realized that this Dallona of Hadron wasn't any ordinary student. She probably had trouble keeping down to the local level of psychic knowledge. So, as soon as she'd learned their techniques, she was allowed to undertake experimental work of her own. I imagine she let herself out on that; as soon as she'd mastered the standard Akor-Neb methods of recovering memories of past reincarnations, she began refining and developing them more than the local yokels had been able to do in the past thousand years. I can't tell you just what she did, because I don't know the subject, but she must have lit things up properly. She got quite a lot of local publicity; not only scientific journals, but general newscasts.

"Then, four days ago, she disappeared, and her disappearance seems to have been coincident with an unsuccessful attempt on her life. We don't know as much about this as we should; all we have is Zortan Brend's account.

"It seems that on the evening of her disappearance, she had been attending the voluntary discarnation feast—suicide party—of a prominent nobleman named Garnon of Roxor. Evidently when the Akor-Neb people get tired of their current reincarnation they invite in their friends, throw a big party, and then do themselves in in an atmosphere of general conviviality. Frequently they take poison or inhale lethal gas; this fellow had his personal trigger man shoot him through the head. Dalla was one of the guests of honor, along with this Harnosh of Hosh.

"They'd made rather elaborate preparations, and after the shooting they got a detailed and apparently authentic spirit-communication from the late

Garnon. The voluntary discarnation was just a routine social event, it seems, but the communication caused quite an uproar, and rated top place on the System-wide newscasts, and started a storm of controversy.

"After the shooting and the communication, Dalla took the officiating gun artist, one Dirzed, into her own service. This Dirzed was spoken of as a generally respected member of something called the Society of Assassins, and that'll give you an idea of what things are like on that sector, and why I don't want to send anybody who might develop trigger-finger cramp at the wrong moment. She and Dirzed left the home of the gentleman who had just had himself discarnated, presumably for Dalla's apartment, about a hundred miles away. That's the last that's been heard of either of them.

"This attempt on Dalla's life occurred while the pre-mortem revels were still going on. She lived in a six-room apartment, with three servants, on one of the upper floors of a three-thousand-foot tower—Akor-Neb cities are built vertically, with considerable interval between units—and while she was at this feast, a package was delivered at the apartment, ostensibly from the Reincarnation Institute and made up to look as though it contained record tapes.

"One of the servants accepted it from a service employee of the apartments. The next morning, a little before noon, Dr. Harnosh of Hosh called her on the visiphone and got no answer; he then called the apartment manager, who entered the apartment. He found all three of the servants dead, from a lethal-gas bomb which had exploded when one of them had opened this package. However, Hadron Dalla had never returned to the apartment, the night before."

IV

Verkan Vall was sitting motionless, his face expressionless as he ran Tortha Karf's narrative through the intricate semantic and psychological processes of the First Level mentality. The fact that Hadron Dalla had been a former wife of his had been relegated to one corner of his consciousness and contained there; it was not a fact that would, at the moment, contribute to the problem or to his treatment of it.

"The package was delivered while she was at this suicide party," he considered. "It must, therefore, have been sent by somebody who either did not know she would be out of the apartment, or who did not expect it to function until after her return. On the other hand, if her disappearance was due to hostile action, it was the work of somebody who knew she was at the feast and did not want her to reach her apartment again. This would seem to exclude the sender of the package bomb."

Tortha Karf nodded. He had reached that conclusion, himself.

"Thus," Verkan Vall continued, "if her disappearance was the work of an enemy, she must have two enemies, each working in ignorance of the other's plans."

"What do you think she did to provoke such enmity?"

"Well, of course, it just might be that Dalla's normally complicated love-life had got a little more complicated than usual and short-circuited on her," Verkan Vall said, out of the fullness of personal knowledge, "but I doubt that, at the moment. I would think that this affair has political implications."

"So?" Tortha Karf had not thought of politics as an explanation. He waited for Verkan Vall to elaborate.

"Don't you see, Chief?" the Special Assistant asked. "We find a belief in reincarnation on many time-lines, as a religious doctrine, but these people accept it as a scientific fact. Such acceptance would carry much more conviction; it would influence a people's entire thinking. We see it reflected in their disregard for death—suicide as a social function, this Society of Assassins, and the like. It would naturally color their political thinking, because politics is nothing but common action to secure more favorable living conditions, and to these people, the term 'living conditions' includes not only the present life, but also an indefinite number of future lives as well. I find this title, 'Independent' Institute, suggestive. Independent of what? Possibly of partisan affiliation."

"But wouldn't these people be grateful to her for her new discoveries, which would enable them to plan their future reincarnations more intelligently?" Tortha Karf asked.

"Oh, Chief!" Verkan Vall reproached. "You know better than that! How many times have our people got in trouble on other time-lines because they divulged some useful scientific fact that conflicted with the locally revered nonsense? You show me ten men who cherish some religious doctrine or political ideology, and I'll show you nine men whose minds are utterly impervious to any factual evidence which contradicts their beliefs, and who regard the producer of such evidence as a criminal who ought to be suppressed.

"For instance, on the Fourth Level Europo-American Sector, where I was just working, there is a political sect, the Communists, who, in the territory under their control, forbid the teaching of certain well-established facts of genetics and heredity, because those facts do not fit the world-picture demanded by their political doctrines. And on the same sector, a religious sect recently tried, in some sections successfully, to outlaw the teaching of evolution by natural selection."

Tortha Karf nodded. "I remember some stories my grandfather told me, about his narrow escapes from an organization called the Holy Inquisition, when he was a Paratime trader on the Fourth Level, about four hundred years ago. I believe that thing's still operating, on the Europo-American Sector, under the name of the NKVD. So you think Dalla may have proven something that conflicted with local reincarnation theories, and somebody who had a vested interest in maintaining those theories is trying to stop her?"

"You spoke of a controversy over the communication alleged to have originated with this voluntarily discarnated nobleman. That would suggest a difference of opinion on the manner or nature of reincarnation or the discarnate state. This difference may mark the dividing line between the different political parties. Now, to get to this Darsh place, do I have to go to Venus, as Dalla did?"

"No. The Outtime Trading Corporation has transposition facilities at Ravvanan, on the Nile, which is spatially co-existent with the city of Ghamma on the Akor-Neb Sector, where Zortan Brend is. You transpose through there, and Zortan Brend will furnish you transportation to Darsh. It'll take you about two days, here, getting your hypno-mech indoctrinations and having your skin pigmented, and your hair turned black. I'll notify Zortan Brend at once that you're coming through. Is there anything special you'll want?"

"Why, I'll want an abstract of the reports Dalla sent back to Rhogom Foundation. It's likely that there is some clue among them as to whom her discoveries may have antagonized. I'm going to be a Venusian *zerfa*-planter, a friend of her father's; I'll want full hypno-mech indoctrination to enable me to play that part. And I'll want to familiarize myself with Akor-Neb weapons and combat techniques. I think that will be all, chief."

V

The last of the tall city-units of Ghamma were sliding out of sight as the ship passed over them—shaft-like buildings that rose two or three thousand feet above the ground in clumps of three or four or six, one at each corner of the landing stages set in series between them. Each of these units stood in the middle of a wooded park some five miles square; no unit was much more or less than twenty miles from its nearest neighbor, and the land between was the uniform golden-brown of ripening grain, crisscrossed with the threads of irrigation canals and dotted here and there with sturdy farm-village buildings and tall, stacklike granaries.

There were a few other ships in the air at the fifty-thousand-foot level, and below, swarms of small airboats darted back and forth on different levels, depending upon speed and direction. Far ahead, to the northeast, was the shimmer of the Red Sea and the hazy bulk of Asia Minor beyond.

Verkan Vall—the Lord Virzal of Verkan, temporarily—stood at the glass front of the observation deck, looking down. He was a different Verkan Vall from the man who had talked with Tortha Karf in the latter's office, two days before. The First Level cosmeticists had worked miracles upon him with their art. His skin was a soft chocolate-brown, now; his hair was jet-black, and so were his eyes. And in his subconscious mind, instantly available to consciousness, was a vast body of knowledge about conditions on the Akor-Neb sector, as well as a complete command of the local language, all hypnotically acquired.

He knew that he was looking down upon one of the minor provincial cities of a very respectably advanced civilization. A civilization which built its cities vertically, since it had learned to counteract gravitation. A civilization which still depended upon natural cereals for food, but one which had learned to make the most efficient use of its soil. The network of dams and irrigation canals which he saw was as good as anything on his own Paratime level.

The wide dispersal of buildings, he knew, was a heritage of a series of disastrous atomic wars of several thousand years before; the Akor-Neb people had come to love the wide inter-vistas of open country and forest, and had continued to scatter their buildings, even after the necessity had passed. But the slim, towering buildings could only have been reared by a people who had banished nationalism and, with it, the threat of total war. He contrasted them with the ground-hugging dome cities of the Khiftan civilization, only a few thousand parayears distant.

Three men came out of the lounge behind him and joined him. One was, like himself, a disguised Paratimer from the First Level—the Outtime Export and Import man, Zortan Brend, here known as Brarnend of Zorda. The other two were Akor-Neb people, and both wore the black tunics and the winged-bullet badges of the Society of Assassins. Unlike Verkan Vall and Zortan Brend, who wore shoulder holsters under their short tunics, the Assassins openly displayed pistols and knives on their belts.

"We heard that you were coming two days ago, Lord Virzal," Zortan Brend said. "We delayed the take-off of this ship, so that you could travel to Darsh as inconspicuously as possible. I also booked a suite for you at the Solar Hotel, at Darsh. And these are your Assassins—Olirzon, and Marnik."

Verkan Vall hooked fingers and clapped shoulders with them. "Virzal of Verkan," he identified himself. "I am satisfied to entrust myself to you."

"We'll do our best for you, Lord Virzal," the older of the pair, Olirzon, said. He hesitated for a moment, then continued: "Understand, Lord Virzal, I only ask for information useful in serving and protecting you. But is this of the Lady Dallona a political matter?"

"Not from our side," Verkan Vall told him. "The Lady Dallona is a scientist, entirely nonpolitical. The Honorable Brarnend is a business man; he doesn't meddle with politics as long as the politicians leave him alone. And

I'm a planter on Venus; I have enough troubles, with the natives, and the weather, and blue-rot in the *zerfa* plants, and poison roaches, and javelin bugs, without getting into politics. But psychic science is inextricably mixed with politics, and the Lady Dallona's work has evidently tended to discredit the theory of Statistical Reincarnation."

"Do you often make understatements like that, Lord Virzal?" Olirzon grinned. "In the last six months, she's knocked Statistical Reincarnation to splinters."

"Well, I'm not a psychic scientist, and as I said, I don't know much about Terran politics," Verkan Vall replied. "I know that the Statisticalists favor complete socialization and political control of the whole economy, because they want everybody to have the same opportunities in every reincarnation. And the Volitionalists believe that everybody reincarnates as he pleases, and so they favor continuance of the present system of private ownership of wealth and private profit under a system of free competition. And that's about all I do know.

"Naturally, as a land-owner and the holder of a title of nobility, I'm a Volitionalist in politics, but the socialization issue isn't important on Venus. There is still too much unseated land there, and too many personal opportunities, to make socialism attractive to anybody."

"Well, that's about it," Zortan Brend told him. "I'm not enough of a psychist to know what the Lady Dallona's been doing, but she's knocked the theoretical basis from under Statistical Reincarnation, and that's the basis, in turn, of Statistical Socialism. I think we'll find that the Statisticalist Party is responsible for whatever happened to her."

Marnik, the younger of the two Assassins, hesitated for a moment, then addressed Verkan Vall: "Lord Virzal, I know none of the personalities involved in this matter, and I speak without wishing to give offense, but is it not possible that the Lady Dallona and the Assassin Dirzed may have gone somewhere together voluntarily? I have met Dirzed, and he has many qualities which women find attractive, and he is by no means indifferent to the opposite sex. You understand, Lord Virzal—"

"I understand all too perfectly, Marnik," Verkan Vall replied, out of the fullness of experience. "The Lady Dallona has had affairs with a number of men, myself among them. But under the circumstances, I find that explanation unthinkable."

Marnik looked at him in open skepticism. Evidently, in his book, where an attractive man and a beautiful woman were concerned, that explanation was never unthinkable.

"The Lady Dallona is a scientist," Verkan Vall elaborated. "She is not above diverting herself with love affairs, but that's all they are—a not too important form of diversion. And, if you recall, she had just participated in a most significant experiment: you can be sure that she had other things on her mind at the time than pleasure jaunts with good-looking Assassins."

The ship was passing around the Caucasus Mountains, with the Caspian Sea in sight ahead, when several of the crew appeared on the observation deck and began preparing the shielding to protect the deck from gunfire. Zortan Brend inquired of the petty officer in charge of the work as to the necessity.

"We've been getting reports of trouble at Darsh, sir," the man said. "Newscast bulletins every couple of minutes: rioting in different parts of the city. Started yesterday afternoon, when a couple of Statisticalist members of the Executive Council resigned and went over to the Volitionalists. Lord Nirzav of Shonna, the only nobleman of any importance in the Statisticalist Party, was one of them; he was shot immediately afterward, while leaving the Council Chambers, along with a couple of Assassins who were with him. Some people in an airboat sprayed them with a machine rifle as they came out onto the landing stage."

The two Assassins exclaimed in horrified anger over this. "That wasn't the work of members of the Society of Assassins!" Olirzon declared. "Even after he'd resigned, the Lord Nirzav was still immune till he left the Government Building. There's too blasted much illegal assassination going on!"

"What happened next?" Verkan Vall wanted to know.

"About what you'd expect, sir. The Volitionalists weren't going to take that quietly. In the past eighteen hours, four prominent Statisticalists were forcibly discarnated, and there was even a fight in Mirzark of Bashad's house, when Volitionalist Assassins broke in; three of them and four of Mirzark's

Assassins were discarnated."

"You know, something is going to have to be done about that, too," Olirzon said to Marnik. "It's getting to a point where these political faction fights are being carried on entirely between members of the Society. In Ghamma alone, last year, thirty or forty of our members were discarnated that way."

"Plug in a newscast visiplate, Karnil," Zortan Brend told the petty officer. "Let's see what's going on in Darsh now."

In Darsh, it seemed, an uneasy peace was being established. Verkan Vall watched heavily-armed airboats and light combat ships patrolling among the high towers of the city. He saw a couple of minor riots being broken up by the blue-uniformed Constabulary, with considerable shooting and a ruthless disregard for who might get shot. It wasn't exactly the sort of policing that would have been tolerated in the First Level Civil Order Section, but it seemed to suit Akor-Neb conditions. And he listened to a series of angry recriminations and contradictory statements by different politicians, all of whom blamed the disorders on their opponents.

The Volitionalists spoke of the Statisticalists as "insane criminals" and "underminers of social stability," and the Statisticalists called the Volitionalists "reactionary criminals" and "enemies of social progress." Politicians, he had observed, differed little in their vocabularies from one time-line to another.

This kept up all the while the ship was passing over the Caspian Sea; as they were turning up the Volga valley, one of the ship's officers came down from the control deck, above. "We're coming into Darsh, now," he said, and as Verkan Vall turned from the visiplate to the forward windows, he could see the white and pastel-tinted towers of the city rising above the hardwood forests that covered the whole Volga basin on this sector.

"Your luggage has been put into the airboat, Lord Virzal and Honorable Assassins, and it's ready for launching whenever you are." The officer glanced at his watch. "We dock at Commercial Center in twenty minutes; we'll be passing the Solar Hotel in ten."

They all rose, and Verkan Vall hooked fingers and clapped shoulders with Zortan Brend.

"Good luck, Lord Virzal," the latter said. "I hope you find the Lady Dallona safe and carnate. If you need help, I'll be at Mercantile House for the next day or so; if you get back to Ghamma before I do, you know who to ask for there."

VI

A number of assassins loitered in the hallways and offices of the Independent Institute of Reincarnation Research when Verkan Vall, accompanied by Marnik, called there that afternoon. Some of them carried submachine-guns or sleep-gas projectors, and they were stopping people and questioning them. Marnik needed only to give them a quick gesture and the words, "Assassins' Truce," and he and his client were allowed to pass.

They entered a lifter tube and floated up to the office of Dr. Harnosh of Hosh, with whom Verkan Vall had made an appointment.

"I'm sorry, Lord Virzal," the director of the Institute told him, "but I have no idea what has befallen the Lady Dallona, or even if she is still carnate. I am quite worried; I admired her extremely, both as an individual and as a scientist. I do hope she hasn't been discarnated; that would be a serious blow to science. It is fortunate that she accomplished as much as she did, while she was with us."

"You think she is no longer carnate, then?"

"I'm afraid so. The political effects of her discoveries—" Harnosh of Hosh shrugged sadly. "She was devoted, to a rare degree, to her work. I am sure that nothing but her discarnation could have taken her away from us, at this time, with so many important experiments still uncompleted."

Marnik nodded to Verkan Vall, as much as to say: "You were right."

"Well, I intend acting upon the assumption that she is still carnate and in need of help, until I am positive to the contrary," Verkan Vall said. "And in the latter case, I intend finding out who discarnated her, and sending him to apologize for it in person. People don't forcibly discarnate my friends with impunity."

"Sound attitude," Dr. Harnosh commented. "There's certainly no positive evidence that she isn't still carnate. I'll gladly give you all the assistance I can, if you'll only tell me what you want."

"Well, in the first place," Verkan Vall began, "just what sort of work was she doing?" He already knew the answer to that, from the reports she had sent back to the First Level, but he wanted to hear Dr. Harnosh's version. "And what, exactly, are the political effects you mentioned? Understand, Dr. Harnosh, I am really quite ignorant of any scientific subject unrelated to *zerfa* culture, and equally so of Terran politics. Politics, on Venus, is mainly a question of who gets how much graft out of what."

Dr. Harnosh smiled; evidently he had heard about Venusian politics. "Ah, yes, of course. But you are familiar with the main differences between Statistical and Volitional reincarnation theories?"

"In a general way," Verkan said. "The Volitionalists hold that the discarnate individuality is fully conscious, and is capable of something analogous to sense-perception, and is also capable of exercising choice in the matter of reincarnation vehicles, and can reincarnate or remain in the discarnate state as it chooses. They also believe that discarnate individualities can communicate with one another, and with at least some carnate individualities, by telepathy

"The Statisticalists deny all this; their opinion is that the discarnate individuality is in a more or less somnambulistic state, that it is drawn by a process akin to tropism to the nearest available reincarnation vehicle, and that it must reincarnate in and only in that vehicle. They are labeled Statisticalists because they believe that the process of reincarnation is purely at random, or governed by unknown and uncontrollable causes, and is unpredictable except as to aggregates."

"That's a fairly good generalized summary," Dr. Harnosh of Hosh said begrudgingly, unwilling to give a mere layman too much credit. He dipped a spoon into a tobacco humidor, dusted the tobacco lightly with dried *zerfa*, and rammed it into his pipe. "You must understand that our modern Statisticalists are the intellectual heirs of those ancient materialistic thinkers who denied the possibility of any discarnate existence, or of any extraphysical mind, or even of extrasensory perception.

"Since all these things have been demonstrated to be facts, the materialistic dogma has been broadened to include them, but always strictly within the frame of materialism. We have proven, for instance, that the human individuality can exist in a discarnate state, and that it reincarnates into the body of an infant, shortly after birth. But the Statisticalists cannot accept the idea of discarnate consciousness, since they conceive of consciousness purely as a function of the physical brain. So they postulate an unconscious discarnate personality, or, as you put it, one in a somnambulistic state.

"They have to concede memory to this discarnate personality, since it was by recovery of memories of previous reincarnations that discarnate existence and reincarnation were proven to be facts. So they picture the discarnate individuality as a material object, or physical event, of negligible but actual mass, in which an indefinite number of memories can be stored as electronic charges. And they picture it as being drawn irresistibly to the body of the nearest non-incarnated infant. Curiously enough, the reincarnation vehicle chosen is almost always of the same sex as the vehicle of the previous reincarnation, the exceptions being cases of persons who had a previous history of psychological sex-inversion."

Dr. Harnosh remembered the unlighted pipe in his hand, thrust it into his mouth, and lit it. For a moment, he sat with it jutting out of his black beard, until it was drawing to his satisfaction. "This belief in immediate reincarnation leads the Statisticalists, when they fight duels or perform voluntary discarnation, to do so in the neighborhood of maternity hospitals," he added. "I know, personally, of one reincarnation memory-recall, in which the subject, a Statisticalist, voluntarily discarnated by lethal-gas inhaler in a private room at one of our local maternity hospitals, and reincarnated twenty years later in the city of Jeddul, three thousand miles away."

The square black beard jiggled as the scientist laughed. "Now, as to the political implications of these contradictory theories: Since the Statisticalists believe that they will reincarnate entirely at random, their aim is to create an utterly classless social and economic order, in which, theoretically, each individuality will reincarnate into a condition of equality with everybody else. Their political program, therefore, is one of complete socialization of all means of production and distribution, abolition of hereditary titles and inherited wealth—eventually, all private wealth—and total government control of all economic, social and cultural activities.

"Of course," Dr. Harnosh apologized, "politics isn't my subject; I wouldn't presume to judge how that would function in practice."

"I would," Verkan Vall said shortly, thinking of all the different time-lines on which he had seen systems like that in operation. "You wouldn't like it, doctor. And the Volitionalists?"

"Well, since they believe that they are able to choose the circumstances of their next reincarnations for themselves, they are the party of the *status quo*. Naturally, almost all the nobles, almost all the wealthy trading and manufacturing families, and almost all professional people, are Volitionalists; most of the workers and peasants are Statisticalists. Or, at least, they were, for the most part, before we began announcing the results of the Lady Dallona's experimental work."

"Ah; now we come to it," Verkan Vall said as the story clarified.

"Yes. In somewhat oversimplified form, the situation is rather like this." Dr. Harnosh of Hosh said. "The Lady Dallona introduced a number of refinements and some outright innovations into our technique of recovering memories of past reincarnations. Previously, it was necessary to keep the subject in a hypnotic trance, during which he or she would narrate what was remembered of past reincarnations, and this would be recorded. On emerging from the trance, the subject would remember nothing; the tape-recording would be all that would be left.

"But the Lady Dallona devised a technique by which these memories would remain in what might be called the fore part of the subject's subconscious mind, so that they could be brought to the level of consciousness at will. More, she was able to recover memories of past discarnate existences, something we had never been able to do heretofore." Dr. Harnosh shook his head. "And to think, when I first met her, I thought that she was just another sensation-seeking young lady of wealth, and was almost about to refuse her enrollment!"

He wasn't the only one whom little Dalla had surprised, Verkan Vall thought. At least, he had been pleasantly surprised.

"You see," Dr. Harnosh continued, "this entirely disproves the Statistical Theory of Reincarnation. For example, we got a fine set of memory-recalls from one subject, for four previous reincarnations and four intercarnations.

In the first of these, the subject had been a peasant on the estate of a wealthy noble. Unlike most of his fellows, who reincarnated into other peasant families almost immediately after discarnation, this man waited for fifty years in the discarnate state for an opportunity to reincarnate as the son of an over-servant. In his next reincarnation, he was the son of a technician, and received a technical education; he became a physics researcher.

"For his next reincarnation, he chose the son of a nobleman by a concubine as his vehicle; in his present reincarnation, he is a member of a wealthy manufacturing family, and married into a family of the nobility. In five reincarnations, he has climbed from the lowest to the next-to-highest rung of the social ladder. Few individuals of the class from whence he began this ascent possess so much persistence or determination. Then, of course, there was the case of Lord Garnon of Roxor."

He went on to describe the last experiment in which Hadron Dalla had participated.

"Well, that all sounds pretty conclusive," Verkan Vall commented. "I take it the leaders of the Volitionalist Party here are pleased with the result of the Lady Dallona's work?"

"Pleased? My dear Lord Virzal, they're fairly bursting with glee over it!" Harnosh of Hosh declared. "As I pointed out, the Statisticalist program of socialization is based entirely on the proposition that no one can choose the circumstances of his next reincarnation, and that's been demonstrated to be utter nonsense. Until the Lady Dallona's discoveries were announced, they were the dominant party, controlling a majority of the seats in Parliament and on the Executive Council.

"Only the Constitution kept them from enacting their entire socialization program long ago, and they were about to legislate constitutional changes which would remove that barrier. They had expected to be able to do so after the forthcoming general elections. But now, social inequality has become desirable: it gives people something to look forward to in the next reincarnation. Instead of wanting to abolish wealth and privilege and nobility, the proletariat want to reincarnate into them." Harnosh of Hosh laughed happily. "So you can see how furious the Statisticalist Party organization is!"

"There's a catch to this, somewhere," Marnik the Assassin, speaking for the first time, declared. "They can't all reincarnate as princes, there aren't enough vacancies to go 'round. And no noble is going to reincarnate as a tractor driver to make room for a tractor driver who wants to reincarnate as a noble."

"That's correct," Dr. Harnosh replied. "There is a catch to it; a catch most people would never admit, even to themselves. Very few individuals possess the will power, the intelligence or the capacity for mental effort displayed by the subject of the case I just quoted. The average man's interests are almost entirely on the physical side; he actually finds mental effort painful, and makes as little of it as possible. And that is the only sort of effort a discarnate individuality can exert. So, unable to endure the fifty or so years needed to make a really good reincarnation, he reincarnates in a year or so, out of pure boredom, into the first vehicle he can find, usually one nobody else wants."

Dr. Harnosh dug out the heel of his pipe and blew through the stem. "But nobody will admit his own mental inferiority, even to himself. Now, every machine operator and field hand on the planet thinks he can reincarnate as a prince or a millionaire. Politics isn't my subject, but I'm willing to bet that since Statistical Reincarnation is an exploded psychic theory, Statisticalist Socialism has been caught in the blast area and destroyed along with it."

VII

Olirzon was in the drawing room of the hotel suite when they returned, sitting on the middle of his spinal column in a reclining chair, smoking a pipe, dressing the edge of his knife with a pocket-hone, and gazing lecherously at a young woman in the visiplate. She was an extremely well-designed young woman, in a rather fragmentary costume, and she was heaving her bosom at the invisible audience in anger, sorrow, scorn, entreaty, and numerous other emotions.

"—this revolting crime," she was declaiming, in a husky contralto, as Verkan Vall and Marnik entered, "foul even for the criminal beasts who conceived and perpetrated it!" She pointed an accusing finger. "This murder of the beautiful Lady Dallona of Hadron!"

Verkan Vall stopped short, considering the possibility of something having been discovered lately of which he was ignorant. Olirzon must have guessed his thought; he grinned reassuringly.

"Think nothing of it, Lord Virzal," he said, waving his knife at the visiplate. "Just political propaganda; strictly for the sparrows. Nice propagandist, though."

"And now," the woman with the magnificent natural resources lowered her voice reverently, "we bring you the last image of the Lady Dallona, and of Dirzed, her faithful Assassin, taken just before they vanished, never to be seen again."

The plate darkened, and there were strains of slow, dirgelike music; then it lighted again, presenting a view of a broad hallway, thronged with men and women in bright varicolored costumes. In the foreground, wearing a tight skirt of deep blue and a short red jacket, was Hadron Dalla, just as she had looked in the solidographs taken in Dhergabar after her alteration by the First Level cosmeticians to conform to the appearance of the Malayoid Akor-Neb people.

She was holding the arm of a man who wore the black tunic and red badge of an Assassin, a handsome specimen of the Akor-Neb race. *Trust little Dalla for that*, Verkan Vall thought. The figures were moving with exaggerated slowness, as though a very fleeting picture were being stretched out as far as possible. Having already memorized his former wife's changed appearance, Verkan Vall concentrated on the man beside her until the picture faded.

"All right, Olirzon; what did you get?" he asked.

"Well, first of all, at Assassins' Hall," Olirzon said, rolling up his left sleeve, holding his bare forearm to the light, and shaving a few fine hairs from it to test the edge of his knife. "Of course, they never tell one Assassin anything about the client of another Assassin; that's standard practice. But I was in the Lodge Secretary's office, where nobody but Assassins are ever admitted. They have a big panel in there, with the names of all the Lodge members on it in light-letters; that's standard in all Lodges.

"If an Assassin is unattached and free to accept a client, his name's in white light. If he has a client, the light's changed to blue, and the name of the client goes up under his. If his whereabouts are unknown, the light's changed to amber. If he is discarnated, his name's removed entirely, unless the circumstances of his discarnation are such as to constitute an injury to the Society. In that case, the name's in red light until he's been properly avenged, or, as we say, till his blood's been mopped up.

"Well, the name of Dirzed is up in blue light, with the name of Dallona of Hadron under it. I found out that the light had been amber for two days after the disappearance, and then had been changed back to blue. Get it, Lord Virzal?"

Verkan Vall nodded. "I think so. I'd been considering that as a possibility from the first. Then what?"

"Then I was about and around for a couple of hours, buying drinks for people—unattached Assassins, Constabulary detectives, political workers, newscast people. You owe me fifteen System Monetary Units for that, Lord Virzal. What I got, when it's all sorted out—I recorded it in detail, as soon as I got back—reduces to this: The Volitionalists are moving mountains to find out who was the spy at Garnon of Roxor's discarnation feast, but are doing nothing but nothing at all to find the Lady Dallona or Dirzed.

"The Statisticalists are making all sorts of secret efforts to find out what happened to her. The Constabulary blame the Statistos for the package-bomb: they're interested in that because of the discarnation of the three servants by an illegal weapon of indiscriminate effect. They claim that the disappearance of Dirzed and the Lady Dallona was a publicity hoax. The Volitionalists are preparing a line of publicity to deny this."

Verkan Vall nodded. "That ties in with what you learned at Assassins' Hall," he said. "They're hiding out somewhere. Is there any chance of reaching Dirzed through the Society of Assassins?"

Olirzon shook his head. "If you're right—and that's the way it looks to me, too—he's probably just called in and notified the Society that he's still carnate and so is the Lady Dallona, and called off any search the Society might be making for him."

"And I've got to find the Lady Dallona as soon as I can. Well, if I can't reach her, maybe I can get her to send word to me," Verkan Vall said. "That's going to take some doing, too."

"What did you find out, Lord Virzal?" Olirzon asked. He had a piece of soft leather, now, and was polishing his blade lovingly.

"The Reincarnation Research people don't know anything," Verkan Vall replied. "Dr. Harnosh of Hosh thinks she's discarnate. I did find out that the experimental work she's done, so far, has absolutely disproved the theory of Statistical Reincarnation. The Volitionalists' theory is solidly established."

"Yes, what do you think, Olirzon?" Marnik added. "They have a case on record of a man who worked up from field hand to millionaire in five reincarnations. Deliberately, that is." He went on to repeat what Harnosh of Hosh had said; he must have possessed an almost eidetic memory, for he gave the bearded psychist's words verbatim, and threw in the gestures and voice-inflections.

Olirzon grinned. "You know, there's a chance for the easy-money boys," he considered. "'You, too, can Reincarnate as a millionaire! Let Dr. Nirzutz of Futzbutz Help You! Only 49.98 System Monetary Units for the Secret, Infallible, Autosuggestive Formula.' And would it sell!"

He put away the hone and the bit of leather and slipped his knife back into its sheath. "If I weren't a respectable Assassin, I'd give it a try, myself."

Verkan Vall looked at his watch. "We'd better get something to eat," he said. "We'll go down to the main dining room; the Martian Room, I think they call it. I've got to think of some way to let the Lady Dallona know I'm looking for her."

The Martian Room, fifteen stories down, was a big place, occupying almost half of the floor space of one corner tower. It had been fitted to resemble one of the ruined buildings of the ancient and vanished race of Mars who were the ancestors of Terran humanity. One whole side of the room was a gigantic cine-solidograph screen, on which the gullied desolation of a Martian landscape was projected; in the course of about two hours, the scene changed from sunrise through daylight and night to sunrise again.

It was high noon when they entered and found a table; by the time they had finished their dinner, the night was ending and the first glow of dawn was tinting the distant hills. They sat for a while, watching the light grow stronger, then got up and left the table.

There were five men at a table near them; they had come in before the stars had grown dim, and the waiters were just bringing their first dishes. Two were Assassins, and the other three were of a breed Verkan Vall had learned to recognize on any time-line—the arrogant, cocksure, ambitious, leftist politician, who knows what is best for everybody better than anybody else does, and who is convinced that he is inescapably right and that whoever differs with him is not only an ignoramus but a venal scoundrel as well.

One was a beefy man in a gold-laced cream-colored dress tunic; he had thick lips and a too-ready laugh. Another was a rather monkish-looking young man who spoke earnestly and rolled his eyes upward, as though at some celestial vision. The third had the faint powdering of gray in his black hair which was, among the Akor-Neb people, almost the only indication of advanced age.

"Of course it is; the whole thing is a fraud," the monkish young man was saying angrily. "But we can't prove it."

"Oh, Sirzob, here, can prove anything, if you give him time," the beefy one laughed. "The trouble is, there isn't too much time. We know that that communication was a fake, prearranged by the Volitionalists, with Dr. Harnosh and this Dallona of Hadron as their tools. They fed the whole thing to that idiot boy hypnotically, in advance, and then, on a signal, he began typing out this spurious communication. And then, of course, Dallona and this Assassin of hers ran off somewhere together, so that we'd be blamed with discarnating or abducting them, and so that they wouldn't be made to testify about the communication on a lie detector."

A sudden happy smile touched Verkan Vall's eyes. He caught each of his Assassins by an arm. "Marnik, cover my back," he ordered. "Olirzon, cover everybody at the table. Come on!"

Then he stepped forward, halting between the chairs of the young man and the man with the gray hair and facing the beefy man in the light tunic. "You!" he barked. "I mean YOU."

The beefy man stopped laughing and stared at him; then sprang to his feet. His hand, streaking toward his left armpit, stopped and dropped to his side as Olirzon aimed a pistol at him. The others sat motionless.

"You," Verkan Vall continued, "are a complete, deliberate, malicious, and unmitigated liar. The Lady Dallona of Hadron is a scientist of integrity, incapable of falsifying her experimental work. What's more, her father is one of my best friends; in his name, and in hers, I demand a full retraction of the slanderous statements you have just made."

"Do you know who I am?" the beefy one shouted.

"I know *what* you are," Verkan Vall shouted back. Like most ancient languages, the Akor-Neb speech included an elaborate, delicately-shaded, and utterly vile vocabulary of abuse; Verkan Vall culled from it judiciously and at length.

"And if I don't make myself understood verbally, we'll go down to the object level," he added, snatching a bowl of soup from in front of the monkish-looking young man and throwing it across the table. The soup was a dark brown, almost black. It contained bits of meat, and mushrooms, and slices of hard-boiled egg, and yellow Martian rock lichen. It produced, on the light tunic, a most spectacular effect.

For a moment, Verkan Vall was afraid the fellow would have an apoplectic stroke, or an epileptic fit. Mastering himself, however, he bowed jerkily. "Marnark of Bashad," he identified himself. "When and where can my friends consult yours?"

"Lord Virzal of Verkan," the Paratimer bowed back. "Your friends can negotiate with mine here and now. I am represented by these Gentlemen-Assassins."

"I won't submit my friends to the indignity of negotiating with them," Marnark retorted. "I insist that you be represented by persons of your own quality and mine."

"Oh, you do?" Olirzon broke in. "Well, is your objection personal to me, or to Assassins as a class? In the first case, I'll remember to make a private project of you, as soon as I'm through with my present employment; if it's the latter, I'll report your attitude to the Society. I'll see what Klarnood, our President-General, thinks of your views."

A crowd had begun to accumulate around the table. Some of them were persons in evening dress, some were Assassins on the hotel payroll, and some were unattached Assassins.

"Well, you won't have far to look for him," one of the latter said, pushing through the crowd to the table. He was a man of middle age, inclined to stoutness; he made Verkan Vall think of a chocolate figure of Tortha Karf. The red badge on his breast was surrounded with gold lace, and, instead of black wings and a silver bullet, it bore silver wings and a golden dagger. He bowed contemptuously at Marnark of Bashad. "Klarnood, President-General of the Society of Assassins," he announced.

"Marnark of Bashad, did I hear you say that you considered members of the Society as unworthy to negotiate an affair of honor with your friends, on behalf of this nobleman who has been courteous enough to accept your challenge?" he demanded.

Marnark of Bashad's arrogance suffered considerable evaporation-loss. His tone became almost servile. "Not at all, Honorable Assassin-President," he protested. "But as I was going to ask these gentlemen to represent me, I thought it would be more fitting for the other gentleman to be represented by personal friends, also. In that way—"

"Sorry, Marnark," the gray-haired man at the table said. "I can't second you; I have a quarrel with the Lord Virzal, too."

He rose and bowed. "Sirzob of Abo. Inasmuch as the Honorable Marnark is a guest at my table, an affront to him is an affront to me. In my quality as his host, I must demand satisfaction from you, Lord Virzal."

"Why, gladly, Honorable Sirzob," Verkan Vall replied. This was getting better and better every moment. "Of course, your friend, the Honorable Marnark, enjoys priority of challenge; I'll take care of you as soon as I have, shall we say, satisfied, him."

The earnest and rather consecrated-looking young man rose also, bowing to Verkan Vall. "Yirzol of Narva. I, too, have a quarrel with you, Lord Virzal; I cannot submit to the indignity of having my food snatched from in front of me, as you just did. I also demand satisfaction."

"And quite rightly, Honorable Yirzol," Verkan Vall approved. "It looks like such good soup, too," he sorrowed, inspecting the front of Marnark's tunic. "My seconds will negotiate with yours immediately; your satisfaction, of course, must come after that of Honorable Sirzob."

"If I may intrude," Klarnood put in smoothly, "may I suggest that as the Lord Virzal is represented by his Assassins, yours can represent all three of you at the same time. I will gladly offer my own good offices as impartial supervisor."

Verkan Vall turned and bowed as to royalty. "An honor, Assassin-President: I am sure no one could act in that capacity more satisfactorily."

"Well, when would it be most convenient to arrange the details?" Klarnood inquired. "I am completely at your disposal, gentlemen."

"Why, here and now, while we're all together," Verkan Vall replied.

"I object to that!" Marnark of Bashad vociferated. "We can't make arrangements here; why, all these hotel people, from the manager down, are nothing but tipsters for the newscast services!"

"Well, what's wrong with that?" Verkan Vall demanded. "You knew that when you slandered the Lady Dallona in their hearing."

"The Lord Virzal of Verkan is correct," Klarnood ruled. "And the offenses for which you have challenged him were also committed in public. By all means, let's discuss the arrangements now." He turned to Verkan Vall. "As the challenged party, you have the choice of weapons; your opponents, then, have the right to name the conditions under which they are to be used."

Marnark of Bashad raised another outcry over that. The assault upon him by the Lord Virzal of Verkan was deliberately provocative, and therefore tantamount to a challenge; he, himself, had the right to name the weapons.

Klarnood upheld him.

"Do the other gentlemen make the same claim?" Verkan Vall wanted to know.

"If they do, I won't allow it," Klarnood replied. "You deliberately provoked Honorable Marnark, but the offenses of provoking him at Honorable Sirzob's table, and of throwing Honorable Yirzol's soup at him, were not given with intent to provoke. These gentlemen have a right to challenge, but not to consider themselves provoked."

"Well, I choose knives, then," Marnark hastened to say.

Verkan Vall smiled thinly. He had learned knife-play among the greatest masters of that art in all Paratime, the Third Level Khanga pirates of the Caribbean Islands. "And we fight barefoot, stripped to the waist, and without any parrying weapon in the left hand," Verkan Vall stipulated.

The beefy Marnark fairly licked his chops in anticipation. He outweighed Verkan Vall by forty pounds; he saw an easy victory ahead. Verkan Vall's own confidence increased at these signs of his opponent's assurance.

"And as for Honorable Sirzob and Honorable Yirzol, I choose pistols," he added.

Sirzob and Yirzol held a hasty whispered conference. "Speaking both for Honorable Yirzol and for myself," Sirzob announced, "we stipulate that the distance shall be twenty meters, that the pistols shall be fully loaded, and that fire shall be at will after the command."

"Twenty rounds, fire at will, at twenty meters!" Olirzon hooted. "You must think our principal's as bad a shot as you are!"

The four Assassins stepped aside and held a long discussion about something, with considerable argument and gesticulation. Klarnood, observing Verkan Vall's impatience, leaned close to him and whispered: "This is highly irregular; we must pretend ignorance and be patient. They're laying bets on the outcome. You must do your best, Lord Virzal; you don't want your supporters to lose money."

He said it quite seriously, as though the outcome were otherwise a matter of indifference to Verkan Vall.

Marnark wanted to discuss time and place, and proposed that all three duels be fought at dawn, on the fourth landing stage of Darsh Central Hospital; that was closest to the maternity wards, and statistics showed that most births occurred just before that hour.

"Certainly not," Verkan Vall vetoed. "We'll fight here and now; I don't propose going a couple of hundred miles to meet you at any such unholy hour. We'll fight in the nearest hallway that provides twenty meters' shooting distance."

Marnark, Sirzob and Yirzol all clamored in protest.

Verkan Vall shouted them down, drawing on his hypnotically acquired knowledge of Akor-Neb dueling customs. "The code explicitly states that satisfaction shall be rendered as promptly as possible, and I insist on a literal interpretation. I'm not going to inconvenience myself and Assassin-President

Klarnood and these four Gentlemen-Assassins just to humor Statisticalist superstitions."

VIII

The manager of the hotel, drawn to the Martian Room by the uproar, offered a hallway connecting the kitchens with the refrigerator rooms; it was fifty meters long by five in width, was well-lighted and soundproof, and had a bay in which the seconds and other could stand during the firing.

They repaired thither in a body, Klarnood gathering up several hotel servants on the way through the kitchen. Verkan Vall stripped to the waist, pulled off his ankle boots, and examined Olirzon's knife. Its tapering eight-inch blade was double-edged at the point, and its handle was covered with black velvet to afford a good grip, and wound with gold wire. He nodded approvingly, gripped it with his index finger crooked around the cross-guard, and advanced to meet Marnark of Bashad.

As he had expected, the burly politician was depending upon his greater brawn to overpower his antagonist. He advanced with a sidling, spread-legged gait, his knife hand against his right hip and his left hand extended in front.

Verkan Vall nodded with pleased satisfaction; a wrist-grabber. Then he blinked. Why, the fellow was actually holding his knife reversed, his little finger to the guard and his thumb on the pommel!

Verkan Vall went briskly to meet him, made a feint at his knife hand with his own left, and then side-stepped quickly to the right.

As Marnark's left hand grabbed at his right wrist, his left hand brushed against it and closed into a fist, with Marnark's left thumb inside of it, He gave a quick downward twist with his wrist, pulling Marnark off balance.

Caught by surprise, Marnark stumbled, his knife flailing wildly away from Verkan Vall.

As he stumbled forward, Verkan Vall pivoted on his left heel and drove the point of his knife into the back of Marnark's neck, twisting it as he jerked it free. At the same time, he released Marnark's thumb.

The politician continued his stumble and fell forward on his face, blood spurting from his neck. He gave a twitch or so, and was still.

Verkan Vall stooped and wiped the knife on the dead man's clothes—another Khanga pirate gesture—and then returned it to Olirzon. "Nice weapon, Olirzon," he said. "It fitted my hand as though I'd been born holding it."

"You used it as though you had, Lord Virzal," the Assassin replied. "Only eight seconds from the time you closed with him."

The function of the hotel servants whom Klarnood had gathered up now became apparent; they advanced, took the body of Marnark by the heels, and dragged it out of the way. The others watched this removal with mixed emotions.

The two remaining principals were impassive and frozen-faced. Their two Assassins, who had probably bet heavily on Marnark, were chagrined. And Klarnood was looking at Verkan Vall with a considerable accretion of respect.

Verkan Vall pulled on his boots and resumed his clothing. There followed some argument about the pistols; it was finally decided that each combatant should use his own shoulder-holster weapon. All three were nearly enough alike—small weapons, rather heavier than they looked, firing a tiny ten-grain bullet at ten thousand foot-seconds. On impact, such a bullet would almost disintegrate; a man hit anywhere in the body with one would be killed instantly, his nervous system paralyzed and his heart stopped by internal pressure. Each of the pistols carried twenty rounds in the magazine.

Verkan Vall and Sirzob of Abo took their places, their pistols lowered at their sides, facing each other across a measured twenty meters.

"Are you ready, gentlemen?" Klarnood asked. "You will not raise your pistols until the command to fire; you may fire at will after it. Ready. *Fire!*"

Both pistols swung up to level.

Verkan Vall found Sirzob's head in his sights and squeezed; the pistol kicked back in his hand, and he saw a lance of blue flame jump from the muzzle of Sirzob's. Both weapons barked together, and with the double report came the whip-cracking sound of Sirzob's bullet passing Verkan Vall's head.

Then Sirzob's face altered its appearance unpleasantly, and he pitched forward. Verkan Vall thumbed on his safety and stood motionless, while the servants advanced, took Sirzob's body by the heels, and dragged it over beside Marnark's.

"All right; Honorable Yirzol, you're next," Verkan Vall called out.

"The Lord Virzal has fired one shot," one of the opposing seconds objected, "and Honorable Yirzol has a full magazine. The Lord Virzal should put in another magazine."

"I grant him the advantage; let's get on with it," Verkan Vall said.

Yirzol of Narva advanced to the firing point. He was not afraid of death—none of the Akor-Neb people were; their language contained no word to express the concept of total and final extinction—and discarnation by gunshot was almost entirely painless. But he was beginning to suspect that he had made a fool of himself by getting into this affair, he had work in his present reincarnation which he wanted to finish, and his political party would suffer loss, both of his services and of prestige.

"Are you ready, gentlemen?" Klarnood intoned ritualistically. "You will not raise your pistols until the command to fire; you may fire at will after it. Ready, *Fire!*"

Verkan Vall shot Yirzol of Narva through the head before the latter had his pistol half raised. Yirzol fell forward on the splash of blood Sirzob had made, and the servants came forward and dragged his body over with the others.

It reminded Verkan Vail of some sort of industrial assembly-line operation. He replaced the two expended rounds in his magazine with fresh ones and slid the pistol back into its holster.

The two Assassins whose principals had been so expeditiously massacred were beginning to count up their losses and pay off the winners.

Klarnood, the President-General of the Society of Assassins, came over, hooking fingers and clapping shoulders with Verkan Vall.

"Lord Virzal, I've seen quite a few duels, but nothing quite like that," he said. "You should have been an Assassin!"

That was a considerable compliment. Verkan Vall thanked him modestly.

"I'd like to talk to you privately," the Assassin-President continued. "I think it'll be worth your while if we have a few words together."

Verkan Vall nodded.

"My suite is on the fifteenth floor above; will that be all right?" He waited until the losers had finished settling their bets, then motioned to his own pair of Assassins.

IX

As they emerged into the Martian Room again, the manager was waiting; he looked as though he were about to demand that Verkan Vall vacate his suite. However, when he saw the arm of the President-General of the Society of Assassins draped amicably over his guest's shoulder, he came forward bowing and smiling.

"Larnorm, I want you to put five of your best Assassins to guarding the approaches to the Lord Virzal's suite," Klarnood told him. "I'll send five more from Assassins' Hall to replace them at their ordinary duties. And I'll hold you responsible with your carnate existence for the Lord Virzal's safety in this hotel. Understand?"

"Oh, yes, Honorable Assassin-President; you may trust me. The Lord Virzal will be perfectly safe."

In Verkan Vall's suite, above, Klarnood sat down and got out his pipe, filling it with tobacco lightly mixed with *zerfa*. To his surprise, he saw his host light a plain tobacco cigarette. "Don't you use *zerfa*?" he asked.

"Very little," Verkan Vall replied. "I grow it. If you'd see the bums who hang around our drying sheds, on Venus, cadging rejected leaves and smoking themselves into a stupor, you'd be frugal in using it, too."

Klarnood nodded. "You know, most men would want a pipe of fifty percent, or a straight *zerfa* cigarette, after what you've been through," he said. "I'd need something like that, to deaden my conscience, if I had one to deaden."

Verkan Vall said. "As it is, I feel like a murderer of babes. That overgrown fool, Marnark, handled his knife like a cow-butcher. The young fellow couldn't handle a pistol at all. I suppose the old fellow, Sirzob, was a fair shot, but dropping him wasn't any great feat of arms, either."

Klarnood looked at him curiously for a moment. "You know," he said, at length, "I believe you actually mean that. Well, until he met you, Marnark of Bashad was rated as the best knife-fighter in Darsh. Sirzob had ten dueling victories to his credit, and young Yirzol four." He puffed slowly on his pipe. "I like you, Lord Virzal; a great Assassin was lost when you decided to reincarnate as a Venusian land-owner. I'd hate to see you discarnated without proper warning. I take it you're ignorant of the intricacies of Terran politics?"

"To a large extent, yes."

"Well, do you know who those three men were?" When Verkan Vall shook his head, Klarnood continued: "Marnark was the son and right-hand associate of old Mirzark of Bashad, the Statisticalist Party leader. Sirzob of Abo was their propaganda director. And Yirzol of Narva was their leading socio-economic theorist, and their candidate for Executive Chairman. In six minutes, with one knife thrust and two shots, you did the Statisticalist Party an injury second only to that done them by the young lady in whose name you were fighting.

"In two weeks, there will be a planet-wide general election. As it stands, the Statisticalists have a majority of the seats in Parliament and on the Executive Council. As a result of your work and the Lady Dallona's, they'll lose that majority, and more, when the votes are tallied."

"Is that another reason why you like me?" Verkan Vall asked.

"Unofficially, yes. As President-General of the Society of Assassins, I must be nonpolitical. The Society is rigidly so; if we let ourselves become involved, as an organization, in politics, we could control the System Government inside of five years, and we'd be wiped out of existence in fifty years by the very forces we sought to control," Klarnood said. "But personally, I would like to see the Statisticalist Party destroyed. If they succeed in their program of socialization, the Society would be finished. A socialist state is, in its final development, an absolute, total, state; no total state can tolerate extra-legal and para-governmental organizations.

"So we have adopted the policy of giving a little inconspicuous aid, here and there, to people who are dangerous to the Statisticalists. The Lady Dallona of Hadron, and Dr. Harnosh of Hosh, are such persons. You appear to be another. That's why I ordered that fellow, Larnorm, to make sure you were safe in his hotel."

"Where is the Lady Dallona?" Verkan Vall asked. "From your use of the present tense, I assume you believe her to be still carnate."

Klarnood looked at Verkan Vall keenly. "That's a pretty blunt question, Lord Virzal," he said. "I wish I knew a little more about you. When you and your Assassins started inquiring about the Lady Dallona, I tried to check up on you. I found out that you had come to Darsh from Ghamma on a ship of the family of Zorda, accompanied by Brarnend of Zorda himself. And that's all I could find out. You claim to be a Venusian planter, and you might be.

"Any Terran who can handle weapons as you can would have come to my notice long ago. But you have no more ascertainable history than if you'd stepped out of another dimension."

That was getting uncomfortably close to the truth. In fact, it *was* the truth.

Verkan Vall laughed. "Well, confidentially," he said, "I'm from the Arcturus System. I followed the Lady Dallona here from our home planet, and when I have rescued her from among you Solarians, I shall, according to our customs, receive her hand in marriage. As she is the daughter of the Emperor of Arcturus, that'll be quite a good thing for me."

Klarnood chuckled. "You know, you'd only have to tell me that about three or four times and I'd start believing it," he said. "And Dr. Harnosh of Hosh would believe it the first time; he's been talking to himself ever since the Lady Dallona started her experimental work here.

"Lord Virzal, I'm going to take a chance on you. The Lady Dallona is still carnate, or was four days ago, and the same for Dirzed. They both went into hiding after the discarnation feast of Garnon of Roxor, to escape the enmity of the Statisticalists. Two days after they disappeared, Dirzed called Assassins' Hall and reported this, but told us nothing more. I suppose, in about three or four days, I could re-establish contact with him. We want the public to think that the Statisticalists made away with the Lady Dallona, at least until the election's over."

Verkan Vall nodded. "I was pretty sure that was the situation," he said.

"It may be that they will get in touch with me; if they don't, I'll need your help in reaching them."

"Why do you think the Lady Dallona will try to reach you?"

"She needs all the help she can get. She knows she can get plenty from me. Why do you think I interrupted my search for her, and risked my carnate existence, to fight those people over a matter of verbalisms and political propaganda?"

Verkan Vall went to the newscast visiplate and snapped it on. "We'll see if I'm getting results, yet." The plate lighted, and a handsome young man in a gold-laced green suit was speaking out of it: "—where he is heavily guarded by Assassins. However, in an exclusive interview with representatives of this service, the Assassin Hirzif, one of the two who seconded the men the Lord Virzal fought, said that in his opinion all of the three were so outclassed as to have had no chance whatever, and that he had already refused an offer of ten thousand System Monetary Units to discarnate the Lord Virzal for the Statisticalist Party. 'When I want to discarnate,' Hirzif the Assassin said, 'I'll invite in my friends and do it properly; until I do, I wouldn't go up against the Lord Virzal of Verkan for ten million S.M.U.'"

Verkan Vall snapped off the visiplate. "See what I mean?" he asked. "I fought those politicians just for the advertising. If Dallona and Dirzed are anywhere near a visiplate, they'll know how to reach me."

"Hirzif shouldn't have talked about refusing that retainer," Klarnood frowned. "That isn't good Assassin ethics. Why, yes, Lord Virzal; that was cleverly planned. It ought to get results. But I wish you'd get the Lady Dallona out of Darsh, and preferably off Terra, as soon as you can. We've benefited by this, so far, but I shouldn't like to see things go much further. A real civil war could develop out of this situation, and I don't want that. Call on me for help; I'll give you a code word to use at Assassins' Hall."

X

A real civil war was developing even as Klarnood spoke; by mid-morning of the next day, the fighting that had been partially suppressed by the Constabulary had broken out anew. The Assassins employed by the Solar

Hotel—heavily reinforced during the night—had fought a pitched battle with Statisticalist partisans on the landing-stage above Verkan Vall's suite, and now several Constabulary airboats were patrolling around the building.

The rule on Constabulary interference seemed to be that while individuals had an unquestionable right to shoot out their differences among themselves, any fighting likely to endanger nonparticipants was taboo. Just how successful in enforcing this rule the Constabulary were was open to some doubt.

Ever since arising, Verkan Vall had heard the crash of small arms and the hammering of automatic weapons in other parts of the towering city-unit. There hadn't been a civil war on the Akor-Neb Sector for over five centuries, he knew, but then—Hadron Dalla, Doctor of Psychic Science, and intertemporal trouble-carrier extraordinary—had only been on this sector for a little under a year. If anything, he was surprised that the explosion had taken so long to occur.

One of the servants furnished to him by the hotel management approached him in the drawing room, holding a four-inch-square wafer of white plastic. "Lord Virzal, there is a masked Assassin in the hallway who brought this under Assassins' Truce," he said.

Verkan Vall took the wafer and pared off three of the four edges, which showed black where they had been fused. Unfolding it, he found, as he had expected, that the pyrographed message within was in the alphabet and language of the First Paratime Level:

Vall, darling: Am I glad you got here; this time I really am *in the middle, but good! The Assassin, Dirzed, who brings this, is in my service. You can trust him implicitly; he's about the only person in Darsh you can trust. He'll bring you to where I am. Dalla*

P.S. I hope you're not still angry about that musician. I told you, at the time, that he was just helping me with an experiment in telepathy. D.

Verkan Vall grinned at the postscript. That had been twenty years ago, when he'd been eighty and she'd been seventy. He supposed she'd expect him to take up his old relationship with her again. It probably wouldn't last any longer than it had, the other time; he recalled a Fourth Level proverb about the leopard and his spots. It certainly wouldn't be boring, though.

"Tell the Assassin to come in," he directed. Then he tossed the message down on a table. Outside of himself, nobody in Darsh could read it but the woman who had sent it; if, as he thought highly probable, the Statisticalists had spies among the hotel staff, it might serve to reduce some cryptanalyst to gibbering insanity.

The Assassin entered, drawing off a cowl-like mask. He was the man whose arm Dalla had been holding in the visiplate picture; Verkan Vall even recognized the extremely ornate pistol and knife on his belt.

"Dirzed the Assassin," he named himself. "If you wish, we can visiphone Assassins' Hall for verification of my identity."

"Lord Virzal of Verkan. And my Assassins, Marnik and Olirzon."

They all hooked fingers and clapped shoulders with the newcomer.

"That won't be needed," Verkan Vall told Dirzed. "I know you from seeing you with the Lady Dallona, on the visiplate; you're 'Dirzed, her faithful Assassin.'"

Dirzed's face, normally the color of a good walnut gunstock, turned almost black. He used shockingly bad language. "And that's why I have to wear this abomination," he finished, displaying the mask.

"The Lady Dallona and I can't show our faces anywhere; if we did, every Statisticalist and his six-year-old brat would know us, and we'd be fighting off an army of them in five minutes."

"Where's the Lady Dallona, now?"

"In hiding, Lord Virzal, at a private dwelling dome in the forest; she's most anxious to see you. I'm to take you to her, and I would strongly advise that you bring your Assassins along. There are other people at this dome, and they are not personally loyal to the Lady Dallona. I've no reason to suspect them of secret enmity, but their friendship is based entirely on political expediency."

"And political expediency is subject to change without notice," Verkan Vall finished for him.

"Have you an airboat?"

"On the landing stage below. Shall we go now, Lord Virzal?"

"Yes." Verkan Vall made a two-handed gesture to his Assassins, as though gripping a submachine-gun; they nodded, went into another room, and returned carrying light automatic weapons in their hands and pouches of spare drums slung over their shoulders. "And may I suggest, Dirzed, that one of my Assassins drives the airboat? I want you on the back seat with me, to explain the situation as we go."

Dirzed's teeth flashed white against his brown skin as he gave Verkan Vall a quick smile. "By all means, Lord Virzal; I would much rather be distrusted than to find that my client's friends were not discreet."

There were a couple of hotel Assassins guarding Dirzed's airboat, on the landing stage. Marnik climbed in under the controls, with Olirzon beside him; Verkan Vall and Dirzed entered the rear seat. Dirzed gave Marnik the co-ordinate reference for their destination.

"Now, what sort of a place is this, where we're going?" Verkan Vall asked. "And who's there whom we may or may not trust?"

"Well, it's a dome house belonging to the family of Starpha; they own a five-mile radius around it, oak and beech forest and underbrush, stocked with deer and boar. A hunting lodge. Prince Jirzyn of Starpha, Lord Girzon of Roxor, and a few other top-level Volitionalists, know that the Lady Dallona's hiding there. They're keeping her out of sight till after the election, for propaganda purposes. We've been hiding there since immediately after the discarnation feast of the Lord Garnon of Roxor."

"What happened, after the feast?" Verkan Vall wanted to know.

"Well, you know how the Lady Dallona and Dr. Harnosh of Hosh had this telepathic-sensitive there, in a trance and drugged with a *zerfa*-derivative alkaloid the Lady Dallona had developed. I was Lord Garnon's Assassin; I discarnated him, myself. Why, I hadn't even put my pistol away before he was in control of this sensitive, in a room five stories above the banquet hall; he began communicating at once. We had visiplates to show us what was going on.

"Right away, Nirzav of Shonna, one of the Statisticalist leaders who was a personal friend of Lord Garnon's in spite of his politics, renounced Statisticalism and went over to the Volitionalists, on the strength of this communication. Prince Jirzyn, and Lord Girzon, the new family-head of

Roxor, decided that there would be trouble in the next few days, so they advised the Lady Dallona to come to this hunting lodge for safety. She and I came here in her airboat, directly from the feast. A good thing we did, too; if we'd gone to her apartment, we'd have walked in before that lethal gas had time to clear.

"There are four Assassins of the family of Starpha, and six menservants, and an upper-servant named Tarnod, the gamekeeper. The Starpha Assassins and I have been keeping the rest under observation. I left one of the Starpha Assassins guarding the Lady Dallona when I came for you, under brotherly oath to protect her in my name till I returned."

The airboat was skimming rapidly above the treetops, toward the northern part of the city.

"What's known about that package bomb?" Verkan Vall asked. "Who sent it?"

Dirzed shrugged. "The Statisticalists, of course. The wrapper was stolen from the Reincarnation Research Institute; so was the case. The Constabulary are working on it." Dirzed shrugged again.

The dome, about a hundred and fifty feet in width and some fifty in height, stood among the trees ahead. It was almost invisible from any distance; the concrete dome was of mottled green and gray concrete, trees grew so close as to brush it with their branches, and the little pavilion on the flattened top was roofed with translucent green plastic. As the airboat came in, a couple of men in Assassins' garb emerged from the pavilion to meet them.

"Marnik, stay at the controls," Verkan Vall directed. "I'll send Olirzon up for you if I want you. If there's any trouble, take off for Assassins' Hall and give the code word, then come back with twice as many men as you think you'll need."

Dirzed raised his eyebrows over this. "I hadn't known the Assassin-President had given you a code word, Lord Virzal," he commented. "That doesn't happen very often."

"The Assassin-President has honored me with his friendship," Verkan Vall replied noncommittally, as he, Dirzed and Olirzon climbed out of the airboat. Marnik was holding it an unobtrusive inch or so above the flat top of the dome, away from the edge of the pavilion roof.

The two Assassins greeted him, and a man in upper-servants' garb and wearing a hunting knife and a long hunting pistol approached. "Lord Virzal of Verkan? Welcome to Starpha Dome. The Lady Dallona awaits you below."

Verkan Vall had never been in an Akor-Neb dwelling dome, but a description of such structures had been included in his hypno-mech indoctrination. Originally, they had been the standard structure for all purposes; about two thousand elapsed years ago, when nationalism had still existed on the Akor-Neb Sector, the cities had been almost entirely underground, as protection from air attack. Even now, the design had been retained by those who wished to live apart from the towering city units, to preserve the natural appearance of the landscape.

The Starpha hunting lodge was typical of such domes. Under it was a circular well, eighty feet in depth and fifty in width, with a fountain and a shallow circular pool at the bottom. The storerooms, kitchens and servants' quarters were at the top, the living quarters at the bottom, in segments of a wide circle around the well, back of balconies.

"Tarnod, the gamekeeper," Dirzed performed the introductions. "And Erarno and Kirzol, Assassins."

Verkan Vall hooked fingers and clapped shoulders with them. Tarnod accompanied them to the lifter tubes—two percent positive gravitation for descent and two percent negative for ascent—and they all floated down the former, like air-filled balloons, to the bottom level.

"The Lady Dallona is in the gunroom," Tarnod informed Verkan Vall, making as though to guide him.

"Thanks, Tarnod; we know the way," Dirzed told him shortly, turning his back on the upper-servant and walking toward a closed door on the other side of the fountain. Verkan Vall and Olirzon followed; for a moment, Tarnod stood looking after them, then he followed the other two Assassins into the ascent tube.

"I don't relish that fellow," Dirzed explained. "The family of Starpha use him for work they couldn't hire an Assassin to do at any price. I've been here often, when I was with the Lord Garnon; I've always thought he had something on Prince Jirzyn."

He knocked sharply on the closed door with the butt of his pistol. In a moment, it slid open, and a young Assassin with a narrow mustache and a tuft of chin beard looked out.

"Ah, Dirzed." He stepped outside. "The Lady Dallona is within; I return her to your care."

Verkan Vall entered, followed by Dirzed and Olirzon. The big room was fitted with reclining chairs and couches and low tables; its walls were hung with the heads of deer and boar and wolves, and with racks holding rifles and hunting pistols and fowling pieces. It was filled with the soft glow of indirect cold light. At the far side of the room, a young woman was seated at a desk, speaking softly into a sound transcriber. As they entered, she snapped it off and rose.

Hadron Dalla wore the same costume Verkan Vall had seen on the visiplate: he recognized her instantly. It took her a second or two to perceive Verkan Vall under the brown skin and black hair of the Lord Virzal of Verkan. Then her face lighted with a happy smile.

"Why, Va-a-a-ll!" she whooped, running across the room and tossing herself into his not particularly reluctant arms. After all, it had been twenty years— "I didn't know you, at first."

"You mean, in these clothes?" he asked, seeing that she had forgotten, for the moment, the presence of the two Assassins. She had even called him by his First Level name, but that was unimportant—the Akor-Neb affectionate diminutive was formed by omitting the *-irz-* or *-arn-*. "Well, they're not exactly what I generally wear on the plantation."

He kissed her again, then turned to his companions. "Your pardon, Gentlemen-Assassins; it's been something over a year since we've seen each other."

Olirzon was smiling at the affectionate reunion; Dirzed wore a look of amused resignation, as though he might have expected something like this to happen.

Verkan Vall and Dalla sat down on a couch near the desk. "That was really sweet of you, Vall, fighting those men for talking about me," she began. "You took an awful chance, though. But if you hadn't, I'd never have known you were in Darsh—Oh-oh! That was why you did it, wasn't it?"

"Well, I had to do something. Everybody either didn't know or weren't saying where you were. I assumed, from the circumstances, that you were hiding somewhere. Tell me, Dalla; do you really have scientific proof of reincarnation? I mean, as an established fact?"

"Oh, yes; these people on this sector have had that for over ten centuries. They have hypnotic techniques for getting back into a part of the subconscious mind that we've never been able to reach. And after I found out how they did it, I was able to adapt some of our hypno-epistemological techniques to it, and—"

"All right; that's what I wanted to know," he cut her off. "We're getting out of here, right away."

"But where?"

"Ghamma, in an airboat I have outside, and then back to the First Level. Unless there's a Paratime-transposition conveyer somewhere nearer."

"But why, Vall? I'm not ready to go back; I have a lot of work to do here, yet. They're getting ready to set up a series of control-experiments at the Institute, and then, I'm in the middle of an experiment, a two-hundred-subject memory-recall experiment. See, I distributed two hundred sets of equipment for my new technique—injection-ampoules of this *zerfa*-derivative drug, and sound records of the hypnotic suggestion formula, which can be played on an ordinary reproducer. It's just a crude variant of our hypno-mech process, except that instead of implanting information in the subconscious mind, to be brought at will to the level of consciousness, it works the other way, and draws into conscious knowledge information already in the subconscious mind.

"The way these people have always done has been to put the subject in an hypnotic trance and then record verbal statements made in the trance state; when the subject comes out of the trance, the record is all there is, because the memories of past reincarnations have never been in the conscious mind. But with my process, the subject can consciously remember everything about his last reincarnation, and as many reincarnations before that as he wishes to. I haven't heard from any of the people who received these auto-recall kits, and I really must—"

"Dalla, I don't want to have to pull Paratime Police authority on you, but, so help me, if you don't come back voluntarily with me, I will. Security of the secret of Paratime Transposition."

"Oh, my eye!" Dalla exclaimed. "Don't give me that, Vall!"

"Look, Dalla. Suppose you get discarnated here," Verkan Vall said. "You say reincarnation is a scientific fact. Well, you'd reincarnate on this sector, and then you'd take a memory-recall, under hypnosis. And when you did, the Paratime secret wouldn't be a secret any more."

"Oh!" Dalla's hand went to her mouth in consternation. Like every Paratimer, she was conditioned to shrink with all her being from the mere thought of revealing to any outtime dweller the secret ability of her race to pass to other time-lines, or even the existence of alternate lines of probability. "And if I took one of the old-fashioned trance-recalls, I'd blat out everything; I wouldn't be able to keep a thing back. And I even know the principles of transposition!"

She looked at him, aghast.

"When I get back, I'm going to put a recommendation through Department channels that this whole sector be declared out of bounds for all Paratime Transposition, until you people at Rhogom Foundation work out the problem of discarnate return to the First Level," he told her. "Now, have you any notes or anything you want to take back with you?"

She rose. "Yes; just what's on the desk. Find me something to put the recording spools and notebooks in, while I'm getting them in order."

Verkan secured a large game bag from under a rack of fowling pieces, and held it while she sorted the material rapidly, stuffing spools of recordings and notebooks into it. They had barely begun when the door slid open and Olirzon, who had gone outside, sprang into the room, his pistol drawn, swearing vilely.

"They've double-crossed us!" he cried. "The servants of Starpha have turned on us." He holstered his pistol and snatched up his submachine-gun, taking cover behind the edge of the door and letting go with a burst in the direction of the lifter tubes. "Got that one!" he grunted.

"What happened, Olirzon?" Verkan Vall asked, dropping the game bag on the table and hurrying across the room.

"I went up to see how Marnik was making out. As I came out of the lifter tube, one of the obscenities took a shot at me with a hunting pistol. He missed me; I didn't miss him. Then a couple more of them were coming up, with fowling pieces; I shot one of them before they could fire, and jumped into the descent tube and came down heels over ears. I don't know what's happened to Marnik."

He fired another burst, and swore. "Missed him!"

"Assassins' Truce! Assassins' Truce!" a voice howled out of the descent tube. "Hold your fire, we want to parley."

"Who is it?" Dirzed shouted, over Olirzon's shoulder. "You, Sarnax? Come on out; we won't shoot."

The young Assassin with the mustache and chin beard emerged from the descent tube, his weapons sheathed and his clasped hands extended in front of him in a peculiarly ecclesiastical-looking manner. Dirzed and Olirzon stepped out of the gunroom, followed by Verkan Vall and Hadron Dalla. Olirzon had left his submachine-gun behind. They met the other Assassin by the rim of the fountain pool.

"Lady Dallona of Hadron," the Starpha Assassin began. "I and my colleagues, in the employ of the family of Starpha, have received orders from our clients to withdraw our protection from you, and to discarnate you, and all with you who undertake to protect or support you." That much sounded like a recitation of some established formula; then his voice became more conversational.

"I and my colleagues, Erarno and Kirzol and Harnif, offer our apologies for the barbarity of the servants of the family of Starpha, in attacking without declaration of cessation of friendship. Was anybody hurt or discarnated?"

"None of us," Olirzon said. "How about Marnik?"

"He was warned before hostilities were begun against him," Sarnax replied. "We will allow five minutes until—"

Olirzon, who had been looking up the well, suddenly sprang at Dalla, knocking her flat, and at the same time jerking out his pistol. Before he could raise it, a shot banged from above and he fell on his face. Dirzed, Verkan Vall, and Sarnax, all drew their pistols, but whoever had fired the shot had vanished. There was an outburst of shouting above.

"Get to cover," Sarnax told the others. "We'll let you know when we're ready to attack; we'll have to deal with whoever fired that shot, first."

He looked at the dead body on the floor, exclaimed angrily, and hurried to the ascent tube, springing upward. Verkan Vall replaced the small pistol in his shoulder holster and took Olirzon's belt, with his knife and heavier pistol.

"Well, there you see," Dirzed said, as they went back to the gunroom. "So much for political expediency."

"I think I understand why your picture and the Lady Dallona's were exhibited so widely," Verkan Vall said. "Now, anybody would recognize your bodies, and blame the Statisticalists for discarnating you."

"That thought had occurred to me, Lord Virzal," Dirzed said. "I suppose our bodies will be atrociously but not unidentifiably mutilated, to further enrage the public," he added placidly.

"If I get out of this carnate, I'm going to pay somebody off for it."

XI

After a few minutes, there was more shouting of: "Assassins' Truce!" from the descent tube. The two Assassins, Erarno and Kirzol, emerged, dragging the gamekeeper, Tarnod, between them. The upper-servant's face was bloody, and his jaw seemed to be broken. Sarnax followed, carrying a long hunting pistol in his hand.

"Here he is!" he announced. "He fired during Assassins' Truce; he's subject to Assassins' Justice!"

He nodded to the others. They threw the gamekeeper forward on the floor, and Sarnax shot him through the head, then tossed the pistol down beside him. "Any more of these people who violate the decencies will be treated similarly," he promised.

"Thank you, Sarnax," Dirzed spoke up. "But we lost an Assassin: discarnating this lackey won't equalize that. We think you should retire one of your number."

"That at least, Dirzed; wait a moment." The three Assassins conferred at some length. Then Sarnax hooked fingers and clapped shoulders with his companions. "See you in the next reincarnation, brothers," he told them, walking toward the gun-room door, where Verkan Vall, Dalla and Dirzed stood. "I'm joining you people. You had two Assassins when the parley began, you'll have two when the shooting starts."

Verkan Vall looked at Dirzed in some surprise. Hadron Dalla's Assassin nodded. "He's entitled to do that, Lord Virzal; the Assassins' code provides for such changes of allegiance."

"Welcome, Sarnax," Verkan Vall said, hooking fingers with him. "I hope we'll all be together when this is over."

"We will be," Sarnax assured him cheerfully. "Discarnate. We won't get out of this in the body, Lord Virzal."

A submachine-gun hammered from above, the bullets lashing the fountain pool; the water actually steamed, so great was their velocity. "All right!" a voice called down. "Assassins' Truce is over!"

Another burst of automatic fire smashed out the lights at the bottom of the ascent tube. Dirzed and Dalla struggled across the room, pushing a heavy steel cabinet between them; Verkan Vall, who was holding Olirzon's submachine-gun, moved aside to allow them to drop it on edge in the open doorway, then wedged the door half-shut against it. Sarnax came over, bringing rifles, hunting pistols, and ammunition.

"What's the situation, up there?" Verkan Vall asked him. "What force have they, and why did they turn against us?"

"Lord Virzal!" Dirzed objected, scandalized. "You have no right to ask Sarnax to betray confidences!"

Sarnax spat against the door. "In the face of Jirzyn of Starpha!" he said. "And in the face of his *zortan* mother, and of his father, whoever he was! Dirzed, do not talk foolishly; one does not speak of betraying betrayers."

He turned to Verkan Vall. "They have three menservants of the family of Starpha; your Assassin, Olirzon, discarnated the other three. There is one of Prince Jirzyn's poor relations, named Girzad. There are three other men, Volitionalist precinct workers, who came with Girzad, and four Assassins, the three who were here, and one who came with Girzad. Eleven, against the three of us."

"The four of us, Sarnax," Dalla corrected. She had buckled on a hunting pistol, and had a light deer rifle under her arm. Something moved at the bottom of the descent tube. Verkan Vall gave it a short burst, though it was probably only a dummy, dropped to draw fire.

"The four of us, Lady Dallona," Sarnax agreed. "As to your other Assassin, the one who stayed in the airboat, I don't know how he fared. You see, about twenty minutes ago, this Girzad arrived in an airboat, with an Assassin and these three Volitionalist workers. Erarno and I were at the top of the dome when he came in. He told us that he had orders from Prince Jirzyn to discarnate the Lady Dallona and Dirzed at once. Tarnod, the gamekeeper"—Sarnax spat ceremoniously against the door again—"told him you were here, and that Marnik was one of your men. He was going to shoot Marnik at once, but Erarno and I and his Assassin stopped him. We warned Marnik about the change in the situation, according to the code, expecting Marnik to go down here and join you.

"Instead, he lifted the airboat, zoomed over Girzad's boat, and let go a rocket blast, setting Girzad's boat on fire. Well, that was a hostile act, so we all fired after him. We must have hit something, because the boat went down, trailing smoke, about ten miles away. Girzad got another airboat out of the hangar and he and his Assassin started after your man. About that time, your Assassin, Olirzon—happy reincarnation to him—came up, and the Starpha servants fired at him, and he fired back and discarnated two of them, and then jumped down the descent tube. One of the servants jumped after him; I found his body at the bottom when I came down to warn you formally. You know what happened after that."

"But why did Prince Jirzyn order our discarnation?" Dalla wanted to know. "Was it to blame the Statisticalists with it?"

Sarnax, about to answer, broke off suddenly and began firing at the opening of the ascent tube with a hunting pistol. "I got him," he said, in a pleased tone. "That was Erarno; he was always playing tricks with the tubes, climbing down against negative gravity and up against positive gravity. His body will float up to the top—Why, Lady Dallona, that was only part of it. You didn't hear about the big scandal, on the newscast, then?"

"We didn't have it on. What scandal?"

Sarnax laughed. "Oh, the very father and family-head of all scandals!

You ought to know about it, because you started it; that's why Prince Jirzyn wants you out of the body—You devised a process by which people could give themselves memory-recalls of previous reincarnations, didn't you? And distributed apparatus to do it with? And gave one set to young Tarnov, the son of Lord Tirzov of Fastor?"

Dalla nodded.

Sarnax continued: "Well, last evening, Tarnov of Fastor used his recall outfit, and what do you think? It seems that thirty years ago, in his last reincarnation, he was Jirzid of Starpha, Jirzyn's older brother. Jirzid was betrothed to the Lady Annitra of Zabna. Well, his younger brother was carrying on a clandestine affair with the Lady Annitra, and he also wanted the title of Prince and family-head of Starpha. So he bribed this fellow Tarnod, whom I had the pleasure of discarnating, and who was an underservant here at the hunting lodge.

"Between them, they shot Jirzid during a boar hunt. An accident, of course. So Jirzyn married the Lady Annitra, and when old Prince Jarnid, his father, discarnated a year later, he succeeded to the title. And immediately, Tarnod was made head gamekeeper here."

"What did I tell you, Lord Virzal? I knew that son of a *zortan* had something on Jirzyn of Starpha!" Dirzed exclaimed.

"A nice family, this of Starpha!"

"Well, that's not the end of it," Sarnax continued. "This morning, Tarnov of Fastor, late Jirzid of Starpha, went before the High Court of Estates and entered suit to change his name to Jirzid of Starpha and laid claim to the title of Starpha family-head. The case has just been entered, so there's been no hearing, but there's the blazes of an argument among all the nobles about it—some are claiming that the individuality doesn't change from one reincarnation to the next, and others claiming that property and titles should pass along the line of physical descent, no matter what individuality has reincarnated into what body.

"They're the ones who want the Lady Dallona discarnated and her discoveries suppressed. And there's talk about revising the entire system of estate-ownership and estate-inheritance. Oh, it's an utter obscenity of a business!"

"This," Verkan Vall told Dalla, "is something we will not emphasize when we get home."

That was as close as he dared come to it, but she caught his meaning. The working of major changes in outtime social structures was not viewed with approval by the Paratime Commission on the First Level. "*If* we get home," he added. Then an idea occurred to him. "Dirzed, Sarnax; this place must have been used by the leaders of the Volitionalists for top-level conferences. Is there a secret passage anywhere?"

Sarnax shook his head. "Not from here. There is one, on the floor above, but they control it. And even if there were one down here, they would be guarding the outlet."

"That's what I was counting on. I'd hoped to simulate an escape that way, and then make a rush up the regular tubes." Verkan Vall shrugged. "I suppose Marnik's our only chance. I hope he got away safely."

"He was going for help? I was surprised that an Assassin would desert his client; I should have thought of that," Sarnax said. "Well, even if he got down carnate, and if Girzad didn't catch him, he'd still be afoot ten miles from the nearest city unit. That gives us a little chance—about one in a thousand."

"Is there any way they can get at us, except by those tubes?" Dalla asked.

"They could cut a hole in the floor, or burn one through," Sarnax replied. "They have plenty of thermite. They could detonate a charge of explosives over our heads, or clear out of the dome and drop one down the well. They could use lethal gas or radiodust, but their Assassins wouldn't permit such illegal methods. Or they could shoot sleep-gas down at us, and then come down and cut our throats at their leisure."

"We'll have to get out of this room, then," Verkan Vall decided. "They know we've barricaded ourselves in here; this is where they'll attack. So we'll patrol the perimeter of the well; we'll be out of danger from above if we keep close to the wall. And we'll inspect all the rooms on this floor for evidence of cutting through from above."

Sarnax nodded. "That's good sense, Lord Virzal. How about the lifter tubes?"

"We'll have to barricade them. Sarnax, you and Dirzed know the layout of this place better than the Lady Dallona or I; suppose you two check the rooms, while we cover the tubes and the well," Verkan Vall directed. "Come on, now."

XII

They pushed the door wide-open and went out past the cabinet. Hugging the wall, they began a slow circuit of the well, Verkan Vall in the lead with the submachine-gun, then Sarnax and Dirzed, the former with a heavy boar-rifle and the latter with a hunting pistol in each hand, and Hadron Dalla brought up in the rear with her rifle.

It was she who noticed a movement along the rim of the balcony above and snapped a shot at it; there was a crash above, and a shower of glass and plastic and metal fragments rattled on the pavement of the court. Somebody had been trying to lower a scanner or a visiplate-pickup, or something of the sort; the exact nature of the instrument was not evident from the wreckage Dalla's bullet had made of it.

The rooms Dirzed and Sarnax entered were all quiet; nobody seemed to be attempting to cut through the ceiling, fifteen feet above. They dragged furniture from a couple of rooms, blocking the openings of the lifter tubes, and continued around the well until they had reached the gunroom again. Dirzed suggested that they move some of the weapons and ammunition stored there to Prince Jirzyn's private apartment, halfway around to the lifter tubes, so that another place of refuge would be stocked with munitions in event of their being driven from the gunroom.

Leaving him on guard outside, Verkan Vall, Dalla and Sarnax entered the gunroom and began gathering weapons and boxes of ammunition. Dalla finished packing her game bag with the recorded data and notes of her experiments. Verkan Vall selected four more of the heavy hunting pistols, more accurate than his shoulder-holster weapon or the dead Olirzon's belt arm, and capable of either full or semi-automatic fire. Sarnax chose a couple more boar rifles.

Dalla slung her bag of recorded notes, and another bag of ammunition, and secured another deer rifle. They carried this accumulation of munitions to the private apartments of Prince Jirzyn, dumping everything in the middle of the drawing room, except the bag of notes, from which Dalla refused to separate herself.

"Maybe we'd better put some stuff over in one of the rooms on the other side of the well," Dirzed suggested. "They haven't really begun to come after us; when they do, we'll probably be attacked from two or three directions at once."

They returned to the gunroom, casting anxious glances at the edge of the balcony above and at the barricade they had erected across the openings to the lifter tubes. Verkan Vall was not satisfied with this last; it looked to him as though they had provided a breastwork for somebody to fire on them from, more than anything else. He was about to step around the cabinet which partially blocked the gun-room door when he glanced up, and saw a six-foot circle on the ceiling turning slowly brown. There was a smell of scorched plastic. He grabbed Sarnax by the arm and pointed.

"Thermite," the Assassin whispered. "The ceiling's got six inches of spaceship-insulation between it and the floor above; it'll take them a few minutes to burn through it." He stooped and pushed on the barricade, shoving it into the room. "Keep back; they'll probably drop a grenade or so through, first, before they jump down. If we're quick, we can get a couple of them."

Dirzed and Sarnax crouched, one at either side of the door, with weapons ready. Verkan Vall and Dalla had been ordered, rather peremptorily, to stay behind them; in a place of danger, an Assassin was obliged to shield his client. Verkan Vall, unable to see what was going on inside the room, kept his eyes and his gun muzzle on the barricade across the openings to the lifter tubes, the erection of which he was now regretting as a major tactical error.

Inside the gunroom, there was a sudden crash, as the circle of thermite burned through and a section of ceiling dropped out and hit the floor. Instantly, Dirzed flung himself back against Verkan Vall, and there was a tremendous explosion inside, followed by another and another. A second or so passed, then Dirzed, leaning around the corner of the door, began firing rapidly into the room. From the other side of the door, Sarnax began blazing away with his rifle. Verkan Vall kept his position, covering the lifter tubes.

Suddenly, from behind the barricade, a blue-white gun flash leaped into being, and a pistol banged. He sprayed the opening between a couch and a section of bookcase from whence it had come, releasing his trigger as the gun rose with the recoil, squeezing and releasing and squeezing again. Then he jumped to his feet.

"Come on, the other place; hurry!" he ordered.

Sarnax swore in exasperation. "Help me with her, Dirzed!" he implored.

Verkan Vall turned his head, to see the two Assassins drag Dalla to her feet and hustle her away from the gunroom; she was quite senseless, and they had to drag her between them.

Verkan Vall gave a quick glance into the gunroom; two of the Starpha servants and a man in rather flashy civil dress were lying on the floor, where they had been shot as they had jumped down from above. He saw a movement at the edge of the irregular, smoking, hole in the ceiling, and gave it a short burst, then fired another at the exit from the descent tube. Then he took to his heels and followed the Assassins and Hadron Dalla into Prince Jirzyn's apartment.

As he ran through the open door, the Assassins were letting Dalla down into a chair; they instantly threw themselves into the work of barricading the doorway so as to provide cover and at the same time allow them to fire out into the central well.

For an instant, as he bent over her, he thought Dalla had been killed, an assumption justified by his knowledge of the deadliness of Akor-Neb bullets. Then he saw her eyelids flicker. A moment later, he had the explanation of her escape. The bullet had hit the game bag at her side; it was full of spools of metal tape, in metal cases, and notes in written form, pyrographed upon sheets of plastic ring-fastened into metal binders. Because of their extreme velocity, Akor-Neb bullets were sure killers when they struck animal tissue, but for the same reason, they had very poor penetration on hard objects. The alloy-steel tape, and the steel spools and spool cases, and the notebook binders, had been enough to shatter the little bullet into splinters of magnesium-nickel alloy, and the stout leather back of the game bag had stopped all of these.

But the impact, even distributed as it had been through the contents of the bag, had been enough to knock the girl unconscious. He found a bottle of some sort of brandy and a glass on a serving table nearby and poured her a drink, holding it to her lips. She spluttered over the first mouthful, then took the glass from him and sipped the rest. "What happened?" she asked. "I thought those bullets were sure death."

"Your notes. The bullet hit the bag. Are you all right, now?"

She finished the brandy. "I think so." She put a hand into the game bag and brought out a snarled and tangled mess of steel tape. "Oh, *blast!* That stuff was important; all the records on the preliminary auto-recall experiments." She shrugged. "Well, it wouldn't have been worth much more if I'd stopped that bullet, myself."

She slipped the strap over her shoulder and started to rise. As she did, a bedlam of firing broke out, both from the two Assassins at the door and from outside. They both hit the floor and crawled out of line of the partly-open door; Verkan Vall recovered his submachine-gun, which he had set down beside Dalla's chair.

Sarnax was firing with his rifle at some target in the direction of the lifter tubes; Dirzed lay slumped over the barricade, and one glance at his crumpled figure was enough to tell Verkan Vall that he was dead.

"You fill magazines for us," he told Dalla, then crawled to Dirzed's place at the door. "What happened, Sarnax?"

"They shoved over the barricade at the lifter tubes and came out into the well. I got a couple, they got Dirzed, and now they're holed up in rooms all around the circle. They—Aah!"

He fired three shots, quickly, around the edge of the door. "That stopped that."

The Assassin crouched to insert a fresh magazine into his rifle. Verkan Vall risked one eye around the corner of the doorway, and as he did, there was a red flash and a dull roar, unlike the blue flashes and sharp cracking reports of the pistols and rifles, from the doorway of the gunroom. He wondered, for a split second, if it might be one of the fowling pieces he had seen there, and then something whizzed past his head and exploded with a soft *plop* behind him.

Turning, he saw a pool of gray vapor beginning to spread in the middle of the room. Dalla must have got a breath of it, for she was slumped over the chair from which she had just risen. Dropping the submachine-gun and gulping a lungful of fresh air from outside, Verkan Vall rushed to her, caught her by the heels, and dragged her into Prince Jirzyn's bedroom, beyond. Leaving her in the middle of the floor, he took another deep breath and returned to the drawing room, where Sarnax was already overcome by the sleep-gas.

He saw the serving table from which he had got the brandy, and dragged it over to the bedroom door, overturning it and laying it across the doorway, its legs in the air. Like most Akor-Neb serving tables, it had a gravity-counteraction unit under it; he set this for double minus-gravitation and snapped it on. As it was now above the inverted table, the table did not rise, but a tendril, of sleep-gas, curling toward it, bent upward and drifted away from the doorway.

Satisfied that he had made a temporary barrier against the sleep-gas, Verkan Vall secured Dalla's hunting pistol and spare magazines and lay down at the bedroom door. For some time, there was silence outside. Then the besiegers evidently decided that the sleep-gas attack had been a success. An Assassin, wearing a gas mask and carrying a submachine-gun, appeared in the doorway, and behind him came a tall man in a tan tunic, similarly masked. They stepped into the room and looked around.

Knowing that he would be shooting over a two hundred percent negative gravitation-field, Verkan Vall aimed for the Assassin's belt-buckle and squeezed. The bullet caught him in the throat. Evidently the bullet had not only been lifted in the negative gravitation, but lifted point-first and deflected upward. He held his front sight just above the other man's knee, and hit him in the chest. As he fired, he saw a wisp of gas come sliding around the edge of the inverted table. There was silence outside, and for an instant, he was tempted to abandon his post and go to the bathroom, back of the bedroom, for wet towels to improvise a mask.

Then, when he tried to crawl backward, he could not. There was an impression of distant shouting which turned to a roaring sound in his head. He tried to lift his pistol, but it slipped from his fingers.

XIII

When consciousness returned, he was lying on his back, and something cold and rubbery was pressing into his face. He raised his arms to fight off whatever it was, and opened his eyes, to find that he was staring directly at the red oval and winged bullet of the Society of Assassins. A hand caught his wrist as he reached for the small pistol under his arm. The pressure on his face eased.

"It's all right, Lord Virzal," a voice came to him. "Assassins' Truce!"

He nodded stupidly and repeated the words. "Assassins' Truce; I won't shoot. What happened?"

Then he sat up and looked around. Prince Jirzyn's bedchamber was full of Assassins. Dalla, recovering from her touch of sleep-gas, was sitting groggily in a chair, while five or six of them fussed around her, getting in each other's way, handing her drinks, chaffing her wrists, holding damp cloths on her brow.

That was standard procedure, when any group of males thought Dalla needed any help. Another Assassin, beside the bed, was putting away an oxygen-mask outfit, and the Assassin who had prevented Verkan Vall from drawing his pistol was his own follower, Marnik. And Klarnood, the Assassin-President, was sitting on the foot of the bed, smoking one of Prince Jirzyn's monogrammed and crested cigarettes critically.

Verkan Vall looked at Marnik, and then at Klarnood, and back to Marnik. "You got through," he said. "Good work, Marnik; I thought they'd downed you."

"They did; I had to crash-land in the woods. I went about a mile on foot, and then I found a man and woman and two children, hiding in one of these little log rain shelters. They had an airboat, a good one. It seemed that rioting had broken out in the city unit where they lived, and they'd taken to the woods till things quieted down again. I offered them Assassins' protection if they'd take me to Assassins' Hall, and they did."

"By luck, I was in when Marnik arrived," Klarnood took over. "We brought three boatloads of men, and came here at once. Just as we got here, two boatloads of Starpha dependents arrived; they tried to give us an argument, and we discarnated the lot of them. Then we came down here, crying Assassins' Truce. One of the Starpha Assassins, Kirzol, was still carnate; he told us what had been going on."

The President-General's face-became grim. "You know, I take a rather poor view of Prince Jirzyn's procedure in this matter, not to mention that of his underlings. I'll have to speak to him about this. Now, how about you and the Lady Dallona? What do you intend doing?"

"We're getting out of here," Verkan Vall said. "I'd like air transport and protection as far as Ghamma, to the establishment of the family of Zorda. Brarnend of Zorda has a private space yacht; he'll get us to Venus."

Klarnood gave a sigh of obvious relief. "I'll have you and the Lady Dallona airborne and off for Ghamma as soon as you wish," he promised. "I will, frankly, be delighted to see the last of both of you. The Lady Dallona has started a fire here at Darsh that won't burn out in a half-century, and who knows what it may consume."

He was interrupted by a heaving shock that made the underground dome dwelling shake like a light airboat in turbulence. Even eighty feet under the ground, they could hear a continued crashing roar. It was an appreciable interval before the sound and the shock ceased. For an instant, there was silence, and then an excited bedlam of shouting broke from the Assassins in the room: Klarnood's face was frozen in horror.

"That was a fission bomb!" he exclaimed. "The first one that has been exploded on this planet in hostility in a thousand years!"

He turned to Verkan Vall. "If you feel well enough to walk, Lord Virzal, come with us. I must see what's happened."

They hurried from the room and went streaming up the ascent tube to the top of the dome. About forty miles away, to the south, Verkan Vall saw the sinister thing that he had seen on so many other time-lines, in so many other Paratime sectors—a great pillar of varicolored fire-shot smoke, rising to a mushroom head fifty thousand feet above.

"Well, that's it," Klarnood said sadly. "That is civil war."

"May I make a suggestion, Assassin-President?" Verkan Vall asked. "I understand that Assassins' Truce is binding even upon non-Assassins; is that correct?"

"Well, not exactly; it's generally kept by such non-Assassins as want to remain in their present reincarnations, though."

"That's what I meant. Well, suppose you declare a general, planet-wide Assassins' Truce in this political war, and make the leaders of both parties responsible for keeping it. Publish lists of the top two or three thousand Statisticalists and Volitionalists, starting with Mirzark of Bashad and Prince Jirzyn of Starpha, and inform them that they will be assassinated, in order, if the fighting doesn't cease."

"Well!" A smile grew on Klarnood's face. "Lord Virzal, my thanks; a good suggestion. I'll try it. And furthermore, I'll withdraw all Assassin protection permanently from anybody involved in political activity, and forbid any Assassin to accept any retainer connected with political factionalism. It's about time our members stopped discarnating each other in these political squabbles."

He pointed to the three airboats drawn up on the top of the dome; speedy black craft, bearing the red oval and winged bullet. "Take your choice, Lord Virzal. I'll lend you a couple of my men, and you'll be in Ghamma in three hours."

He hooked fingers and clapped shoulders with Verkan Vall, bent over Dalla's hand. "I still like you, Lord Virzal, and I have seldom met a more charming lady than you, Lady Dallona. But I sincerely hope I never see either of you again."

XIV

The ship for Dhergabar was driving north and west; at seventy-thousand feet, it was still daylight, but the world below was wrapping itself in darkness. In the big visiscreens, which served in lieu of the windows which could never have withstood the pressure and friction heat of the ship's speed, the sun was sliding out of sight over the horizon to port. Verkan Vall and Dalla sat together, watching the blazing western sky—the sky of their own First Level time-line.

"I blame myself terribly, Vall," Dalla was saying. "And I didn't mean any of them the least harm. All I was interested in was learning the facts. I know, that sounds like 'I didn't know it was loaded,' but—"

"It sounds to me like those Fourth Level Europo-American Sector physicists who are giving themselves guilt-complexes because they designed an atomic bomb," Verkan Vall replied. "All you were interested in was learning the facts. Well, as a scientist, that's all you're supposed to be interested in. You don't have to worry about any social or political implications. People have to learn to live with newly-discovered facts; if they don't, they die of them."

"But, Vall; that sounds dreadfully irresponsible—"

"Does it? You're worrying about the results of your reincarnation memory-recall discoveries, the shootings and rioting and the bombing we saw."

He touched the pommel of Olirzon's knife, which he still wore. "You're no more guilty of that than the man who forged this blade is guilty of thc death of Marnark of Bashad; if he'd never lived, I'd have killed Marnark with some other knife somebody else made. And what's more, you can't know the results of your discoveries. All you can see is a thin film of events on the surface of an immediate situation, so you can't say whether the long-term results will be beneficial or calamitous.

"Take this Fourth Level Europo-American atomic bomb, for example. I chose that because we both know that sector, but I could think of a hundred other examples in other Paratime areas. Those people, because of deforestation, bad agricultural methods and general mismanagement, are eroding away their arable soil at an alarming rate. At the same time, they are breeding like rabbits. In other words, each successive generation has less and less food to divide among more and more people, and, for inherited traditional and superstitious reasons, they refuse to adopt any rational program of birth-control and population-limitation.

"But, fortunately, they now have the atomic bomb, and they are developing radioactive poisons, weapons of mass-effect. And their racial, nationalistic and ideological conflicts are rapidly reaching the explosion point. A series of all-out atomic wars is just what that sector needs, to bring their population down to their world's carrying capacity; in a century or so, the inventors of the atomic bomb will be hailed as the saviors of their species."

"But how about my work on the Akor-Neb Sector?" Dalla asked. "It seems that my memory-recall technique is more explosive than any fission bomb. I've laid the train for a century-long reign of anarchy!"

"I doubt that; I think Klarnood will take hold, now that he has committed himself to it. You know, in spite of his sanguinary profession, he's the nearest thing to a real man of good will I've found on that sector. And here's something else you haven't considered. Our own First Level life expectancy is from four to five hundred years. That's the main reason why we've accomplished as much as we have. We have, individually, time to accomplish things. On the Akor-Neb Sector, a scientist or artist or scholar or statesman will grow senile and die before he's as old as either of us.

"But now, a young student of twenty or so can take one of your auto-recall treatments and immediately have available all the knowledge and experience gained in four or five previous lives. He can start where he left off in his last reincarnation. In other words, you've made those people time-binders, individually as well as racially. Isn't that worth the temporary discarnation of a lot of ward-heelers and plug-uglies, or even a few decent types like Dirzed and Olirzon? If it isn't, I don't know what scales of values you're using."

"Vall!" Dalla's eyes glowed with enthusiasm. "I never thought of that! And you said, 'temporary discarnation.' That's just what it is. Dirzed and Olirzon and the others aren't dead; they're just waiting, discarnate, between physical lives. You know, in the sacred writings of one of the Fourth Level peoples it is stated: 'Death is the last enemy.' By proving that death is just a cyclic condition of continued individual existence, these people have conquered their last enemy."

"Last enemy but one," Verkan Vall corrected. "They still have one enemy to go, an enemy within themselves. Call it semantic confusion, or illogic, or incomprehension, or just plain stupidity. Like Klarnood, stymied by verbal objections to something labeled 'political intervention.' He'd never have consented to use the power of his Society if he hadn't been shocked out of his inhibitions by that nuclear bomb.

"Or the Statisticalists, trying to create a classless order of society through a political program which would only result in universal servitude to an omnipotent government. Or the Volitionalist nobles, trying to preserve their hereditary feudal privileges, and now they can't even agree on a definition of the term 'hereditary.' Might they not recover all the silly prejudices of their past lives, along with the knowledge and wisdom?"

"But...I thought you said—" Dalla was puzzled, a little hurt.

Verkan Vall's arm squeezed around her waist, and he laughed comfortingly. "You see? Any sort of result is possible, good or bad. So don't blame yourself in advance for something you can't possibly estimate."

An idea occurred to him, and he straightened in the seat. "Tell you what; if you people at Rhogom Foundation get the problem of discarnate Paratime Transposition licked by then, let's you and I go back to the Akor-Neb Sector in about a hundred years and see what sort of a mess those people have made of things."

"A hundred years: that would be Year Twenty-Two of the next millennium. It's a date, Vall; we'll do it."

They bent to light their cigarettes together at his lighter. When they raised their heads again and got the flame glare out of their eyes, the sky was purple-black, dusted with stars, and dead ahead, spilling up over the horizon, was a golden glow—the lights of Dhergabar and home.

PARATIME PARASITES

JOHN F. CARR

I

1951 A.D.

Verkan Vall had just returned from a ten-day vacation outtime, visiting his private island home of Nerros on Fourth Level Europo-American, Hispania Subsector. On this subsector, the Spanish Armada had conquered the island of Britain, which had resulted in the Spanish domination of Europe and a bad case of culture paralysis after the Heresy Wars ended the Protestant movements on the Major Land Mass. The Office of the Holy Inquisition was still in operation in both the Old World and New World and the mechanical arts had not evolved much above the windmill and the waterwheel.

There had been little development on most of the Caribbean Islands and Verkan had purchased the one called Cayman Brac on most Hispano-Columbian subsectors for his vacation home. He had named it

Nerros after his hereditary home on Venus. Most Paratimers preferred to have their outtime villas on uninhabited Fifth Level time-lines, but Verkan didn't like the choices represented: one could either relax in a villa populated by robot servers, or dragoon some poor outtimers, usually rescued from some local disaster on the Fourth Level, into becoming one's servants. Like Chief Tortha had done on his Fifth Level island of Sicily, as it was called on Fourth Level, Europo-American.

Earlier in his career, Verkan had rescued a party of Paratime tourists on the Hispano Subsector, who had run afoul of the local Inquisition, and had made the acquaintance of Grandee, Luis Fernández de Córdoba y Salabert, Duke of Medinaceli. In thanks for saving his clients and himself from the *Tribunal del Santo Oficio de la Inquisición*, Duke Fernández had granted Verkan Vall the small island some thirty years ago. Under Verkan's stewardship, Nerros had prospered and the villagers considered him their protector as well as their patron.

After the reincarnation fracas on Second Level Akor-Neb Subsector, Verkan had invited Hadron Dalla, his former wife, to stay with him there for a short vacation. Dalla had agreed and they'd had a wonderful time together, walking the beach, eating sumptuous local dishes and getting to know each other again. Of course, as one of the universal axioms throughout all the Paratime levels put it: *All good things must come to an end.* So, no sooner than he'd arrived back at the Paratime Building, he had received a call on his hand-phone directing him to see the Chief—at once.

The Chief's secretary waved him on and Verkan nodded to the guards outside Paratime Police Chief Tortha Karf's office as he went through the door. Inside, Chief Tortha, smoking a cigarette, was seated behind his horseshoe desk.

"Hi, Vall, have a seat."

"Thanks, Chief."

"Want a cigarette?" Tortha asked.

"No," Verkan answered, pulling out several of his own cigarettes, rolled in tobacco leaf, from the inside pocket of his green jacket. "I brought some with me from Nerros."

"You've got your own tobacco plantation!" the Chief exclaimed.

Verkan nodded. "A small one; for one thing, the island isn't that big. The locals know that I like good leaf, and it's their way of thanking me. I've also got a couple of boxes of hand-rolled cigars back at the apartment. I'll bring some in for you, if you'd like."

"Thanks," the Chief said, as he put out his own. "Let me try one now."

"Sure," Verkan said, passing him one of the dark-brown cigarettes.

They both lit up and drew in a lungful of smoke.

"Hmm," Tortha said, his face breaking into a smile. "Nice flavor! Now, if only I could teach those worthless peasants of mine at my retreat on Fifth Level to do likewise."

Verkan shook his head. Tortha was actually quite fond of his 'tribe,' as he called them, and spoiled them outrageously. "Wrong climate zone, Chief. Besides, I've got more than enough to share."

"Thanks. How was your vacation?" the Chief asked, raising his eyebrows. Tortha was quite familiar with his and Dalla's previous companionate marriage, as Verkan had leaned on his shoulder a number of times before their first breakup.

"Actually, it was nice, very nice!" Verkan smiled as he reviewed his memories of the evenings they'd shared.

"I don't doubt it," Tortha replied grumpily, "as long as it doesn't affect your work for the Department—"

"We haven't made any plans, yet. Still, Dalla seems to have grown up a bit since we were last together."

Tortha's brow furrowed as if he were thinking, *'I've heard this before!'*

"Plus, it was important to keep Dalla away from the Rhogom Institute," Verkan said. "I was finally able to convince her that her scientific evidence, proving that death is just a cyclic condition of continued individual existence, might be agitating the same nest of rattlesnakes on First Level that she kicked over on the Akor-Neb subsector."

"Hey, you didn't put that into your report!" Tortha exclaimed.

"Too dangerous. Despite regulations, too many people in the Department read those reports—some are even leaked to the newsies."

Tortha made a reluctant nod. "You might be right. The last thing we need are a bunch of proles discarnating themselves, hoping to become

Home Time-liners in their next reincarnation!"

"It could happen. The time-line we were on went nuclear after the news was released."

"Dalla at work again," Tortha said with disgust. "She's a one woman Typhoid Mary!"

"Hey, don't blame her," Verkan stated. "Dalla was only doing her job."

"I've heard that excuse before. Problems seem to run in the Hadron family. That brother of hers just got busted by Metro for some Ponzi scheme he was working on."

"What's a 'Ponzi scheme'?" Verkan asked.

"It's one of those pyramid selling plans," Tortha said, "which uses money from new investors to pay people, who've already invested, instead of using real profit to pay them off. Typically, the later investors get nothing for their funds, while the authors make a fortune. It's a common confidence game in many Europo-American subsectors."

"That sounds like something Tharn would glom onto. But I believe Dalla's turned a new page," Verkan said. "She even agreed to sit on her work for the time being. Of course, it helped that most of her notes and records were destroyed before we were able to escape the Volitionalist assassins. Still, she actually admitted: 'My memory-recall technique is more explosive than any fission bomb.'"

"Phew, that is some admission, coming from Dalla. Maybe she has changed. For your sake, I hope so."

"So, Chief, what's so important that you gave me a red priority call the moment I entered the building?"

Tortha grimaced. "You know that one of my goals as Chief has been to clear up past discrepancies in the Outtime Survey Records Division."

"Sure," Verkan said. "Every chief since Untar Zand has been promising to do just that very thing. Of course, none of them ever found the time to do it."

"I know. I assigned a promising new agent to the job, Kostran Galth, and he's discovered something that's been overlooked since the early days of Paratime exploration."

Verkan winced. "What are you talking about? More nonsense about time-lines beyond the Hesthor Limit." The Barthov Uncertainty Principle established a limit as to how far a Ghaldron-Hesthor conveyer could go. This was called the Hesthor Limit and it corresponded to time-lines that were identical to Home Time Line until less than fifty thousand years ago. A time-line that varied from Home Time Line fifty-one thousand years ago, or five hundred thousand, etc. was beyond the Hesthor limit and could never be reached by a Ghaldron-Hesthor conveyer.

Most Paratime theorists agreed there were time-lines beyond the Hesthor Limit, and referred to them as the "Sixth Level." Hence there was a steady leakage of time-lines out of *reachable* Paratime. The leakage was slow, which meant Paratime would not 'evaporate' completely for several billion years, and waiting for it to happen was like waiting for the sun to use up all its hydrogen. In other words, sheer silliness, as far as Verkan was concerned. Not surprisingly, the Sixth Level was a favorite topic of Home Time Line fantasy authors and Tri-D producers.

Tortha Karf shook his head in the negative. "This has nothing to do with the Hesthor Limit. Kostran found a record of an early recon mission to the Fifth Level, and noted nobody had filed an end-status report on it: No end-status report, no crew returned, no Paratime conveyer back to where it belonged and accounted for."

That got Verkan's attention: A missing conveyer and crew was a direct threat to the Paratime secret, something that could not be ignored even after ten thousand years. "What do you want to do about it, Chief?"

"This 'lost' conveyer could be a political hot potato, to use a particularly apt Fourth Level aphorism."

"How would it embarrass the Department?" Verkan asked.

"The head of Paratime Survey at that time was one of the founding members of the Management Party. The Opposition would have a field day with this tidbit."

"Who? Talron Warth!"

"Exactly. Or the Great Leader as he's usually called."

"It's highly unlikely we'll find anything after ten thousand years," Verkan said. "Unless you have evidence otherwise."

"No. It's just an embarrassing loose end that needs to be snipped. And you're just the man to do it," Tortha finished.

II

The air shimmered, much like a distant heat distortion, then solidified as the Ghaldron-Hesthor transposition field collapsed revealing a thirty-foot hemispherical device that appeared to be made of an intricate metal mesh. A door slid open and several armed men dressed in Paratime Police green stepped out of the conveyer. Among them were Verkan Vall and Ranthar Jard, on leave from his position as sub-chief of the Esaron Sector.

Verkan studied the landscape, both visually and with the scanner on his wrist. There was a significant array of bio-signatures ranging from the microbial all the way up to something large enough to be a Mammoth, but no indications of power generation or communications broadcasting. While there was always the possibility that the technology of this time-line was shielded or so alien as to defy identification, Verkan had good reason to suspect that was not the case.

Fifth Level time-lines were invariably inhabited by primitive hominids who rarely achieved even bow and arrow technology, which wasn't to say that they couldn't be extremely dangerous. One of those hominids, dubbed Neanderthal Man on many Fourth level time-lines, was incredibly strong and capable of throwing a spear twice as far as any First Level athlete, and with impressive, not to mention lethal, accuracy.

Satisfied that there was no immediate danger, Verkan holstered his pistol. All but two men followed his example; it was standard procedure for at least two men to be at the ready in an unexplored time-line. At least here they didn't have to worry about appropriate costumes or languages, he reflected.

Verkan nodded at Ranthar Jard. Ranthar pulled a box out of the conveyer and opened it. Inside were several spherical objects known as Boomerang Balls. Boomerang balls, or BBs as some people called them, were designed to fly around under their own power recording and transmitting imagery. The dozen or so BBs in the box, when activated, would cover more territory in a few hours than a hundred men on foot could do in a month or more. Preprogrammed targeting information would limit the sensory data transmitted back to Jard and his crew for quick analysis, though all the data would be stored for more thorough inspection when they returned to the Home Time Line.

"You do know this is a long shot," Ranthar Jard said. "Ten thousand years is a very long time. I would guess that even if there is anything left, it could be buried under thousands of years of accumulated earth and rock."

Verkan nodded. "Just between you and me, I think the whole mission is a wash. But when the Chief says jump, you ask 'how high' and start jumping."

Ranthar smiled and nodded as he watched the BBs float up, then shoot out in every direction. Sunar Gand opened up a teleview screen. The main display screen gave a real time view of the local terrain as seen from one thousand feet above ground. Twelve miniature boxes, four above, four below, and two on the right and left showed the imagery that each individual BB was relaying.

"You would think they would have kept better track of these conveyers back when Paratime travel was invented," Ranthar said.

Verkan shrugged. "It was a new science. What impresses me is that Kostran Galth found a record of this particular recon mission. There was no end-status report, no crew returned and no Paratime conveyer back where it belonged."

"Still, Verkan, after ten thousand years, what could be left of the conveyer?" Ranthar looked out at the landscape. "According to the records it was an all-male crew, so no descendants were possible. Unless one of them had a thing for, um, ape men."

"Get stranded on a desert time-line and there's no telling what would start looking attractive after a few years," Verkan countered. "Still, even if they were inter-fertile with the locals, the genetic contribution would likely have been bred out of the race by now."

"That also assumes," Ranthar said, with a laugh, "that the locals didn't think that they were crunchy and delicious."

Verkan shook his head. Ranthar Jard had the strangest sense of humor. Still, things were never dull when he was around.

"But seriously, Verkan, what are the odds that we'll find anything?"

Verkan Vall mentally reviewed what he knew from the ten thousand year old report. A team of explorers had taken one of the earliest prototypes of the Paratime Transposition conveyer and set out for as far as it would go downwhen. It was the farthest Paratime journey on the books. Certainly the farthest Verkan had ever taken, even if one accounted for round trips. The scenery had been interesting enough, at the beginning, watching trees, buildings, and even people appear and vanish. Once they hit Fifth level, all he saw was industrial complexes, mining operations and private villas. At least at first. As the conveyer got closer to the designated time-line, fewer and fewer examples of First Level civilization appeared. The last several hundred thousand parayears had been completely empty of any evidence of exploitation.

The prototype had been constructed before the advent of collapsed metal, so it was most likely made of polysteel, a corrosion-resistant alloy capable of retaining its shape and durability for a very long time. However, it had never been tested under these conditions. Could the poly-steel hull resist degradation brought on by heat, cold, humidity and animal depredation for thousands of years?

Verkan took a large breath, then released it slowly. "The odds are not good, I think. But if there is anything here, we for damned sure had better find it before we go back."

Ranthar nodded in agreement. "I guess I'll get some of the guys to work on the camp. I suspect we'll be here for a while."

III

From a ridge, hidden in the foliage, two humanoids observed the men in green. They watched with interest as the two men opened the side of the silvery round thing and something floated out. The floating thing came to rest several paces from the sphere and large square wafer thin segments were set into place by long arms on the floating thing. In short order a dome grew from the aggregate sections of wafer squares large enough to house all the men in green.

After a time, one tapped the other on the shoulder, gestured, and the pair stealthily crawled away, keeping a wary eye out for the round things that floated away as if by magic.

The sun was sinking low on the horizon when Jard ordered the men to button up the conveyer and file into the enclosure. Once the hatch on the metal 'igloo' was sealed, they were safe from anything short of a direct strike from a meteorite or nuclear blast. The square wafers that the enclosure was made of were all super-thin sheets of polysteel laminated with a micron-thick collapsium shell.

The insulating properties of the collapsium were such that the men's own body heat soon made the interior of the igloo stifling, at which point Jard activated the air-cooler. In moments, the device sucked in all the extraneous heat and even acted as an oxygen scrubber keeping the air purified of excess carbon dioxide.

"So what was on the equipment list of this lost mission?" Ranthar asked. "They must have gone loaded for Venusian Nightwolves back in the pioneer days of paratravel."

Verkan said, "They did. I was surprised at how little the technology and names of devices have changed in the last ten thousand years, but even with the unfamiliar ones it isn't hard to recognize the purpose of what they carried. Standard tool kit, pioneering equipment, firearms, stunners, recording devices, compact computers, a teaching machine, translator, first aid kits—"

"Wait," Ranthar interrupted. "Teaching machines? As in hypno-mech? What on Mars for?"

Verkan shrugged. "Maybe to teach the indigenes our language so they could communicate. The subjects could always be mind-wiped afterwards. We didn't have the vast store of language tapes from all the different sectors, let alone sub-sectors, back then. We can't teach ourselves something we don't already know, so we would have had to teach the indigenous population what we did know."

"Now, of course, we have much stricter guidelines about that sort of thing," Ranthar noted.

"Back then we didn't even have Paratime Police," Verkan added.

"Weren't there a bunch of crazies who thought we should go out as some sort of missionary force to enlighten the poor unfortunates of the lower levels?" Ranthar asked. "As I heard it, they wanted to bring everyone outtime up to our cultural and technological level."

Verkan shuddered at the mental image. "In no time at all, they would have all been in the same boat we're in, and with no other time-lines to draw resources from. Second Level at least developed space travel, and there are predictions that some of the Fourth Level subsectors will make it into interstellar space within a few decades, or less. None of that would have happened if we interfered with their natural development to the degree you just mentioned."

Ranthar laughed out loud. When the others looked at him, he explained, "Maybe our missing pioneers were missionary types. They scooted back here to teach these ape men how to be civilized, and then got invited to dinner. As the main course."

Verkan and the rest looked at Ranthar with mixed reactions. "You might have a point there. That would explain the teaching machines, too."

"Well," Ranthar offered, "if they did come here and try to teach the locals, I would say they failed miserably. So far, there hasn't been any indication of a higher civilization."

The other officers nodded in agreement and joked about super-intelligent apemen while Verkan quietly considered the possible ramifications of technologically developed Neanderthals or some other hominid. He didn't like where his thoughts took him.

The next morning the men made breakfast from the stores while Ranthar checked the readouts and Verkan inspected the conveyer. The likelihood of damage was remote, but inspections were SOP in the Paratime Police manual. Satisfied that all was as it should be, Verkan joined the men for breakfast.

After a quick meal of pre-packaged, self-heating eggs, sausage and something called grits on Fourth Level Europo-American Sector, Verkan selected six field agents to join him on a short recon of the surrounding area. Valton Rotar, Tortha 'no-relation-to-Karf' Melk, Yandar Barv, Khandat Vith, Martak Klarj and Qixtor Zinn were instructed to draw stunners as well as their own rifles. Ranthar Jard would stay with the conveyer and establish a safe-zone around it.

When not undercover or operating covertly on more developed time-lines Paracops would often arm themselves with their own personal rifles. There was no regulation against it and familiarity with one's weapon was always desirable. Jard noted that Rotar and Melk favored automatics from Fourth Level Europo-American Hispano-Columbian Subsector used in something called the Korean War. Barv used a regulation issue semi-automatic rifle, Vith and Klarj both favored Second Level Akor-Neb rifles and Zinn had some strange contraption of his own design. Verkan hoped it wouldn't blow up in Zinn's face the first time he fired it. He preferred the Caulnor 12mm, one of the better First Level automatics.

The squad moved out and performed a quick sweep of the area. There was no actual requirement for the men to do so as the Boomerang Balls already surveyed the immediate area, but it was good practice and would break the monotony of waiting for something to happen. Verkan regretted leaving Dalla back on First Level. So far, this expedition was more a picnic than a military operation and it would have been nice to spend some down-time with her.

It was too early to determine if they had a future together, but deep down inside Verkan hoped they did. While at times Dalla might be considered a natural catastrophe in action, it was one he enjoyed being around. Living with her was never dull.

A low roar caught Verkan's attention. Thirty meters ahead and to the right was a big feline with phenomenally large fangs. It was one of the great cats that were extinct on every level but Fifth Level, and only in the subsectors where they weren't hunted for sport by Home Time Line thrill seekers.

Valton and Qixtor Zinn had already put the big cat in their sights, but waited for orders.

"Tortha and Yandar draw stunners and take aim," ordered Jard. "If he leaves us alone, we'll leave him alone, but if not, I'd rather not have to dig our bullets out of his carcass in the interest of preventing further cross-time contamination."

Rotar nodded while Zinn looked disappointed. Zinn likely wanted to bag a trophy with his newly-designed rifle.

The saber-toothed tiger moved in a sideways fashion, as if sizing up the seven men. Alone, none of them would look particularly dangerous, but as any predator knows, numbers are not to be ignored, especially when they don't turn and run.

After a moment, the tiger moved toward the squad, slowly, as if sizing up what they might do. Verkan was about to order Melk and Barv to stun the beast when it suddenly leaped forward. Before anybody could react, two spears struck the big cat; one in the center of mass, the second in the right haunch. The tiger dropped dead in his tracks.

Verkan turned to the source of the spears and spotted what appeared to be four Neanderthal males. They were too developed for apemen or any of the earlier hominids. They were hairy, slope-shouldered, low-browed and had under-slung chins. Two were unarmed from throwing their spears, the other two held their spears in a neutral position.

"Should we stun them, Verkan?" whispered Rotar.

Verkan threw a disgusted look at Rotar then whispered back, "Since they probably just saved our lives, I think stunning them might be considered rude."

"Point," Rotar nodded. "So what do we do? I don't speak any Neanderthalis, even if the local language is similar to the higher sub-sectors variety. Do you?"

Verkan admitted he didn't. Neither did any of the others. He was annoyed that he hadn't thought to get a hypno-mech of the local language, then realized that this far downwhen it was unlikely that any tapes on Lingua-Neanderthalis would match the local language.

"We'll have to go with sign language," Verkan said. "They killed the tiger instead of us, so I'm going to assume that they're friendly until they give us reason to suspect otherwise."

Everybody agreed. Melk and Zinn pulled the spears out of the carcass and held them out in a neutral position for their owners to recover. Verkan watched the faces of the newcomers for any sign of hostile intent. It was difficult to be sure; the faces were so different from upwhen humans. At least they weren't growling and baring their teeth.

Two of the heavily-browed Neanderthals handed their spears to their comrades, then went over and hoisted the saber-toothed tiger on their shoulders. Jard estimated that the cat had to weigh at least eight to nine hundred pounds. They didn't make it look easy, but they still managed to carry the brute between them. No doubt they planned to carve it up and share it with their tribe when they got back.

Verkan decided to risk a communication. He slowly pulled his radio off his belt and signaled Rotar.

"Verkan, I was about to call you," came Ranthar Jard's voice from the radio. The Neanderthals looked at him. He wasn't sure, but he thought they looked startled. "The BBs found something. There is a tribe of apemen over the rise about two kilometers out at the base of that mountain. They must have been in that cave when we arrived and only came out this morning or the Boomerang Balls would have spotted them sooner. And get this, they have something shiny and metallic looking on some sort of, um, well, portable altar would be my guess. It looks like they are taking it into the cave."

"Why was it outside in the first place?" Verkan asked.

"Religious ritual would be my guess," Ranthar suggested. "The ritual is over, now, so the holy whatzit goes back in the closet."

"Jard, see if anybody back at the camp was ever hypno-meched for Lingua-Neanderthalis." Ranthar Jard gave a 'yes, sir' and the radio went quiet for a moment. "Lindar Marth used to work on Fifth Level managing Neanderthal servants on a private estate before becoming a Paracop."

"Good. Have him track our signal and meet up with us. Warn him that we have company and not to make any sudden or hostile movements. I wouldn't want to offend our new friends."

"Right. He's on his way. Anything else?"

"Not now, but stay in touch and post some guards. Just in case. Vall out."

Verkan and his men followed the natives while keeping a wary eye out for an ambush. The fact that the two carrying the big cat and the two holding the spears were in the lead was a good sign. He would have been more worried if one or more of them had brought up the rear where they could attack from behind. Marth joined the procession making a big show of keeping his hands chest high and spread open, showing he wielded no weapons. The Neanderthals grunted something and Marth fell in next to Verkan.

"Are we prisoners?" Marth asked.

Verkan shook his head. "Guests, it would seem. They haven't made any hostile gestures that I could see. That smilodon they are hauling away was sizing us up for brunch when these nice fellows changed its mind. That says friend, to me, but I won't take it on faith until I see what kind of reception we get from their tribe, village or whatever."

Marth nodded. "Do you think they'll have us over for dinner, or for dinner?"

"You tell me. You're the expert, here."

"I wouldn't go that far, but I take your point." Marth thought for a moment before speaking, as if to arrange his thoughts. "The 'thals I worked with upwhen were a nice enough bunch, really. I never heard of them engaging in casual cannibalism, to be honest, though they did like to eat a lot of meat. I've spoken with some guys who worked on other time-lines where they had to fight with 'thals. Stunners only seem to piss them off, and it takes a fair amount of firepower to put them down. Anything less than a .38 just annoys them. You may have noticed that they have a lot of muscle mass. Well, it ain't for show like on a bodybuilder. Every ounce of it is like rock. And their bones are thicker and harder than ours, too. Mortally wounded, they'll still come after you as long as they can draw breath."

Verkan didn't like the sound of any of that. "Are they typically hostile to strangers?"

Lindar Marth shook his head in Fourth Level fashion. "No. Every story I heard about them going to war with our people was a direct result of human ignorance or arrogance. Some idiot starts building a factory or private villa without finding out if the natives might object. Maybe the land is sacred, or the best place for good hunting or maybe they just don't like strangers coming in and tearing up the scenery. Well, next thing you know they come in to ask what's going on and some fool takes a shot at them. Things go downhill real fast from there."

"But not where you worked?" Verkan asked.

"Nope. My boss Glintov Hulva was way smarter than that. He sent in a team of anthropologists to study the natives, then just asked them nicely if they would mind letting him have some land they weren't using. Something along those lines. He paid them in cattle and had the anthropologists teach them about farming and ranching. Now he has friendly neighbors and a good source of day laborers."

Verkan reflected that his and other Paratime Polices' jobs would be a lot easier if everybody was as enlightened as this Glintov Hulva. Far too many Paratime travelers seemed to think that all lower sectors inhabitants were just there to be exploited. That attitude had put many a Paratimer in serious danger—and killed more than a few.

"How well do you think you'll be able to communicate with these, um, 'thals?"

"Don't know," replied Marth. "Haven't heard them say anything, yet."

Verkan realized that Lindar Marth was right. In fact, none of the natives had uttered a single syllable aside from that grunt. So far they'd only used sign language. *Could it be this bunch hasn't developed language, yet? No, cogent thought required workable symbolism. Intelligent beings thought in words and symbols, didn't they? Back in his university days there was an ongoing argument as to which came first; sapience or language. One side argued that language was necessary for sapient cogitation while the opposing case was that sapience was a prerequisite for developing language.*

Verkan suddenly remembered another theory he heard in university; the Inverse Intelligence Paradigm. The theory was that First Level was the most successful colony not only because they landed safely on Terra, but because they were up against the least intelligent competition. The idea was that the further downwhen one went, the more intelligent the indigent population was, which might explain why colonization from Mars failed in Fifth Level. By Fourth Level the Neanderthals lacked the brain power to compete with the colonists and either died out or were wiped out by the Martian colonists, mistakenly identified as Cro-Magnon Man. Unfortunately, no funds were ever allocated to do empirical research on the theory.

If the theory held true, these would be the smartest ape-men of the lot. He wasn't comforted by the possibility. But if that were the case, why weren't they talking?

IV

Verkan took this opportunity to study the locals. They were clean enough, suggesting they bathed, at least occasionally. Hard to sneak up on prey that can smell you coming, he guessed. The waist coverings were tanned animal hides held in place with leather straps, like knotted belts. They clearly hadn't developed weaving for clothes, yet. They also didn't show any sign of bow and arrow technology; but given the accuracy they demonstrated with the spears, and the power they threw them with, they may not have needed anything more sophisticated.

Necessity was the mother of invention, after all.

Verkan and his squad were led to a cave opening, when the Neanderthals in the lead stopped and gestured for them to wait. The two with the saber-toothed tiger and one other went into the cave while the one that had done all the gesturing remained with Jard and his crew. The Neanderthal made no threatening moves, and Jard ordered his men to show the same courtesy. There was no point in setting off useless and unnecessary hostilities.

After several nervous minutes of waiting, the three natives returned with three more. One in an elaborate headdress made of a saber-toothed tiger skull and decorated with shiny stones and feathers, and two that looked like an honor guard with spears and ornate bone necklaces.

Marth whispered to Verkan, "This has to be the chief. The decoration is different, but the basics are there; the skull of a dangerous animal adorned to look impressive and a guard with him in case of trouble. This is definitely the guy calling the shots."

The Chief said something and the natives spread out in front of the cave entrance. That proved they were capable of speech, at least. Jard watched and decided they weren't being hostile, just wary. He looked at Marth, who shook his head. He would need to hear a lot more of the language before he could start acting as translator.

The Chief stepped forward with his elbows at his sides and hands thrust forward, palms up. Marth took the initiative and duplicated the gesture, stepping forward to face the chief, but stopping two paces away. Verkan wanted to ask what he was doing, but suspected any talking could upset the chief and his people. Better to let Marth do his part and hope for the best. The chief said something and Marth replied. They went back and forth a few times, then Marth smiled and turned to Jard.

"We're in luck, Assistant Chief. There is about as much difference between the 'thal languages I learned and this one as there is between Fourth Level Europo-American Sector Hitler Victory Belt German and Dutch on the same subsector. I can make out most of what he is saying, and he seems able to follow me well enough to get along."

"Great. What have you two been talking about?"

"Oh, the usual. 'We come in peace', 'we are seeking a thing made of shiny rock'...they don't have a word for metal, you know. Chief Mighty Cat, I think that's the name, says they have some of this shiny rock, but don't want to part with it. I think it might be part of something sacred to these people."

Sacred? That's just great, Verkan thought. "Ask him if we can see this shiny rock, but phrase it so they won't take offence. Tell them we are seekers of knowledge, or something. Just try not to provoke them. If they say 'no', just accept it and we'll think of something else."

Marth nodded and turned back to the chief and made his request. Jard couldn't tell what was being said, of course, but he could read the chief's reaction well enough. It was no surprise when Marth relayed that they would be allowed to see the shiny rock.

"The Chief recognizes that you are the leader, Special Chief's Assistant—"

"Just call me Verkan, Marth. It'll be less confusing."

"Right. Anyway, the chief knows you're the boss, so you and I will be allowed inside to look at this holy relic. You, because you're the boss, me because I speak the language. The rest will have to stay out here."

Verkan looked around at his men and the natives. He didn't like leaving them behind. Not one little bit.

"Do you think you can change his mind?" Ranthar Jard asked.

"Not a chance. He's bending the rules, so to speak, just for us," Marth replied. "Even a chief has to consider the will of the tribe, Verkan."

Verkan thought for a moment. If the shiny rock was a piece of the ten-thousand year-old conveyer, it had to be either confiscated or destroyed to reduce the contamination and keep the Paratime secret. Even if it meant wiping out the whole tribe.

"When do we see it?"

Marth turned back to the Chief. After a short dialogue, he replied, "Tomorrow morning. Something about the angle of the sun or something."

That made sense. The early morning sun would be positioned to shine directly into the cave, illuminating the interior better than a few torches. That also gave Verkan time to set a few things up.

"Thank the chief and see if we should bring any gifts or offerings," he said. "We can bag a deer or antelope or whatever is around these parts and leave it on the altar or just give it to the chief, here."

After another brief exchange, Verkan and his squad were escorted back to their camp. One of the natives stayed near the camp after the rest returned to the cave.

"What's with Ogg over there?" Ranthar Jard asked as he studied the Neanderthal escort.

"He'll escort us back in the morning," Marth explained. "I think the chief wants him to spy on us and report back anything suspicious."

"Ha!" Ranthar snorted. "What about us isn't suspicious—at least to them?"

Verkan thought about it and realized that he was right. The native acted like nothing was out of place, yet here was one great big shiny rock in the form of the conveyer, and then there was the collapsium-laminated 'igloo'. Ogg, as Ranthar had named him, was taking everything with remarkable stoicism. Had there been other, more recent Paratime travelers here? Or was he just keeping his poker face on?

"Ranthar, do we have anything that will accelerate corrosion on metal? Particularly polysteel?"

He thought for a moment. "There's some Branx solvent in the conveyer."

"Branx?!" Valton Rotar exclaimed. "That's a heavy duty metal cleaning agent. How would that corrode the metal?"

"It's designed to remove grease and rust and sticky residue from almost anything," Sundar Gand explained. "But it has to be thoroughly cleaned off after use or it will damage the metal."

"Hmm. And what would it do to a piece of ten-thousand-year-old polysteel if it wasn't cleaned off in a hurry?" he asked.

Ranthar smiled. "Eat through it in about a month, more or less. Depends on how clean it is when the solvent is applied, and what it was cleaned with. Humidity in the air is also a factor." Ranthar paused as he considered the local tech level. "Water and maybe animal fat would be my guess, here. Branx would rip through the fat in no time flat. Yeah, Branx would do the job, but how do you apply it without getting killed in the attempt?"

Everybody joined in trying to figure out how to apply the Branx covertly. Ideas were tossed in and thrown out. Finally, Zinn came up with an idea.

"We use the hypo-spray mist gun. It's small, hides under the sleeve, and activated with a palm button. Just get your arm within three feet of the relic and fire."

"Two problems," Melk noted. "One, hypo-spray is almost completely invisible and odorless; Branx smells up the joint and is faintly yellowish."

"I can dilute it enough to reduce the color and smell, and still be effective," Yandar Barv said. "I just hope these 'thals don't have noses any more sensitive than ours."

"Okay, but the whole point of using Branx is that it is a corrosive solvent, right?" Melk looked around at everybody. They were missing the point. "How long will the spray gun stay functional once you load that stuff into it?"

"Damn! He's right," Verkan said. "Hypo-sprayers aren't even made of polysteel."

Everybody was silent for a moment while they thought of other possibilities. It was Valton Rotar who broke the silence.

"Wait, all we need is a simple squirt gun that sprays a mist rather than a stream, right? Well, we can just take a plastic hose, rig it to a rubber bladder, and put a mist nozzle on the end."

"Where do we get the hose and bladder?" Melk asked.

"We can pull the hose from the atmosphere scrubber on the conveyer," Valton said. "The bladder will come off of the hypo-sprayer, since it isn't metal, and we can use the sprayer's mist nozzle. It only has to last long enough for one or two shots. It should certainly last that long."

"And if we have to bug out of here in a hurry, what about the atmosphere scrubber?" Melk asked.

Verkan thought Melk might soon get a reputation as a nay-sayer, but his point was valid.

"We can go about twenty minutes without the scrubbers. Plenty of time to stop in another time-line and replace the hose. We can rinse it out in transit so as not to get any solvent in the machinery."

Valton Rotar looked about for any other objections, then looked at Verkan. "What do you think, boss?"

Verkan smiled and said, "I think we don't have any better ideas, Valton. It's this or we start killing the locals. I'd rather not commit any atrocities during this mission. So let's get busy and make this work."

Ogg, as Gand had named him, watched the entire discussion with great interest, though his face had remained expressionless throughout.

V

Verkan and his team were up with the sun. Ogg had remained in his spot the entire night. There was no indication that he had slept, nor any indication that he suffered from the lack of sleep. *These guys are tough*, he thought.

Lindar Marth and Verkan Vall were to accompany Ogg, while a team of six would follow at a distance in case of trouble. Verkan would leave his radio on and transmitting, but muted so as not to disturb their hosts. During the previous evening, Klarj and Melk went out and bagged a cave bear. It was too heavy to carry back, so they had to use the anti-grav lifter that built the igloo. The mechanical arms, designed to lift and assemble the collapsium enclosure, easily managed the thousand-pound carcass and transported it to the campsite.

"Damn," Verkan said, as he looked at the cave bear draped over the lifter. "How do we take this to the chief without creating a panic?"

Marth pointed to Ogg. "He doesn't seem to be bothered in the least."

Verkan looked over at the Neanderthal and realized that Marth was right. He wasn't panicking, or even nervous. "Marth, have you noticed that Ogg is taking everything we do very calmly? On some Fourth Level time-lines a floating machine would cause a riot, maybe even get somebody burned at the stake. This guy acts like it's business as usual."

Marth nodded and walked over to Ogg, who squatted down as he approached. The two spoke briefly, then Marth returned. "I can't be sure, but I think he believes that we are gods or something."

"Gods?"

"Yeah," Lindar Marth nodded. "As such, miracles are to be expected."

"Gods," Verkan repeated. He remembered the time he had been stranded on a barely inhabited Second Level subsector that had never recovered from a world-wide nuclear war. After he had used his sigma-ray needler to kill a few that were aggressively coveting his possessions, the rest of the tribe had treated him as a god. It had been offsetting and uncomfortable, but had kept him from harm until a rescue team arrived.

"I can't say I'm thrilled about the idea, but we can use it to our advantage. We'll bring the bear on the lifter, drop it off wherever Chief Big Cat wants and then send the lifter back to camp. We might all wind up as deities in the local pantheon, but that sort of thing happens every so often and isn't considered a threat to the Paratime secret."

Marth glanced over at Ogg, then said, "Given how easily he accepts us as gods, do you think others from First Level have been here? More recently?"

"Like who? Your run of the mill thieves or slavers aren't going to search for victims this far downwhen." Verkan considered the question, but couldn't think of anything else that made sense. Of course there were always the misguided do-gooder types who wanted to enlighten the poor ignorant downwhen peoples. They were carefully monitored and arrested when they overstepped their bounds. "We'll keep our eyes open for other signs of contamination. Maybe these Neanderthals just aren't prone to amazement, or maybe they've had a lot of visitors."

Verkan made a mental note to report his suspicions when he returned to Home Time Line. Missionaries could be just as bad as criminals, if not worse since their misdeeds and false doctrines often lasted long their deaths.

Ogg tapped his spear on the ground three times to get Ranthar's attention, then gestured that it was time to go. Ogg, Verkan, Marth and the lifter holding the bear proceeded to the cave while a six-man team followed at a discrete distance. As planned, Verkan kept his radio on and muted. If he or Marth ran into trouble, help would be on its way in seconds.

At the cave opening, Chief Mighty Cat and his honor guard greeted them. They seemed suitably impressed with the offering of the bear, or maybe the way the bear was delivered. Relieved of its load, the lifter floated away back to the campsite while two natives collected the bear. This time the carcass was dragged instead of carried, which suggested the upper limit of their strength.

Marth spoke with the Chief and after a few pleasantries he and Verkan were escorted inside. The first thing that struck him was the walls of the cave. He had expected something like animal skins and cave drawings. Instead, the walls were festooned with what looked like uncut gemstones, catching the light of the morning sun and reflecting the rays in every direction.

"Marth, do you know what these are?"

"Some. The larger stones are quartz crystals. The smaller white and yellowish stones are uncut diamonds. The red ones are rubies and the green are emeralds. All cleaned and polished and embedded in the rock walls. See the yellow glassy substance holding them in place? That's amber; hardened tree sap. The veins of golden metal running through the cave wall aren't gold, I don't think. Pyrite would be my guess."

Verkan was impressed, and looked about. "Where do you think they found all these gems?"

"In caves, most likely. I would guess it took centuries to get this many without actual mining." Marth noticed that the concentration of gems thinned out as they proceeded deeper into the cave. "I would guess this cave has been home base for this tribe at least a thousand years. Look there." Marth pointed to a young Neanderthal dipping an uncut ruby into a bowl of something sticky, then planting it on the bare rock on the wall. Next he held a small torch near enough to speed the drying process of the sap.

"Junior there just made his contribution to the family fortune. Notice how he holds the torch close enough to dry the sap, but not so close as to cause it to crack from overheating. He's been well taught."

"Do you think this is the shiny rock they were talking about?" Verkan asked.

"I don't think so," Marth said, as he looked about. "The gems on the wall didn't even get pointed at as we passed through, and we're still going. Chief Mighty Cat is definitely taking us to see something else."

Jard nodded then started when he realized that the torch was the first example of fire he had seen among the natives. For that matter, where were their living places? How did the smoke vent from the cave? He watched the trail of smoke go up into a darkened crevice. That had to be path to the outside. A quick glance around the ceiling revealed several such fractures. The mountain had to be lousy with them.

VI

As the group went deeper into the cave it opened into a wide natural cavern. Verkan could hear the sound of water flowing in the distance. Torches were set all around to add to the ambient light reflected from the entrance. There was a large pool near the center of the cavern, and a few cook fires near the edge. The smoke all went up and escaped through a series of fissures.

Water, no doubt rainwater that filtered through the crevasses in the mountain, flowed into the pool where a couple small streams carried away the overflow. In one stream a hairy female Neanderthal was bathing herself and an infant. By the other stream a young male was urinating into the water. Nobody bathed in the main pool, let alone relieved themselves. It was the source of the drinking and cooking water and kept pristine. It appeared that only the overflow streams were used for sanitation purposes.

Verkan also noticed that the surrounding area was neat and tidy; no sign of squalor, anywhere. Refuse was most likely hauled out of the cavern and buried somewhere so as not to attract vermin or scavengers, or possibly used as bait to attract the next meal. Two big Neanderthals were already skinning and gutting the bear near the same stream the boy urinated in. The blood was directed into the water where it was carried away. *That will keep the ant population down*, Verkan decided.

There was a distinct animal smell to the cavern, almost musty. However, it wasn't too unpleasant. *Good air circulation.*

Across the pool Verkan could barely make out what had to be the altar. The light was too dim to see any real detail at that distance, but he thought he saw some shiny metal and some bones.

Human sacrifice? No, there were no humans on this level, he concluded. Did the natives kill their own in religious ceremonies?

The chief motioned for them to follow. As they approached, Verkan could see a lot more of the gemstones decorating the wall behind the altar. What he had thought was metal was actually the reflection from the gems. The actual metal was lying flat on a bench-like affair on top of a bearskin. The slightly curved metal was being used to capture water that dripped from the ceiling.

Damn, he thought. *The water will reduce the effectiveness of the Branx, not to mention poison anybody who drank from it. Now what am I going to do?*

"Verkan, you said the records showed a five-man team came here ten thousand years ago, right? All male?"

"Yes," Verkan said.

Marth nodded without taking his eyes off the metal relic. "The records were wrong."

Verkan pulled his eyes away from the metal and looked where Marth was pointing. The bones he had seen were neatly arranged skeletons preserved in clear amber: ten skeletons, five male and five female if the rib count and pelvis formations could be believed. He was too stunned to even swear.

Five breeding pairs!

Marth looked over the skeletons. The amber was clear enough to make out a lot of details. "Do you think the locals found them and decided, um, that they were crunchy and delicious like Ranthar said?"

Verkan examined the bones then shook his head. "No, these guys lived long enough to break bones and reset them. Look at that female's leg. That break wasn't healed on First Level or there wouldn't be any trace of the injury. And look how smooth the bones are, no signs of being gnawed on. No, my guess is that they died of old age or disease."

Marth looked relieved.

"Ask them about the skeletons?" Verkan ordered. "They must be pretty important to be kept on display like this, especially with the altar."

Marth nodded and turned to Chief Mighty Cat and asked the question. The Chief went into preacher mode, Verkan guessed, from the way he spoke and gestured. Marth interrupted occasionally, probably to ask for clarification on something since the language was still different from what he had learned on another time-line.

It took a while, but the story got told, and Marth summarized for Verkan. "I'll spare you the hokum and hex part and tear it down to what I understood were the basics. The story was passed down from father to son for ten millennia, so there is a lot of hocus pocus added to the story over time. A great shiny rock, that would be the conveyer, appeared from thin air long ago bringing two hands of gods in it."

Marth jerked a thumb towards the amber encased skeletons. "That would be these guys, of course. They came as teachers and showed the Neanderthals how to make fire safer to use, demonstrated how to use the tree sap as a glue, better ways to tan hides, sanitation, that sort of thing. The gods promised to show them even greater things, but then they became sick and died."

"All of them?" Verkan asked.

"All. There must be some kind of bug here that we didn't vaccinate for, back then. They got sick and keeled over in weeks, if I have the time frame understood right."

"Damn. We might be in danger, too. And that's not all." Verkan looked at the skeletons. "We have to either destroy these bones or take them with us. We can't leave them here."

"I was afraid you would say that. How do we convince the chief here to let us take them? Wars have been fought on numerous time-lines over less of a religious offence than destroyed venerated relics."

How indeed? Verkan thought it over, then hit on an idea. "We'll tell them that we are going to take them home and restore them to life."

"What?" Marth thought it over. "Well, maybe they'll buy that. We're supposed to be gods, right?"

Marth turned back to the Chief and started talking. Verkan still didn't understand a word they were saying, but he could tell that Marth was laying it on thick by the tone of his voice and the gestures he used. At one point he pulled his pistol and fired into the air. The sound was nearly deafening in the confines of the cavern, but had the desired effect. Everybody squatted down and placed their hands on their chests.

Verkan assumed it was the local equivalent to kneeling and bowing. That explained why Ogg did that so much back at the campsite.

Marth holstered the pistol and put a hand out to the Chief and helped him back up. That would be the whole "I am not a wrathful deity" ploy. The two spoke some more, then the Chief clapped his hands and yelled something. Another female, naked to the waist, approached from the front of the cave.

"What's going on?" Verkan asked.

"Good news, bad news, boss," replied Marth. "The Chief wants proof that we can restore the dead. I managed to convince him that we could only restore life to long-dead bones if they belong to the gods and we take them back to heaven first. He bought that quick enough. Unfortunately we have to restore something more recently dead to prove our power. So, he wants us to kill this female and restore her to life as proof of our claims. I managed to talk him out of restoring the bear since the bear would be too dangerous, not to mention too dead for us to fake it."

Verkan didn't like where this was going. "Do you think ultrasonic paralysis will fool them?"

Marth looked at the female. "No, I can't even be sure it will affect her. I've seen 'thals take a point blank hit from an ultrasonic gun and keep right on going. Something about the way their brains are arranged keeps them going when a more sensible creature would just lie down."

"Electroshock, then?"

"Hmm...that would stop her heart, probably," Marth nodded. "How are you going to restart it?"

"Cardio-pulmonary resuscitation. We'll pass it off as the laying on of the hands." Verkan inspected the female. She had the kind of musculature often attributed to male body builders on Fourth Level or palace guards on Third Level. He had no doubt she was strong enough to survive the procedure, but questioned if he or Marth were strong enough to kick start her heart with chest compressions. If that didn't work, he would have to hit her with another jolt of electricity, like a defibrillator.

"Tell the chief we want, oh, call it a talisman of power, or something." Verkan spoke as if to Marth, but directed his next request to the radio. "Ranthar, send a shocker and some adrenalin in a chest needle, just in case."

Verkan couldn't hear any reply, but was confident that Jard had received the message and was acting on it. Ten tense minutes later, Marth had to go to the cave mouth to receive the 'talismans of power.' The Chief still refused entrance to anybody else; being a god only carried so much weight.

"There's about a million safer ways we could have done this, had we packed the right equipment," Marth observed.

"This was a recon mission," Verkan said. "We'll just have to improvise. You ready?"

"Yeah, but I dislike adding murder to my resume." Marth put the shocker on his left hand and walked over to the female. He said something, she replied, then he placed his hand on her chest where her heart should be.

There was a sizzling sound, then the female seemed to jump back several feet and fall to the cave floor. The tribe muttered and several stepped back a few feet. They were impressed. The chief crouched down and placed his ear on the woman's chest, then bolted up with eyes wide.

"Nalk!"

Marth translated. Dead.

"Let's get busy," Verkan ordered, and the two men started CPR on the female. Verkan did chest compressions while Marth did the breathing. After about thirty seconds, he decided to risk the adrenalin. He plunged the needle into her chest where the chief's ear had been moments before. He wasn't taking a chance on anatomical differences between the species.

No reaction.

"We'll have to defibrillate," Verkan said. "Use the shocker when I say 'clear'."

Marth nodded and placed his palm above the female's chest. Before Jard could give the command, the female started breathing on her own. After a moment, she opened her eyes and said, "Nalk?"

Marth made a gesture and said, "Tal." Alive.

The tribe, at first silent, all roared something then squatted with their arms over their chests.

Marth looked over the tribe and sighed. "Looks like we're in the pantheon, boss. Wanna bet, I'm the Grim Reaper and you're the bringer of life."

Verkan looked about at the tribe then back to Marth. "When we get back to Olympus, or Asgard, or whatever, I'm putting in for a vacation."

VII

Things went smoothly after that. The amber-encased skeletons were lovingly taken to the conveyer by the tribe, and all the Paratime Policemen were invited to a great feast. The bear was roasted over a pit, fruits and tubers were served raw along with various nuts and even a bowl of worms. Paratime cops are trained to eat a lot of things that would make the average Home Time-liner sick.

After the feast, Marth made a big speech and gave the chief a bow and arrow he had constructed the day before with the help of the fabricator in the conveyer. Verkan had allowed it as it wasn't something that violated the Paratime Secret. The materials would rot away in time. The chief tried a shot and launched an arrow high into the air. Verkan suspected the bird population would soon be added to the local cuisine.

With the igloo dismantled, the boomerang balls recalled and the bones along with the metal relic (a plastic bowl that would slowly disintegrate after 100 years was traded for it) stowed in the storage lockers, Marth made the farewells and dogged the hatch behind him.

"They'll get a real kick out of what comes next," Zinn observed as he activated the conveyer controls. "I wish I could see their faces as we fade out."

"The chariot of the gods returning to heaven," Yandar Barv said. He was about to say something else when he put a hand over his mouth and ran to the sanitation closet.

Melk commented that Barv never could hold his cave bear, then he, too, became ill. One by one, the Paratime cops became sick.

"Marth, didn't the chief say that their 'gods' became ill and died?" Verkan asked.

Marth nodded, afraid to open his mouth lest more than words came out. "Zinn, turn on the emergency beacon and set the auto-control to stop at Fifth Level Police Terminal in case we can't do it ourselves. We must have picked up the same damned bug that killed the first team. They'll have to quarantine us as soon as we get back. Melk, break out the broad spectrum antibiotics and anti-virals."

Verkan sank back in his seat, then passed out.

Verkan awoke in the hospital. He could tell by the sounds and smells. A device above his bed beeped quietly. After a moment, a doctor walked in.

"Verkan Vall? I am Doctor Zardal. You had a rather nasty virus you picked up on your last mission, but we managed to get it all cleaned out. You'll need a few weeks of medical leave, though."

Verkan moved his mouth but had difficulty speaking. After a few tries he managed to ask about his men.

"Oh, they all came out of it in one piece. Those anti-virals all of you took before leaving helped. I spoke with Chief Tortha. He said we'll have to quarantine that time-line you were on."

"Why?" Verkan asked with a raspy voice.

"The pathogen that infected you is one nasty little germ," Dr. Zardal explained. "We don't have a vaccine for it and it was damned difficult to beat. If you go back you'll likely contract it again. Anybody staying there would eventually die from it. With endless numbers of safer time-lines to exploit that one is not worth the risk, nor the bother to create a vaccine."

"Where...did the virus...come from?"

"We think it is a hybrid of something those first travelers took with them to that subsector crossed with a local germ. After ten thousand years the locals must have developed immunity, but the rest of us aren't so lucky."

"Hmm."

"Oh, and I've got a visitor for you. She's been ringing my communicator for hours to get to see you."

Just before Verkan closed his eyes, he heard Dalla's voice in the background. Just before drifting back to sleep he couldn't help thinking it was a shame. The 'thals had seemed like a nice bunch of people.

VIII

The tribe watched as the conveyer faded away until nothing was left but thin air.

"Is it safe, yet?" the one they called Ogg asked.

The chief removed his headdress and extracted a small device from within. He read the display and nodded. "They're gone."

The tribe let out a cheer. Several removed their wigs while others took out the prosthetic overlays that made their teeth look crooked and damaged.

The chief slapped Ogg on the back. "Good job, 'Ogg'."

"Gah! What kind of name is that anyway, 'Chief Fearsome Feline'? Ogg. It sounds like something is stuck in your throat."

"Come on, Tarv," the Chief said. "First round's on me."

The 'tribe' all filed back into the cave. Tarv pressed an uncut ruby on the wall and a section of rock receded to form a passage. Inside, there was an elevator with glass walls. Tarv, the chief and his honor guard filed inside. Tarv pressed a button and the elevator started downward. Through the glass they looked out over the vast subterranean metropolis. The power, which had been shut down to avoid detection, was coming back up and the lights turned on. There were several anti-gravity craft moving about above the city.

Tarv looked out over his home. "We really pulled it off, didn't we, Karx?"

Karx nodded. "And I can put this damned headdress back in the props room. I wasn't sure the humans would buy the whole 'primitive apeman' line at all. Are our counterparts really that stupid in the other time-lines?"

Tarv shrugged. "They didn't have the advantage of the Teachers like we did. The Teachers warned us long ago that we might be visited by their people again, and that they might come back as conquerors or thieves.

Better to make them think that we are as helpless and ignorant as the other time-line primitives."

"And slip them the Garka virus." Karx didn't look happy about that. "Too bad the Teachers and their descendants died out."

"Oh, some of them may have mixed with our ancestors. They just didn't have a large enough genetic base to keep a pure line going."

The elevator stopped and the four men filed out. Tarv and Karx waved to the 'honor guard' as they separated.

The two walked down a passage passed a large display. It was the ancient conveyer the Teachers had come in, complete save for a small section of the hull that was missing. Tarv and Karx glanced at it and kept on walking. They had seen it many times before.

"The alarm worked perfectly. Main power dropped off almost immediately when the humans arrived. Now that they are gone do you think we can start building above ground?"

Tarv shrugged. "Maybe, but I doubt we will. Fear of the Other Timers is too deeply ingrained in us. We don't even build on the surface of Mars, because of it. Screw it, let's go get those drinks."

"Should we change before hitting the bar?" Karx asked. He looked down at his hairy chest and leather skins. Others passed by him, similarly bare-chested, but wearing a kilt-like wrap at the waist and manufactured boots on their feet.

"Nah. We might attract a few females and regale them with tales of our bravery," Tarv said. "We just sent those humans running with runny noses. We're heroes!"

"They'll beat the virus, you know," pointed out Karx.

"But they won't be able to vaccinate. If they return, they'll just get sick again. No, they're done with this time-line. Too dangerous for them."

Once in the bar they took seats at a table and ordered two alcoholic drinks that were nothing like anything consumed by humans. Their costumes drew a few glances, and one female winked at Tarv.

Tarv winked back.

"I feel a bit bad about the humans, though," Karx said. "That leader of theirs, Verkan, spoke pretty freely in front of me since he thought I didn't understand him. He was doing everything he could to avoid a fight. And I really hated putting Tinti in danger, like that."

"Hey, she volunteered and survived. If the humans hadn't restarted her heart, we would have gotten her out of there and to the med-center as soon as we could chase the outtimers out of the cave." Tarv took a drink then shrugged. "She'll likely get a promotion and medical leave after this. That kind of courage is rare."

"Still, after ten thousand years, do you really think these outtimers are as dangerous as the Teachers said in the histories?" Karx took a long drink, then added, "For that matter, the Teachers came from that same time-line, and they gave us the tools to push our civilization forward. These costumes wouldn't be just for show without their help and guidance."

Tarv looked squarely at Karx and pointed a massive finger at him. "These creatures from the fourth planet are parasites, and sooner or later either a parasite kills its host, or the host finds a way to kill the parasite. Either way, the parasite is bad for the host. The Teachers said that these people used up their home world, then used up this one in their time-line. Now they seek to do the same with all the other time-lines. We need to keep them out of this one until we either move out among the stars, or become too strong to mess with."

Tarv nodded and took another long drink. "Now, let's go thump our chests and find some women and celebrate."

TEMPLE TROUBLE

H. Beam Piper

I

1951 A.D.

Through a haze of incense and altar smoke, Yat-Zar looked down from his golden throne at the end of the dusky, many-pillared temple. Yat-Zar was an idol, of gigantic size and extraordinarily good workmanship; he had three eyes, made of turquoises as big as doorknobs, and six arms. In his three right hands, from top to bottom, he held a sword with a flame-shaped blade, a jeweled object of vaguely phallic appearance and, by the ears, a rabbit. In his left hands were a bronze torch with burnished copper flames, a big goblet and a pair of scales with an egg in one pan balanced against a skull in the other. He had a long bifurcate beard made of gold wire, feet like a bird's and other rather startling anatomical features.

His throne was set upon a stone plinth about twenty feet high, into the front of which a doorway opened; behind him was a wooden screen, elaborately gilded and painted.

Directly in front of the idol, Ghullam the high priest knelt on a big blue and gold cushion. He wore a gold-fringed robe of dark blue, and a tall conical gold miter and a bright blue false beard, forked like the idol's golden one; he was intoning a prayer, and holding up, in both hands, for divine inspection and approval, a long curved knife. Behind him, about thirty feel away, stood a square stone altar, around which four of the lesser priests, in light blue robes with less gold fringe and dark-blue false beards, were busy with the preliminaries to the sacrifice.

At considerable distance, about halfway down the length of the temple, some two hundred worshipers—a few substantial citizens in gold-fringed tunics, artisans in tunics without gold fringe, soldiers in mail hauberks and plain steel caps, one officer in ornately gilded armor, a number of peasants in nondescript smocks, and women of all classes—were beginning to prostrate themselves on the stone floor.

Ghullam rose to his feet, bowing deeply to Yat-Zar and holding the knife extended in front of him, and backed away toward the altar. As he did, one of the lesser priests reached into a fringed and embroidered sack and pulled out a live rabbit, a big one, obviously of domestic breed, holding it by the ears while one of his fellows took it by the hind legs. A third priest caught up a silver pitcher, while the fourth fanned the altar fire with a sheet-silver fan.

As they began chanting antiphonally, Ghullam turned and quickly whipped the edge of his knife across the rabbit's throat.

The priest with the pitcher stepped in to catch the blood, and when the rabbit was bled, it was laid on the fire.

Ghullam and his four assistants all shouted together, and the congregation shouted in response.

The high priest waited as long as was decently necessary and then, holding the knife in front of him, stepped around the prayer-cushion and went through the door under the idol into the Holy of Holies. A boy in novice's white robes met him and took the knife, carrying it reverently to a fountain for washing. Eight or ten underpriests, sitting at a long table, rose and bowed, then sat down again and resumed their eating and drinking. At another table, a half-dozen upperpriests nodded to him in casual greeting.

Crossing the room, Ghullam went to the Triple Veil in front of the House of Yat-Zar, where only the highest of the priesthood might go, and parted the curtains, passing through, until he came to the great gilded door. Here he fumbled under his robe and produced a small object like a mechanical pencil, inserting the pointed end in a tiny hole in the door and pressing on the other end. The door opened, then swung shut behind him, and as it locked itself, the lights came on within.

Ghullam removed his miter and his false beard, tossing them aside on a table, then undid his sash and peeled out of his robe. His regalia discarded, he stood for a moment in loose trousers and a soft white shirt, with a pistol-like weapon in a shoulder holster under his left arm—no longer Ghullam the high priest of Yat-Zar, but now Stranor Sleth, resident agent on this time-line of the Fourth Level Proto-Aryan Sector for the Transtemporal Mining Corporation.

Then he opened a door at the other side of the anteroom and went to the antigrav shaft, stepping over the edge and floating downward.

II

There were temples of Yat-Zar on every time-line of the Proto-Aryan Sector, for the worship of Yat-Zar was ancient among the Hulgun people of that area of Paratime, but there were only a few which had such installations as this, and all of them were owned and operated by Transtemporal Mining, which had the fissionable ores franchise for this sector.

During the ten elapsed centuries since Transtemporal had begun operations on this sector, the process had become standardized. A few First Level Paratimers would transpose to a selected time-line and abduct an upperpriest of Yat-Zar, preferably the high priest of the temple at Yoldav or Zurb. He would be drugged and transposed to the First Level, where he would receive hypnotic indoctrination and, while unconscious, have an operation performed on his ears which would enable him to hear sounds well above the normal audible range.

He would be able to hear the shrill sonar-cries of bats, for instance, and, more important, he would be able to hear voices when the speaker used a First Level audio-frequency step-up phone. He would also receive a memory-obliteration from the moment of his abduction, and a set of pseudo-memories of a visit to the Heaven of Yat-Zar, on the other side of the sky. Then he would be returned to his own time-line and left on a mountain top far from his temple, where an unknown peasant, leading a donkey, would always find him, return him to the temple and then vanish inexplicably.

Then the priest would begin hearing voices, usually while serving at the altar. They would warn of future events, which would always come to pass exactly as foretold. Or they might bring tidings of things happening at a distance, the news of which would not arrive by normal means for days or even weeks. Before long, the holy man who had been carried alive to the Heaven of Yat-Zar would acquire a most awesome reputation as a prophet, and would speedily rise to the very top of the priestly hierarchy.

Then he would receive two commandments from Yat-Zar. The first would ordain that all lower priests must travel about from temple to temple, never staying longer than a year at any one place. This would insure a steady influx of newcomers personally unknown to the local upper-priests, and many of them would be First Level Paratimers.

Then, there would be a second commandment: A house must be built for Yat-Zar, against the rear wall of each temple. Its dimensions were minutely stipulated; its walls were to be of stone, without windows, and there was to be a single door, opening into the Holy of Holies, and before the walls were finished, the door was to be barred from within. A triple veil of brocaded fabric was to be hung in front of this door.

Sometimes such innovations met with opposition from the more conservative members of the hierarchy: when they did, the principal objector would be seized with a sudden and violent illness; he would recover if and when he withdrew his objections. Very shortly after the House of Yat-Zar would be completed, strange noises would be heard from behind the thick walls.

Then, after a while, one of the younger priests would announce that he had been commanded in a vision to go behind the veil and knock upon the door. Going behind the curtains, he would use his door-activator to let himself in, and return by Paratime conveyer to the First Level to enjoy a well-earned vacation. When the high priest would follow him behind the veil, after a few hours, and find that he had vanished, it would be announced as a miracle.

A week later, an even greater miracle would be announced. The young priest would return from behind the Triple Veil, clad in such raiment as no man had ever seen, and bearing in his hands a strange box. He would announce that Yat-Zar had commanded him to build a new temple in the mountains, at a place to be made known by the voice of the god speaking out of the box. This time, there would be no doubts and no objections.

A procession would set out, headed by the new revelator bearing the box, and when the clicking voice of the god spoke rapidly out of it, the site would be marked and work would begin. No local labor would ever be employed on such temples; the masons and woodworkers would be strangers, come from afar and speaking a strange tongue, and when the temple was completed, they would never be seen to leave it.

Men would say that they had been put to death by the priest and buried under the altar to preserve the secrets of the god. And there would always be an idol to preserve the secrets of the god. And there would always be an idol of Yat-Zar, obviously of heavenly origin, since its workmanship was beyond the powers of any local craftsman. The priests of such a temple would be exempt, by divine decree, from the rule of yearly travel. Nobody, of course, would have the least idea that there was a uranium mine in operation under it, shipping ore to another time-line.

The Hulgun people knew nothing about uranium, and neither did they as much as dream that there were other time-lines. The secret of Paratime Transposition belonged exclusively to the First Level civilization which had discovered it, and it was a secret that was guarded well.

III

Stranor Sleth, dropping to the bottom of the antigrav shaft, cast a hasty and instinctive glance to the right, where the freight conveyers were. One was gone, taking its cargo over hundreds of thousands of parayears to the First Level. Another had just returned, empty, and a third was receiving its cargo from the robot mining machines far back under the mountain.

Two young men and a girl, in First Level costumes, sat at a bank of instruments and visor-screens, handling the whole operation, and six or seven armed guards, having inspected the newly-arrived conveyer and finding that it had picked up nothing inimical en route, were relaxing and lighting cigarettes. Three of them, Stranor Sleth noticed, wore the green uniforms of the Paratime Police.

"When did those fellows get in?" he asked the people at the control desk, nodding toward the green-clad newcomers.

"About ten minutes ago, on the passenger conveyer," the girl told him.

"The Big Boy's here. Brannad Klav. And a Paratime Police officer. They're in your office."

"Uh huh; I was expecting that," Stranor Sleth nodded. Then he turned down the corridor to the left. Two men were waiting for him, in his office. One was short and stocky, with an angry, impatient face—Brannad Klav, Transtemporal's vice president in charge of operations. The other was tall and slender with handsome and entirely expressionless features; he wore a Paratime Police officer's uniform, with the blue badge of hereditary nobility on his breast, and carried a sigma-ray needler in a belt holster.

"Were you waiting long, gentlemen?" Stranor Sleth asked. "I was holding Sunset Sacrifice up in the temple."

"No, we just got here," Brannad Klav said. "This is Verkan Vall, Mavrad of Nerros, Special Assistant to Chief Tortha of the Paratime Police, Stranor Sleth, our resident agent here."

Stranor Sleth touched hands with Verkan Vall. "I've heard a lot about you, sir," he said. "Everybody working in Paratime has, of course. I'm sorry we have a situation here that calls for your presence, but since we have, I'm glad you're here in person. You know what our trouble is, I suppose?"

"In a general way," Verkan Vall replied. "Chief Tortha, and Brannad Klav, have given me the main outline, but I'd like to have you fill in the details."

"Well, I told you everything," Brannad Klav interrupted impatiently. "It's just that Stranor's let this blasted local king, Kurchuk, get out of control. If I—" He stopped short, catching sight of the shoulder holster under Stranor Sleth's left arm. "Were you wearing that needler up in the temple?" he demanded.

"You're blasted right I was!" Stranor Sleth retorted. "And any time I can't arm myself for my own protection on this time-line, you can have my resignation. I'm not getting into the same jam as those people at Zurb."

"Well, never mind about that," Verkan Vall intervened. "Of course Stranor Sleth has a right to arm himself; I wouldn't think of being caught without a weapon on this time-line, myself. Now, Stranor, suppose you tell me what's been happening, here, from the beginning of this trouble."

"It started, really, about five years ago, when Kurchuk, the King of Zurb, married this Chuldun princess, Darith, from the country over beyond the Black Sea, and made her his queen, over the heads of about a dozen daughters of the local nobility, whom he'd married previously. Then he brought in this Chuldun scribe, Labdurg, and made him Overseer of the Kingdom—roughly, prime minister. There was a lot of dissatisfaction about that, and for a while it looked as though he was going to have a revolution on his hands, but he brought in about five thousand Chuldun mercenaries, all archers—these Hulguns can't shoot a bow worth beans—so the dissatisfaction died down, and so did most of the leaders of the disaffected group.

"The story I get is that this Labdurg arranged the marriage, in the first place. It looks to me as though the Chuldun emperor is intending to take over the Hulgun kingdoms, starting with Zurb.

"Well, these Chulduns all worship a god called Muz-Azin. Muz-Azin is a crocodile with wings like a bat and a lot of knife blades in his tail. He makes this Yat-Zar look downright beautiful. So do his habits. Muz-Azin fancies human sacrifices. The victims are strung up by the ankles on a triangular frame and lashed to death with iron-barbed whips. Nasty sort of a deity, but this is a nasty time-line. The people here get a big kick out of watching these sacrifices. Much better show than our bunny-killing. The victims are usually criminals, or overage or incorrigible slaves or prisoners of war.

"Of course, when the Chulduns began infiltrating the palace, they brought in their crocodile-god, too, and a flock of priests, and King Kurchuk let them set up a temple in the palace. Naturally, we preached against this heathen idolatry in our temples, but religious bigotry isn't one of the numerous imperfections of this sector. Everybody's deity is as good as anybody else's—indifferentism, I believe, is the theological term. Anyhow, on that basis things went along fairly well, till two years ago, when we had this run of bad luck."

"Bad luck!" Brannad Klav snorted. "That's the standing excuse of every incompetent!"

"Go on, Stranor; what sort of bad luck?" Verkan Vall asked.

"Well, first we had a drought, beginning in early summer, that burned up most of the grain crop. Then, when that broke, we got heavy rains and hailstorms and floods, and that destroyed what got through the dry spell. When they harvested what little was left, it was obvious there'd be a famine, so we brought in a lot of grain by conveyer and distributed it from the temples—miraculous gift of Yat-Zar, of course. Then the main office on First Level got scared about flooding this time-line with a lot of unaccountable grain and were afraid we'd make the people suspicious, and ordered it stopped.

"Then Kurchuk, and I might add that the kingdom of Zurb was the hardest hit by the famine, ordered his army mobilized and started an invasion of the Jumdun country, south of the Carpathians, to get grain. He got his army chopped up, and only about a quarter of them got back, with no grain. You ask me, I'd say that Labdurg framed it to happen that way. He advised Kurchuk to invade, in the first place, and I mentioned my suspicion that Chombrog, the Chuldun Emperor, is planning to move in on the Hulgun kingdoms. Well, what would be smarter than to get Kurchuk's army smashed in advance?"

"How did the defeat occur?" Verkan Vall asked. "Any suspicion of treachery?"

"Nothing you could put your finger on, except that the Jumduns seemed to have pretty good intelligence about Kurchuk's invasion route and battle plans. It could have been nothing worse than stupid tactics on Kurchuk's part. See, these Hulguns, and particularly the Zurb Hulguns, are spearmen. They fight in a fairly thin line, with heavy-armed infantry in front and light infantry with throwing-spears behind. The nobles fight in light chariots, usually at the center of the line, and that's where they were at this Battle of Jorm. Kurchuk himself was at the center, with his Chuldun archers massed around him.

"The Jumduns use a lot of cavalry, with long swords and lances, and a lot of big chariots with two javelin men and a driver. Well, instead of ramming into Kurchuk's center, where he had his archers, they hit the extreme left and folded it up, and then swung around behind and hit the right from the rear. All the Chuldun archers did was stand fast around the king and shoot anybody who came close to them: they were left pretty much alone. But the Hulgun spearmen were cut to pieces. The battle ended with Kurchuk and his nobles and his archers making a fighting retreat, while the Jumdun cavalry were chasing the spearmen every which way and cutting them down or lancing them as they ran.

"Well, whether it was Labdurg's treachery or Kurchuk's stupidity, in either case, it was natural for the archers to come off easiest and the Hulgun spearmen to pay the butcher's bill. But try and tell these knuckle-heads anything like that! Muz-Azin protected the Chulduns, and Yat-Zar let the Hulguns down, and that was all there was to it. The Zurb temple started losing worshipers, particularly the families of the men who didn't make it back from Jorm.

"If that had been all there'd been to it, though, it still wouldn't have hurt the mining operations, and we could have got by. But what really tore it was when the rabbits started to die. Stranor Sleth picked up a cigar from his desk and bit the end, spitting it out disgustedly. "Tularemia, of course," he said, touching his lighter to the tip. "When that hit, they started going over to Muz-Azin in droves, not only at Zurb but all over the Six Kingdoms.

"You ought to have seen the house we had for Sunset Sacrifice, this evening! About two hundred, and we used to get two thousand. It used to be all two men could do to lift the offering box at the door, afterward, and all the money we took in tonight I could put in one pocket!" The high priest used language that would have been considered unclerical even among the Hulguns.

Verkan Vall nodded. Even without the quickie hypno-mech he had taken for this sector, he knew that the rabbit was domesticated among the Proto-Aryan Hulguns and was their chief meat animal. Hulgun rabbits were even a minor import on the First Level, and could be had at all the better restaurants in cities like Dhergabar. He mentioned that.

"That's not the worst of it," Stranor Sleth told him. "See, the rabbit's sacred to Yat-Zar. Not taboo; just sacred. They have to use a specially consecrated knife to kill them—consecrating rabbit knives has always been an item of temple revenue—and they must say a special prayer before eating them. We could have got around the rest of it, even the Battle of Jorm—punishment by Yat-Zar for the sin of apostasy—but Yat-Zar just wouldn't make rabbits sick. Yat-Zar thinks too well of rabbits to do that, and it'd not been any use claiming he would. So there you are."

"Well, I take the attitude that this situation is the result of your incompetence," Brannad Klav began, in a bullyragging tone. "You're not only the high priest of this temple, you're the acknowledged head of the religion in all the Hulgun kingdoms. You should have had more hold on the people than to allow anything like this to happen."

"Hold on the people!" Stranor Sleth fairly howled, appealing to Verkan Vall. "What does he think a religion is, on this sector, anyhow? You think these savages dreamed up that six-armed monstrosity, up there, to express their yearning for higher things, or to symbolize their moral ethos, or as a philosophical escape-hatch from the dilemma of causation? They never even heard of such matters. On this sector, gods are strictly utilitarian. As long as they take care of their worshipers, they get their sacrifices: when they can't put out, they have to get out.

"How do you suppose these Chulduns, living in the Caucasus Mountains, got the idea of a god like a crocodile, anyhow? Why, they got it from Homran traders, people from down in the Nile Valley. They had a god, once, something basically like a billy goat, but he let them get licked in a couple of battles, so out he went. Why, all the deities on this sector have hyphenated names, because they're combinations of several deities, worshiped in one person. Do you know anything about the history of this sector?" he asked the Paratime Police officer.

"Well, it develops from an alternate probability of what we call the Nilo-Mesopotamian Basic sector-group," Verkan Vall said. "On most Nilo-Mesopotamian sectors, like the Macedonian Empire Sector, or the Alexandrian-Roman or Alexandrian-Punic or Indo-Turanian or Europo-American, there was an Aryan invasion of Eastern Europe and Asia Minor about four thousand elapsed years ago. On this sector, the ancestors of the Aryans came in about fifteen centuries earlier, as neolithic savages, about the time that the Sumerian and Egyptian civilizations were first developing, and overran all southeast Europe, Asia Minor and the Nile Valley.

"They developed to thc bronze-age culture of the civilizations they overthrew, and then, more slowly, to an iron-age culture. About two thousand years ago, they were using hardened steel and building large stone cities, just as they do now. At that time, they reached cultural stasis. But as for their religious beliefs, you've described them quite accurately. A god is only worshiped as long as the people think him powerful enough to aid and protect them; when they lose that confidence, he is discarded and the god of some neighboring people is adopted instead."

He turned to Brannad Klav. "Didn't Stranor report this situation to you when it first developed?" Verkan asked. "I know he did; he speaks of receiving shipments of grain by conveyer for temple distribution. Then why didn't you report it to Paratime Police? That's what we have a Paratime Police Force for."

"Well, yes, of course, but I had enough confidence in Stranor Sleth to think that he could handle the situation himself. I didn't know he'd gone slack—"

"Look, I can't make weather, even if my parishioners think I can," Stranor Sleth defended himself. "And I can't make a great military genius out of a blockhead like Kurchuk. And I can't immunize all the rabbits on this time-line against tularemia, even if I'd had any reason to expect a tularemia epidemic, which I hadn't because the disease is unknown on this sector;

this is the only outbreak of it anybody's ever heard of on any Proto-Aryan time-line."

"No, but I'll tell you what you could have done," Verkan Vall told him. "When this Kurchuk started to apostatize, you could have gone to him at the head of a procession of priests, all Paratimers and all armed with energy-weapons, and pointed out his spiritual duty to him, and if he gave you any back talk, you could have pulled out that needler and rayed him down and then cried, 'Behold the vengeance of Yat-Zar upon the wicked king!' I'll bet any sum at any odds that his successor would have thought twice about going over to Muz-Azin, and none of these other kings would have even thought once about it."

"Ha, that's what I wanted to do!" Stranor Sleth exclaimed. "And who stopped me? I'll give you just one guess."

"Well, it seems there was slackness here, but it wasn't Stranor Sleth who was slack," Verkan Vall commented.

"Well! I must say; I never thought I'd hear an officer of the Paratime Police criticizing me for trying to operate inside the Paratime Transposition Code!" Brannad Klav exclaimed.

Verkan Vall, sitting on the edge of Stranor Sleth's desk, aimed his cigarette at Brannad Klav like a blaster. "Now, look," he began. "There is one, and only one, inflexible law regarding outtime activities. The secret of Paratime Transposition must be kept inviolate, and any activity tending to endanger it is prohibited. That's why we don't allow the transposition of any object of extraterrestrial origin to any time-line on which space travel has not been developed. Such an object may be preserved, and then, after the local population begin exploring the planet from whence it came, there will be dangerous speculations and theories as to how it arrived on Terra at such an early date.

"I came within inches, literally, of getting myself killed, not long ago, cleaning up the result of a violation of that regulation. For the same reason, we don't allow the export, to outtime natives, of manufactured goods too far in advance of their local culture. That's why, for instance, you people have to hand-finish all those big Yat-Zar idols, to remove traces of machine work. One of those things may be around, a few thousand years from now, when these people develop a mechanical civilization.

"But as far as raying down this Kurchuk is concerned, these Hulguns are completely nonscientific. They wouldn't have the least idea what happened. They'd believe that Yat-Zar struck him dead, as gods on this plane of culture are supposed to do, and if any of them noticed the needler at all, they'd think it was just a holy amulet of some kind."

"But the law is the law—" Brannad Klav began.

Verkan Vall shook his head. "Brannad, as I understand, you were promoted to your present position on the retirement of Salvan Marth, about ten years ago; up to that time, you were in your company's financial department. You were accustomed to working subject to the First Level Commercial Regulation Code. Now, any law binding upon our people at home, on the First Level, is inflexible. It has to be. We found out, over fifty centuries ago, that laws have to be rigid and without discretionary powers in administration in order that people may be able to predict their effect and plan their activities accordingly. Naturally, you became conditioned to operating in such a climate of legal inflexibility.

"But in Paratime, the situation is entirely different. There exist, within the range of the Ghaldron-Hesthor Paratemporal-field generator, a number of time-lines of the order of ten to the hundred-thousandth power. In effect, that many different worlds. In the past ten thousand years, we have visited only the tiniest fraction of these, but we have found everything from time-lines inhabited only by subhuman apemen to Second Level civilizations which are our own equal in every respect but knowledge of Paratemporal Transposition. We even know of one Second Level civilization which is approaching the discovery of an interstellar hyperspatial drive, something we've never even come close to. And in between are every degree of savagery, barbarism and civilization.

"Now, it's just not possible to frame any single code of laws applicable to conditions on all of these. The best we can do is prohibit certain flagrantly immoral types of activity, such as slave-trading, introduction of new types of narcotic drugs, or out-and-out piracy and brigandage. If you're in doubt as to the legality of anything you want to do outtime, go to the Judicial Section of the Paratime Commission and get an opinion on it. That's where you made your whole mistake. You didn't find out just how far it was allowable for you to go."

IV

He turned to Stranor Sleth again. "Well, that's the background, then. Now tell me about what happened yesterday at Zurb."

"Well, a week ago, Kurchuk came out with this decree closing our temple at Zurb and ordering his subjects to perform worship and make money offerings to Muz-Azin. The Zurb temple isn't a mask for a mine: Zurb's too far south for the uranium deposits. It's just a center for propaganda and that sort of thing. But they have a House of Yat-Zar, and a conveyer, and most of the upper-priests are Paratimers.

"Well, our man there, Tammand Drav, alias Khoram, defied the king's order, so Kurchuk sent a company of Chuldun archers to close the temple and arrest the priests. Tammand Drav got all his people who were in the temple at the time into the House of Yat-Zar and transposed them back to the First Level. He had orders"—Stranor Sleth looked meaningly at Brannad Klav—"not to resist with energy-weapons or even ultrasonic paralyzers. And while we're on the subject of letting the local yokels see too much, about fifteen of the under-priests he took to the First Level were Hulgun natives."

"Nothing wrong about that: they'll get memory-obliteration and pseudo-memory treatment," Verkan Vall said. "But he should have been allowed to needle about a dozen of those Chulduns. Teach the beggars to respect Yat-Zar in the future. Now, how about the six priests who were outside the temple at the time? All but one were Paratimers. We'll have to find out about them, and get them out of Zurb."

"That'll take some doing," Stranor Sleth said. "And it'll have to be done before sunset tomorrow. They are all in the dungeon of the palace citadel, and Kurchuk is going to give them to the priests of Muz-Azin to be sacrificed tomorrow evening."

"How'd you learn that?" Verkan Vall asked.

"Oh, we have a man in Zurb, not connected with the temple," Stranor Sleth said. "Name's Crannar Jurth; calls himself Kranjur, locally. He has a swordmaker's shop, employs about a dozen native journeymen and apprentices who hammer out the common blades he sells in the open market. Then, he imports a few high-class alloy-steel blades from the First Level, that'll cut through this local low-carbon armor like cheese. Fits them with locally-made hilts and sells them at unbelievable prices to the nobility.

"He's Swordsmith to the King; picks up all the inside palace dope. Of course, he was among the first to accept the New Gospel and go over to Muz-Azin. He has a secret room under his shop, with his conveyer and a radio.

"What happened was this: These six priests were at a consecration ceremony at a rabbit-ranch outside the city, and they didn't know about the raid on the temple. On their way back, they were surrounded by Chuldun archers and taken prisoner. They had no weapons but their sacrificial knives." He threw another dirty look at Brannad Klav. "So they're due to go up on the triangles at sunset tomorrow."

"We'll have to get them out before then," Verkan Vall stated. "They're our people, and we can't let them down; even the native is under our protection, whether he knows it or not. And in the second place, if those priests are sacrificed to Muz-Azin," he told Brannad Klav, "you can shut down everything on this time-line, pull out or disintegrate your installations, and fill in your mine-tunnels. Yat-Zar will be through on this time-line, and you'll be through along with him. And considering that your fissionables franchise for this sector comes up for renewal next year, your company will be through in this Paratime area."

"You believe that would happen?" Brannad Klav asked anxiously.

"I know it will, because I'll put through a recommendation to that effect, if those six men are tortured to death tomorrow," Verkan Vall replied. "And in the fifty years that I've been in the Police Department, I've only heard of five such recommendations being ignored by the commission. You know, Fourth Level Mineral Products Syndicate is after your franchise. Ordinarily, they wouldn't have a chance of getting it, but with this, maybe they will, even without my recommendation. This was all your fault, for ignoring Stranor Sleth's proposal and for denying those men the right to carry energy weapons."

"Well, we were only trying to stay inside the Paratime Code," Brannad Klav pleaded. "If it isn't too late, now, you can count on me for every co-operation." He fiddled with some papers on the desk. "What do you want me to do to help?"

"I'll tell you that in a minute." Verkan Vall walked to the wall and looked at the map, then returned to Stranor Sleth's desk. "How about these dungeons?" he asked. "How are they located, and how can we get in to them?"

"I'm afraid we can't," Stranor Sleth told him. "Not without fighting our way in. They're under the palace citadel, a hundred feet below ground. They're spatially co-existent with the heavy water barriers around one of our company's plutonium piles on the First Level, and below surface on any unoccupied time-line I know of, so we can't transpose in to them. This palace is really a walled city inside a city. Here, I'll show you."

Going around the desk, he sat down and, after looking in the index-screen, punched a combination on the keyboard. A picture appeared on the viewscreen. It was an air-view of the city of Zurb—taken, the high priest explained, by infrared light from an airboat over the city at night. It showed a city of an entirely pre-mechanical civilization, with narrow streets, lined on either side by low one- and two-story buildings. Although there would be considerable snow in winter, the roofs were usually flat, probably massive stone slabs supported by pillars within.

Even in the poorer sections, this was true except for the very meanest houses and out-buildings, which were thatched. Here and there, some huge pile of masonry would rear itself above its lower neighbors, and, where the streets were wider, occasional groups of large buildings would be surrounded by battlemented walls.

Stranor Sleth indicated one of the larger of these. "Here's the palace," he said. "And here's the temple of Yat-Zar, about half a mile away." He touched a large building, occupying an entire block; between it and the palace was a block-wide park, with lawns and trees on either side of a wide roadway connecting the two.

"Now, here's a detailed view of the palace." He punched another combination; the view of the City was replaced by one, taken from directly overhead, of the walled palace area.

"Here's the main gate, in front, at the end of the road from the temple," he pointed out. "Over here, on the left, are the slaves' quarters and the stables and workshops and store houses and so on. Over here, on the other side, are the nobles' quarters. And this"—he indicated a towering structure at the rear of the walled enclosure—"is the citadel and the royal dwelling. Audience hall on this side; harem over here on this side. A wide stone platform, about fifteen feet high, runs completely across the front of the citadel, from the audience hall to the harem. Since this picture was taken, the new temple of Muz-Azin was built right about here."

He indicated that it extended out from the audience hall into the central courtyard. "And out here on the platform, they've put up about a dozen of these triangles, about twelve feet high, on which the sacrificial victims are whipped to death."

"Yes. About the only way we could get down to the dungeons would be to make an airdrop onto the citadel roof and fight our way down with needlers and blasters, and I'm not willing to do that as long as there's any other way," Verkan Vall said. "We'd lose men, even with needlers against bows, and there's a chance that some of our equipment might be lost in the melee and fall into outtime hands. You say this sacrifice comes off tomorrow at sunset?"

"That would be about actual sunset plus or minus an hour; these people aren't astronomers, they don't even have good sundials, and it might be a cloudy day," Stranor Sleth said. "There will be a big idol of Muz-Azin on a cart, set about here." He pointed. "After the sacrifice, it is to be dragged down this road, outside, to the temple of Yat-Zar, and set up there. The temple is now occupied by about twenty Chuldun mercenaries and five or six priests of Muz-Azin. They haven't, of course, got into the House of Yat-Zar; the door is made of impervium steel, about six inches thick, with a plating of collapsed nickel under the gilding. It would take a couple of hours to cut through it with our best atomic torch; there isn't a tool on this time-line that could even scratch it. And the insides of the walls are lined with the same thing."

"Do you think our people have been tortured, yet?" Verkan Vall asked.

"No." Stranor Sleth was positive. "They'll be fairly well treated, until the sacrifice. The idea's to make them last as long as possible on the triangles; Muz-Azin likes to see a slow killing, and so does the mob of spectators."

"That's good. Now, here's my plan. We won't try to rescue them from the dungeons. Instead, we'll transpose back to the Zurb temple from the First Level, in considerable force—say a hundred or so men—and march on the palace, to force their release. You're in constant radio communication with all the other temples on this time-line, I suppose?"

"Yes, certainly."

"All right. Pass this out to everybody, authority Paratime Police, in my name, acting for Tortha Karf. I want all Paratimers who can possibly be spared to transpose to First Level immediately and rendezvous at the First Level terminal of the Zurb temple conveyer as soon as possible. Close down all mining operations, and turn over temple routine to the native under-priests. You can tell them that the upper-priests are retiring to their respective Houses of Yat-Zar to pray for the deliverance of the priests in the hands of King Kurchuk. And everybody is to bring back his priestly regalia to the First Level; that will be needed."

He turned to Brannad Klav. "I suppose you keep spare regalia in stock on the First Level?"

"Yes, of course; we keep plenty of everything in stock. Robes, miters, false beards of different shades, everything."

"And these big Yat-Zar idols: they're mass-produced on the First Level? You have one available now? Good. I'll want some alterations made on one. For one thing, I'll want it plated heavily, all over, with collapsed nickel. For another, I'll want it fitted with antigrav units and some sort of propulsion-units, and a loud-speaker and remote control.

"And, Stranor, you get in touch with this swordmaker, Crannar Jurth, and alert him to co-operate with us. Tell him to start calling Zurb temple on his radio about noon tomorrow, and keep it up till he gets an answer. Or, better, tell him to run his conveyer to his First Level terminal, and bring with him an extra suit of clothes appropriate to the role of journeyman-mechanic. I'll want to talk to him, and furnish him with special equipment. Got all that?

"Well, carry on with it, and bring your own Paratimers, priests and mining operators, back with you as soon as you've taken care of everything. Brannad, you come with me, now. We're returning to First Level immediately. We have a lot of work to do, so let's get started."

"Anything I can do to help, just call on me for it," Brannad Klav promised earnestly. "And, Stranor, I want to apologize. I'll admit, now, that I ought to have followed your recommendations, when this situation first developed."

V

By noon of the next day, Verkan Vall had at least a hundred men gathered in the big room at the First Level Fissionables refinery at Jarnabar, spatially co-existent with the Fourth Level temple of Yat-Zar at Zurb. He was having a little trouble distinguishing between them, for every man wore the fringed blue robe and golden miter of an upper-priest, and had his face masked behind a blue false beard.

It was, he admitted to himself, a most ludicrous-looking assemblage; one of the most ludicrous things about it was the fact that it would have inspired only pious awe in a Hulgun of the Fourth Level Proto-Aryan Sector. About half of them were priests from the Transtemporal Mining Corporation's temples; the other half were members of the Paratime Police.

All of them wore, in addition to their temple knives, holstered sigma-ray needlers. Most of them carried ultrasonic paralyzers, eighteen-inch batonlike things with bulbous ends. Most of the Paratime Police and a few of the priests also carried either heat-ray pistols or neutron-disruption blasters; Verkan Vall wore one of the latter in a left-hand belt holster. The Paratime Police were lined up separately for inspection, and Stranor Sleth, Tammand Drav of the Zurb temple, and several other high priests were checking the authenticity of their disguises.

A little apart from the others, a Paratime Policeman, in high priest's robes and beard, had a square box slung in front of him; he was fiddling with knobs and buttons on it, practicing. A big idol of Yat-Zar, on antigravity, was floating slowly about the room in obedience to its remote controls, rising and lowering, turning about and pirouetting gracefully.

"Hey, Vall!" he called to his superior. "How's this?" The idol rose about five feet, turned slowly in a half-circle, moved to the right a little, and then settled slowly toward the floor.

"Fine, fine, Horv," Verkan Vall told him, "but don't set it down on anything, or turn off the antigravity. There's enough collapsed nickel-plating on that thing to sink it a yard in soft ground."

"I don't know what the idea of that is," Brannad Klav, standing beside him, said. "Understand, I'm not criticizing. I haven't any right to, under the circumstances. But it seems to me that armoring that thing in collapsed nickel was an unnecessary precaution."

"Maybe it is," Verkan Vall agreed. "I sincerely hope so. But we can't take any chances. This operation has to be absolutely right. Ready, Tammand? All right; first detail into the conveyer."

He turned and strode toward a big dome of fine metallic mesh, thirty feet high and sixty in diameter, at the other end of the room. Tammand Drav, and his ten Paratimer priests, and Brannad Klav, and ten Paratime Police, followed him in. One of the latter slid shut the door and locked it; Verkan Vall went to the control desk, at the center of the dome, and picked up a two-foot globe of the same fine metallic mesh, opening it and making some adjustments inside, then attaching an electric cord and closing it. He laid the globe on the floor near the desk and picked up the hand battery at the other end of the attached cord.

"Not taking any chances at all, are you?" Brannad Klav asked, watching this operation with interest.

"I never do, unnecessarily. There are too many necessary chances that have to be taken, in this work." Verkan Vall pressed the button on the hand battery. The globe on the floor flashed and vanished.

"Yesterday, five paratimers were arrested. Any or all of them could have had door-activators with them. Stranor Sleth says they were not tortured, but that is a purely inferential statement. They may have been, and the use of the activator may have been extorted from one of them. So I want a look at the inside of that conveyer-chamber before we transpose into it."

He laid the hand battery, with the loose-dangling wire that had been left behind, on the desk, then lit a cigarette. The others gathered around, smoking and watching, careful to avoid the place from which the globe had vanished. Thirty minutes passed, and then, in a queer iridescence, the globe reappeared. Verkan Vall counted ten seconds and picked it up, taking it to the desk and opening it to remove a small square box. This he slid into a space under the desk and flipped a switch.

Instantly, a viewscreen lit up and a three-dimensional picture appeared—the interior of a big room a hundred feet square and some seventy in height. There was a big desk and a radio; tables, couches, chairs and an arms-rack full of weapons, and at one end, a remarkably clean sixty-foot circle on the concrete floor, outlined in faintly luminous red.

"How about it?" Verkan Vall asked Tammand Drav. "Anything wrong?"

The Zurb high priest shook his head. "Just as we left it," he said. "Nobody's been inside since we left."

VI

One of the policemen took Verkan Vall's place at the control desk and threw the master switch, after checking the instruments. Immediately, the Paratemporal-Transposition field went on with a humming sound that mounted to a high scream, then settled to a steady drone. The mesh dome flickered with a cold iridescence and vanished, and they were looking into the interior of a great fissionables refinery plant, operated by Paratimers on another First Level time-line. The structural details altered, from time-line to time-line, as they watched. Buildings appeared and vanished.

Once, for a few seconds, they were inside a cool, insulated bubble in the midst of molten lead. Tammand Drav jerked a thumb at it, before it vanished. "That always bothers me," he said. "Bad place for the field to go weak. I'm fussy as an old hen about inspection of the conveyer, on account of that."

"Don't blame you," Verkan Vall agreed. "Probably the cooling system of a breeder-pile."

They passed more swiftly, now, across the Second Level and the Third. Once they were in the midst of a huge land battle, with great tank-like vehicles spouting flame at one another. Another moment was spent in an air bombardment. On any time-line, this section of East Europe was a natural battleground. Once a great procession marched toward them, carrying red banners and huge pictures of a coarse-faced man with a black mustache—Verkan Vall recognized the environment as Fourth Level Europo-American Sector.

As the transposition-rate slowed, they saw a clutter of miserable thatched huts, in the rear of a granite wall of a Fourth Level Hulgun temple of Yat-Zar—a temple not yet infiltrated by Transtemporal Mining Corporation agents. Finally, they were at their destination. The dome around them became visible, and an overhead green light flashed slowly on and off. Verkan Vall opened the door and stepped outside, his needler drawn.

The House of Yat-Zar was just as he had seen it in the picture photographed by the automatic reconnaissance-conveyer. The others crowded outside after him. One of the regular priests pulled off his miter and beard and went to the radio, putting on a headset. Verkan Vall and Tammand Drav snapped on the visiscreen, getting a view of the Holy of Holies outside.

There were six men there, seated at the upper-priests' banquet table, drinking from golden goblets. Five of them wore the black robes with green facings which marked them as priests of Muz-Azin; the sixth was an officer of the Chuldun archers, in gilded mail and helmet.

"Why, those are the sacred vessels of the temple!" Tammand Drav cried, scandalized. Then he laughed in self-ridicule. "I'm beginning to take this stuff seriously, myself; time I put in for a long vacation. I was actually shocked at the sacrilege!"

"Well, let's overtake the infidels in their sins," Verkan Vall said. "Paralyzers will be good enough."

He picked up one of the bulb-headed weapons, and unlocked the door. Tammand Drav and another of the priests of the Zurb temple following and the others crowding behind, they passed out through the veils, and burst into the Holy of Holies. Verkan Vall pointed the bulb of his paralyzer at the six seated men and pressed the button; other paralyzers came into action, and the whole sextet were knocked senseless.

The officer rolled from his chair and fell to the floor in a clatter of armor. Two of the priests slumped forward on the table. The others merely sank back in their chairs, dropping their goblets.

"Give each one of them another dose, to make sure," Verkan Vall directed a couple of his own men. "Now, Tammand; any other way into the main temple beside that door?"

"Up those steps," Tammand Drav pointed. "There's a gallery along the side; we can cover the whole room from there."

"Take your men and go up there. I'll take a few through the door. There'll be about twenty archers out there, and we don't want any of them loosing any arrows before we can knock them out. Three minutes be time enough?"

"Easily. Make it two," Tammand Drav said.

He took his priests up the stairway and vanished into the gallery of the temple. Verkan Vall waited until one minute had passed and then, followed by Brannad Klav and a couple of Paratime Policemen, he went under the plinth and peered out into the temple. Five or six archers, in steel caps and sleeveless leather jackets sewn with steel rings, were gathered around the altar, cooking something in a pot on the fire.

Most of the others, like veteran soldiers, were sprawled on the floor, trying to catch a short nap, except half a dozen, who crouched in a circle, playing some game with dice—another almost universal military practice. The two minutes were up. He aimed his paralyzer at the men around the altar and squeezed the button, swinging it from one to another and knocking them down with a bludgeon of inaudible sound.

At the same time, Tammand Drav and his detail were stunning the gamblers. Stepping forward and to one side, Verkan Vall, Brannad Klav and the others took care of the sleepers on the floor. In less than thirty seconds, every Chuldun in the temple was incapacitated.

"All right, make sure none of them come out of it prematurely," Verkan Vall directed. "Get their weapons, and be sure nobody has a knife or anything hidden on him. Who has the syringe and the sleep-drug ampoules?"

Somebody had them, it developed, who was still on the First Level, to come up with the second conveyer load. Verkan Vall swore. Something like this always happened, on any operation involving more than half a dozen men. "Well, some of you stay here: patrol around, and use your paralyzers on anybody who even twitches a muscle."

Ultrasonics were nice, effective, humane police weapons, but they were unreliable. The same dose that would keep one man out for an hour would paralyze another for no more than ten or fifteen minutes. "And be sure none of them are playing 'possum."

He went back through the door under the plinth, glancing up at the decorated wooden screen and wondering how much work it would take to move the new Yat-Zar in from the conveyers. The five priests and the archer-captain were still unconscious; one of the policemen was searching them.

"Here's the sort of weapons these priests carry," one policeman said, holding up a short iron mace with a spiked head. "Carry them on their belts." He tossed it on the table, and began searching another knocked-out hierophant.

"Like this—*Hey!* Look at this, will you!" He drew his hand from under the left side of the senseless man's robe and held up a sigma-ray needler.

Verkan Vall looked at it and nodded grimly.

"Had it in a regular shoulder holster," the policeman said, handing the weapon across the table. "What do you think?"

"Find anything else funny on him?"

"Wait a minute." The policeman pulled open the robe and began stripping the priest of Muz-Azin; Verkan Vall came around the table to help. There was nothing else of a suspicious nature.

"Could have got it from one of the prisoners, but I don't like the familiar way he's wearing that holster," Verkan Vall said. "Has the conveyer gone back, yet?"

When the policeman nodded, he continued: "When it returns, take him to the First Level. I hope they bring up the sleep-drug with the next load. When you get him back, take him to Dhergabar by strato-rocket immediately, and make sure he gets back alive. I want him questioned under narco-hypnosis by a regular Paratime Commission psycho-technician, in the presence of Chief Tortha Karf and some responsible Commission official. This is going to be hot stuff."

Within an hour, the whole force was assembled in the temple. The wooden screen had presented no problem—it slid easily to one side—and the big idol floated on antigravity in the middle of the temple.

Verkan Vall was looking anxiously at his watch. "It's about two hours to sunset," he said, to Stranor Sleth. "But as you pointed out, these Hulguns aren't astronomers, and it's a bit cloudy. I wish Crannar Jurth would call in with something definite."

Another twenty minutes passed. Then the man at the radio came out into the temple. "O. K.!" he called. "The man at Crannar Jurth's called in. Crannar Jurth contacted him with a midget radio he has up his sleeve; he's in the palace courtyard now. They haven't brought out the victims, yet, but Kurchuk has just been carried out on his throne to that platform in front of the citadel. Big crowd gathering in the inner courtyard; more in the streets outside. Palace gates are wide open."

"This is it!" Verkan Vall cried. "Form up; the parade's starting. Brannad, you and Tammand and Stranor and I in front; about ten men with paralyzers a little behind us. Then Yat-Zar, about ten feet off the ground, and then the others. Forward—*ho-o!*"

VII

They emerged from the temple and started down the broad roadway toward the palace. There was not much of a crowd, at first. Most of Zurb had flocked to the palace earlier; the lucky ones in the courtyard and the late comers outside. Those whom they did meet stared at them in open-mouthed amazement, and then some, remembering their doubts and blasphemies, began howling for forgiveness.

Others—a substantial majority—realizing that it would be upon King Kurchuk that the real weight of Yat-Zar's six hands would fall, took to their heels, trying to put as much distance as possible between them and the palace before the blow fell. As the procession approached the palace gates, the crowds were thicker, made up of those who had been unable to squeeze themselves inside. The panic was worse, here, too. A good many were trampled and hurt in the rush to escape, and it became necessary to use paralyzers to clear a way.

That made it worse: everybody was sure that Yat-Zar was striking sinners dead left and right. Fortunately, the gates were high enough to let the god through without losing altitude appreciably. Inside, the mob surged back, clearing a way across the courtyard. It was only necessary to paralyze a few here and the levitated idol and its priestly attendants advanced toward the stone platform, where the king sat on his throne, flanked by court functionaries and black-robed priests of Muz-Azin. In front of this, a rank of Chuldun archers had been drawn up.

"Horv; move Yat-Zar forward about a hundred feet and up about fifty," Verkan Vall directed. "Quickly!"

As the six-armed anthropomorphic idol rose and moved closer toward its saurian rival, Verkan Vall drew his needler, scanning the assemblage around the throne anxiously.

"*Where is the wicked King?*" a voice thundered—the voice of Stranor Sleth, speaking into a midget radio tuned to the loud-speaker inside the idol. "*Where is the blasphemer and desecrator, Kurchuk?*"

"There's Labdurg, in the red tunic, beside the throne," Tammand Drav whispered. "And that's Ghromdur, the Muz-Azin high priest, beside him."

Verkan Vall nodded, keeping his eyes on the group on the platform. Ghromdur, the high priest of Muz-Azin, was edging backward and reaching under his robe. At the same time, an officer shouted an order, and the Chuldun archers drew arrows from their quivers and fitted them to their bowstrings. Immediately, the ultrasonic paralyzers of the advancing Paratimers went into action, and the mercenaries began dropping.

"*Lay down your weapons, fools!*" the amplified voice boomed at them. "*Lay down your weapons or you shall surely die! Who are you, miserable wretches, to draw bows against Me?*"

At first a few, then all of them, the Chulduns lowered or dropped their weapons and began edging away to the sides. At the center, in front of the throne, most of them had been knocked out. Verkan Vall was still watching the Muz-Azin high priest intently; as Ghromdur raised his arm, there was a flash and a puff of smoke from the front of Yat-Zar—the paint over the collapsed nickel was burned off, but otherwise the idol was undamaged.

Verkan Vall swung up his needler and rayed Ghromdur dead; as the man in the green-faced black robes fell, a blaster clattered on the stone platform.

"Is that your puny best, Muz-Azin?" the booming voice demanded. *"Where is your high priest now?"*

"Horv; face Yat-Zar toward Muz-Azin," Verkan Vall said over his shoulder, drawing his blaster with his left hand. Like all First Level people, he was ambidextrous, although, like all Paratimers, he habitually concealed the fact while outtime.

As the levitated idol swung slowly to look down upon its enemy on the built-up cart, Verkan Vall aimed the blaster and squeezed. In a spot less than a millimeter in diameter on the crocodile idol's side, a certain number of neutrons in the atomic structure of the stone from which it was carved brokc apart, becoming, in effect, atoms of hydrogen. With a flash and a bang, the idol burst and vanished.

Yat-Zar gave a dirty laugh and turned his back on the cart, which was now burning fiercely, facing King Kurchuk again.

"Get your hands up, all of you!" Verkan Vall shouted, in the First Level language, swinging the stubby muzzle of the blaster and the knob-tipped twin tubes of the needler to cover the group around the throne, "Come forward, before I start blasting!"

Labdurg raised his hands and stepped forward. So did two of the priests of Yat-Zar. They were quickly seized by Paratime Policemen who swarmed up onto the platform and disarmed them. All three were carrying sigma-ray needlers, and Labdurg had a blaster as well.

King Kurchuk was clinging to the arms of his throne, a badly frightened monarch trying desperately not to show it. He was a big man, heavy-shouldered, black-bearded; under ordinary circumstances he would probably have cut an imposing figure, in his gold-washed mail and his golden crown. Now his face was a dirty gray, and he was biting nervously at his lower lip.

The others on the platform were in even worse state. The Hulgun nobles were grouped together, trying to disassociate themselves from both the king and the priests of Muz-Azin. The latter were staring in a daze at the blazing cart from which their idol had just been blasted. And the dozen men who were to have done the actual work of the torture-sacrifice had all dropped their whips and were fairly gibbering in fear. Yat-Zar, manipulated by the robed Paratimer, had taken a position directly above the throne and was lowering slowly.

Kurchuk stared up at the massive idol descending toward him, his knuckles white as he clung to the arms of his throne. He managed to hold out until he could feel the weight of the idol pressing on his head. Then, with a scream, he hurled himself from the throne and rolled forward almost to the edge of the platform. Yat-Zar moved to one side, swung slightly and knocked the throne toppling, and then settled down on the platform. To Kurchuk, who was rising cautiously on his hands and knees, the big idol seemed to be looking at him in contempt.

"*Where are my holy priests, Kurchuk?*" Stranor Sleth demanded in to his sleeve-hidden radio. "*Let them be brought before me, alive and unharmed, or it shall be better for you had you never been born!*"

The six priests of Yat-Zar, it seemed, were already being brought onto the platform by one of Kurchuk's nobles. This noble, whose name was Yorzuk, knew a miracle when he saw one, and believed in being on the side of the god with the heaviest artillery. As soon as he had seen Yat-Zar coming through the gate without visible means of support, he had hastened to the dungeons with half a dozen of his personal retainers and ordered the release of the six captives.

He was now escorting them onto the platform, assuring them that he had always been a faithful servant of Yat-Zar and had been deeply grieved at his sovereign's apostasy.

"*Hear my word, Kurchuk,*" Stranor Sleth continued through the loudspeaker in the idol. "*You have sinned most vilely against me, and were I a cruel god, your fate would be such as no man has ever before suffered. But I am a merciful god; behold, you may gain forgiveness in my sight. For thirty days, you shall neither eat meat nor drink wine, nor shall you wear gold nor fine raiment, and each day shall you go to my temple and beseech me for my forgiveness. And on the thirty-first day, you shall set out, barefoot and clad in the garb of a slave, and journey to my temple that is in the mountains over above Yoldav, and there will I forgive you, after you have made sacrifice to me. I, Yat-Zar, have spoken!*"

The king started to rise, babbling thanks.

"*Rise not before me until I have forgiven you!*" Yat-Zar thundered. "*Creep out of my sight upon your belly, wretch!*"

VIII

The procession back to the temple was made quietly and sedately along an empty roadway. Yat-Zar seemed to be in a kindly humor; the people of Zurb had no intention of giving him any reason to change his mood. The priests of Muz-Azin and their torturers had been flung into the dungeon. Yorzuk, appointed regent for the duration of Kurchuk's penance, had taken control and was employing Hulgun spearmen and hastily-converted Chuldun archers to restore order and, incidentally, purge a few of his personal enemies and political rivals.

The priests, with the three prisoners who had been found carrying First Level weapons among them and Yat-Zar floating triumphantly in front, entered the temple. A few of the devout, who sought admission after them, were told that elaborate and secret rites were being held to cleanse the profaned altar, and sent away.

Verkan Vall and Brannad Klav and Stranor Sleth were in the conveyer chamber, with the Paratime Policemen and the extra priests; along with them were the three prisoners. Verkan Vall pulled off his false beard and turned to face these. He could see that they all recognized him.

"Now," he began, "you people are in a bad jam. You've violated the Paratime Transposition Code, the Commercial Regulation Code and the First Level Criminal Code, all together. If you know what's good for you, you'll start talking."

"I'm not saying anything till I have legal advice," the man who had been using the local alias of Labdurg replied. "And if you're through searching me, I'd like to have my cigarettes and lighter back."

"Smoke one of mine, for a change," Verkan Vall told him. "I don't know what's in yours beside tobacco."

He offered his case and held a light for the prisoner before lighting his own cigarette. "I'm going to be sure you get back to the First Level alive."

The former Overseer of the Kingdom of Zurb shrugged. "I'm still not talking," he said.

"Well, we can get it all out of you by narco-hypnosis, anyhow," Verkan Vall told him. "Besides, we got that man of yours who was here at the temple when we came in. He's being given a full treatment, as a presumed outtime native found in possession of First Level weapons. If you talk now it'll go easier with you."

The prisoner dropped the cigarette on the floor and tramped it out. "Anything you cops get out of me, you'll have to get the hard way," he said. "I have friends on the First Level who'll take care of me."

"I doubt that. They'll have their hands full taking care of themselves, after this gets out." Verkan Vall turned to the two in the black robes. "Either of you want to say anything?" When they shook their heads, he nodded to a group of his policemen; they were hustled into the conveyer.

"Take them to the First Level terminal and hold them till I come in. I'll be along with the next conveyer load."

The conveyer flashed and vanished. Brannad Klav stared for a moment at the circle of concrete floor from whence it had disappeared. Then he turned to Verkan Vall. "I still can't believe it," he said. "Why, those fellows were First Level Paratimers. So was that priest, Ghromdur: the one you rayed."

"Yes, of course. They worked for your rivals, the Fourth Level Mineral Products Syndicate; the outfit that was trying to get your Proto-Aryan Sector fissionables franchise away from you. They operate on this sector already; have the petroleum franchise for the Chuldun country, east of the Caspian Sea. They export to some of these internal-combustion-engine sectors, like Europo-American. You know, most of the wars they've been fighting, lately, on the Europo-American Sector have been, at least in part, motivated by rivalry for oil fields.

"But now that the Europo-Americans have begun to release nuclear energy, fissionables have become more important than oil. In less than a century, it's predicted that atomic energy will replace all other forms of power. Mineral Products Syndicate wanted to get a good source of supply for uranium, and your Proto-Aryan Sector franchise was worth grabbing.

"I had considered something like this as a possibility when Stranor, here, mentioned that tularemia was normally unknown in Eurasia on this sector. That epidemic must have been started by imported germs. And I knew that Mineral Products has agents at the court of the Chuldun emperor, Chombrog: they have to, to protect their oil wells on his eastern frontiers. I spent most of last night checking up on some stuff by video-transcription from the Paratime Commission's library at Dhergabar. I found out, for one thing, that while there is a King Kurchuk of Zurb on every time-line for a hundred parayears on either side of this one, this is the only time-line on which he married a Princess Darith of Chuldun, and it's the only time-line on which there is any trace of a Chuldun scribe named Labdurg.

"That's why I went to all the trouble of having that Yat-Zar plated with collapsed nickel. If there were disguised Paratimers among the Muz-Azin party at Kurchuk's court, I expected one of them to try to blast our idol when we brought it into the palace. I was watching Ghromdur and Labdurg in particular; as soon as Ghromdur used his blaster, I needled him. After that, it was easy."

"Was that why you insisted on sending that automatic viewer on ahead?"

"Yes. There was a chance that they might have planted a bomb in the House of Yat-Zar, here. I knew they'd either do that or let the place entirely alone. I suppose they were so confident of getting away with this that they didn't want to damage the conveyer or the conveyer chamber. They expected to use them, themselves, after they took over your company's franchise."

"Well, what's going to be done about it by the Commission?" Brannad Klav wanted to know.

"Plenty. The syndicate will probably lose their Paratime license; any of its officials who had guilty knowledge of this will be dealt with according to law. You know, this was a pretty nasty business."

"You're telling me!" Stranor Sleth exclaimed. "Did you get a look at those whips they were going to use on our people? Pointed iron barbs a quarter-inch long braided into them, all over the lash-ends!"

"Yes. Any punitive action you're thinking about taking on these priests of Muz-Azin—the natives, I mean—will be ignored on the First Level. And that reminds me: you'd better work out a line of policy, pretty soon."

"Well, as for the priests and the torturers, I think I'll tell Yorzuk to have them sold to the Bhunguns, to the east. They're always in the market for galley slaves," Stranor Sleth said.

He turned to Brannad Klav. "And I'll want six gold crowns made up, as soon as possible. Strictly Hulgun design, with Yat-Zar religious symbolism, very rich and ornate, all slightly different. When I give Kurchuk absolution, I'll crown him at the altar in the name of Yat-Zar. Then I'll invite in the other five Hulgun kings, lecture them on their religious duties, make them confess their secret doubts, forgive them, and crown them, too. From then on, they can all style themselves as ruling by the will of Yat-Zar."

"And from then on, you'll have all of them eating out of your hand," Verkan Vall concluded. "You know, this will probably go down in Hulgun history as the Reformation of Ghullam the Holy. I've always wondered whether the theory of the divine right of kings was invented by the kings, to establish their authority over the people, or by the priests, to establish *their* authority over the kings. It works about as well one way as the other."

"What I can't understand is this," Brannad Klav said. "It was entirely because of my respect for the Paratime Code that I kept Stranor Sleth from using Fourth Level weapons and other techniques to control these people with a show of apparent miraculous powers. But this Fourth Level Mineral Products Syndicate was operating in violation of the Paratime Code by invading our franchise area. Why didn't they fake up a supernatural reign of terror to intimidate these natives?"

"Ha, exactly because they *were* operating illegally," Verkan Vall replied. "Suppose they had started using needlers and blasters and antigravity and nuclear-energy around here. The natives would have thought it was the power of Muz-Azin, of course, but what would you have thought? You'd have known, as soon as they tried it, that First Level Paratimers were working against you, and you'd have laid the facts before the Commission, and this time-line would have been flooded with Paratime Police. They had to conceal their operations not only from the natives, as you do, but also from us. So they didn't dare make public use of First Level techniques.

"Of course, when we came marching into the palace with that idol on antigravity, they knew, at once, what was happening. I have an idea that they only tried to blast that idol to create a diversion which would permit them to escape—if they could have got out of the palace, they'd have made their way, in disguise, to the nearest Mineral Products Syndicate conveyer and transposed out of here. I realized that they could best delay us by blasting our idol, and that's why I had it plated with collapsed nickel.

"I think that where they made their mistake was in allowing Kurchuk to have those priests arrested, and insisting on sacrificing them to Muz-Azin. If it hadn't been for that, the Paratime Police wouldn't have been brought into this, at all.

"Well, Stranor, you'll want to get back to your temple, and Brannad and I want to get back to the First Level. I'm supposed to take my wife to a banquet in Dhergabar, tonight, and with the fastest strato-rocket, I'll just barely make it."

BACK FROM THE DEAD

John F. Carr

I

1955 A.D.

Ulvarn Rarth parked his aircar on the twelfth floor of the Old Town Dhergabar City Garage, where he walked to the corner antigrav shaft and dropped to the bottom level. From there, he stepped onto Main Street. Old Town was the only section of the city that had ground access; in fact, it resembled nothing so much as one of the Fourth Level cities housing millions, although its current population was somewhere around five hundred thousand—mostly Serv Sec Proles and petty criminals. It was the oldest section of the City dating back to the pre-Paratime Era.

He understood why Hadron Tharn liked to use it for private meetings. Here the doors opened without ident-keys or thumb-locks, providing the necessary anonymity the grounders required.

Ulvarn wore his loose-fitting tunic with a hood that covered most of his face. There were sky-eyes above to keep watch for the Metropolitan Police for any street-level criminal activity. Fortunately, despite all their efforts, Metro hadn't been able to get spy-eyes and ear-taps installed inside the clip joints, honkytonks, drug emporiums, cabarets, juke joints, flash-bars, taprooms, nightclubs, gambling dens and barrooms that proliferated throughout Old Town.

This decade Fourth Level Europo-American was all the rage and the streets were lined with dim streetlights and neon signs. It was time for the evening rain and the bright florescent lights appeared smeared and luminescent. The tallest buildings, mostly brownstones, were only twelve stories high and they looked squat and foreboding. When he was growing up, Second Level Vathroff Sector had been at the peak of its influence and as adolescents his gang had their faces morphed into animal shapes and had worn multi-colored tattoos all over their bodies. It had later cost him a small fortune to have his entire epidermis removed and re-grafted. He still kept his old lynx face mask and wore it to costume parties and pantomimes.

Ulvarn saw the garish blue and red neon sign flashing *Speakeasy* and knew he'd found Hadron Tharn's latest "hangout." He had to knock on the door and provide the code word "Bebop," which Hadron had left on his voice-drop, before entering. Inside the door he was frisked by two men wearing Fourth-Level wide-lapelled brown suits each carrying a Tommy gun. A neon-bubbling jukebox was playing a piano rag and several men in trench coats and fedoras were dancing the Lindy Hop with their molls.

In the rear corner, facing the door, Ulvarn saw Hadron Tharn hunched over a mug of beer with his favorite henchman, Warntha, at his side. Warntha—who never bothered with disguises—was rumored to be an ex-military Strike Team commander, who'd been cashiered after the last Prole Uprising for use of excessive force which, considering the usual Strike Team practices, probably meant outright murder and torture. He certainly wasn't a man any sane person would cross.

Today Hadron Tharn's face was covered by a skin-mask that hid his identity and was dressed in an all-black Fourth-Level style paramilitary uniform. He had tiny silver death-head's as collar tabs. "You're late, Ulvarn."

"I'm sorry, Leader. I thought someone might be following so I took an air-cab from the Paratime Building and made a couple of false stops and turns before stopping at my residence."

Hadron nodded. Warntha smiled and he shivered.

The tableau froze for a moment when a bartender, in a leather apron, came over to take their drink order. He ordered a beer, Old Milwaukee, same as Hadron's.

After the bartender left, he said, "I gave Hasthor your instructions."

"What did he have to say for himself?"

"He wasn't happy about them. I think he'll do what he's told—for now. Still, I think he's more afraid of Tortha Karf and the Paratime Police than he is of the Organization."

Warntha shook his head slowly.

"That's a mistake," Hadron Tharn said.

"Warntha, I want you to set up an action-team, just in case Hasthor gets cold feet somewhere along the line. These politicians are soft sisters, when the blood starts to flow."

Ulvarn found himself shivering. How did he get involved with this lunatic? It had happened five years ago after he'd been threatened with expulsion from the University for a practical joke. He'd gone to a politically connected friend of his father's, who'd recommended he visit Hadron Tharn. Tharn'd taken care of his problems in exchange for some errands. Later Hadron had put him on his payroll and helped him when he needed to pick up some easy Paratemporal Exchange Credits so that he could afford an outtime honeymoon. His life hadn't been his own since then....

"Rarth, stop your wool gathering. I want you to hang close. I might need you for another errand, soon."

II

Verkan Vall stood at the front of Tortha Karf's antebellum white mansion and thought—and not for the first time—at how much it resembled one of the Southern plantations he'd seen so often during his service as a drummer boy in Virginia during the Europo-American Civil War.

The war had been over on most Subsectors by the time he had reached recruitment age, but had still been raging on Europo-American, Confederate States Subsector, where the Confederacy had kept the war going for another six years, finally forcing the Union into a draw. With both sides bled white, the United States and Confederate States of America had both been thrown into an economic depression that neither country would recover from until after what most subsectors on Europo-America called the First World War.

Verkan Darl had believed that by exposing his son to war he would experience war's horror and senselessness. His father had been a lifelong pacifist and believed, as strongly as any Quaker, that early exposure to the ugliness of war would bring about a lifelong aversion. So, against the wishes of his mother, his father had dropped him off on a Confederate States timeline and had him mustered in as a drummer boy in Robert E. Lee's Army of Northern Virginia. There Vall had learned courage as well as a close-at-hand knowledge of fear and death, and admiration for his fellow comrades.

Obviously, his father's plan had backfired. After finishing his schooling, Verkan had joined the Army Strike Force at his majority, but had not reenlisted as his service had been during a very peaceful period; the prole problem was just beginning to rear its ugly head again. And he craved danger and action.

Verkan and his father hadn't exchanged a civil word, much less seen each other, since he had joined the Paracops over seventy-five years ago.

Having vacationed at Tortha Karf's Fifth Level Estate for almost a ten-day, Verkan was already bored to distraction. Dalla and Zinna were off at the beach, enjoying a warm summer's day sunbathing, while he and Kostran were supposedly relaxing. Kostran, who was still discovering the delights that were Zinganna, was having the time of his life; Verkan wished he could say the same thing. True, he was enjoying the time alone with Dalla, but he was unable to take his mind off recent events.

He was absolutely convinced that the Organization, while they might have temporarily stung by the Paratime Police, was a cancerous blight that threatened not only the Paratime Secret but the very fundament of Home Time Line itself.

Verkan was supposedly out here to plink at rabbits, which were savaging Tortha's truck gardens and newly planted lemon tree seedlings, with a .22 caliber rifle—more of a toy than a weapon, unless used up close. In reality, it was just an excuse for him to get away from Tortha's servants, who appeared offended if he did not visibly appear to be having a good time twenty-four hours a day.

The Altides were descended from a Madagascar tribe, from a time-line on the Afro-Sinic Sector, who were about to be taken as slaves by Chinese pirates when they were rescued by Tortha Karf's father. The Chief's father had been a shipping magnate, owner of Trans-Planetary Lines, and wealthy enough to own his own Fifth Level time-line. After he'd rescued them, he'd had the Altides sleep gassed and transposed to Fifth Level Sicily where they had resided ever since. They now numbered in the thousands, but only the most comely and industrious were 'invited' to work on the Tortha Plantation.

It wasn't surprising the Altides viewed their master as some sort of minor deity and showered his guests with the same largesse. Somehow all that attention and slavering got Verkan's goat; he supposed that some of his father's egalitarian teachings may have taken root after all.

As time-liners they lived a precarious existence, living off their hosts' bounty while at the same time keeping the Paratime Secret inviolate. It was stressful ploy, and he was beginning to believe—unnecessary. Now that Home Time Line had access to unlimited Fifth Level uninhabited time-lines, with far more resources than they could ever begin to depreciate, parasitism was no longer needed for mere survival. No, living off host time-lines had become a way of life. It was also, as the Wizard Trader case had demonstrated, outmoded.

This is what had brought him to calling an ad hoc meeting of all the high level Paracops that he trusted with his life. And, here and now was the time and place.

Verkan turned and walked back into the mansion. The inside was filled with Greek and Roman statuary and other antiquities, such as a Minoan wall frieze and a row of Roman death-masks that included originals of Caesar, Mark Anthony and Augustus. He paused to call out to Kostran

Garth, who was eating in the kitchen, which he determined by the fawning sounds coming from that direction of the mansion.

Kostran emerged from the hallway with a mug off steaming coffee. "I don't know where Tortha gets his beans, but I've got to find his supplier!"

"Jamaican Blue Beans, only the best for the Chief. Tortha says good coffee and blended Scotch are the only two liquids worth imbibing."

Kostran hoisted his mug. "I'll drink to that! I must say, I'm getting spoiled by the Chief's domestics; I only wish my robot servant was half as attentive."

Verkan turned away from the sweeping staircase that rose to the second story mezzanine to traverse the long corridor past the spacious kitchen, which lead to the basement entryway. The entrance was blocked by a collapsed-metal door, meant to keep out any curious servants or unexpected visitors.

Verkan pressed the thumb-lock and the door pneumatically opened; he was one of only three people who could open that door, the other two were Tortha himself and his wife Dalla. He walked downstairs to the small conveyer-head with a fifteen-foot mini-conveyer sitting on one of two permanent pads. The other pad was big enough for a sixty-foot conveyer, and was where his guests would be arriving shortly from First Level Police Terminal. Besides the landing pads, there were stands of weapons, both edged and gunpowder, a large food pantry and kitchen, multiple doors leading to storage rooms and a meeting alcove large enough for twenty chairs and a circular table.

The outline of a large conveyer dome suddenly appeared, coruscating and shimmering, as it materialized in the basement. Ranthar Jard, pipe in mouth, was the first one out of the conveyer; he was followed by Altarn Vor, whose jowls hung like a basset hound, Field Agent Dalon Sath, Vordran Larn, Kiro Soran, Maldar Dard, Skordran Kirv and finally, Dr. Nentrov Dard, the Paratime Police Psychist.

"What's going on, Verkan?" Ranthar asked.

"It looks like a Paratime Police coup!" Maldar Dard joked.

"Close," Verkan replied. He turned and activated the robot bartender with a push of his hand controller. The robot squawked and beeped; in response, a full-service bar folded out of one of the walls.

"Sing now or be sorry," Verkan cried. "Have a seat. This is the most secure room on the time-line."

Everyone called out a drink order, as they took a seat at the table. The headless robot squawked again, turned on its wheels and waited while the autobar filled the appropriate glasses with the requested colored fluids. Once the drinks were done and put on a tray, the robot bartender wheeled around and served each man with his glass using its spindly arms and graspers.

"Now, I know you're all wondering why I called you here together."

"You got it, Vall," Ranthar said, as he removed his pipe and began to tap it against the heel of his hand to remove the dottle.

"Why isn't the Chief here, Verkan?" Vlasthor asked.

"I wanted to get the ball rolling before I involve Chief Tortha. Also, because I think he's part of the problem."

There was a hushed silence.

"No, I don't mean he's lost his marbles, or has begun dribbling down his chin in public! I just think Tortha's taking the wrong approach to the Organization Affair by attempting to create a secondary Paratime Police Force."

"We've got to do something, Verkan," Kiro Soran said. He was a tall man, half a head taller than even Ranthar Jard, and wore a short goatee. "This Wizard Trader outfit's big enough to practically quarantine an entire sector by itself! What's wrong with doubling the Police Force; you all know we can use more field agents and detectives."

"I agree," Verkan said forestalling more questions. "However, where are we going to get them from? Recruitment for the Paratime Police has been down for the past three centuries; we're lucky to muster half a million agents. Half of these are deskbound. And, considering the number of sectors and time-lines we have to police, that's just a drop in the bucket."

Everyone nodded in agreement. The Paratime Police had been understaffed probably since the first decade after the discovery of the Ghaldron-Hesthor Paratemporal Transposition field.

"We'd probably accomplish more against the Organization by having all of our officers go under narco-hypnosis. Isn't that right, Dr. Nentrov."

The lantern-jawed Psychist nodded. "Yes, I already suggested that, but the Chief won't go for it. I told him, from the way the Organization was able to penetrate Police security and kill Salgarth Trod with fake officers, they've clearly infiltrated the Paratime Police. The Chief just blew his stack, when I brought up the possibility—"

"And, that gentlemen, is why we have to take matters into our own hands."

"And how are we going to do that, Vall?" Ranthar asked, pointing his pipe stem at Verkan like a pistol barrel.

"Since we can't trace our own moles, without alerting both the Chief and the Organization to our game plan, we're going to have to follow the trail—the money trail. Most of you weren't there, but I got a good gander at the Organization's setup on the Abzar Sector. They had enormous holding pens for the slaves, scores of transposition pads and conveyer landing stages. To say nothing of their storage facilities and warehouses. You should have seen the size of that armed air freighter that almost put paid to our whole operation! There are entire countries on Second Level that couldn't afford an operation that size."

Several of the Paracops nodded in agreement, while others looked skeptical.

"From what I saw on the visiscreen, they must have invested a billion and a half P.E.U. in that sector alone. What I want to know is: How are we supposed to track down the financiers, Special Chief's Assistant?" Altarn Vor asked, his tight lips pursed.

"Deputy Altarn, you've headed the Financial Fraud Division for decades," Verkan said. "I believe you are just the man to find out."

Altarn nodded. "It could be done, but it would take a lot of extra manpower and Exchange Credits."

"My plan is to take some of the funding that the Chief was able to squeeze out of the Executive Council, once they realized how heavily they'd been compromised by the Organization, and set up a Special First Level Fraud Investigation. I'd want you to head it, Altarn."

"Hmm. I have some finance boys I trust, but I'd need a lot more."

"I can use some of the discretionary funds the Chief gave me to create a double force to hire you some fast guns. We'll have Dr. Nentrov set up a special Psychist unit for Internal Affairs and have him narco-hypno test all the applicants."

"As fast as the Organization got information about the Salgarth Assassination," Nentrov Dard said, "I think all of us might want to do random testing and a department test of our agents every ten ten-days."

"Thank you, Doctor. Excellent point. In addition, I want every new recruit to the Special First Level Fraud Division to be tested by Nentrov's special Psychist unit. Nor would it be a bad idea if we ourselves were tested every ten ten-days, starting with myself."

There were nods of agreement from everyone at the table.

"Ranthar, I want you to oversee the interrogation of all the Organization prisoners. I know a lot of them are suffering from memory obliteration and hypnotic blocks, but get together with Dr. Nentrov and create a special force to root out all the information you can."

III

Hadron Tharn paced back and forth, like a caged dire wolf, in his penthouse apartment as he waited for his sister, Hadron Dalla's, call. He still couldn't believe the news she'd left on his answer device. A Hadron in the Paracops! His great-grandfather must be spinning like a top in his crypt in the family mausoleum. What was Dalla thinking, or better yet—was she thinking at all?

Tharn heard the phone clang, then the cheep, cheep of his robot servant as it picked up the phone and wheeled it over to where he was now standing—in front of the picture wall that showed most of the tall towers and spires of Dhergabar City. He saw Dalla's face in the telescreen, her dark hair was wet, with stringy strands of hair hanging in her face. Not a good look, even for her. She must have been swimming in the ocean.

He'd heard she was on vacation at Tortha Karf's family demesne and had wheedled the phone number out of a mutual acquaintance.

"Hi, little brother." Then she must have seen his frown: "What is it, Tharn?"

"Sis, why is it that I always have to hear the family news from some cock-sure newsie on the visiscreen?"

"Maybe, because you don't take my good news well—"

"Is that what you think?"

"Well, after the way you blew up when I announced that Verkan and I were getting back together—"

"That professional assassin you call a husband! You knew I never liked him—"

"Irrationally hated him, might be a better way to put it!"

"Now, sis, I didn't call to berate you about past errors; I'm more concerned with what you're doing joining the Paracops. Why did you do it—to hurt me, again?"

Dalla sighed, not even attempting to keep it off screen. *Maybe I've gone too far, this time. Still, if Dalla'd had the ten-day I've had, she might understand.*

"Look, I like the work, and it gives me more time with Vall. I know you don't understand; I don't even expect you to."

"How about time for me, sis?"

"Tharn, you're never home. I've tried a dozen times in the past six ten-days to call you; not once have you returned my calls—"

"I was outtime, Dal. I've had some business reverses. Somebody's got to tend the family fortune."

Dalla threw up her hands. "I know, but I don't care about the family investments. Vall makes more than enough credits to satisfy my wants. I want more time with my little brother."

"Not while you're married to *that* man!"

"Well, I'm not going to leave him again—count on it! I love him."

Tharn cringed, then saw Dalla wince in response. Now that he had her reacting emotionally, it was time to grill her. "What's going on with all this Wizard Trader stuff, anyway? It's all the newsies are talking about anymore."

"It's a big cross-time slavery ring—run by an outfit that calls itself the Organization. They've been selling slaves across different sectors. It's got both the Paratime Police and the Executive Council in an uproar."

"How did you get in the middle?" Tharn asked.

"I was helping Vall do some narco-hypnosis on some of the Organization prisoners. Most of them committed suicide before we could question them. You probably heard; they managed to assassinate the Opposition Party leader, Salgarth Trod, before we could get anything out of him."

"Too bad, big sis. How did you go from Psychist helper, to Paracop?"

"Chief Tortha liked the job I was doing with Zinganna, Salgarth's former mistress. We used her in a scam to set up the Organization and throw them off balance."

"Did it work?"

"Partially, however, they came at as from a different angle. The best news is that I made a new friend and sister."

"Sister! What are you talking about?"

"Well, Zinna and I got along so well, I decided to adopt her—"

"ADOPT HER—without talking to me! Isn't she a prole?"

Dalla visibly cringed. "I'm sorry..."

"Tell me you haven't actually, done the ceremony yet? Have you? Without telling me—"

She made her sorry face; he wanted to smash it right through the visiscreen! "You did do it, didn't you?"

"Yes, I'm sorry—"

"You should be, all my life you've been telling me how sorry you are... you're not the only one who carries the family name, Hadron. A prole—I won't be able to go out in public anymore! Our family can trace its lineage back five thousand years; there's never been a prole in our genealogy—"

"I said, I'm sorry, Tharn—I don't know what else to do."

"Sometimes I have a hard time believing *we're* even related, sis. Do you ever use that head of yours for anything more than a hatrack for one of your pretty hats? Think—think about what our parents would say about this if they were still alive... Think about what it does to our social standing! Think about how it makes me look!"

Dalla was now in tears, which made him feel a little better.

"I'm sorry, Tharn, but I have to break-off. I just can't talk to you when you're like this—"

"You mean, when I'm crazy mad, or when you don't have a good answer for another of your dumb stunts—"

This time Dalla hung up on him; well, she'd pay for that. Her Paracop husband, too. One of these days, *they'd* all pay!

IV

Danar Sirna knocked on her husband's door; she knew better than to push the pneumatic release—he'd already bitten her head off twice today! She suspected something had gone wrong at work. Ulvarn Rarth had already held three positions since leaving the University of Dhergabar, but something always went awry: his boss was too unrealistic, nepotism was rampant or the work too trivial. She knew deep down he wanted to be in politics, that's why his new position with Hadron Tharn, as his personal lobbyist and assistant, had seemed too good to be true... *Has he already been fired?*

"Rarth, you need to eat something. Something to keep up your strength."

Again, he didn't answer. She knocked some more: sometimes he acted like such a child. Maybe that's why she was considering dissolving their marriage. That and his inability to hold a job, his moodiness and habit of blaming others for his faults. Still, Zarn was the most handsome man she'd ever met, although his petulance had begun to spoil his looks. Maybe she was finally beginning to see beyond the surface façade.

Suddenly the door whooshed open, knocking her off balance. She teetered for a moment, then regained her footing.

Rarth stood before her, his tunic disheveled, face pale and anemic. "Leave me alone: How many times do I have to tell you?"

"What's going on? I'm your wife; I have a right to know."

The robot servant came down the hall, beeping twice. "Dinner is ready, Mister and Madam."

When it came into range, Rarth shoved it hard; it smashed into the wall—the robot squawked, then tottered to the floor. It hit the marble tiles with a sound like that of breaking dishes, beeped again, sputtered—then died, sending out a dark cloud of astringent smoke.

"Now you've done it. We just got that robot as a Year-End Day gift from my parents. What will they say?"

"Robots are passé," Rarth responded. "Just like your phony parents."

"They've always liked you."

He smirked. "The more fools, they. If they wanted to gift us a present, they should have given us a prole with a ten-year labor contract. None of my friends have robots anymore..."

"Your boss does."

"You had to mention *him.* I haven't seen him in three ten-days; no one else has either. He's been outtime on Fifth Level Industrial Sector. That's what you'll tell anybody who asks."

"That's not true! I saw you talking with him on the visiphone just a couple of days ago; I recognized his penthouse."

Rarth's face turned brick red. "You never saw anything! Remember that. Nothing. Hadron Tharn's been outtime; that's all you know. Understand?"

If looks could kill, I'd be a corpse, Sirna thought. For the first time in their marriage, she was deathly afraid of her husband.

V

Verkan Vall took aim at the target head-and-shoulders silhouette with his Europo-American Colt Python .357 Magnum with the eight-inch barrel, one of the finest revolvers ever produced on any time-line. When he retrieved his target, he saw a tight grouping at the head for the first five hits, with one miss. He was going to have to spend more time at the range, which was conveniently located in the basement of the Paratime Building. It was unusual for him to be off by even a single shot.

It was all the paperwork they had him doing, he thought. He was much more valuable in the field than sitting at his desk making charts of transtemporal interpenetration events and pickup graphs. At least his shooting skills hadn't completely atrophied. Most of his shots were grouped in the target's mid-facial area.

Verkan took a deep breath, enjoying the smell of cordite from the spent rounds. This was as close to the outside as he was going to get for a while.

"Vall, it's me." a familiar voice said from behind.

He took off his ear protectors, then turned around to discover Inspector Ranthar Jard. They touched hands in greeting. "What crisis has you chasing me down here at the range?"

Ranthar laughed, showing large well-formed white teeth underneath a trim mustache. "It's something to do with the Organization."

"Oh, yeah," Verkan said, all ears. "That's different."

"We've been hypno-meching the Wizard Trader suspects for the last two ten-days; most of them either know nothing or refer us to other individuals—most of whom we find discorporated or missing. We traced one, an employee of Outtime Exotic Beverages, who has mysteriously disappeared."

"That's a familiar refrain with this case."

Ranthar paused while another officer fired off about twenty rounds from an automatic. Once it was quieter, he continued, "Agreed. However, one of the techs, while going over his work computer discovered that one Citizen, a Valar Karnath, made an unscheduled transposition to a time-line on Fourth Level Europo-American, Hartley Belt."

"Hartley Belt? That's a new one on me." Which wasn't a surprise, as there were tens of thousands of small belts throughout Europo-American, less than a tenth of which the Paratime Police Survey Division had visited.

"Hey, Vall, we're not the Paratime exploration corps."

"No, but sometimes we have to act as if we are. Maybe that is what's needed to take some of the pressure of the Department."

"Right, I can just see Chief Tortha taking that proposal to the Executive Council. As soon as the Speaker reaches the budget expenditures, the Council will have the Chief up on charges of trying to loot the Treasury."

Verkan grinned wryly. The sad part was the Treasury Bureau was filled to overflowing with Home Time Line's Outtime Trade Tax and import revenues collected over thousands of years. The Council acted as if the credits were coming out of their own bank accounts instead of the State's.

"So what's the Survey Division have on this Hartley Belt?" he asked.

"First, it's a very recent Europo-America Belt, post the War against Hitler. It appears to be a divarication of the Islamic Caliphate Subsector, where there are three major power blocs, instead of two as on most of the Europo-American Subsector. They are the recently formed Islamic

Caliphate, the Soviet Union and the United States. The unusual aspect of this Hartley Belt is the appearance in the United States of an outfit that calls itself Associated Enterprises, a cartel that's one of the Hartley Belt's largest industrial conglomerates. From all Survey evidence of the para-area, it appears that the actual divarication took place less than a decade ago."

"I assume then," Verkan said, "that the Hartley family is the key. I've been all over Fourth Level Europo-American and I don't recall ever hearing mention of either Associated Enterprises or the Hartley family."

"Yes, it's one of those sudden success stories so popular in Europo-America cinema, and sometimes in real life. As far as our man could learn, the principal, Blake Hartley, was a nonentity—a small town lawyer in Williamsport, Pennsylvania. Suddenly, he came into money; Survey doesn't give any information on how he got it. He began buying ownership in small companies, then later larger ones. Since it wasn't flagged, Survey only did a very basic overview of the Belt."

"What caused the break-off?"

Ranthar shook his head. "Not enough information. Survey is too overtaxed to do more than a cursory appraisal of most new belts—especially on Fourth Level. We may never know the exact divarication trigger or date."

"Why would the Organization be interested in this particular Belt?" Verkan asked.

"Maybe, because no one else is. If you want to do something nefarious, do it in the middle of a big city in a deserted building."

"I believe you're on to something, Ranthar. Just how large is the Hartley Belt?"

"About three parayears."

"That's manageable," Verkan said. "We should be able to monitor all transposition conveyer activity there quite easily. I want you to stop what you're doing now and head up a Hartley Team on Pol-Term. First monitor the entire Belt for outtime conveyer traffic, in-bound and out-bound; those are the time-lines where we'll concentrate our energies. I want a dozen five-man field teams to start. Once we have a target, we can focus our energies on seeing just what the Organization is doing there. We'll start in Williamsport; learn everything we can about Blake Hartley, then go from there.

"Obviously, it's no two-bit slaving operation like on Third Level Esaron Sector. They're up to something *big* here; I can feel it."

Ranthar paused to take out his pipe and fill it with tobacco from his pouch. "Do you think the Organization's behind this new conglomerate, Associated Enterprises?"

"Could be; this Blake Hartley might be an outtimer working as a stalking horse, or maybe the Organization's attempting to create a pocket Belt where they can get themselves into all kinds of mischief and devilment—without anyone being the wiser. They know how overextended the Department is on Fourth Level. Or maybe this Hartley just wants to be deified. We've run into megalomaniacs before whose ambition is to be the Dictator of an entire time-line; well, maybe this one wants his own Belt. And, if he's this Hartley fellow; the Paratime Police Survey Division has just given him his heart's desire by naming the entire Belt after him!"

VI

Chief's Assistant Verkan Vall had barely sat down in his seat, after his time on the firing range, when his office visiphone chirped. He keyed it on and saw Kaldron Zarn, Deputy Chief of the Bureau of Outtime Fraud, whose blocky visage took up most of the screen.

"Hello, Chief's Assistant. Congratulations on your recent promotion."

"Thanks, Kaldron. What's up?"

"I got your interdepartmental memo on the Organization, asking for help identifying unusual trends or outtime activities."

Verkan nodded, thinking get to the point.

"The Department has been picking up a lot of information from our informants about famous artworks and masterpieces appearing on the black market. As you know, Chief's Assistant, there's been a flood of rare artworks on the market since the Fourth Level Europo-American war against Hitler began—the one the outtimers like to call World War II. The Nazis, under the Reichsleiter Rosenberg Institute for the Occupied Territories, looted many museums and private collections during the War. Both Outtime Art Works, Ltd. and Holnyt Art House extensively looted the Nazi crèches and storage depots, increasing the number of rare art treasures from Fourth Level by tenfold. Much of the loot came from the Neuschwanstein Castle, in Bavaria right after the war."

"I remember," Verkan said. "I also recall the public outcry by the Concerned Citizens Against Outtime Cultural Theft and the resultant newsie feeding frenzy."

Kaldron gave a pained look. "Yes, even our Bureau got a black eye from not doing more to stem the flow of these quasi-illegal thefts. I remember Chief Tortha's response, 'We're a damn good bunch of parasites and it's our job to take what our hosts can't keep. It's when we forget who we are, that we get in trouble.'"

Verkan nodded, trying to keep the smile off his face. That was a Karfism, if there ever was. It did stir up a bad publicity storm for a while, but no one could refute what the Chief said—that is, nobody who wasn't a complete hypocrite or total ass, which included most of the Opposition Party.

"What we've noticed is a sudden increase in the number of art treasures and masterpieces that have been popping up on the secondary markets, private exchanges and collectors auctions. For example, a Mona Lisa was recently auctioned off for less than ten thousand Paratime Exchange Credits!"

"What!" Verkan, thanks to his friend Thalvan Dras and his wife Dalla, had quite an education on outtime and First Level artworks. He'd even visited the Louvre on several occasions and was quite familiar with the Mona Lisa.

"Yes, from our initial survey over a thousand of them appear to be in private hands."

"A thousand originals! I thought there were only three; one in the Dhergabar Museum of Outtime Treasures, one in the Home Time Line Repository and one in the World Museum of Art in Vendaran."

"That's what I also believed, until recently. Those three copies were stolen from Vincenzo Peruggia, the Louvre employee who originally took the Mona Lisa from the museum by putting it under his coat. He held it for two years intending to return it to Italy, when he was caught attempting to sell it to the Uffizi Gallery in Florence. Of course, on three time-lines it was never recovered, but that theft was over forty years ago and the painting was recovered everywhere else—that we know of."

"I thought the Nazis had refrained from looting the Louvre and other major museums because of all the bad publicity."

"Yes, that was true throughout most of Europo-American; but not so true on those subsectors in the Hitler Victory Belt, where Nazi Germany won the war. The Mona Lisa originals have to be coming from that Belt, or we've got more problems than we know about."

Verkan nodded. "The Hitler Victory Belt time-lines are on the Proscribed List of time-lines by the Paratime Commission—especially for trading and retrieval operations."

"Yes, for all *legitimate* trading and retrieval firms and operations. However, I believe it's possible this may be another one of the Organization's operations."

"We've had problems on that Belt before. Thank you, Kaldron for bringing this to my attention."

"Should I put my operatives to work on the Hitler Belt?"

"Not for now. The last thing I want to do is tipoff the Organization that we're interested in that area. Until I inform you otherwise, keep your suspicions to yourself."

He keyed off the visiscreen, his thoughts in a jumble. He was certain there was at least one high-placed mole in the Department—if not more. But, until he could convince Chief Karf of that, he couldn't have everyone in the Department hypno-meched, which meant he had to keep things close to his vest. The problem with Tortha was that he viewed the request as a black mark against administration; in other words, he was too ego-involved. The old Chief was like one of the nomad chieftains of Central Asia on Indo-Turanian, in that he'd rather cut off his toes than admit one of his men was a thief.

Verkan needed to talk to someone who knew most of the major players in the art field. Of course, there was his old friend Thalvan Dras. It might be better, though, if Dalla questioned him.

He keyed in her code and a few moments later Dalla's face appeared in his visiscreen.

"Hi, Vall," Dalla said, looking pert in her new Police greens. "Or should

I call you, Special Chief's Assistant, here at work?" There was a twinkle in her eye.

Verkan smiled. "Call me Vall. If anybody complains, I'll transfer them to Second Level Second Level Khiftan. I've got a special assignment."

"Already. Oh goodie! What is it?"

He told her about Deputy Kaldron Zarn's call and what it implied. "What I want you to do is set up an interview with Thalvan Dras and see what he can tell you about the underground art market."

"Thalvan Dras is a good choice. He buys a lot of art and knows most of the Dhergabar artist community. But why don't you talk with him, since he's your childhood friend?"

"We both know that Dras skirts the letter of the law in a lot of his outtime operations and he always gets nervous, or clams up, when I question him about his outtime activities."

"You're right. A lot of your friends do that. Hmm. Does that mean, now that I'm your Assistant, I can expect that, too?"

"Probably, but word won't get out for a while. Besides, Dalla, you have the people knack; people you don't even know go out of their way to confide in you."

"Well, if you put it like that, how can I refuse? I'll give him a call now. Bye, Vall. Oh, what do you want to do about dinner?"

"How about meeting me at the Constellation House at 1900 hours?"

"Sounds good, but only if we hold off on the shop talk until after dinner."

"Agreed. We've got a deal."

VII

Barton Shar felt groggy as he surfaced out of a heavy sleep. The room was graveyard dark and the only thing he could hear was the thump-thump of his beating heart. His mind was whirling and he had a headache; too much drinking at the Speakeasy last night. He'd forgotten his alcodote tabs, as well. With Verkan Vall nosing around at work, he needed all the sleep he could get.

"Hello, Shar. Are you awake now?" asked a disembodied voice.

"What are you doing in here! Who are you?" Barton asked, bolting upright in his bed. His heart was beating so fast he was afraid it might leap right out of his chest.

"It's just me, Hadron Tharn. I thought it was time we talked again."

"What in Fasif's name are you doing here in my bedroom?" Barton shouted.

Tharn made an unpleasant laugh. "Barton, just where would you rather see me? In that Old Town dive you frequent, the Speakeasy, where there are more Metro agents than customers? At your office at Police Headquarters in the Paratime Building? Or maybe at the Constellation House for a few drinks?"

"Stop it, please! You're making my headache worse. We agreed not to meet again, since I was promoted to Deputy Bureau Chief."

"Congratulations on that. But something urgent has come up. Which reminds me, that promotion was over a decade ago...wasn't it? What happened to your ambition to be Special Chief's Assistant and Police Chief? We all know Old Tortha isn't going to be around for more than another decade."

"It's that damn brother-in-law of yours, Tharn—Verkan Vall."

Barton's neck was suddenly in the grip of iron hard fingers. He couldn't breathe and his heart started thumping wildly. Suddenly the pressure was released and he began gasping for air and choking.

"Don't ever call him that again, Shar!"

"Yes, yes...I'm sorry, Your Lordship," Barton sputtered.

"That's better. We're allies, you know. You want to be Paratime Chief and I want to own the Paracops!"

Tharn made a barking noise that reminded Barton of the hacking noise of a wild dog or wolf on the scent of prey. It sent shivers up and down his spinal cord. Why did he allow himself to get into the debt of this wild man? It was his damnable gambling losses that started it all—

"Enough reminiscing. I came here to obtain some information."

"But, I could get in real trouble—"

"You're already in trouble up to your eyebrows! You've been neglectful in keeping me posted on the Department's progress on the 'Wizard Traders'—isn't that your Department's fanciful name for the Organization?"

"Yes, but they've blocked access. Verkan, with the Chief's backing, has put together a special team to— Don't tell me, you have anything to do with that slave trading operation?"

"You don't need to know, Shar. You don't *want* to know. But, just to quiet your worries, some *friends* of mine have invested heavily in the Organization and they don't want to take any heavy losses because of the Paracops can't leave well enough alone. Understood?"

All Barton knew was that this was bad news and the less he knew, the better he'd sleep. "I'm glad you're not involved because the Chief's made busting this outfit his number one priority. He's even given Verkan orders to make a shadow department to follow up on it because there are so many leaks in the Department."

Hadron giggled. "He's only now figured that out. Well, we've got a big one right here!"

Barton felt Tharn's cupped fingers strike the spot right beneath where his breastbones met. His lungs emptied of air and his heart felt as if it had just entered free fall. The pain was almost unbearable— He began gasping, trying desperately to catch his breath.

Tharn waited patiently until he caught his breath. "That was just a reminder of whose side you're on. The worst punishment the Paracops will ever do to you is send you to Bureau of Psy-Hygiene for psycho-rehab; me, I'll just have your entrails ripped right out of your stomach and eaten by rats—while you watch!"

Barton felt as if he were going to pass out; his head was swimming and his thoughts were all awhirl.

He heard Tharn rustling around the room while he tried to catch his breath and keep his heart from leaping out of his chest. Tomorrow, he was going to see his medico and demand a heart transplant; this one had gone bad faster than the last two. *If I live that long?*

"Wh...What do you want me to do?"

"Answer a few questions."

"Anything, anything...if you'll only leave."

"Enough! Shar, you're so pathetic you're hardly any fun. If Old Tortha is so worried about leaks in the Department, why doesn't he have all the Paracops hypno-meched?"

Barton would have laughed, if his head hadn't been so airy. "Tortha and Naldor Larn despise each other. The last thing the Chief wants is to have Naldor and his psychists poking around in Police internal affairs. And, there aren't enough Department psychists in Internal Affairs to screen the ranks in anything less than twenty years—we're talking over half a million men here. No, that's one thing we don't have to worry over.

"Of course, we don't know what Karf's successor might do—"

"Don't worry about the next Chief; he'll be taken care of when the time comes. However, it would be most beneficial if you were to step into that vacancy."

"I don't know how. The way things stand with the Chief—what's that Europo-American expression—not until Hell freezes over."

"The one universal constant is: things change. My other question is, what's the latest news on the Organization probe?"

"Like I said, Your Lordship, I don't know very much about this operation. The only thing I've seen was a Chief's Memo making inquiries about some Europo-American belt, called the Hartley Belt—"

He felt Hadron grab him again, this time around the wrist. He knew that he'd unknowingly struck another nerve.

"Where did you see this Memo?"

"It was while I was meeting with Sandor Jiral, who's head of Conveyer Dispatch and Scheduling. He had a flimsy on his desk, when he turned to talk to one of his subordinates I read it. It was a Chief's Memo. He wanted Sandor to survey the Hartley Belt and keep an eye out for unscheduled transpositions."

"Very interesting. This has been a most enlightening visit. Shar, I want you to keep your ears open for any news about either the Wizard Traders or the Hartley Belt. You can pass it on to my associate, Ulvarn Rarth."

VIII

Thalvan Dras was seated in his favorite chair, which looked to Dalla like a throne; it was high-backed wooden chair with a panel carved from teak, displaying a royal couple and their retainers, and two large arm rests. Certainly, Thalvan sat himself down as if he were a Fourth Level Europo-American potentate from the last century might, or an actor playing one in a theatrical play. Nor did his clothes, a black suit with a cloth-of-gold sash and a long red velvet coat, discourage the comparison.

He rose majestically to greet her with a hug and quick kiss.

Dalla quickly turned her face to the side so the kiss hit her check instead of her lips.

"Hello, Dalla, my favorite lady. What brings you here by your lonesome to my demesne?"

Something about Thalvan's tone made the whole encounter seem smarmy and cheap. Vall always accused her of exaggerating when she told him that she thought Thalvan was interested in more than just her companionship. Well, she at least, knew better.

"I was thinking of buying a few special paintings, something to set off our new apartment. You did know that we're moving from the Turquoise Towers, didn't you?"

Thalvan look surprised. "No, I did not. That's one of the best addresses in Dhergabar: Why move now?"

"Well, now that Vall's been promoted and all, we decided we needed larger digs. So we're going to be moving to the new Space Spire."

"Ahh. That's very expensive, but quite nice. They have excellent security as well. If I didn't own this old tower outright, I might move there myself."

"Nothing like home ownership," Dalla said. *'Old tower,' my foot*, she thought. It was state of the art construction, rose up into the sky for a quarter mile, with luxury apartments and townhouses for over five thousand lessees.

"How many square feet?"

"Fifteen thousand."

"That's more than twice the space of your old apartment. Planning any additions?"

How Thalvan could ask that and leer at the same time was beyond Dalla's comprehension, but he managed. She needed to get the conversation back on track.

"I was thinking the parlor needed four or five select pieces of art. Maybe Post-Impressionist pieces from Europo-American."

"Not many of those on the open market these days, Dalla. You're about five decades too late. Why don't you have Vall 'find' one on one of his outtime excursions? I'm sure it wouldn't be too difficult for a man in his position."

Dalla shook her head. "You know Vall. As honest as they come. Was he always like that?"

Thalvan withdrew into himself for a moment. "I believe so. We were at the same First School together. In those days, the fad was live births for women of *our* class. Of course, it caused a lot of needless suffering, I dare say. Vall's mother, for one, I understand she was never the same afterwards."

"I never met her; she died in a rocket crash some years before I met Vall."

"I remember that, a really nasty crash. Some fool forgot to take the antigrav lifter off his industrial conveyer and when it arrived at the conveyer head, it went straight up! A tragedy for everyone involved. But, Vall's mother, was strange long before then. As I said, she never got over Vall's childbirth; the few times I saw her she was like a pale ghost—one of the most ineffective human beings I've ever witnessed."

"And you know Vall's father, Verkan Darl?"

"Yes," Thalvan said. "Vall's father was not someone who thought much of children; he treated Vall like a strike-team recruit. When Darl got the idea that his son should join the drum and bugle corps, his mother didn't even try to talk him out of it. Poor Vall; here he was just ten or eleven years old and shipped out to Confederate States Belt. He was a light-hearted and friendly little boy; the young man that came back from those wars was a completely different person. So sad, so serious, so earnest. The horrors he must have witnessed! It's no wonder he joined the Paratime Police. We were all sure that he'd join the Army Strike-Teams for good, but something changed his mind. Still, he must have missed the military, as the Paratime Police are a quasi-military force."

She nodded. The few times she talked to Verkan's father, in futile attempts at reconciliation between him and Vall, she'd found him to be the most stubborn human being—after Chief Tortha—she'd ever met.

"Now, stop it. Vall has always done just what he's wanted." She felt guilty about letting Thalvan, who wasn't man enough to wear Vall's boots, run him down. Still, she was there not as a friend, but as an interrogator.

"I'm not defaming Vall, he's one of my best friends. Still, it wouldn't hurt if he lightened his load."

Dalla was starting to get angry about the way Thalvan was talking about her husband, as if he were so superior—Ha! She made a determined effort to get this conversation back on course. "As I said, I'm really looking to find a few special pieces of art. I know you know lots of people in the business and I thought maybe you'd have some ideas."

"For what you want to pay, I don't think so."

That remark angered her; he had no idea of their financial resources. "That's not what I hear, Thalvan. A friend picked up a late Modigliani and a Cezanne for less than a hundred thousand Paratime Exchange Credits."

He looked real interested. "Ah, yes but on the Black Market. You couldn't touch a good one from Bralavar's House of Auctions for less than a million, five hundred thousand P.E.U.s."

"How do I go about *getting* on the Black Market lists?" she asked.

"Not easily, my dear. Especially, with your and Verkan's connections to the Paratime Police Department. I do know some people, who know some people, who may be able to help. If you're really serious, I'll put out some feelers."

"Would you, Thalvan? That would be divine," she exaggerated.

"Of course, anything for *you* Dalla," he said, his eyebrows arching upward.

The look on his face made her stomach cringe. "Thank you so much."

"Ahh. But in exchange, you have to share some gossip with me. I know that Vall tells you all sorts of things."

IX

Dalla arrived at his table in a swirl of Chanel No. 5 and chiffon. Verkan couldn't help but notice that almost every male head in the top floor of the Constellation Room had turned to watch and follow her entrance. He rose up and gave her a big hug.

The waiter was hovering at their table before Verkan could sit back down.

Dalla ordered a martini, extra-dry with an olive, while he ordered a rum and Coke with a twist of lime. Outtime Food and Beverages had made a fortune with their Coca-Cola franchise alone. Even though they'd stolen the Coca-Cola secret formula more than fifty years ago, everyone still wanted the real thing and most Coke was transposed in from Fourth Level.

"How was your meeting with Dras?" he asked.

"Oh, Mr. Ego. I'd forgotten how much in love with himself he was. I think he was more interested in helping himself to me, than in helping an old friend."

Verkan laughed. "That sounds like Dras, all right. If you don't encourage him, he's harmless."

"Yeah, like a toothless old lion; he could maul a girl to death."

"He didn't actually—"

"No, of course not. But only because I didn't give him an opening. Really, Vall, just what kind of friend is he?"

"An old friend; one of the few people who's made the effort to keep in touch through the decades. I know he's full of himself and a bit grating, but he means well—and he always comes through on a promise."

"What I want to know is: How did Dras every pass his Bureau of Psy-Hygiene Character Profile tests?" Dalla asked.

Verkan shook his head. The Character Profile was also known as the Majority Test; every First Level Citizen had to undergo a BuPsy-Hyg Character Profile at age twenty-five before they could receive full Citizenship, which included longevity treatments, full medical profiles and a stockpile of replacement organs and an outtime travel pass.

"Considering some of the whackos the Department runs into I wonder if the Character Profiles are of any help. Tortha's been lobbying the Executive Committee to sanction required Character Profiles at each century mark. He says it takes at least a hundred years before a man's true character wins out. He may be right, but the sun will stop shining long before the Committee passes that resolution."

Dalla nodded. "I'm not even sure I could pass a Character Profile exam today."

"Well, if *you* couldn't, I'd say it's time to scrap the entire test—and the Bureau of Psych-Hygiene, as well!"

"You won't find me disagreeing. Here's the waiter, let's order dinner."

Verkan ordered a Kobe beefsteak with new potatoes and a Caesar Salad, while Dalla ordered grilled salmon and curried Rice Pilaf.

Afterwards they smoked cigarettes, had another round of drinks and watched the constellations pass overhead on the sky screens, while Dalla gave him the highlights over her conversation with Thalvan Dras. She finished with, "Dras'll do his best to find me a black market dealer, not because he's that well-connected, but because he wants me to think he is."

"That's a good observation, dearest. Maybe that will give us some leads as to which Europo-American Subsector all these masterpieces are stolen from."

"Which, in turn, will give us a searching point for the Organization."

"You're getting this police jargon down, my dear. The Wizard Traders were too well financed and organized to be localized only at the Esaron Sector. Besides, they'd only been there for a few months. I suspect they search out an isolated subsector or belt, work it for a while, then move on before anyone's the wiser. This is a well-rooted criminal conspiracy, and it's aimed at the heart of First Level."

"Okay, Vall. Enough preaching; I'm with the choir now. Remember, we were going to leave work at the Paratime Building and just enjoy the evening?"

"Yes, darling. How about another round of drinks?"

"Now, you're talking."

***

Ulvarn Rarth looked around at the modern art, Picassos, Klees, a Marc Chagall, two Jackson Pollocks and others, hanging on the walls of Thalvan Dras' penthouse with naked envy. To own all this, like Thalvan Dras, as well as his own tower and penthouse; plus, several major outtime firms, like Consolidated Outtime Foodstuffs and Holnyt Art House, the premier purveyor of fine art in Dhergabar City or anywhere else on First Level. He had it all.

A prole servant dressed in Thalvan's red and gold livery appeared, asking, "How are you, Citizen? May I bring you a beverage?"

"Not now. I'm here to see Mavrad."

"Certainly. What name shall I give him?"

Rarth, who'd already given the code name Vislur at the door, didn't give him Hadron Tharn's name, as the Mavrad didn't know him by name. He was the "messenger." And, not always of good tidings.

"Tell him, a *Mutual Friend* is here."

When the servant turned, he began to examine the parlor more closely. The book and spool shelves were all made out of rare woods, mostly teak and mahogany. The furniture was handmade, each piece a work of art. The folding screens were all made of ivory, hand-carved elephants and tigers, crafted on Fourth Level Indo-Kirsh. This was what he wanted for himself and Sirna—*Why couldn't she see that?* Instead she wanted him housebound like a neutered cat, tenured at the University of Dhergabar, lecturing bored-out-of-their-skulls students who didn't want to be there anymore than he had during his undergraduate days. He had dreams: he wanted to be somebody, Speaker of the Executive Council; not a party hack for the Opposition Party like his father, or a lowly professor like Sirna's parents.

Being Hadron Tharn's assistant gave him the opportunity to meet important people, sit on the sidelines of big deals—to see how serious units were made. Certainly Hadron was one of the wealthiest men on Home Time Line; even if it wasn't publicly acknowledged. Many of Tharn's *investments* were with Old Town syndicates and mob bosses, as well as with outtime gangs and scam clans. But, nobody truly cared where it all came from; it was the units in Hadron's accounts that mattered and the way he manipulated politicians and industrialists alike.

Working for Tharn made him a junior kingpin. One day, when his boss went down for one of his many crimes—probably a crime of passion, it would all be his. Tharn was known to go into manic frenzies and didn't care who he hurt. During those spells, he was certifiably insane and even he kept his distance. So far Hadron's sister and his political connections had kept him out of the Bureau of Psy-Hygiene's clutches, but that wouldn't continue indefinitely—then it would be Rarth's turn. He knew all Tharn's connections and connectors between legitimate and illegitimate business interests. Then Sirna would see just what a big man he truly was. Her talk of divorce was nonsense—

"Who are you?" Thalvan Dras—who had just entered the room—asked. He was looking down at him as if he were a cheap used-robot salesman. "I was told a Mutual Friend had entered."

"Our Mutual Friend shall remain nameless, as always. To jog your memory, remember five years ago, when certain investments you made at the Trade Exchange proved imprudent? It was our Mutual Friend's units that kept you out of trouble."

Thalvan nodded reluctantly.

"I was told that you sent a red-code message to our Mutual Friend's voice-drop."

"Yes, you must be his *latest* errand boy. Do you prefer to remain nameless, as your predecessor did?"

"Yes." He already disliked Thalvan's attitude. He'd have to relay it to Hadron Tharn, who tended to take such things personally, when he returned. Although, Tharn gave his fellow nobles more leeway in these matters than major industrialists and corporate chairmen. Rarth also knew that if Thalvan *really* wanted to know his identity, he could surreptitiously put a tell-tale on him or a sticky dot.

He didn't worry about being bugged—a most useful Europo-American expression—because, in reality, none of Tharn's *business* partners truly wanted to know where he was for fear of igniting his legendary temper.

"Tell our Mutual Friend that his sister and the new Chief's Assistant, Assistant of the Paratime Police, has been making disturbing inquiries, both to myself and other known acquaintances, about our mutual import business. Tell him that I will no longer require any new inventory until this matter is resolved. I will make a stock exchange in his favor of his account to cover costs of any current inventory in order so that he will not be adversely affected by this new development. Until this matter is resolved, I will consider our balance sheets balanced."

The Mavrad had him out the door so fast it made his head swim. Hadron wasn't going to take this setback lightly; especially, since it was his sister who was meddling in his affairs—the one person he couldn't, or wouldn't touch. No, Tharn was not going to be happy with this new development. Ever since the raid on the Esaron Sector, the Paracops had taken far too much interest in the Organization's outtime activities. Now, it was affecting his Home Time Line interests.

He wouldn't want to be in Hadron's new slave girl's chains tonight!

X

As soon as Verkan Vall arrived at his office desk in the morning, he found the red-flagged message from Ranthar Jard, which he had sent him by way of message-ball from Fourth Level Hispano-Columbian, Europo-American Subsector, Hartley Belt.

Verkan slipped the data wafer into the visiphone slot and Ranthar's face appeared on the screen. "Chief's Assistant, this is Inspector Ranthar Jard reporting in: It is one-nine-seven day at 1100 hours, Hartley Prime. The Hartley Headquarters Unit arrived on one-eight-six day at Hartley Prime, the time-line serving as the nucleus of the Departmental probe into the Hartley Belt. As ordered, we are currently conducting an investigation into the criminal enterprise known as the 'Organization.'

"Before arrival, we were informed by the Department of Conveyer Dispatch and Scheduling that there were several reported incidences of conveyer traffic between the Hartley Belt and Fifth Level. However, all such traffic has ceased through the Belt since our arrival on the Hartley Prime. It is almost as if they anticipated our arrival. We now have teams on some two thousand time-lines throughout the Hartley Belt. We have already identified several anomalies in this belt. The most important of which is the Organization appears to have infiltrated the Vanadium Corporation, a Canadian mining firm that mines uranium among other metals. Since the takeover in 1948, the New Vanadium Corporation has opened mines in the Colorado Plateau, the Jackpile mine in New Mexico, the Athabasca Basin in northern Saskatchewan, as well as a heavy expansion in Africa, primarily South Africa, Rhodesia, and Niger. Currently, they're making big inroads into Australia—"

Verkan stopped the message. He was going to have to visit the Hartley Belt himself, clearly there were a number of disturbing Paratime Code violations going on there. The big question was: what were they doing with all the uranium? First Level procured most of its fissionables from Fifth Level Industrial Sector, where there was no possibility of outtime locals getting involved. Outtime fissionable mining had been a violation of the Paratime Code, Section 143, for several thousand years.

He was going to have to inform the military to put several strike teams on alert, rotate more investigators to Hartley Prime, inform Chief Tortha of the latest developments and contact Dalla. This case was like the proverbial tar baby; the more you pushed and pulled, the more it pulled back.

Verkan pressed the controller and Ranthar continued: "In most respects, Hartley Prime is your typical Europo-American Subsector time-line. The two major powers are the Soviet Union and the United States of America; both diametrically opposed and armed to the teeth with everything from conventional weapons to atomic bombs. However, on this Belt we see the recent emergence of a third power bloc, the Islamic Caliphate.

"The origins of the Caliphate can be traced to the assassination of King Abdullah the Hashemite king of Jordan and his young grandson, Prince Hussein on July 20, 1951 Europo-American Standard Dating (E.A.S.D.). The Arab dynasty of the Hashem trace their bloodline back from Hashim ibn Abd al-Manaf, the great-grandfather of the Islamic prophet Mohammed.

"After the murder of his father and son in Jerusalem, the new King Talal, Abdullah's oldest son, was forced to step down due to mental fatigue. Shortly afterwards he was institutionalized as a schizophrenic. There was about a year of instability before a compromise candidate was put forth, Khalid ibn Hussein, a distant cousin. He appears to have inspired leadership qualities; Khalid has created a new bloc of Arab states which he has named the Islamic Caliphate, out-maneuvering Abdel Nasser of Egypt by co-opting the emerging Republic of Egypt into the Caliphate. Earlier this year later Nasser was found shot dead by a prowler in his bedroom.

"On most Europo-American Subsectors, young Prince Hussein survived the gunshots that killed his grandfather, when they struck a medal that his grandfather had awarded him. This appears to be spurious data and legend-building encouraged by the Royal advisors. However, the young Prince Hussein of Jordan has stabilized Jordan throughout most of the Subsector and appears much more modest in his ambitions than Khalid.

"Verkan, there's something very strange going on here. It's almost as if someone anticipated our questions—maybe the Organization, maybe some other party. I sent a team of our best field agents to Williamsport, home of Blake Hartley, to dig up information. It appears, up until right after the war, he was your usual ex-veteran small-town lawyer. About eight years ago, he started to play the horses; or at least, that's the gossip around town. He made a couple of big killings on a horse named Assault. In August 5, 1945, he made his first big bet at the Flash Stakes. Assault started at odds of 70 to 1.

"In 1946 Assault had an uneven record, even though he won the Triple Crown. Interesting, our man didn't wager on any of the losing races, except one which he won with another horse. Later in the year, between the Pimlico Special and the Westchester Handicap races he pulled in half a million dollars. And that's just for starters. Blake was unbeatable in 1947, winning every major race he bet upon.

"He's tried to cover all this up. But a lot of this information is based on public and private records and interviews with track officials and race-track touts. It appears that his betting went underground during the years of 1948 through 1951 when it ceased completely. By that time Associated Enterprises was up and running with a number of novel patents, many of them decades beyond what any other comparable Europo-American Subsector has developed. Hartley's also made a lot of investments in computer firms, primarily International Business Machines, and recently took over a photographic paper company named the Haloid Company. He now owns majority stock in both companies through his umbrella conglomerate, Associated Enterprises.

"It's possible Blake Hartley is a precog, or maybe that most unlikely possibility—a time traveler! This is just one of a number of anomalies that characterize this new Belt. We are in the process of setting up a private meeting with Chairman Hartley of Associated Enterprises in a ten-day. It would be most helpful if you and Chief's Assistant, Assistant Hadron Dalla were present for this meeting. I would highly recommend that you transpose to Hartley Prime as soon as work permits. Inspector Ranthar Jard, signing off."

Verkan knew he wasn't making much progress towards prosecuting the Organization from his desk at Department of Paratime Police Headquarters, as opposed to Inspector Ranthar on Hartley Prime. Of course, it never took very much to wrest him away from deskwork, he thought wryly. Although, in this case, he had sufficient cause; enough even to convince even Tortha Karf, the old taskmaster himself.

It was time to call Dalla. He keyed in her number and a few moments later she filled his view screen. "Hi, dearest. How would you like to go on a distant journey?"

"I'd love to, Vall. But is it work-related?"

"Caught red-handed. Yes, there are some interesting anomalies that have popped up on the Hartley Belt. We may have need of your Psychist talents."

"What have you found?"

"A typical small-town attorney suddenly picks the winner of every race he bets on, going from a five-figure income to a seven-figure one in two years. How does that smell to you?"

"Like Denmark, as the Bard would say. Your lucky track player wouldn't happen to be Blake Hartley—would it?"

"Great guess. Now you know why I want you along."

"You couldn't keep me away," she said. "Have you contacted the Rhogom Foundation about this?"

"No, and we're not going to. I know you're a Fellow of the Foundation and have your responsibilities, but this case has Departmental Top Priority.

I'm not even letting Conveyer Dispatch know we're leaving. We'll take our private conveyer."

She saluted him. "Yes, sir. I take it you have some doubts as to internal security."

"You nailed it. I'll see you tonight. We'll make it an early evening. Take-off is at 0600."

XI

The next morning Verkan, Dalla and Verkan's bodyguard Dalon Sath took a private conveyer to Fifth Level Police Terminal, Dhergabar Equivalent. At Pol-Term they took a rocket to Vendaran Equivalent, which was the Philadelphia, Pennsylvania equivalent on almost all Fourth Level Europo-American sectors, belts and time-lines. There was a large conveyer rotunda-head at Vendaran Equivalent with a lot of traffic going in and out. An Army strike team brigade had already arrived and Verkan was quickly escorted to their temporary headquarters about a half mile away from the rotunda.

The 12th Strike Team Brigade temporary headquarters were made out of pulse rock, still warm to the touch. Verkan was quickly ushered into the office of Colonel Sordar Kran.

"Welcome, Chief's Assistant Verkan. I've been given orders to put my brigade under your command, sir." Sordar didn't look happy about that, as if he didn't trust civilians with military assets. "I was given a very short briefing, some trouble with an outtime paramilitary force. That's all I was told, sir."

Verkan's rank in the Paratime Police was the equivalent of Major General in the Army, although no military man thought they were in any way equal.

Verkan quickly briefed Colonel Sordar on his previous encounter with the Organization's forces in First Level Abzar Sector, very little of which for security reasons had been reported in the media or anywhere else. Then he brought the Colonel up-to-date, without mentioning any specifics, of their operation on Hartley Prime.

"Now, I understand why you requested a backup force, sir."

"Colonel, I really hope that the Department of Paratime Police doesn't require the 12th's services, because if we do it's going to get messy. After all, this is a densely populated Belt; any major incursion might involve one or two competing sovereignties. I don't believe that the Organization wants the publicity an all-out war on Hartley would bring about. I know *we* don't. On the other hand, we don't really know who the enemy is or what they're truly capable of doing."

"If needed, we're only an hour away, sir. The general has transferred another ten Strike Team Brigades to Pol-Term; they'll be quartered around Vendaran Equivalent, for quick transposition, in case trouble develops on any of the other time-lines in the Hartley Belt."

"Excellent, Colonel."

After his meeting with the Strike Team commander, they made the hour-long conveyer journey to the Hartley Belt. While in transit, he and Dalla discussed Blake Hartley.

"I'd like to join you when you meet with Hartley," Dalla said.

"I want you there. We've got a private meeting setup about selling him a semiconductor patent that we have pending. I'm supposed to be Dr. Verkan who was one of the engineers working for the Regency Division of the Industrial Development Engineering Associates; they're currently working on the first practical transistor radio and plan to bring it out before the end of the year. It's something Jard's team cooked up; it's just the kind of thing to pique Hartley's interest—if he's who we think he is."

"That should hook him if he truly has precognitive abilities. Did it occur to you that if he's a true precog, we might be able to mine information out of him that would be helpful to the Department?"

Verkan made a big grin. "Maybe..."

Dalla lightly punched him on the shoulder. "You big lug. Who knows what he could tell us...?"

"Almost anything would make our job easier. If there's going to be a big war, when to pull our operatives off this belt or even the Caliphate Subsector."

"What if he's a time traveler?" she asked. "That might be more problematic."

"I'll believe it, when he's given us solid data we can verify. It would certainly shake things up back on First Level. We've been working on linear time travel for over twelve thousand years; it would make a lot of people unhappy to discover some outtimer worked up a time machine in his basement!"

"Still, think of all the things we could learn."

"Or all the new headaches that would come with it," returned Verkan.

They were welcomed at the temporary rotunda-head by Ranthar Jard and Inspector Kostran Garth.

"We've got the 12th Strike Team on call at Police Terminal; they're only a message ball away. However, I don't want to bring them in except under dire circumstances."

"Understood, Chief's Assistant," Ranthar Jard replied. "Hartley has his Associated Enterprises headquarters here in Philadelphia. He still maintains a residence in Williamsport, but for logistical reasons operates out of here. Associated Enterprises is making a big splash locally; they finished the new sixty-story Associated Tower in the Penn Center. They and their subsidiaries are now Pennsylvania's biggest employer. He's also making a lot of political contacts within the Republican Party, this Belt's version of Management."

"Is there any evidence that he's either working with or aware of the Organization or their mining activities?"

Ranthar shook his head. "I'm not sure how the Organization discovered this Belt, but I doubt they know the divarification trigger; if they did, Hartley would already be under their control. It only took the Department a million man-hours of Survey Division research time to discover Blake Hartley."

"How does he factor in on the other Europo-American Subsectors, like Hispano-Columbian?"

"That's another anomaly, boss. We've been unable to discover any living Blake Hartley on any Hispano-Columbian time-line. We know his father was named Herbert Hartley and he had two children, one who died at birth, and Blake Orr Hartley who was born on April 18, 1911. Blake is reported to have died of the flu at age eight during the Influenza Pandemic of 1918 on every time-line outside of the Hartley Belt we investigated."

"That pretty much rules out the time traveler theory," Dalla offered.

"Not completely. Through some fluke, he didn't catch the flu and die on this particular Belt. He also has a son, Allan Hartley, who was born on July 18, 1932 in Williamsport to Blake and Amanda Hartley."

"What happened to Amanda?" Dalla asked.

"She died in an automobile accident in 1942. Drunk driver ran her over as she was crossing a Williamsport downtown street. Died instantly."

Dalla shuddered.

Verkan put his arm around her. Sometimes it was easy to forget how fragile life was on these primitive Fourth Level sectors.

"Blake, with the help of a housekeeper, one Eileen Stauber, raised young Allan by himself. The boy is quite precocious; he graduated from high school at fifteen and by eighteen had a Bachelor's Degree in Engineering from the Massachusetts Institute of Technology. It only took him another year to get his master's. At nineteen Allan went to work for his father at the Blake Institute of Engineering Research in State College, Pennsylvania. Of course, we know who put up the money for that. The son is considered a local genius, according to his fellow engineers, who teasingly refer to him as Young Edison."

"Is the son brilliant because he's recycling the father's precognitions, or is he a precog, too?" Dalla asked.

"Good question," Verkan said. "This is something we can broach after you hypno-mech the father. "What about the Organization: Are there any cells on this time-line?"

Ranthar paused to fill his pipe with tobacco. He used a local lighter, in a metal case, to ignite it, then said, "We found a big open-pit uranium mining operation in the Namib Desert, some thirty miles from Swakopmund, South Africa. It was discovered in 1928, but not mined until the Vanadium Corporation started operations about five years go. Rössing Uranium Mine's a massive operation, employing three to four thousand employees. They have their own refining and processing plant. They've pretty much depleted all the surface ore. The uranium deposits at Namib haven't been developed on most of the contiguous Europo-American Sectors, which again points to

Organization infiltration of this Belt.

"Since the plant was relatively isolated, we thought it would be an ideal place to raid. We've got a tactical operation set for later today.

"Good," Verkan replied. "Maybe we can get to the bottom of all this."

XII

Kostran Garth left immediately to arrange the Rössing Uranium Mine raid on Police Terminal. When it got dark, Verkan left Dalla in Philadelphia with the Hartley Team while he and Ranthar Jard transposed back to Fifth Level Police Terminal.

Colonel Sordar was waiting for them at the Vendaran Equivalent conveyer-head.

"Are your sure you're not going to need air support, sir?"

"From our surveillance sky-eyes and tell-tales, Colonel, we know there are roughly six hundred guards at the mine, all of them are Organization out-time hires brought here for this operation. It appears that the Organization doesn't trust the local Afrikaners or the black workers. I don't foresee any need for strike team air-cavalry that some local might mistake for flying saucers! We want to keep a very low profile on this mission."

"I'll send a squad to the conveyer-head anyway. Just in case you need backup."

"If we do, all the demons will blast out of the Pits of Kunargh! These Europo-American time-lines are saturated with newsies and reporters."

The Colonel shook his head. "I don't envy the Department on this, not even one little bit."

After telling Colonel Sordar they didn't need his assistance, they picked up another hundred Paratime Police troopers and took a large transport plane to twenty miles outside the Swakopmund Equivalent where there was a temporary conveyer-head already laid out. It was 2300 hours when Verkan's forces arrived at the temporary camp two miles outside Rössing Uranium Mine's open-pit mine and processing plants.

There were already two hundred Paratime Police field agents and tactical officers at the conveyer-head awaiting their arrival.

Kostran approached him after they exited the conveyer. "It's been pretty quiet so far, boss. The local workers are shut in their barracks at 2100 hours. They're not allowed to let off any steam until Friday night, when the brothel tents and gambling pavilions are flown in. These poor laborers get paid terrible wages, then the company uses its own prostitutes and gamblers to skim their pathetic pay."

"How'd you find that out?"

"We took a laborer captive, who was outside the perimeter fence, as well as one of the outtime guards."

"Good thinking, Garth. What else did you learn?"

"The guards here are lax. Other than a riot, a few years back when they first took over, there's been no trouble. Most of these workers are just glad to have a place to rest their heads and earn a few credits. Any mine workers who complain, start trouble or talk strike are conveniently gone the next day; I'm sure if we wanted to we could find their burial pit somewhere in the desert. The managers and production people live in those houses over there behind the razor-wire fences. They're unguarded, too. It's an easy post for the First Level managers and engineers. According to our informant, most of them were chronic complainers and time-wasters who were facing sentencing with the Bureau of Psy-Hygiene when they were 'offered' a job outtime with no questions asked."

"That's ominous. Who, in Fasif's name, is supplying the Organization with that kind of information? Only the Department, Metro, BuPsy-Hygiene and the Executive Council have access to those files. The Chief's not going to be happy when he hears of this."

"I'm just stunned at the size of this operation, boss. And this is just one time-line out of thousands. Of course, not all of them will have this depth of infiltration by the Organization, but—"

"I know, Kostran. We've got our work cut out for us."

At exactly 0400 hours, Verkan gave the order to commence the raid. The orders were to hit the management compound first since they held all the time-liners from First Level. At the same time, a hit team of fifty men were to hit the conveyer rotunda-head just in case there were any working conveyers. The largest force of some three hundred men were to neutralize the workers' barracks with sleep gas. They'd be left to awaken in the morning, to find the processing plants and management housing in ruins, wondering where all the staff had disappeared to. The Vanadium stockholders back in Toronto would be left holding the bag....

The outside guards were neutralized at once. Any who showed initiative or tried to resist were garroted or needled. Everything went according to plan until one of the rotunda guards opened up with submachine gun fire; then everything went to Shpeegar!

Lights started popping on and guns opened up in the manager's compound. Armed guards started pouring out of tunnels and buildings.

Verkan took a ten-man team with him to the compound. The razor wire was already cut and Kostran shot one guard with his needler, while they finessed their way through the sharp wire and entered the compound. He ran up to the main house and set a timed charge. He raised his arm and the team pulled back; moments later the porch and front doorway disappeared in a burst of fire and black smoke.

Two guards, their gray uniforms wreathed in flames, ran out of the building screaming and flailing their arms.

Verkan swept them both off their feet with his sawed-off shotgun.

He quickly re-loaded his shotgun with special 12-gauge micro-flechette shells that disintegrated upon contact and followed Kostran into the smoldering house. There was automatic fire coming from the back bedroom area; they crept through the hallway on the ground wearing oxy-masks. The air was filled with smoke and heating up.

A woman dressed in a blue nightgown ran out of the bedroom and before she could reach them a dozen shots rang out. She jerked and dropped to the ground in a heap like a rag doll.

Verkan clenched his hands twice and started backpedaling. The others followed. When the team had vacated the hallway, a rocket launcher fired and the back of the house disappeared in a wall of flames and dense smoke.

By the time they were back outside, the fight was over. Some of the field agents were rounding up a few dozen prisoners, but most of the compound was on fire with flames reaching toward the sky. He was glad they were so far from Swakopmund or they'd already be swamped with police and reporters.

Ranthar, who had led the raid on the conveyer-head, came running up. "Verkan, we've got the conveyer-head secured. No conveyers inside. All the guards are down or captured. It appears the top brass left yesterday. I don't know how they found out we were coming, but there's a big leak somewhere."

"Tell me about it!" Verkan replied, through gritted teeth.

"I don't think we're going to learn much from this crowd." Ranthar grimaced. "We've interrogated, or tried to, a few of the managers. I've seen some criminal overdoses of Zanithax before, but nothing like this! Some of these poor bastards had their memory stripped to the point they didn't even know their own names.... These Organization people don't give a spent shell about their own troops! A lot of the technicians—I guess they hadn't had time to transpose them out—were given noodles behind the ear—execution style. We got a few IDs we can check back on First Level, but I doubt we'll learn anything new. We're sending most of the prisoners to Pol-Term, as it would cause a world-class public relations nightmare if the local newsgrids got wind of this. Great Blaxthakka help us, if the newsies back on First Level ever learned about it! This outfit is deathly serious about maintaining security."

"What I want to know is: Where are they sending the yellow-cake?" Verkan asked. "It's not going to Home Time Line; we've got all the radioactives there we'll ever need. Somewhere someone is building a lot of atomic bombs. We've got to find out where and quick."

By 0450 they were rounding up the last of the prisoners, some eighty-five all together. Fourteen had already committed suicide. Verkan suspected post-hypnotic commands were responsible. He had all the remaining prisoners, except two, sleepgassed so they wouldn't kill themselves.

"What are our losses?" Verkan asked.

"Three dead and five seriously wounded, all on their way to Pol-Term with Crash med-units. The butcher's bill would have been lower if that idiot with the machine gun hadn't opened fire."

Kostran shoved a tall man, trussed up with sticky fiber, through the door of the large transport aircraft where Verkan was waiting impatiently.

"We don't have a lot of time, boss. This is the head engineer; apparently, he wasn't important enough to transpose out yesterday. Survey just picked up two helicopters coming from Swakopmund. They're about twenty miles out."

"What did the Deception Team come up with to cover-up all this," Verkan asked, pointing to the smoldering ruins and burning houses inside the compound.

"They set it up to look like a worker's revolt turned nasty. They've burned most of the evidence, removed the collapsed metal shielding and blown up the conveyer head. Deception threw most of the corpses into the flames. Just before we left they planted some Kalashnikovs and grenades in the barracks, along with some Communist books and pamphlets, and some illegal alcohol stills—which will explain their hangovers. The Team shot up several hundred of the workers; the authorities wouldn't buy it if only the guards and managers were discorporated. Then they hit the survivors with the sleep gas antidote. Most of the survivors will be wide-awake and wandering around in a daze when the authorities arrive. It'll look like just another Communist-sponsored revolt against the Capitalist system."

Verkan could think of a dozen operations in the Europo-American Subsector where bungled operations in Malaysia and Kenya, in particular, had been covered up by so-called Communist insurrections.

"That ploy almost always works on this Sector," Verkan said.

"It's even easier the other way around," Kostran chuckled. "The Communists in this sector are even more paranoid than their Capitalist opponents. It's unfortunate that the laborers are going to take most of the blame for this massacre, but there won't be any Transtemporal Contamination."

"Good. It's unfortunate for the miners, but it's not the disaster it might have been had the Wizard Traders decided to move out on their own. From what we've seen, they're not in the habit of leaving witnesses behind."

Ranthar nodded in agreement.

XIII

Raids were made throughout the Hartley Belt over the next ten-day, but the results were hardly illuminating. Many of the Organization's operations were abandoned, others were destroyed by fire or bombs. It was obvious that somebody had tipped them off. Still, the Paratime Police took thousands of prisoners, none of whom knew anything about the Organization or what they were doing with the fissionable ores they were shipping out of the Belt. There didn't appear to be any connection between Blake Hartley and the Organization itself, but they wouldn't know for certain until after their interview.

The Associated Enterprises Building was surprisingly well guarded and Verkan and Dalla were passed through three security checks before they reached the top floor and Blake Hartley's private office. Blake was on the tall side and wore a tailored gray suit; his hair was streaked with gray but his mustache was still brown. After greetings were exchanged, Verkan put his hand out. When Blake reached over the desk to shake hands, Verkan jerked him forward and injected him in the neck with a pneumatic hypo with his left hand.

Blake Hartley slumped over his desk.

"This is supposed to be a private meeting," Verkan said, "so we'll have about twenty minutes before he gets a phone call or someone barges in. I'll cover the door in case we get an intruder."

Blake was regaining consciousness when Dalla moved her chair up to the desk.

He shook his head back and forth. "Whattt...happened?" he slurred.

Dalla held up the gold flower ring she wore on her finger. It began to spin, catching and holding Blake's eyes.

She began her hypnotic induction, speed up by the drugs: "Your arms are loose and limp, just like a rag doll. As I raise your hand, let all of the weight hang limply in my fingers. When I drop it, send a wave of relaxation all across your body. As you feel your hand touch your body, send that wave of relaxation from the top of your head all the way down to the very tips of your toes.

"And as you do, you find that you double your previous level of relaxation. Now, once again, with the other hand."

She turned to Verkan. "He's under. Now, I'll interrogate him. Blake, what's the name of your housekeeper?"

"Mrs. Stauber."

"And how long has she been with you?"

"Thirteen years."

"Very good. Blake, where did you obtain the funds to start Associated Enterprises?"

"By winning money at the track."

"How did you pick your horses?"

"Allan gave me the dates and winners. It was his idea to begin with."

"Is this your son, Allan, who provided you with the names of the winning horses?"

"Yes, my son."

"How was he able to determine which horse would win each race?"

"He knew. He's already lived the future."

Dalla bolted upright. Verkan motioned for her to hurry up.

"What exactly do you mean, when you say Allan has 'already lived the future'?"

"On August 5th, 1945 Allan woke up with the memories of his forty-three year-old self. He died in a nuclear explosion—at least, that's what he's told me. My little boy was gone and in his place was a grown-up in a child's body; a man of forty-three, an army officer, former chemist and best-selling novelist. He proved the truth of it to me by telling me of future events that I got to watch come to fruition. It was Allan's decision to start Associated Enterprises in an attempt to stop the world from World War III. I've been helping him the best I can."

It sounded insane, but Verkan believed he was telling the truth. Hartley continued in this vein, giving chapter and verse of some of their deals and just how they built Associated Enterprises block by block.

"Have you been contacted by any unusual persons who may want to help you in your goal or invest in Associated Enterprises?"

"No. Allan and I put all this together by ourselves. We're doing much better now that he's an *official* adult and can manage the skunk labs out in State College. Allan's goal is to get me elected President. The next step is winning the Governorship of Pennsylvania. It's too late for the 1956 election as George Leader has the office all but wrapped up. But I'm planning to run as a Republican in 1960."

Verkan snapped his fingers to get her attention. "Wrap it up. Our time's almost over."

Dalla quickly began to terminate the session: "When you wake up, you will remember nothing except that you offered us engineering positions with Associated Enterprises We were both very qualified and you were anxious to add us to your roster. Now, I'm going to count from one to five, and then I'll say, 'Fully awake.' At the count of five, your eyes are open, and you are then fully aware, feeling calm, rested, refreshed, relaxed. All right. One: you are slowly, calmly regaining consciousness... Two: you're coming awake...."

She continued in this vein until Blake was waking up, ending with: "Five: you're *fully awake*. Eyelids open. Take a good, deep breath, fill up your lungs and stretch."

After yawning, Blake exclaimed, "Excuse me! I don't know what got into me. I need more sleep."

"Don't we all," Verkan replied. "We both want to thank you for your generous offer of employment. Before we make a decision we'll need to think this over and have our lawyer go over our employment agreements to see if our employment with Associated will go against any of the disclosure clauses in our contacts with Industrial Development Engineering Associates."

"Of course," Blake answered. "Now, I hope you don't mind if I tackle some of this paperwork." He gave a boyish grin as he looked down at his desk which was covered with almost a linear foot of documents, folders and memos.

As they got into the backseat of the 1954 Buick Roadmaster, Dalla said, "I thought that went quite well."

"Yes, I liked him. I was glad to find out he isn't part of the Organization."

"I need to interview Allan. He's the one."

"I'll get Ranthar to set up an interview out at the Blake Institute of Engineering and Applied Research. Allan's the one who'll be interested in our semiconductor research."

"Vall, I really feel I should inform the Rhogom Foundation about Allan Hartley. This is the first case I've ever encountered where a future personality came to inhabit his younger self. It's unique and worth the kind of study that only the Foundation can undertake."

"Yes, and destroy young Hartley's life. It's bad enough we have the Organization to deal with without adding in the Rhogom Foundation and their screwball Fellows to mess with his life."

Dalla frowned. "Of which, I'm one. Sometimes you're as thickheaded as a blockwall."

Verkan laughed. "Yes, and I aim to stay that way."

XIV

Thalvan Dras tossed the last of his stolen masterpieces, Rembrandts' Man With The Golden Helmet, frame and all, into the portable disintegrator where it was ripped apart to its constituent atoms. The last of his secret fine art collection was gone; he felt sick, as if his guts were poisoned. His secret art museum and greatest private pleasure destroyed! To be forced by circumstances to destroy more than fifty great works of art; it would have been far easier for him to shoot down passing aircars from his penthouse.

It was all he could do to not break down and weep.

This desecration had been forced upon him by Verkan's meddling wife, Dalla—a woman as dangerous and ingenious as she was beautiful. Thalvan had learned a lot about her deviousness when a mutual friend informed him that she was now working for the Department of Paratime Police. A fact Dalla never bothered to tell him.

When he visiphoned Verkan's office, he'd learned they both were due to return to Home Time Line by the end of the ten-day. He had three days to act. Once Dalla was back, she would put all of her formidable gifts to work in finding out the identity of the persons selling proscribed artwork in

Dhergabar.

The names he had given her previously were low-level thieves with no direct ties back to himself, but she would eventually find a link if she dug deep enough. And she would—of that, he had no doubt. He'd listened to far too many of Verkan's tales about the beautiful and clever Dalla to ever underestimate her talents, especially now that she had something to focus them on.

Unfortunately, that focus would eventually fall upon him.

He'd been careful to use middlemen to make all his sales, but conceivably they too could be linked back to him. However, with all the evidence destroyed, no one would dare prosecute someone of his stature, except Hadron Dalla, who in her own way was as dangerous as her deranged brother was reputed to be. Not even Thalvan's ties to Verkan would save him....

To fully protect himself, there was one final action to be completed. He used his visiphone to contact Ulvarn Rarth; his contact with the shadowy world of the illicit art trade. Ulvarn was a puffed-up little man, filled with his own self-importance, a political hack in training to the Opposition Party. A bunch of nobodies who'd been out of power for centuries. Still, Ulvarn was a useful man, as he had connections to many of the syndicate and crime bosses in Old Town Dhergabar.

He'd also been his point of contact with the mystery man who'd provided him with his illicit masterpieces, so many that he could sell them at bargain prices. Not that he needed the money; it was the privilege of being able to dispense great works of art like party favors that had most appealed to him. Watching behind his masked identity, as friends humbled themselves for the privilege of purchasing a Van Gogh at a thousandth of its true value, knowing all the while they were illicit, was a thrill the likes of which he'd never experienced. *You never truly knew your friends*, he thought, *until after you'd watched them grovel and beg.*

He used his scrambler to leave a message at Ulvarn's drop. "This is Art Critic, meet me at the usual spot at 2200 hours."

XV

Thalvan Dras arrived on time at the usual spot, named Rick's Café by the owner, Jorand Rarth, an Old Town mob boss rumored to have connections to the Novilan Syndicate. It was one of four clubs and three casinos Jorand owned in Old Town Dhergabar. Thalvan sat at the long mahogany bar, watching as a poorly dressed trio of outtime musicians attempted to play their instruments, while the one in the middle caterwauled in the Europo-American tongue known as American.

He couldn't wait until the cultural barometer made another bellwether change; he was sick of Europo-America's backwards culture and its *things*. Jorand came over to ask how he was doing, but at least this time he didn't do his usual Bogart impression. He waved him off and looked around for Ulvarn, who was always punctual.

Ulvarn staggered in about five minutes later, his face haggard. "I need a double, Rick," he said to the prole bartender. He added, "The usual."

The bartender nodded and returned with a scotch on the rocks.

Thalvan used his First Level mental processes to keep his pulse from racing off the clock. "What's up?" he asked.

"It's my damn wife, Sirna—she left me, the bitch! I didn't think she had the guts."

He laughed in relief. "I felt the same way about my first two wives. You'll get used to it. It's the price we men of action pay for our deeds."

"She'll regret it someday," Ulvarn said, as if he were concluding some private conversation he'd been having with himself.

"I'm sure she will," Thalvan said, not believing it for a second.

"Hey, man, look at that trio, it's Elvis, Scotty and Bill—the Hillbilly Cats! Yo, Jorand," he called, signaling the mobster.

"Yo, Ulvarn. Slip me some skin."

"Cool, Daddy-O!" Ulvarn cried out.

They did some ridiculous handshake, then laughed together in some private communion that made him feel completely like an outsider—probably their intention.

"Where'd you find your own Hillbilly Cats?"

Jorand leaned close and lowered his usual harsh voice to a throaty whisper. "I heard about their new platter for Sun Records, "That's All Right," from some outjacker. He said this Elvis cat was the cat's pajamas. He's the one who discovered Frank Sinatra for me; so I told him: 'Bring me the whole trio, if you can find 'em.' Damned, if he didn't!"

"Wow. I just saw the Trio on Europo Trends on Media Six. It must have cost you a bundle to have them time-jacked?"

"You don't wanna know. Besides, this cat owed me."

Ulvarn nodded. "Dig that crazy beat! He makes Hillbilly Haley look like yesterday's news."

"Everybody's got a Haley, but this is the first Presley."

"I'll pass the word."

They did another complicated series of hand maneuvers that Thalvan couldn't follow before Jorand left to go over and talk with another customer.

He leaned over. "Ulvarn, I need our Mutual Friend's help."

"For what?"

"I need a good Psychist—I mean one who's willing to skirt the law."

"Why would our Mutual Friend do you any favor?" Ulvarn said, not even attempting to keep the insolence out of his voice.

"Because he came to me and I provided him with information he needed to hear, that's why!" he said pointedly, noticing that Ulvarn looked startled. Sometimes the lower orders forgot the gulf that separated them from their betters and needed a reminder.

"Tell him, that I have Hadron Dalla on my trail. I need help, or we're all going to go down."

XVI

Dalla arrived promptly at the Blake Institute of Engineering and Applied Research on Waupelani Drive at 1400 hours. It was a big two-story building that covered about half a city block, an anomaly in the small college town of State College. It was out of the way and a perfect place to conduct research out of the public eye, with the added benefit of the nearby main campus of

Pennsylvania State University from which to draw scientific talent.

Verkan couldn't join her; he was busy dismantling another illegal uranium mine on Hartley Belt Prime, this one at the Colorado Plateau on an Indian Reservation. The Organization had mostly cleared out of Four Corners, but Verkan wanted to personally oversee the cleanup. She thought it was because he didn't like it when she used narco-hypnotism to interrogate suspects; the sessions that followed often made him uncomfortable.

One of these days they'd have to figure out why—whether he liked it or not.

Dalla left her name at the reception desk and before she had time to sit down a young man in suit and hat came to escort her to Mr. Hartley's office. Allan's office looked like that of a college dean, with more space devoted to bookshelves than plaques, photos and mementos. Then she recalled that in his previous "life" he'd been a successful writer. From the amount of paperwork and files on his desk, she doubted he was writing anything these days.

Allan rose up from his desk, removing his hat, as she entered. "Welcome, Hadron Dalla, to the heart of the Blake Institute."

"Thank you," she said, noticing that he didn't put his hand out for a handshake.

She had a micro-needler inside a pocket in her short dress-jacket and a full-sized one in her purse. She also noticed that besides his regular, almost handsome features, Allan had the piercing eyes of a man twice his age—which was appropriate, all things considered. It reminded her, despite his youthful appearance, that he was not a man to be underestimated; for the first time, she regretted not insisting that Verkan join her.

"Please take a seat, Miss Hadron—or is it Mrs.?"

Somehow, Dalla had the feeling, he knew everything there was to know about her identity and job with Regency that was available on this timeline. She hadn't been off-balance like this outtime in many years, and she didn't like it.

"Miss Dalla Evon Hadron, if you don't mind." She needed to ease his suspicions. She made sure that he got an eyeful of her cleavage. This timeline had some revealing ladies' wear and she had done some serious shopping in the big New York department stores while Verkan was in South Africa.

After she was seated, Allan said, "Okay, let's cut the charade." He removed one of the big file bundles and underneath was a Colt Police Special. He didn't touch it, but it was aimed in her direction.

He continued: "I don't intend to hurt you, I just don't want you to underestimate me, or what I know. After you and Dr. Vincent Verkan—now, that's a very strange last name; I've had a top-flight linguist trying to trace its derivation ever since my father's call. He's the tops in his field and he hasn't had a bit of luck finding out the root tongue or where it came from."

Dalla shrugged. "He's just a colleague. How would I know?"

"You know a lot more than you're pretending, Dr. Hadron. No luck with your name either; next time you travel to the past, I suggest you do a better job of finding aliases."

Dalla's heart was racing: how many people would he have informed of their impersonation? Probably no one; he was still unmarried and other than his father didn't have any close friends. Well, being chronologically three times older than all your friends probably made forming lasting attachments difficult. Despite the pistol, she was tempted to pull out her needler and finish Allan here and now, then find his father and discorporate him as well.

Still, he was *much* more interesting alive....

"As I was about to say," he continued, his hand only inches away from the Colt, "after your visit, my father had some blank spots in his memory. He also remembered feeling dizzy when Dr. Verkan shook his hand. He put one and one together and came up with three—he suspected you two doped him up and interrogated him. He called me and we discussed it. I contacted Regency and their head of personnel sent me to the Division of the Industrial Engineering Associates. Their records for both of you are very vague; the school records did not hold up under close scrutiny; they were obvious forgeries. That brought up more questions: I hired a PI to check out both your backgrounds.

"Some of your colleagues could remember you two, but everything was too sketchy. Especially for a woman who looks like a movie star and a man as distinctive as your Mr. Verkan, who could pass for a pro quarterback. My PI even had you both photographed; still, people had trouble remembering you, or got a sudden memory about some trivial thing. You two are like non-porous surfaces—nothing sticks. I talked it over with my father and we decided that the two of you must be time travelers and that I've unwittingly violated some time travel protocol or my actions will somehow upset the future. Am I in the ballpark?"

Dalla briefly considered denying everything, but what was the use? He wasn't going to tell anyone, at best. At worst, she'd have to discorporate him now, or someone else would have to do it later. In a way, it was a relief to drop her cover and all the usual lies: "You're in the ballpark, just the wrong one."

"What do you mean?" he asked.

"We are not from *here*—you're right about that. However, we're not from the future, either. We came to *here* across time." Dalla felt a frisson, as she realized she had just broken the most sacred commandment of Home Time Line; *thou shalt never disclose the Paratime Secret!* If anyone but Verkan ever learned of it, she would be immediately discorporated by authority of the Paratime Commission—no matter how much time had passed, or even if it was the wisest course of action. She shook it off.

"You mean there are really parallel worlds?"

She hadn't expected him to comprehend it so quickly. "You read science fiction?"

His face colored, then he nodded, saying: "Yes, I do. I used to read some before, but now I read it a lot; not the pulps, mostly *Astounding* and *Galaxy Science Fiction*. It helps me feel like I'm not alone—I guess, that's the way to put it."

"Yes, we've come here, but not for you."

"You're kidding! Don't tell me, you stumbled across me while visiting our world—right?"

"Something like that. Just because we're technologically advanced and can travel across time doesn't mean that human nature has changed much. We still have our criminals and outlaws, beggars, thieves and murders. We can treat the criminal mind where we come from, but *they* don't always cooperate. A group of *our* criminals, who call themselves the Organization, set up shop on your time-line. We came here to stop it. It was while our people, call us the cross-time police, were researching your time-line that we discovered an anomaly—you, Allan Hartley."

"Where?"

"Did you hear about the big fuss in South Africa, outside Swakopmund in the desert?"

"Yes, there was supposed to be some sort of Communist-supported takeover of the local uranium digs. They've been going crazy at the U.N. all week. I gotcha; you're saying it was your criminals who were behind the snatch—not the Reds."

"Bright boy. The Communist angle was just a convenient cover-up. We use it a lot in this Sector."

"Oh, man. This is so deep. What does it have to do with us?"

Dalla sighed. "Nothing, really. It's just we don't like outtime mysteries, especially ones that change the future and could come back and bite us in the rear. Besides being a time cop, I'm also an expert on parapsychological phenomenon. My colleague and I thought it might be valuable to learn exactly who you were and if or if not you presented a threat. At first, we thought you might be one of our people, or someone who'd been picked up by one of our time travel vehicles and accidentally dropped off on this time-line."

"That happens?!"

"Yes, rarely, but it happens. But, once we ruled those options out; then we thought *you* might be a time traveler—which by the way we have not been able to accomplish. Now that we know you're not a threat, well, we can all go our separate ways."

"I don't think so. You did something to my father, took some of his memories or got into his head somehow. I want to know how and why." His fingers closed in on the pistol.

"Do you mind if I smoke," she asked, coyly. She knew that leaning forward in her purposely low-cut blouse to pick up her purse would catch his attention; at least, it had always worked before.

"No! Don't—I guess it's okay."

She took out a pack of Lucky Strikes and her hypno-injector disguised as a Lady's Slim Zippo lighter.

Allan now had the gun in his hand and pointed at her chest. She purposely took a deep breath and held out her pack of cigarettes, shuffling it so several came forward. Without thinking, Allan lowered his gun hand and reached for the nearest cigarette with his other hand.

Just as he took the cigarette in his fingers, Dalla leaned further, her cleavage drawing his eyes like twin bulls-eyes. She lit her lighter; at the same time the pneumatic-injector inside shot a narcotic into his neck. She'd used the full dosage, so she had to grab the cigarette out of his mouth as he fell face-first onto the desk. The last thing she needed in his office now was a fire.

When it was out, Dalla stood up and walked around to the front of his large walnut desk. She started opening doors; in the bottom desk drawer she discovered a reel-to-reel briefcase-sized tape recorder. She took it out and pressed the stop record button. Then she rewound it, shuffled through her purse, found the de-magnetizer and blanked the tape. Then she put it back on the spindle and into the desk. Allan would have fun figuring that one out.

Allan still appeared dazed, but he was holding himself up right now. She searched through his drawers until she found his day book; inside was the phone number of the detective he'd hired. Kostran or Ranthar would have to pay him a visit.

When he was ready, Dalla began the hypnotic induction. Allan went under very quickly.

"What is your name?"

"Hartley, Allan; Captain, G5, Chem. Research AN/73/D. Serial, SO-23869403J."

"Very good, Allan."

"Where are you right now?"

"I'm on the battlefield, outside Syracuse, New York. We're getting thrown back! My men are dying! The city is gone? The light! My god—"

"It's all right. You are now back in your old home in Williamsport. In fact, you're in your bedroom. What do you see now?"

"My bedroom. It's sunny outside, even through the tan curtains. I can see the chintz-covered chairs. Ahh. Now I remember; I came back a long time ago, to be with my dad, to be safe again...."

"Very good, Allan."

"Believe me, it wasn't easy convincing him that it was me, a forty-three year old man in my adolescent body. He believed me when I switched pistols and saved Mrs. Gutchall—"

"Yes, Allan. I want you to go back to that other time—"

"Nooo!" he cried. "Not the war!"

"Not the war, but before it began. Long before. And I want you to tell me all about what you see and what you know."

Dalla got back to the Broadwood Hotel in Philadelphia just before dusk. After the four-hour debriefing of Allan Hartley—whom she awoke with no side effects except for a headache and no memory of their conversation—she was exhausted. Verkan was sitting at the hotel desk writing some notes on his mini electro-tablet.

"How did it go, darling? You look beat."

She sighed. "It was touch and go there for a while." Dalla quickly gave him a complete debriefing, only to pause when he suggested dinner. They ate an uninspired meal in the hotel dining room.

Back in their room, Verkan said, "Do you think this will come back on us?"

"What do you mean? My slip of the tongue...?"

He nodded.

"No, I found the tape recorder and went over the room with a tell-tale alert. He didn't have any backup on any microwave, light pulse or other spectrum that I could find. I completely hypno-blanked all of the relevant memories of my interview. You will want to visit the private detective I told you about."

"Yes, I'll go to his suite later tonight with Ranthar. Hartley's detective's got a twenty-man firm; not quite the Pinkertons, but nothing I'd want to fool with. We'll remove and erase all records relating to the Hartley request and hypno-mech all the operatives involved, including the principal. We should be out of here by tomorrow evening with a clean slate."

"Good. I take it you've finished the Four Corners job?"

"Yes, that's the last trace of the Organization on this time-line. Some of the Hartley Teams are still working their way through the Belt; they should have it cleared in another ten-day."

"How were our losses?" she asked.

"Overall, we've only lost about two hundred and seventy field agents. Not bad for an operation this size. Now, what are we going to do about some of that data you peeled out of Hartley?"

"I don't know," Dalla replied. "He told me about something called the Philadelphia Project and Operation Triple Cross, the Indonesian Campaign of 1962 and 1963 E.A.S.T. How much of his future prognostication is particular to this time-line, or even this Belt is problematical? Much less the rest of Europo-America, where the Hartleys don't exist, nor does the Islamic Caliphate...."

"We'll fill in the Chief and let him make the call," Verkan said.

Dalla let out a sigh of relief. "Good idea, hubby."

"What, are you going native? Calling me *hubby*—Fangs of Fasif, no!"

She laughed. Then quickly sobered. "What do I tell the Rhogom Foundation about young Hartley?"

Verkan shook his head. "Not a word."

"Look, I know you don't like Director Volzar Darv, but the Foundation does a great deal of good work in psychic research, which nobody else is doing. And, don't kid yourself, it's always going to be a part of my life."

"I know that, Dalla. But if we were to tell them about Allan Hartley; it's not going to do them any good. It's not like he can go back and forth between the past and the future—"

"We *don't* know that. Maybe with the proper stressors—"

"Like another A-bomb going off! That's what scares me about you...I mean, the Foundation. Your Fellows keep at it, worry the subject to death. Okay, what if Hartley can move his ego component through time, but only under a credible threat of discorporation? The Foundation will keep almost-killing the poor son of a bitch until they actually succeed. And, what do you believe they're going to learn from all that? Probably, not a bloody thing. Allan, from what you told me, is the kind of guy I'd like to meet, have a cup of coffee with. I liked his father, too.

"Give the guy a break. All the poor bastard is trying to do is save his world from nuclear annihilation—not a bad goal. He's one of the good guys. I'd hate to see Allan broken, twisted in some cell in the Foundation's basement, hidden away in shame."

Dalla threw up her hands. "This is some male identification or connection thing: Isn't it? Okay, I'll keep it to myself. Not because you brought it up, but because I too believe that's exactly what will happen if the Foundation gets hold of Allan. From what I heard, Allan doesn't want to go back—even if he could—which I thoroughly doubt. And I liked the guy, too."

A PARATIME PARADOX

JOHN F. CARR

I

1955 A.D.

As the Paratime Police Special Chief's Assistant, Verkan Vall was used to receiving late night calls and getting odd assignments, but that didn't mean he liked it. This call from the Paratime Police Chief Tortha Karf had come in at 0400 hours and was red coded. He managed to slip out of bed without waking his wife Dalla. It took him another twenty minutes to fly his air-car from the Space Spire to the Paratime Building.

After landing in his usual spot, Verkan took the grav-lift down to the Chief's Office. Inside, Tortha Karf was staring at a screen behind his horseshoe desk. His jowly face turned away from the screen and he looked up as Verkan came through the door.

"What's got you working this late, Chief?" Verkan asked.

Tortha shook his nearly bald head wearily and grumbled: "More trouble on Europo-American. That damn subsector is more trouble than it's worth."

Verkan nodded. "I agree, but the outtime trading firms will fight you tooth and claw to keep it open. They're getting more innovations and new products out of the subsector than all the other sectors on Fourth Level combined."

"I know, I know. I had a talk with Executive Councilman Zortan Harn of Management before you came in. He said that we must make every attempt to keep the 'commercial and innovation pipelines flowing,' his words, not mine. Those coonskin hats and that *Davy Crockett* show that spawned them have become the latest craze among the youngsters of Home Time Line. I don't even want to talk about those Superman capes, yo-yos or Mickey Mouse caps!"

Tortha paused to shake his weary head, reminding Verkan of an old hound dog he'd had as a lad when he had served as a drummer boy during the American Civil War. He had joined up with the 13th Pennsylvania Reserves, also known as the bucktails for their habit of wearing a deer tails on their hats—not so different, he guessed, from the coonskin caps of the Crockett craze.

"I know it's not Mickey Mouse ears and coonskin caps that have kept you up all night. What's the problem, Chief?"

"It's a real anomaly, but you've got to promise not to tell that wife of yours about it."

Verkan looked askance. "What do you mean by that, Tortha?"

"It's more of this psychic mumbo jumbo, you know the kind of thing Dalla likes to sink her teeth into and worry to death. You can't have forgotten that Abkor-Neb business, nor this Hartley thing…."

"No, I came this close," he paused to hold out his index finger and thumb which were almost touching, "to losing her to an uprising she single-handedly orchestrated on Abkor-Neb."

"Then you do understand," Tortha replied. "The Bureau of Outtime Intelligence has been keeping a close watch over the entire Europo-American Subsector for the past twenty years."

Verkan nodded; the Bureau of Outtime Intelligence was the office that tried to anticipate outtime wars, political changes, cultural changes and anything else that might disturb trade and extraction elements outtime.

"One of the Bureaus' new 'duties' has been to keep an eye on these 'science-fiction' publications, as they call them. Most of these magazines are pure puffery or adolescent tales filled with derring-do and wish-fulfillment fantasy. However, a few of them contain articles and stories that march awfully damn close to the truth. The premier example is a magazine titled, *Astounding Science Fiction*. Don't be misled by the title; the editor is a top flight amateur theorist and technology booster. Some of the stories that have appeared in this magazine feature time travel as well as travel to alternate worlds. Sound familiar?"

"Yeah, we don't need anyone stumbling onto the truth and finding out that there is a civilization that travels laterally, robbing them of their resources and goods."

"Exactly, the Paratime Secret," Tortha concurred. "Unfortunately, one writer has done more than stumble onto the truth; he's tripped over it, kicked it and thrown it out for everyone to examine. The only good news is that few people—other than a few kooks—take this science-fiction stuff seriously."

"What do you mean, 'stumbled onto the truth'?" Verkan asked.

"In the latest issues of *Astounding* there's a two-part story titled, "Time Crime." Guess what it's about?"

"I have no idea, Chief?"

Tortha scrunched his face up. "It's a retelling of your experience last year with the Wizard Traders right down to the names and events. It's uncanny...."

"You've got to be joking! Who's been talking?"

"No one, Verkan. Those files are under lock and key."

"Then how?" he asked.

"It's even worse than you suspect. The author, H. Beam Piper, even names me, you, Dalla and other Paratimers. It's as if there's some kind of psychic linkage between you and this fellow, Piper."

"You're starting to sound like Dalla, Chief," Verkan said, recoiling. "This is too weird...."

"The Bureau of Outtime Intelligence went back and checked out some earlier *Astounding* issues; they only started this science-fiction magazine oversight operation this year. They found mentions of our operations in three previous issues of *Astounding*; remember the Venusian Nighthound Operation, well, it's all there. And the Hagan Temple fracas, the Abkor-Neb fiasco—them, too."

Verkan shook his head. "Impossible. There are only three people, two of whom are in this room, who know anything about what really happened on Second Level Abkor Neb—"

"I know, I know," Tortha replied, as he puffed away on his cigar.

"What are we going to do about it, Chief? We can't just ignore this and hope it goes away...."

"I was thinking, maybe you ought to meet up with this Piper and see how seriously he takes his own work."

Tortha slotted a data wafer into his visiscreen and a picture of Piper appeared. He was a tall, thin man with a pencil mustache, wearing a nicely cut suit and smoking a pipe. He didn't appear deranged to Verkan. His eyes were dark and sparkled with intelligence.

Tortha continued, "Piper has to have some kind of precognitive gift, but I've never heard of a precog that can cross Paratime time-lines, much less sectors and entire levels! If anyone on his home time-line ever took his stories seriously, it could cause us no end of grief."

"Oh, I get that," Verkan replied. "There are some awfully gullible characters on Europo-American; they even publish flying saucer magazines, about unidentified flying objects, or 'UFOs' as they call them. Plus, Europo-America is rife with conspiracy theorists, like the John Birch Society. They've served us well in the past as covers for various operations, but I'd hate to see them sniff out our trail because of Piper's yarns."

"Yes, it would be an unmitigated disaster."

"How many time-lines are infected with this contagion?" he asked.

Tortha rubbed his jowls before answering. "So far, only one. The Bureau checked a sizeable sample of time-lines with over a hundred different H. Beam Pipers all within a five paraminute area. As you'd expect, most of them are writers with various degrees of success. The most successful

Piper has made a very good living, writing bestselling mysteries. Another specializes in historical fiction and is quite well respected. About a third of them are authors and most work as night watchmen at the car yards of the Pennsylvania Railroad in Altoona, Pennsylvania. Not too far from where that Venusian Nighthound Case took place—"

"You think there's a connection?"

The Chief scrunched up his eyes in thought. "I don't know; it's too nebulous."

"If there's only one of them who has demonstrated this ability, maybe we should just take him out."

Tortha Karf shook his head. "Too drastic; plus, if we disappear him or have him killed, some of his fans—that's what they call most of the readers of these science-fiction stories—might start taking his yarns more seriously. Fans, being short for fanatics, you just can't predict where this might end. Even if it's confined to just one time-line, it's one damn time-line too many."

"I agree," Verkan said. "Besides, we don't have the manpower to check out every single time-line on the Europo-American Subsector. There might be thousands of Pipers, just like this one, exposing our secrets as science fiction! So, Chief, where do you want to go from here?"

"I want you to go to the Piper time-line—that's what we're calling it now—and have a talk with Mr. Piper. You want him to take you seriously, so I suggest you pose as a nuclear engineer who just happens to be on vacation and occasionally reads *Astounding*. These science-fiction writers are always impressed when they're approached by a real working scientist, although more than a few of them are actual scientists and engineers—if you can believe that. I read a few issues of that damn science-fiction magazine and almost got hooked on it myself! That Campbell fellow, editor of *Astounding*, makes some sound observations. We could use him around here!"

"Okay, but you'd better give me a good cover story for Dalla. If she ever pokes her nose into this, who knows where it'll end?"

"By Blaxtha's Beard, you're right. Give me a minute and I'll come up with something...."

II

Verkan took a transtemporal conveyer from First Level to Fourth Level, Tergostar, the Europo-American Altoona equivalent transposition depot. During the journey, Verkan had a hypno-mech dump on the time-line's science fiction magazines, Piper's stories and the field's major works and writers. He wasn't sure how much of this information he'd need to convince Piper that he was a knowledgeable fan, but he was sure it would pay off.

The depot was located in the basement of a large warehouse where he was met by Senior Field Agent, Maldar Dard. After securing the depot they took the stairs to the first floor which was practically empty.

"Not much business going on in there anymore," Verkan stated.

"No, the local railroad company put its faith in the past, or in this case the steam locomotive. Now, they're as out-of-date as horse-drawn buggies. So the shops are mostly empty and the jobs are going or gone."

Verkan nodded. It was common happenstance in areas where technological growth was out of control. The rush towards the future in this subsector made industries and people obsolescent faster than they could be retrained.

Maldar continued, "Tharmax Trading Corporation used to use this time-line for their cigarette imports. They almost lost their Paratime import license over it."

"I remember. It was quite a mess, especially when they started distributing counterfeit petrol coupons during Hitler's War. It looks like they've pretty much closed up shop here."

Maldar nodded. He pointed to some flats piled high with cardboard boxes. "Cigarettes are about all they ship out of here anymore."

Verkan's first impression of downtown Altoona was of a dreary and decaying industrial city that had seen better times. Everything was coated in soot or coal dust, while the streets were surprisingly empty. According to his data dump, the city had been prosperous during the war and shortly thereafter. Now, it was in a deep decline, as the Pennsylvania Railroad tottered towards bankruptcy, which was always a problem with one-industry towns.

"Chief's Assistant, I've reserved you a room at the Penn Alto, the city's premier hotel. But don't expect too much; like everything else in this burg it's seen better days."

"Why the Penn Alto?" Verkan asked.

"It's one of Piper's watering holes. He likes to come to the bar, knows Eddie the bartender quite well. And, it's not too far from here on the corner of 12th Street and 13th Avenue."

"That's confusing."

"No kidding. Whoever laid out this town had a wicked sense of humor."

The inside of the Penn Alto bar was nicer than Verkan had expected, comparable to a similar bar in New York or D.C. on most Europo-America time-lines. They both ordered highballs and found a booth near the back where they could watch the entrance in case Piper came in for a drink.

"It's the middle of the week, so we probably won't see Piper tonight. He works through the weekend and gets the middle of the week off. He usually takes the railroad to New York City and spends time with his new lady friend, Elizabeth Hurst—or Betty, as he calls her."

"You've talked with him?" Verkan probed.

Maldar shook his head. "No, but I've been talking with Jack McGuire, his former friend and writing partner. He's been quite a font of information."

"Tell me about it?"

"Jack's a barely functioning alcoholic. And, like most with this malady, he can't keep his mouth shut."

Verkan nodded. "There's no alcodote or mental reprogramming on this subsector. Alcoholism can be a real problem."

"It is in this guy's case. Apparently, the two of them had some kind of row over a gun McGuire *borrowed* from Piper's apartment without asking first. When Piper found out about it, he cut McGuire off."

"I don't blame him," Verkan said.

"Nor do I. I think Piper was already fed up with McGuire; all he does is whine about his job at a local school and all the problems some of the kids are giving him. Still, at one time he and Piper were good friends; they collaborated on a number of yarns, although most of them still haven't sold.

He says that Piper's head-over-heels in love with a new lady, living in New York. 'No fool, like an old fool,' to quote Jack."

"He's probably said the same thing to Piper; no wonder they're not getting along. Did McGuire tell you anything about Piper's writing?"

"He described how they worked out ideas together with a couple of friends and how he usually got stuck with writing the first draft. Then Piper would come along and give the story the final polish that would make it salable. McGuire's unhappy that so many of their stories never sold, and I believe he blames Piper for it—'he's too damn fussy!' It appears McGuire could use the money, too."

"Did he give you any hint as to how Piper comes up with his story ideas?"

"Not really. McGuire mentioned that Piper spends a lot of alone time late at night in the Pennsy railyards as a guard. He often uses this time to worry out story lines. When I asked him about 'Time Crime,' McGuire just shook his head. I think he was upset that Piper didn't ask him to work on it with him."

"Piper appears to hold his cards close to his vest."

"Yes," Maldar concurred. "He's an odd duck; a life-long bachelor who lives with his ninety-year-old mother. McGuire thought it was amusing that Piper has been seeing this New York gal for almost a year, and still hasn't told his mother about her."

"Hmm. Maybe Piper's keeping the romance to himself. That way there won't be any embarrassing questions if things don't work out. There were times during my first companionate marriage to Dalla where I wished I hadn't told anyone, either. You should have heard old Tortha give me the business when we broke up!"

"I notice he's been a lot more reticent since the two of you got back together."

"Yeah, I think he's grown to like Dalla, or at least appreciate her more. And, Dalla's grown up a lot, too. It looks like the only thing left to do is to question Piper himself."

III

Verkan Vall had Senior Field Agent Maldar stake out the Piper residence, a second story apartment, at 35 Wordsworth Avenue. It wasn't until Thursday night that Verkan learned Piper had returned from New York. They discussed the best way to meet him face to face in Verkan's room at the Penn Alto Hotel.

"Do you think it's wise to let him see you?" Maldar asked.

"Oh, you think he might recognize me from his visions, or whatever it is he's tapping into."

"Yes, I do. I studied the background you brought and read the stories, too; Piper seems to have you, Dalla, Ranthar and Chief Tortha down pretty well. His attention to detail is excellent; I only wish most of our field agents were as observant."

"Good point, Maldar." Verkan paused to mentally run through the published Paratime stories. "I don't recall any mention of you."

"No, I wasn't involved in any of those cases."

"Then maybe you should be the one to interrogate him at the bar. Do you think he'll be there tonight?"

"I've been shadowing Piper for three ten-days. I've noticed he usually comes here to meet with friends or have a few drinks after one of his New York sojourns. I've seen his fiancée and Betty's quite attractive. I'm not sure what she thinks about their bi-city romance, but, when they're together, they're like a couple of teenagers in love."

"Has Piper been writing much?"

"No, I gave his agent, Harry Altshuler, a call last time I was in New York City. I claimed I was going to be the editor of a new science-fiction magazine, 'Wondrous Stories,' and I was looking for some good writers."

"I like it," Verkan enthused. "Although I'm glad you didn't try to contact John W. Campbell; I understand he's a pretty sharp bird.

"Me, too. I mentioned to Altshuler that my friend Fred Pohl—Piper's former agent—had suggested I give him a call. He gave me a list of his clients who wrote science fiction, including H. Beam Piper. I told him I was specifically interested in Piper and his agent pointed out that he was writing mostly mystery stories, but could be convinced to do more science fiction. Then, he tried to sell me on a couple of his other writers who he claimed were more prolific. I suspect, of late, Piper hasn't been writing much."

"Probably not. I bet he has his mind on closer interests, like his new lady friend, which may solve our problem. Let's take the elevator down and see if Piper shows up tonight."

The Penn Alto bar was much busier than it had been the night before, probably because it was closer to the weekend, a local semi-holiday. Many of the inhabitants of Europo-American didn't divide the year up by ten-days like the Home Time-Liners did. The local measurement for time here was: day, week, month and year—all based on the life and death of an obscure Jewish carpenter who had been elevated to godhood. The only thing more dangerous than a woman seeking revenge over an adulterous affair was a true believer in some cockamamie religion. One of the reasons religions of any kind were outlawed on Home Time Line.

IV

Verkan took his usual seat in front of the Chief's horseshoe-shaped desk. Chief Tortha was engrossed in something on his viewscreen and didn't look up for a few minutes. Verkan took the time to review his findings on the Piper Case.

The Chief looked up, and reared back. "Why didn't you say something, Vall? Let me know you were here."

Verkan took a moment to take a cigarette out of its pack, a Chesterfield, and light up. "I didn't want to disturb your concentration, Chief."

Tortha shook his head. "Nothing important, just some budgetary figures from Accounting. Say, you're back early. What did you learn about the Piper paradox?"

"That's a good way to put it. I think we can safely file it as closed."

"What do you mean 'closed?'"

"Well, I had Maldar Dard question Piper—"

"I thought you were going to take care of that," Tortha interrupted.

"I was until Maldar brought up the fact that Piper described me, you and Dalla in his stories, and that he very likely would recognize me the moment we met."

"By The Pits of Kunargh! That would have been grounds for instant termination.'

"Exactly, and this Piper's savvy enough he might have caused a fuss before we could isolate him, since I was going to meet with him in a public place.... Fortunately, Maldar pointed this problem out well before I left my hotel room."

"Good. This Maldar is pretty sharp. Why is he still a field agent?"

"Senior Field Agent, Chief. He's a field agent because he hates paperwork and prefers to work in the field; I don't blame him. Otherwise, he'd have been promoted to Inspector decades ago."

"I get it, but we could use more inspectors like him."

"Before meeting Piper, we did some research on his financials. He's a part-timer at the Pennsylvania Railroad—or Pennsy, as the locals call it—and doesn't make much money at the best of times. The only reason he's able to survive at all is that he lives with his mother, who has a small pension. Harriet Piper also takes care of the housework and makes sure he eats. The future does not appear bright for Mr. Piper; it appears the Pennsy is about to lay off most of its employees. The car shops will take a big hit."

Tortha nodded. "You don't need guards to protect worthless property and railroad engines."

"Nor does it help that Piper's not writing these days."

"Do you think he's expecting his new wife to help out?"

Verkan shook his head. "This Piper is almost pathologically independent. He'd most likely work as a ditch-digger before he'd let his new wife support him. However, he does have a world-class gun collection that should keep him afloat for a while."

"If he'd deign to sell them," Tortha added.

"Exactly. Anyway, Maldar interviewed Piper and used my cover as a science-fiction fan passing through town. He presented himself as a nuclear scientist from Los Alamos. He and Piper 'opened a bag of talk,' as Piper likes to put it. It turns out there's a good reason Piper hasn't written any new Paratime stories lately. It seems that John W. Campbell almost didn't buy 'Time Crime.' He told Piper that he was no longer interested in his police procedural stories; he wanted something dealing with psionics—it seems that's his latest preoccupation, or hobby horse, as they'd say on Europo-American. Campbell told Piper that unless he can come up with a new slant, he doesn't want to see any more of his Paratime stories."

"Well, that's good to hear," Tortha said.

"I had Maldar miked and listened in on their conversation and found myself liking the guy. Piper's a gun enthusiast, as well as a hunter and outdoorsman."

"That's all well and good, Vall. But, did he say anything about how he came up with those Paratime yarns?"

"Yes, it seems they came to him while he was sleeping. He believes they were dreams, not anything real. His subconscious working overtime."

"Phew! Did any of his other stories come to him as dreams?"

Verkan shook his head. "No, just the Paratime stories. He doesn't appear to put any significance to that fact. Now that Campbell isn't interested in them anymore, Piper's lost interest as well. So, I think we can safely put this case to rest."

Tortha nodded. "Just as long as Piper doesn't come up with a 'new slant.'"

"Good point."

"If he does, you know what that means?"

"Right," Verkan said. "Find a way to discarnate him that won't trigger an investigation."

"Yes, for a starving writer, suicide's always a good option."

THE TRANSTEMPORAL MAN

John F. Carr

I

1959 A.D.

Armathan looked around in despair at the unfamiliar men dressed in long white robes, with alternating red and blue stripes, and the black-robed women with veils covering their faces. Where in Fythnar's name was he now? This was no place he'd ever *jumped* before; the tongue spoken here resembled nothing so much as the rasping noise of a metal file being dragged over a whetstone.

Dressed in brown trousers and tunic—outlandish dress to these folks; he could tell by the glances and glares thrown his way—he was already attracting too much notice.

Attention was a very bad thing; it could get a man killed, or put away.

He looked around for an alleyway or vacant stall to hide in. He had arrived in a marketplace in the center of a small town. He was surrounded by booths and stalls filled with household wares, jewelry, leather goods and cooking foods. Most of the goods were simple handcrafted items.

It had been a long time since he'd been on a world with machines that ran on iron rails and sailed the seas. What world had he materialized on this time?

A young boy in a dark robe brushed up against him and he felt fingers light as feathers passing over his pockets, searching for a purse or bag of coins. From long habit, his hand snaked out and grabbed the boy's wrist, jerking it hard enough that he heard the crack of snapping bones.

The boy screamed, turned and ran away cradling his arm.

More eyes peered at him, some with accusation. A tall man spewed out a mouthful of dissonant sounds ending on a questioning note. Soon the "officials" would be notified and he'd be escorted to a dark holding cell. He already knew its every dank corner, smell and stink. Even in the bright overhead sun he could feel its chill penetrating through his muscles to the bone underneath.

A man wearing a blue robe, with a black beard, topped by a red fez pushed through the growing crowd and approached him, jabbering questions in their foreign tongue. He knew the drill: The question he needed answered was: What role would he play in *this* world? Idiot, madman, sage from a far-off land, possessed by the gods, deaf and dumb, or the lost stranger? He'd played them all at one time or another: When you never knew when or where you might suddenly be taken away and dropped off in a strange land, you learned to cultivate many identities. He could do elementary healing, carpentry, silversmithing, tanning and lock-breaking.

One also learned to carry a fat purse, as well as sew gold threads into his garments, for when things got *really* bad.

This looked like one of those times. His last four *jumps*—which is what he called them for lack of any other term—had been to worlds where he knew the tongues and could communicate. It was too much to ask the gods for such good fortune to continue. If only he knew why he *jumped.*

The man in blue with the solid line of black eyebrow and tombstone-shaped white teeth was insistent. Armathan needed time...to think, to plan—

Now the man in the blue robe was pointing. Where: To jail? To that section of town reserved for strangers and foreigners? To the local house for the insane?

The official wrapped his fingers around his bicep and began to lead him away. Several boys in the crowd made catcalls and peacock-like screeches. He tried desperately to organize his thoughts and come up with a plan.

He yanked his arm out of the man in blue's grasp, elbowed him "accidentally" in the eye—and began to throw a fit in the dirt streets. Faces loomed over him. Then he saw a blue arm with a club coming down and drew his knees up to his chest. He felt a blow on the leg, another to his ribs; he flipped over. Suddenly there was a terrible pain at the back of his head—

II

Paratime Police Chief Tortha Karf, with a cigar jutting out of his mouth, was sitting behind his desk staring blankly at a Tri-D photograph depicting a High Shaman of Fasif on his office wall titled, "The Sacrifice of Fasif," when Verkan Vall came into the Chief's office.

Verkan Vall thought it was a tawdry picture: it featured a crimson-faced priest, with sharpened and blackened teeth, about to plunge a crystal dagger into the chest of a young maiden thrown naked over a large obsidian block. On some time-lines it might have passed as the cover to some cheap space opera novel.

Tortha had told him that he'd taken the photo as a young undercover Paratime Police operative attempting to find the whereabouts of a malfunctioning conveyer of First Level tourists who had been mistakenly whisked to Second Level Khiftan Sector. This was where he had found the first one; in fact, he'd arrived too late to do anything more than take a picture of the horrific scene.

It didn't help the young girl, but he'd taken the priest captive and tortured him until he revealed the location of the other twenty-three tourists. The irony was that this was the case that had made the Chief's bones in the Department and a semi-legend among those field agents who'd spent any time at all on Second Level Khiftan Sector—the nastiest outtime sector the Paratime Police had surveyed in ten thousand years. Rumor had it that Tortha had fallen half-in-love with an image of the girl before he'd found her; the truth was far less romantic.

Verkan Vall was seated before Paratime Police Chief Tortha Karf's horseshoe desk at his office in the Paratime Building on First Level. As Special Chief's Assistant, one of his duties was to go over the previous ten-day's cold cases with the Chief. Today it was One-Eight-One Day and there were five red-flagged cases of paratemporal displacement, which happened when two paratemporal conveyers met unexpectedly going in opposite "directions." Their transposition fields would interpenetrate and briefly weaken; occasionally, when this happened, the conveyers involved would pick up objects or hitchhikers—sometimes hostile. It was why Paratimers kept weapons at hand and why all conveyers were checked in detail upon materializing at the First Level depots.

It could be a serious problem, say in the case of a Fourth Level, Europo-American physicist pickup landing on Second Level Triplanetary Empire, where interplanetary space travel was taken for granted. Once the language issue was resolved, when one and one added up to three; the Paratime Secret would be out—and then their problems would multiply geometrically. That was just one of the many problems that bedeviled the Paratime Police, whose primary mission was to keep the secret of Paratime travel inviolate.

The Paratime Police's other job was keeping the outtimers safe from Home Time Line predators and con artists. They were still clearing up an outtime slaving operation, the Wizard Traders, that had reached its tentacles all the way into the Home Time Line's ruling body—the Executive Council. Axiom Number One: If a culture was to be a successful parasite it had to protect its victims; and their culture had survived for ten thousand years, siphoning off labor, resources, machinery, products, entertainment products, cultural treasures and rare works of art.

Keeping track of outtime pickups, and sometimes even discorporating them, was all part of the job.

"We had another pickup, off Fourth Level Europo-American, Anglo-Columbian Belt—"

"Which Subsector is that one?" Tortha asked. Even the Chief, after a lifetime of overseeing the Paratime Police, was unfamiliar with many of the minor trading subsectors and their belts.

"It's an off-shoot of the Hispano-Columbian Subsector; in this Belt, instead of Columbus discovering America for Queen Isabella; he did it for Henry the Seventh of England. The predominant Anglo civilization there is post-mechanical and quite advanced in some areas, very backward in others. When our conveyers interpenetrated they picked up a young boy, approximately eight to ten—"

He heard the squawk of the intercom as the Chief's secretary tried to make an announcement, but before he could get a word out—a whoosh of air announced they had a visitor, Verkan's wife, Hadron Dalla.

"Hi, boys. Chief, is the coffee fresh?"

That was like asking a surgeon if his scalpel was sharp.

Tortha Karf nodded and said, "A fresh pot, Jamaican Blue Mountain beans."

One of Verkan's first jobs as Chief's Assistant had been to ensure that Tortha's five-pound bags of fresh Blue Mountain beans were transposed—regardless of political insurrections, economic downturns, or even poor harvests—every ten-day from the Fourth Level, Europo-American time-line where they were grown on a plantation selected in person by the Chief over a century ago.

While Dalla was filling a mug with the Paratime Police insignia on the front (two black crossed figure-eights—signifying infinity signs—inside a red circle), he asked, "What brings you into the Chief's office today?"

She held up a flimsy. "I just got this transmission from the Rhogom Foundation and I thought I should share it with you both."

Dalla was a Doctor of Psychic Science and only a few years ago—after her study on reincarnation on the Second Level Akor-Neb Sector—had been made a Fellow of the Rhogom Memorial Foundation of Psychic Science. She had completed her doctorate during the period after their divorce, before they both grew up about twenty-five years ago. A big advantage of being a member of a long-lived race was that you had time to learn from both your youthful indiscretions and the passage of time. One thing

Verkan had learned was how much he loved Dalla and how important it was to have her in his life again.

It was also nice being able to share the same work; a recent development due to her involvement in the Wizard Traders' affair, when Dalla narco-hyped some suspects and provided a few crucial insights that led to a big break in the case. In gratitude for her service, Chief Tortha had appointed Dalla as the Chief's Assistant, Special Assistant in the Department of Paratime Police.

"What's that, Dalla?" Tortha asked, looking up from his viewscreen. The Chief was over three hundred years old and coming to the end of middle age; he still had most of his hair although it was thinning in front and now all gray. He was a big man with a body like an oak barrel with too much wine, but still stronger than many men half his age.

"It's a report on an outtimer who the Foundation calls the 'Transposition Man.'"

"What's that mean?" Verkan asked, his interest piqued.

"It's the first I've heard about him," Dalla reported. "From what this transmission says, he's an outtimer on a Fourth Level Indus-Ganges-Irrawaddy Sector, Indo-Mauryan Subsector who has somehow been able to transpose himself from one time-line to another. Just from my reading of it, I'd say he's been flagged by the Rhogom Foundation for quite some time. I'll need to go out to the Foundation to access their secure files to learn the whole story."

"Can you do that?" Tortha asked, looking impressed.

"I can, now that I'm a Foundation Fellow," Dalla replied. "There shouldn't be any restrictions on my access pass."

"I take it, Dalla, the Regents don't know you've recently joined the Department."

Dalla shook her head. "No, and I don't know what the Board of Regents will do when they find out, but I don't believe they'll be amused. When you first offered me the position, I did some checking at the Records Division and couldn't locate any precedent."

There was a long history of tension between the Rhogom Memorial Foundation of Psychic Science and the Department of Paratime Police, usually over matters of jurisdiction. About twelve thousand years before, when Ghaldron was attempting to work up a spacewarp drive for interstellar travel, Hesthor was working out how to develop linear time-travel to go back to a time before their ancestors had despoiled the planet. Between pollution and depletion of resources, things had gotten desperate and First Level civilization was in danger of collapse.

Rhogom, a few centuries earlier, had tried to explain the presence of precognition with a theory of multidimensional time. Hesthor had read some of Rhogom's papers and when he'd learned what Ghaldron was working on, he contacted him and together they discovered Paratemporal Transposition, the ability to travel between an almost infinite number of worlds of alternate probability. There was a near infinity of time-lines, all on the same planet and each needing to be policed.

Once Paratemporal Transposition was discovered, the First Level race began to send its conveyers to this near-infinity of parallel worlds, bringing wealth and unlimited resources back to Home Time Line. Over the course of twelve thousand years, First Level civilization developed a parasitic culture so nearly perfect that the host worlds never suspected its existence. This was the Paratime Secret, Home Time Line's one vulnerability and the Paratime Police's primary mission. If this secret were to be exposed, the very existence of the First Level race would be in jeopardy—to say nothing of the anger and devastation that knowledge of their millennia of plundering would cause the populations of billions of host worlds.

When it didn't interfere with their primary duty, the Paratime Police also tried to prohibit flagrantly immoral conduct by First Level traders, tourists, observers, criminals and out-and-out fools. It was a difficult job, and it sometimes seemed the Paratime Police spent more time covering up dislocations than apprehending and punishing wrongdoers.

Second Level had been civilized almost as long as the First, but there had been dark-age interludes. A few Second Level civilizations had developed technologically above First Level, such as Second Level Gryphyx Sector where they had colonized distant worlds. Except for paratemporal transposition, most of its sectors equaled First Level, and from many, Home Time Line had learned much. The Third Level civilizations were more recent, but still of respectable antiquity and advancement.

Fourth Level was the biggest level. It was divided into a number of sector groups based on where human civilization had first reappeared. There were four major sector groups: Nilo-Mesopotamian, Indus-Ganges-Irrawaddy, Yangtze-Mekong and Andean-Mississippi-Valley of Mexico. The Nilo-Mesopotamian Sector Group, the largest, was the home of Europo-American, Alexandrian-Roman, Sino-Assyrian, Macedonian Empire Sectors and so many others they hadn't had the time in ten thousand years to visit them all.

Fifth Level was the most backward level; on a few sectors, early hominids, speechless and fireless, were barely eking out a grim existence. On most of Fifth Level nothing even vaguely humanoid had appeared. It was on Fifth Level Industrial Service Sector that Home Time Line produced most of their finished heavy machine goods that couldn't be easily stolen outtime. The proles who did the work were the survivors of calamities and wars on Fourth Level, particularly primitives just out of Stone Age savagery. They were transposed en masse to the Service Sector time-lines.

Fifth Level was also home to the Paratime Police Terminal, where a duplicate of Paratime Police Headquarters had been built. Police Terminal was covered with transposition depots at the site of every major city, town and important junction that existed on every major Level and Sector within Paratime, enabling the Paratime Police to transpose to any place they were needed.

Despite the practical applications of its research, the Rhogom Foundation of Psychic Science had continued to focus its resources and energies into psychic and telepathic research. Their studies into the paranormal had been anchored in their developments and studies of normal and abnormal psychology, making them the premier institute on First Level for studies on the human mind, psychic or otherwise. Possibly due to its sporadic nature, most of their investigations into psychic research, telepathy, precognition and telekinesis, had been tenuous at best, and in most of his fellow officers' minds a waste of resources—certainly, that was Tortha Karf's view.

Verkan wasn't so sure, especially after Dalla's researches into reincarnation on the Second Level Akor-Neb Sector.

"What else is in that report on the Transtemporal Man?" he asked.

"His name is Armathan and it is believed that he was born on Fourth Level Indo-Mauryan, Gupta Empire Belt about forty-two or three years ago," Dalla said. "What makes him unique is that he has the ability to make transtemporal transpositions without a conveyer."

"You don't mean that he transposes with his mind?" Tortha asked, his bushy gray-streaked eyebrows raised in an arc.

"No one knows for certain," Dalla replied. "That's the best conclusion the Rhogom Foundation has been able to come up with. But, Chief, just think of it—if we could mentally transpose ourselves, we could go to any time-line anywhere, any time."

The Chief's usually pink face was as white as a sheet. "Is everybody at that bloody Foundation a complete moron? This "—he paused a moment to use his First Level total recall—"Armathan could unwittingly spill the Paratime Secret at any moment. Didn't anyone over there ever think about that and maybe, just maybe, think of contacting us?"

Dalla shook her head. "Chief, as soon as I read the transmission, it struck me that it might be a Paratime Code violation, but that's only because I'm working for the Department. Over at Foundation headquarters they have a different outlook. They see the Department as a hindrance, at best—an enemy, at worst. Let me see what I can learn at the Rhogom Foundation Library and Research Department."

"Dalla, as of this moment, you're cleared from all current assignments," the Chief replied. "I want you to take a strato-rocket over to the Foundation headquarters this afternoon."

"Yes, Chief," Dalla replied with a mock salute.

Tortha Karf frowned. "I'm serious, Dalla. This may be the most important case you'll ever work on."

Dalla turned her shapely backside and left the Chief's office.

"Now, Verkan, what about this pickup off the Anglo-Columbian Belt you were telling me about?"

III

Armathan came to slowly; the back of his head felt as if it had been caved in. He felt something moving, when he turned his head, at the back of his skull. His thoughts kept fading in and out; he'd been hit in the head before—but never this hard... *Maybe I'll die this time,* he thought. It would be a blessing from the gods.

He slowly opened his eyes; it was difficult as they were crusted and everything was blurred. He tried to move his hands to clear them, but his arms were tied down—or paralyzed!

His heart began to race and he felt his mind descending into the darkness again. *Stop it!* he commanded. Slowly his pulse slowed and he noticed that the small room, almost a cell, was whitewashed. Prison cells were usually made of stones or bricks—

They've put me in a madhouse again, Armathan thought bitterly. The last time, seven cycles ago, that he'd been put into one of these asylums it had taken him a whole cycle to learn the language well enough before he could talk his way into freedom. Less than a moon later, he'd *jumped* again. But he still didn't know why. However, he did know that as long as he was incarcerated or an inmate of an asylum, he never *jumped.* It was as if one of the gods were using him as a game piece, or in some pattern that was indecipherable to him.

Did the gods want him to spend his life as a prisoner? Had he committed some heinous crime in a past life?

Armathan tried to push away the black cloud that threatened to engulf his mind. The problem now was that he knew his future only too well. He would either die of his injuries, or they would isolate him for a moon or two, then try some outlandish treatments. He remembered the time they dunked him in cold water every morning, as if the shock would awaken him from his madness....

Of course, he'd undergone worse; he remembered the one world where they'd bled him with leeches until he could barely stand without falling. Another time in a more advanced world they'd put some kind of "electrical" device over his head and shocked him unconscious; that was the worst. He still had problems remembering how and when he'd jumped into that world. It was only when one of the attendants took pity on his feeble attempts to communicate and started working with him that he'd ever gotten a chance to demonstrate his dilemma.

But he had been younger and stronger then, too. Not injured. All the beatings, the harsh treatment, the starvation and long-term isolation had taken its toll. When he was anxious now, his heart would beat like a drum—sometimes it wouldn't stop for a long time, or miss beats. This was not good. He might die here, with no one to care, or even notice....

The sad part was that he could no longer remember his parents' faces, or even his wife's. Once, he'd actually stayed in one place long enough to build a business, find and court a wife—even sire two children, both boys—the gods be praised! Where were they now? What happened to them after he *jumped*? He hoped they weren't cursing him for deserting them.

It was a good thing they had him strapped down to the bed. He might have hurt himself otherwise: *Death, what sweet oblivion. If only I had more courage....*

IV

When Dalla arrived at her desk at the Paratime Building the next morning there was a note on her visiscreen with a red tag reading:

Dalla, come to my office at once! Chief Tortha.

Dalla took the antigrav shaft to the Chief's office. For the first time since she'd met him, Chief Tortha actually rose to his feet as she entered his office. "What did you find out?" he asked, waving his cigar with his right hand.

She started to speak, but he interrupted. "I'd better get Verkan in to hear this—or did you fill him in last night?"

Dalla shook her head. "I didn't get back from Thalna-Jarvizar until after Vall was asleep. He was already gone when I arose this morning."

The Chief called Verkan's office and she got a fresh cup of coffee for herself, Verkan and Tortha while they were waiting. Verkan strode into the office, took the mug of coffee Dalla proffered and asked, "What's up, Chief?"

"Dalla's going to bring us up-to-date about her visit to the Rhogom Foundation. I wanted you to hear it firsthand. Dalla?"

"I arrived at the Foundation at 13:40 and, as a Fellow of the Foundation, I didn't have any trouble accessing the secure files on Armathan: Code Name—*The Transtemporal Man*. His first appearance was twenty-four years ago." She reeled off the shorthand symbols for the particular Fourth Level Indo-Mauryan Subsector, Gupta Empire Belt time-line. "He was a young man, estimated age between seventeen and nineteen.

"Armathan was first noted by Tandrath Dorn, a trader for a small out-time trading firm, Varnax Novelties, who actually saw him vanish in the middle of a transaction at his market stall. His disappearance raised quite a fuss locally and Tandrath stayed there an extra ten-day waiting to see if he'd return. He didn't, and Tandrath, who's an Associate Member, reported it in a message ball to the Foundation." Associate Members were people sympathetic to the Foundation's goals of psychic research and reported suspected outtime parapsychological events. In most cases, these volunteers were the Paratime eyes and ears of the Rhogom Foundation.

"The boy's leave-taking caused quite a sensation in the small town of Hagtha, where he was raised," she said. "Tandrath was able to pick up the lad's local history. His father was a tanner and Armathan was the second son of four. He was an apprentice tanner and a reliable worker—not prone to flights of fancy, excess drinking or sudden disappearances. The family was devastated by his disappearance as well as the rumors of witchcraft running through the town.

"When Tandrath returned to Home Time Line, they had him do a visual recall under narco-hypnosis and had an artist draw a reconstruction of the lad to send everyone who traveled to the Gupta Empire Belt. He wasn't identified for another four years; he was on another Gupta time-line less than a parasecond from the first. There he was identified again and once again vanished before the Foundation could intervene. This time the Associate informed the Foundation immediately and agents were sent out to all the time-lines within thirty paraseconds of the time-line he disappeared from. They were cautioned not to approach him directly as it seems the associates might be somehow responsible for his transposing."

"That's going to make him as slippery as a greased eel to catch," Verkan said.

"Somehow he dropped off the Foundation's screens for about ten years," Dalla said. "One of their agents located him, but he transposed again! The agent met with him at Armathan's silverware shop several times before he vanished. So it wasn't the agent's presence that caused the transposition as the Foundation had suspected."

"Maybe he caught on that he was being watched," Tortha remarked, "and transposed himself to lose the agent tailing him."

"I don't believe so," Dalla said. "The agent was acting as a customer; in fact, originally he was. Our boy's a very talented silversmith. Furthermore, this time Armathan left behind a wife and two sons; he had a local reputation as a good father and provider. His family was quite grief-stricken and stood to lose everything when he disappeared."

Dalla paused to shake her head in disgust: "Women are forbidden ownership of property throughout most of the Gupta Belt. Armathan would have known that voluntarily transposing would leave his family destitute. Besides, he had his own silver shop and was doing quite well."

"I agree, it doesn't sound like he left voluntarily," Verkan reflected.

Tortha didn't look convinced.

"The family was distraught," Dalla said. "That was the last time Armathan was observed until this latest sighting about a ten-day ago. This time the Associate was under orders not to approach him or do anything he might think is suspicious. But something happened; he disappeared in the town square—gone."

"Twenty-four years!" Chief Tortha shouted, no longer able to restrain his temper. "That's how long the Foundation has known about this Armathan. Wind heads, all of them. Too damn smart for their own good, I tell you. Not a word of this to the Department.... If this Armathan is ever transposed to—say, one of the Fourth Level Europo-American time-lines, where time travel and alternate worlds are not completely suspect; well, I don't need to tell you what might happen once he started to blab about all the 'worlds' he's been in with details so complete that only a cross-time traveler would know them... Whoosh—there goes the Paratime secret!"

"Then, Chief, you believe that he is able to achieve Paratemporal Transposition with just his mind?" Dalla asked.

"I don't know and don't care. The important thing is that somehow Armathan has found a way to travel between alternate time-lines by some mechanism we haven't yet identified; I'll leave it to the researchers to answer the question of how. As for his impact on this Department, he is the greatest threat to the Paratime Secret I've encountered in over two hundred and fifty years with the Paratime Police!"

"What are we going to do about it?" Verkan asked.

"Find out where he's transposed, locate him and terminate him as quickly as possible," Tortha replied.

"You can't do that!" Dalla cried. "He's possibly the most marvelous psychic we've ever encountered! We need to find him and study how he transposes between time-lines."

"The Pits of Kunargh, we do! We need to put an end to Armathan's transposing before he inadvertently blows the whole Paratime shebang. The last thing we need are civilians popping in and out of time-lines like kangaroos."

Dalla turned to Verkan. "What do you think?"

"The Chief's right. We need to discorporate him as soon as possible."

"The two of you! You're both as stubborn as a couple of priests of Fasif." She turned and stormed out of the office.

"You don't think she'll do anything stupid do you?" Tortha asked.

Verkan shook his head. "Ten years ago, yes. But Dalla's grown up a lot in the last decade. Almost getting her head shot off on the Akor-Neb Sector was a big learning experience."

"Yes, but she's still a Fellow of the Rhogom Foundation."

"She may be rooting for them privately, Chief, but she won't violate any Department rules."

"If she does, old son, it's on your head!"

V

Verkan was sitting frozen in a trance state on his favorite recliner in their apartment, reminding Dalla of nothing so much as the Holy Man, Ramana Chandara, she had once interviewed during a two ten-day stay at an ashram on Fourth Level Indus-Ganges-Irrawaddy Sector Vedanta Subsector, Advaita Belt.

On this Belt the Pandyan Empire had extended itself from Central Asia all the way into Europe and the caste-bound culture had remained in a state of cultural paralysis for the last millennium. Technology was stuck at the pre-mechanical state. Poverty and large families were endemic; the land was so overpopulated that ritual mass suicide of elders, every Year-End Day, was all but mandatory in large over-populated areas of India and China.

There it was believed that the most holy of the Sadhus and Swamis, who followed the cults of Shakta on Fourth Level Advaita, were able to periodically dematerialize out of thin air.

Dalla had received a grant from the Rhogom Foundation to travel to Benares near the Ganges River to Chandaraji's ashram, where she'd planted several spy-eyes on the Sadhu's private sanctorum to see if he did truly dematerialize—other than on the spiritual plane. Her cameras had actually shown him vanishing, blurring, then—suddenly gone. This happened on four separate occasions during her stay.

Unfortunately, Chandaraji could not dematerialize at will: he explained his disappearance with a bunch of gobbledygook about the will of the gods and breaking the veil of the Maya that made no sense on *her* plane of existence. In the end, Dalla was unable to determine the triggering event, which was either a mental or physical state. One day she hoped to return and complete her studies.

At the moment, Verkan was as motionless and expressionless as any Sadhu or Rishis she'd ever seen. If she hadn't known him better, she'd have thought he was still mad at her for her outburst in the Chief's office.

Suddenly, he looked up and shook his head, like a surfacing seal, and said, "I think I've got it."

Finally, she thought to herself. He isn't any fun when he's in this state.

"Fact: we know for a certainty that Armathan has been paratemporally transposed on seven recorded occasions to seven different time-lines, even if they were located within the same Fourth Level Indo-Mauryan Gupta Empire Belt. We have reason, due to his long and unexplained absences, to believe that he has transposed himself on numerous other occasions. We also know that on not one observable occasion did he have access to a trans-temporal conveyer or other means of mechanical transposition.

"Therefore, he has somehow been born with or mentally developed the ability to move cross-time to one time-line or another by himself—without any physical or material aids. The question now is: How?

"Fact: we know that he has no conscious control over his ability, or he would not continually transpose himself into places where he neither knows anyone or how to speak the language, often finding himself placed in jail cells or institutions for the insane.

"Therefore, there must be an outside catalyst or stimulus that causes his Paratemporal transposing. We know it isn't one of the Home Time Liners who occasionally meet with him, or he would have transposed himself immediately to First Level. Now, all we need to do is isolate this catalyst and maybe we'll have our clue as to how and where he will transpose next."

"That's good, Verkan. You've narrowed down the variables and clarified the problem, but we still don't have a solution."

"Well, Dalla, you're the intuitive one in the family; I'm looking for you to come up with the answer."

She smiled. "Don't put all that responsibility on my shoulders. Still, there has to be one thing in common on all those time-lines, something that unknowingly triggers his jumps. For a while, the Foundation thought it might be his proximity to other Paratimers from First Level, but we had to rule that out when one Associate was actually able to interview him several times. Unfortunately, their talks were cut short when Armathan transposed again before our agent could build up enough trust to get any answers."

"Was the agent present when he transposed?"

"No," Dalla answered. "It was a few days after one of their visits."

"Why didn't he just narco-hypnotize him and question him then?"

"Armathan was in a jail cell and our man, who presented himself as a wealthy family member, was unable to visit him without supervision. By the time he'd paid enough bribes, Armathan had vanished from that time-line."

Verkan shook his head. "Amateurs. If the Paratime Police had been involved, we would have isolated him, discretely removed him from jail and dispatched him immediately to First Level."

"Or you would have disincarnated him," she said angrily.

"Dalla, we've already argued this out last night! Our first duty as Paratime Police officers is to obey the Prime Directive. Once the Paratime Secret gets out, there will be no stopping it. It will end life as we know it on First Level, and elsewhere."

She shrugged. "I still think the importance of the Transtemporal Man's gift far outweighs the danger."

"You're not the only one. Somehow the Rhogom Foundation has learned of our involvement...." Verkan looked questioningly at his wife.

Dalla shook her head. "I'm not the leak! Unless they've tagged the files I was requesting and someone upstairs knew I'd been admitted to the Department and put two and two together."

"Regardless, Director Volzar Darv contacted the Chairman of the Paratime Commission and Armathan's fate is now in the hands of the Commission. It's up to them to determine whether or not we discorporate him."

"Well, I feel better," she said.

"Eliminating him would have solved the problem and he wouldn't still be a threat to the Paratime Secret."

"I just wish I'd known about this case earlier."

"You probably wouldn't have done anything," Verkan said. "You were always a contrarian."

Dalla frowned. "Maybe because I didn't understand; I used to think this whole Paratime Secret business was overemphasized, a way for the Paratime Police to keep their budget high. Now I know better—"

"I'm glad it's finally sunk in. Are we good?"

"For now, until the Paratime Commission comes up with a ruling." Dalla knew in the past she wouldn't have been able to drop it. Even now the injustice of disincarnating Armathan, just because he could transpose from one time-line to another, still rankled, but there was a lot riding on her husband's shoulders and Verkan needed her support.

"Great," Verkan replied. "Now, if you can just use that famous intuition of yours to come up with a clue as to how he transposes without a conveyer."

She shook her head. "I'm sorry Vall, but I'm not getting any kind of a clue. Maybe it's some sort of atmospheric condition, or ground vibration—like how some animals respond just before an earthquake."

"That's good. You're thinking out of the circle. Vibration, I like that. Maybe it is something physical in the environment."

"I can link up to the Foundation's computer and see what that gives us."

"Does our office computer have enough capacity?" he asked.

"No, I'll have to go to headquarters and use one of their big machines. Even for such a limited sample of Fourth Level time-lines, there will be umpteen-millions of time-lines. And most of them probably won't have detailed weather and physical histories."

"That sounds like a dead-end. I know there aren't that many heavily exploited time-lines."

She shook her head. "Almost all of these Indo-Mauryan time-lines are at the pre-mechanical development stage and are merely exploited for handicrafts and primitive artworks. The ruling governments are primarily backed by a theocracy that encourages spiritual advancement at the expense of technical innovation or advancement—similar to Indo-Turanian. The outfits that work these places are small firms; bottom feeders, that move materials from one line to another, hoping to find something that they can cash in on. Still, it's worth noting that Armathan keeps turning up on time-lines with a Paratimer presence."

"What are they selling in Gupta Empire Belt where Armathan keeps transposing?"

"Mostly stuff from nearby time-lines. Nothing from First Level—they're way too backward on his Belt. There's a small profit to be made there, but no one's making any real units."

Verkan's face lit up. "I think I've got it! You've heard of metal memory, right?"

"Sure, Vall. I remember reading that you can bend a wire or foil from certain alloys, nickel and titanium for one, and it will return to its previous shape when heated."

"Exactly, Dalla. What I'm thinking is that some materials also might have a trace time-line memory; that is, they are comprised of elements and molecules particular to a single time-line and exposure to an outtime item might trigger Armathan's transposing to that particular time-line."

"Vall, that's an absolutely brilliant explanation—even if it's wrong!—because it's a hypothesis we can actually test. That is, if we can ever locate our Transtemporal Man."

VI

Chief Tortha Karf shook his head back and forth in admiration. "Great work, Vall. This isn't the kind of thing I usually expect from you, but now that you're back with Dalla maybe some of her intuition has rubbed off."

"Listening to you, the Europo-American phrase 'damning with faint praise' comes to mind. Still, we have a big hurdle before we can test my hypothesis. We need to locate Armathan."

"Wasn't he last seen on Indo-Mauryan Gupta Empire Belt?" the Chief asked.

Verkan nodded.

"So why don't we blanket that Belt with boomerang balls, it can't be all that deep."

That meant pelting each time-line in that Belt grouping with photographic auto-return balls dropped from aircars on Police Terminal over the spatial equivalents of towns and villages where Armathan cropped up most often. The difficulty was they'd have to send out several thousand balls each to millions of time-lines.

"Sorry, Chief, but we don't have enough air cars or boomerang balls to cover the area under investigation. We have to cover, at a minimum, an area of over two million individual time-lines.

"What do you suggest?" the Chief asked.

"Let's start from Armathan's last known sighting and work from there.

First, we need to contact every firm that sells or trades items on that particular time-line; once we've identified where those items come from—we send agents out and blanket each of those time-lines with boomerang balls. While the agents are there, they can contact all the local Paratimers in that area and find out which time-line they get their goods from. With a little bit of luck, most of the goods will come from under a hundred thousand nearby time-lines; we should be able to track him down in a year or two. Shpeegar help us, if any come from other Sector groupings! Then Armathan could be anywhere—"

"Actually, that's a damn good idea, Vall. Maybe it's time I vacated this desk and put someone else on it." He looked straight into Verkan's eyes.

"Don't look in my direction, Chief! I'd much rather work in the background; I hate deskwork. I enjoy going outtime and working on multiple cases: I'm a field agent at heart, and that's all."

"Well, if you like it so much, then you can organize the teams and give them their assignments."

"I'm on it, Chief."

VII

Armathan slowly came to as feeling returned to his fingers and toes. He had a really bad headache, but not as bad as the last time he'd come to. He used his fingers to explore his head; it was still covered with wrappings. He wondered how badly his head had been damaged. Every time he moved it, it felt as if something was loose inside his skull—

He tried to remember what had happened: The man in the blue robes had hit him hard on the head when he threw his fit on the street. They had judged him insane and now he was bound and in an asylum. *I'm getting too old for this...*

Still, it was good that he could remember his name and most of the details after his *jump* until he was hurt.

He remembered waking before, but now he felt as if he were in a dream state. Slowly he raised his eyelids, forcing them to remain open; they must have given him some drug to calm him down.

He was in a different small room with open-rafters and whitewashed walls, which were not very clean. There were splatters of squished bugs and other long-dried fluids. His arms and legs were strapped to the bed so moving his hands and feet was about all he could manage for the moment.

Someone must have been waiting for him to wake, as a young lady, wearing a white robe that ran from her neck to the floor, entered the room. She was unveiled and couldn't, or wouldn't, meet his eyes.

She spoke a few words in that harsh incomprehensible tongue that barely resembled human speech to his ears. He shook his head and spoke his name, "I'm Armathan. Do you understand?"

She shook her head back and forth and appeared confused. She repeated a few words, but this time with a cough-like emphasis.

He shook his head again, nodded and repeated his name.

She said, "Arm..at...han," pointing at his chest in the area of the heart.

He repeated it again.

This time she was closer. "Armath—an!"

He nodded, saying "Yes, yes. Armathan."

"Armathan!"

"Yes, yes, very good." He smiled at her, and she broke eye contact.

If this went true to form, they'd remove his bindings in three or four days; once he'd demonstrated that he wasn't going to have a fit every time the straps were removed. They might continue to give him herbs or other tinctures during that time; it varied from world to world. Some healer or nurse—maybe this one—would take pity on him, or feel a connection of some sort, and slowly as the moon-cycles went by would teach him their language. It would help his learning greatly when they released him into the common population of the asylum.

As a survival trait, he had developed the ability to learn new languages very quickly, although some were much more difficult than others. It might take him four to six cycles—depending on how soon they released him from his room—before he would speak well enough that he could explain his predicament.

The fact that he was a foreigner would eventually be determined, and that would aid his cause. Still, he was weary to death of being thought mad, strapped onto beds and cots, then having to learn new languages....

Maybe it would be better if he kept his eyes closed and stopped eating. Would they let him starve to death? Or would some compassionate caretaker force-feed him?

That depended upon how much these people valued life. He knew that the value he placed upon his own was decreasing *jump* after *jump*, year after year. Only hope kept him alive: the hope that he might return to his home and see his wife and children again. Hope that he would never *jump* again. Hope that he was not mad after all.

VIII

Verkan was going over a report from Maldar Dard on the first hundred time-lines his team had covered in the Transtemporal Man search. So far there hadn't been any trace of Armathan, but his teams had reports on over a thousand discrete time-lines and they were making progress, even if only in eliminating negatives. The other teams would be reporting in soon.

Zulthran Torv, the mathematician in charge of the Paratime Police Computer Office, had just supplied him with a list of most of the First Level companies that had dealings in that two-hundred parayear area centered around Armathan's transpositions. He needed to send Maldar and the other Transtemporal Man teams a copy of the list via the next wave of outgoing message balls.

The intercom squawked and Verkan looked up from his visiscreen. His secretary informed him that he had a visitor: "A Volzar Darv from the Rhogom Foundation."

"Send him in, Karoth."

Volzar Darv was of indeterminate age, probably in his mid-second century, with a thin ascetic face, hawk-like nose and black eyes that looked as if they could turn flesh into stone.

Verkan rose and they touched hands in greeting. "I assume you're here in regards to the Transtemporal Man affair."

"You assume correctly, Special Chief's Assistant. By the way, I am addressed either as Director Volzar or Scholar Volzar."

"Very well, Director Volzar. What can I do for you?" Verkan forced himself to be polite, although he already disliked Volzar's condescending manner. The two men had never met before, but he'd heard Dalla gripe at length about the Director's heavy-handed management style.

"The Foundation has received information that you are making inquiries into Armathan's present location. Is this true?"

"Yes it is, Director. We have reason to believe that Armathan is a threat to the Paratime Secret, which gives the Paratime Police the authority to override all previous directives and restrictions in regards to this individual or anyone else."

"Are you people mad? Armathan was born and has lived, with few exceptions, in a pre-mechanical culture and wouldn't understand the Paratime secret if it was spelled out for him. However, he does have an ability that would be of inestimable value to both the Foundation and to the welfare of Home Time Line society in general. We are Armathan's proper custodians and I implore you to call off this misguided search before he is captured or his abilities damaged—"

"We're no more likely to damage his so-called abilities than you are," Verkan replied, using First Level breathing techniques and mind control to keep his temper in check.

"That's not what we've heard from Commissioner Vardran Lydar."

So that's where the Paratime Commission leak is, Verkan thought to himself. "Just what did you hear from the Commissioner?"

"That Paratime Police Chief Tortha Karf had requested permission to kill the Transtemporal Man on sight! He even got the backing of the rest of the Commission to commit this heinous act...."

"The Chief is worried that Armathan might transpose to a time-line where his knowledge would be catastrophic for all of First Level," Verkan replied, "since we still don't know how or why he is able to travel from one time-line to another."

"That's why he should be protected, not harmed! The Transtemporal Man may well have the most important parapsychological genetic trait that we have ever discovered—the ability to travel transtemporally without mechanical aids. It will be *your* Department's responsibility if this great treasure is lost or destroyed!"

"First of all, Armathan is a human being, not a treasure," Verkan noted. With all his talk of protection, the Director had not once referred to Armathan by name. "True," he continued, "Armathan may or may not have the ability to transpose without a conveyer; however, whether he does or does not have this capacity has not been proven conclusively. Nor will it be until he has been located and isolated."

"We are certain that he does have this gift; it's been verified by the readings of three of our top psychics."

"If you can't locate him, then how can your psychics 'read' him?" Verkan asked.

Director Volzar shook his head with a look of dismay, as if he were dealing with an idiot or blind man. "Precogs don't have to be on a time-line to read a person; they just have to be able to 'touch' something that has passed through his hands. Precognition is a recognized psychic ability—"

Verkan quickly interrupted before he got the full spiel. "Recognized by whom? The Rhogom Foundation and several million crackpots. No reputable scientist accepts precognition as a verifiable phenomenon."

Volzar shook his head. "None are so blind— I'm used to this hostility from the uninformed. By its very nature, 'seeing into the future,' is a cognitive perception which cannot be repeated like some rat pressing a lever. The very act of 'seeing' re-determines the future event! It's along the same lines as quantum mechanics. On Fourth Level they have a very quaint term for it: Schrödinger's Cat."

"I'm familiar with that particular feline and the state of the cat itself would be a quantum superposition—hypothetically, either alive or dead. Although I doubt it has anything to do with any theoretical psychic phenomenon.

"The real question, Director is: why haven't your agents been able to find Armathan after two decades of searching? I can tell you why, your people are rank amateurs when it comes to locating people who don't want to be found. That is our Department's specialty. The crime here is that we weren't notified of this man as soon as his ability was discovered!"

"We were afraid of just this kind of harassment and interference that both you and Chief Tortha are noted for," Director Volzar said, his voice rising. "We have made it our mission to find and nurture the Transtemporal Man's talents."

"Well, it's hard to nurture something you don't have, Volzar. I will grant you this: if Armathan does have half the abilities the Foundation's credited him with, he's the most important human being in the universe. And, to that end, we will comb the parayears where we suspect he's hidden, even if we have to visit every time-line on the Indo-Mauryan Subsector."

"Just don't let your officers hurt even one strand of hair on his head! If your people bungle this operation, I will see to it that it's brought to the attention of the Executive Council."

"You're a little late, Director Volzar. I've already taken the liberty of informing the Paratime Commission of the Rhogom Foundation's violation of the Paratime Code; they are quite aware that you've wasted decades of navel gazing on this matter. We'll see who comes out of this with a black eye!"

IX

Verkan looked up from his viewscreen as Paratime Police Inspector Kostran Garth barged into his office unannounced.

"Verkan, I think you're going to want to come with me."

"Garth, what's this all about?"

"It's Armathan, we've found the time-line where he formerly resided until two ten-days ago." Kostran ran off a group of numerical and symbol coordinates that represented the exact Indo-Mauryan, Gupta Empire time-line.

"That's great!" Verkan exclaimed, as he took his green uniform jacket out of the auto-closet in his desk drawer and shook the wrinkles out. It was about time, too; the Transtemporal Man Teams had already investigated over a hundred thousand discrete time-lines. The heat coming down on the Department from above was red hot. "Did you find any clues that might indicate where he transposed?"

"Not yet, but we took your advice about showing his picture to everyone within a twenty mile radius of Garat Village. Garat is about a hundred and fifty miles south of Ravartol Equivalent, usually referred to on Europo-America as Istanbul; however, on most Indo-Mauryan Subsectors it's named Byzantium. The Greeks were conquered by the Persians throughout the Indus-Ganges-Irrawaddy Sector Grouping and Byzantium's usually a backwater town on the Anatolian peninsula. Within five parayears, there are three major languages, one Indo-European and two Semitic derivatives, which have not made things easy on our boy. Still, most of the First Level operations on this subsector are small independent firms; few import anything farther than a dozen parayears away. We've got agents combing their records now."

"That makes our job a lot easier," Verkan said, as they entered the anti-grav shaft and floated down to Terminal Dispatch on the ground floor.

"We had five identity hits on three time-lines within a two parayear radius from his last known transposition," Kostran Garth said. "Here's the really interesting fact: so far, none of the Armathan Teams have found *any* other Armathan on any time-line they've visited."

Verkan felt his heart race over that news and automatically slowed his heartbeat. First Time Line thought processes allowed conscious thought control over most of the body's autonomic responses. "That means we've found ourselves a real anomaly, a unique Paratemporal Personality."

"Which is why Doctor Nentrov says we've only discovered one Transtemporal Man on Indo-Mauryan. Nentrov believes Armathan's a genetic sport, a once in an eon phenomenon. He may well be the first man or animal with this talent in our Parauniverse. And the last, if we don't find him fast. The Rhogom Foundation has their own teams looking for him; if they get hold of him first—well, you know what will happen."

Verkan nodded. Armathan would conveniently disappear on some Fifth Level time-line where the Foundation would poke and prod him until he either died or they discovered what they were looking for.

"The Paratime Commission is split right down the middle over this case and jurisdiction will go to the first one who finds him," he said.

"Well, we've got the manpower," Kostran said. "The Foundation's already wasted twenty-four years diddling around trying to find him. I wouldn't worry, boss."

"I'm not worried about finding him first; it's all the political monkeyshines on Home Time Line that are worrying me. This Transtemporal Man case should be a straightforward case of a Paratime Code violation."

"Nothing stays simple the moment politics get involved."

"And that's the damn truth. Do I need to pick up clothing from Stores?" Verkan asked.

"No, we'll have the appropriate tunic and trousers you can wear at our temporary conveyer depot. All the teams are wearing local products until the Transtemporal Man is found."

They were now on the ground floor moving on the slideway through the two-story oval portal leading to the conveyer rotunda room looming overhead. The portal was faced with glassine bricks on both sides, each containing the face of a Paratime Police officer lost in the line of duty. Both men automatically saluted as they passed under the entrance. Many of the faces were new, the result of a recent full-blown shoot out on First Level Abzar Sector.

The hanger-sized Terminal Dispatch room was overflowing with field agents and operatives, as it had been every moment of every day for the last ten thousand years. Police officers were checking in or out, with the jukebox shaped robot clerks or human attendants, at the large dispatch desk at the center of the room. Many were in standard Paratime Police greens, like themselves, or wore civilian tunics. Others were dressed in outtime costumes from time-lines all over Paratime: Aryan-Transpacific breastplates and morion helmets spouting multi-colored plumes, black and yellow hooded robes from Styphon's House Subsector, sunbonnets and striped robes of the Third Level Esaron Sector, conical caps and fringed robes from Second Level Khiftan Sector, silver-mesh skinsuits from Second Level Triplanetary Empire and several hundred operatives in full Legionnaire's kit from Macedonian Empire Sector.

There must be something going down on Fourth Level Macedonian, Verkan thought, making a mental note to check with Records upon his return to Police HQ. Kostran led him to a small conveyer waiting in the Reserve Annex; he gave a chit to the conveyer tech and opened the portal granting them entrance. It was a fixed-route conveyer which shuttled operatives only between Home Time Line and Fifth Level Police Terminal, from which most of the Paratime Police operations were routed.

Inside Kostran shoved in the starting lever, while Verkan relaxed in one of the chairs, waiting for the transposition field to build up around them. While they waited, Kostran said, "I brought a hypno-mech for the Dyrald language so you can question the locals yourself."

As the mesh dome of the conveyer vanished, Kostran opened the cabinet from behind the passenger seat on his side, removed one of the blue plastic helmets on swinging arms, placing it on Verkan's head. The transposition to Fifth Level Police Terminal from the Paratime Building would take enough time for hypnotic-mechanical language instruction. To learn the culture and its idiosyncrasies would have required another three or four hours or more of hypnotic indoctrination, but Verkan didn't need to pass for a local for this mission.

Kostran took out an injector and gave him a quick pneumatic-hypno injection. Verkan promptly fell asleep. While he was in R.E.M. sleep, the Dyraldic language, with all its vocabulary and grammar, became part of his subconscious knowledge; he needed only the mental pronunciation of a trigger symbol, or to hear Dyrald spoken, to bring it into consciousness.

When Verkan woke up the conveyer was already arriving at Dhergabar Equivalent, showing flickering images through the slowly materializing mesh. From there it was just a quick rocket trip to the Ravartol Equivalent where they were quickly shuttled via aircar to another conveyer in an underground bunker. From that rotunda-head they took another transtemporal jaunt to the temple basement on the Gupta Empire time-line they wanted to visit.

The moment the conveyer materialized it was surrounded by several Paratime Police field operatives, all armed and checking for accidental pickups, which was standard operating procedure. Verkan and Kostran quickly changed into the local costume, beige tunics and brown woolen trousers. Then they were quickly taken upstairs for a conference with Dr. Nentrov Dard, Paratime Police Psychist; he was a tiny man with a distinguished face and graying goatee. He looked a bit like photos Verkan had seen of Sigmund Freud, an outtime quack who was famous on the Fourth

Level Europo-America Subsector where he'd investigated the Nighthound Incident. Every time he saw Dr. Nentrov, Verkan wondered if this resemblance was accidental, or an affectation.

"Chief's Assistant Verkan. Good to have you here. I understand you're responsible for the success of the Transtemporal Man Operation."

"I won't call it a success until we collar our man. I am pleased that we've identified the time-line he last transposed from. That should make locating him a lot easier."

Nentrov nodded. "Armathan may well prove to be the most important living human being in all of Paratime. I find it hard to believe the audacity of the Rhogom Foundation in covering up his very existence; it's an outrage! They have always been reticent in sharing the results of their research so I shouldn't be surprised—"

"Doctor, we're not here to adjudicate the misdeeds of the Foundation, but to find Armathan before he transposes again, maybe this time to a sector where his knowledge might jeopardize the Paratime secret."

"Yes, you're right. I do get caught up with the spirit of scientific inquiry— But enough of that. Since I sent you the last message ball, one of the Teams has discovered his family."

"We were wondering if they'd turn up," Verkan said.

"So was I, until Team 687 transposed to their time-line with a picture of the Transtemporal Man and he was identified. Our informant knew the family and told us where to find them. Since Armathan's departure, they've fallen on hard times. They were transposed here less than an hour ago and secured in the safe-house above. I decided it was best to wait until you arrived before interrogating the family."

"Kostran, have them released and brought to me."

"Yes, sir. But there's someone you should see first." He turned and went up the brick stairs to the temple floor.

X

A few minutes later, Dalla walked down the stairs. She was still angry with Verkan, but knew it was misdirected; after all, he was only following orders. Still, he was so damn inflexible.

"What are you doing here?" Verkan asked. They hadn't talked much, either in the office or at home, for the past two ten-days.

She looked him right in the eye. "The same thing you are, buster. I want to make sure that you or one of your team members doesn't disincarnate the Transtemporal Man or his family."

Verkan shook his head. "The standing orders from above are: 'Don't harm anyone unless it appears they are about to transpose. Then shoot to kill.' This is straight from the Paratime Commissioner. Is that clear enough for you?"

Dalla looked sick. "Verkan—"

Then he winked at her. "We don't have time to talk, now. This is our job. We follow orders—even if we don't always like them, *or* agree with them."

Suddenly she got it! What Verkan was trying to tell her was that he would only follow orders if he absolutely thought Armanthan endangered the Paratime secret. Besides, if someone was about to transpose, they would do it in a nanosecond—so fast, there wouldn't be any time to shoot. Dalla felt lightheaded with relief.

Verkan leaned over and in their own language, whispered, "All this is being recorded. We'll talk later."

She smiled.

Kostran came back downstairs with a woman he introduced as Elsandrana, and two boys. She appeared to be in her early fifties, but was probably a decade or two younger, dressed in fresh robes provided by the Team. From the ground-in dirt and disheveled appearance of her hair, it wasn't hard to tell that the family was from the lowest strata of society. The oldest boy appeared to be in his early teens, while not shaving yet—certainly just entering puberty.

"Elsandrana, how long has it been since you've seen Armathan, your husband?"

She scowled, then spat on the floor. "That dung-sucking weasel, he deserted us. He left us with an empty purse and an empty larder." Her voice was too weary to display any of the anger or antipathy her words contained.

Verkan didn't bother to explain the circumstances, Dalla noted. Elsandrana couldn't have understood Armathan's disappearance; even he didn't. Dalla doubted that Armathan had left on purpose; he had probably been as distressed as his family to find himself once again on a new time-line. Maybe more so. All his years transposing from one time-line to another could only have left him with a void inside and few attachments to any one time-line—except maybe this one where he had left a family and a prosperous business.

"How long was your husband with you?" Verkan asked.

"Who are you people? Rich men, that much I know. You take us from our village; then put us to sleep, and now we're in this old temple I've never seen before. What is—"

Verkan removed a silver coin from a fat pigskin purse on the table. "Please sit down."

Her eyes widened and she promptly sat on the chair. Kostran indicated to the boys that they were to sit as well.

"Let's set some ground rules, Elsandrana," Verkan said in a voice that brooked no dissent. "You are here at our command. I am a noble of the House of Varnayan; if your answers please me, you will leave here with much silver. If not—" he gave her his most rakish grin.

Elsandrana shuddered. "Yes, Lord. Please forgive me." She lowered her head.

The boys looked as if they were about to break out into tears.

Dalla knew that Verkan hated to bully people who couldn't fight back, but in this case they were short of time and ideas so he really didn't have much choice—not with the Paratime Commission looking over their shoulders and demanding a speedy resolution.

"It's been eight, maybe nine, years since he disappeared," the woman answered, tears tracing a path down her dirty cheeks. "It's hard for me to talk of...Armathan. I was a good wife, I made sacrifices to the Goddess. I don't understand..."

Armathan's last known disappearance had been around eight years ago. It looked like they were making good progress.

"Did your husband ever leave before?"

"No, that's why I was so distressed. Armathan was a good provider and a good father to his sons. He had a good job as a silversmith and owned his own shop. It was small, but we lived well and I was happy; the Goddess had showered us with gifts. So I had no warning that my husband was so displeased with us..." She began to sob.

Verkan gave her a short time to compose herself. It was obvious she knew nothing that might help them locate her husband; however, that did lead him to the next question.

"Did he take anything with him when he left?"

"No. He was on his way home from his shop when he took off."

"So there was no warning?"

"No, and the man who worked for him didn't notice anything unusual. I've had many years to ponder over his leaving, and to this day it doesn't make sense."

"Elsandrana, did you ever consider he might have been kidnapped?"

She pulled back. "No, Your Lordship. We had no bags of silver for ransom. True, my husband made a modest income, but nothing to attract that kind of attention. He must have deserted us."

Dalla could tell by the pain reflected in her eyes that she had considered some of the more unpleasant reasons he might have disappeared. Even in small backwaters, there were swift and dark currents that were best not brought into the light.

"One last question. Have either of your boys ever taken off or disappeared suddenly?"

She shook her head. "They're good boys and they do as they're told."

Verkan looked at the boys. They both shook their heads as though the idea had never come up.

Dalla would hypno-mech them later; although, she doubted either of them had inherited their father's talent. Still, it was worth checking out.

She wanted to do a thorough job, since her files would be going to both the Paratime Police files as well as the Foundation's archives. Of course, the boys would be monitored carefully for the rest of their lives, just in case there was some age-related factor to psychic transposition. Would they let her publish a paper about this? If so, she would call this new talent—teletransporting....

No, that was too controversial... If she brought it up, Old Tortha would have a stroke!

When the interrogation was over and they went back upstairs to the temporary office, she asked, "Verkan, what do you think will happen to them?"

He gave her a hug. "I'm glad you're talking to me, again." He nodded very slightly. "Let's go outside and smoke a cigarette."

That was his code for talking in private. The spy-eyes and tell-tales were so prevalent on First Level that one almost took them for granted.

Once they were in the market square, safe from prying cameras and recorders for the moment, she said, "I'm not mad at you, darling—you just happen to be the only one I can safely vent my emotions on. And sometimes it's so maddening! The way we have to conduct our business...I don't always like it."

Verkan pulled away and looked into her eyes. "I don't either. I hated intimidating that poor woman, but there was no nice way to do the job. It's the nature of police business. You'll get used to it, even if you don't always like it."

"Is that what you've done?"

He nodded.

"So what about your orders to shoot Armathan on sight if he appears to be transposing?"

"Tortha's orders were to shoot him on sight. It's probably the smartest thing we can do as far as protecting the Paratime secret is concerned. On the other hand, the Foundation Director, Volzar Darv, has convinced the Paratime Commissioner that Armathan's some sort of sacred cow. Now we're supposed to tag him with a tell-tale and not fire unless he appears to be transposing—"

"How are you supposed to know?" Dalla asked.

Verkan shrugged. "We can't tell. That's why it's such a farce. Now that I've gone over the records and heard the family; I don't think he's much of a threat."

She exhaled loudly. "I'm glad to hear you say that. What are we going to do with the family?"

Verkan paused to light his pipe and then said: "The Rhogom Foundation has botched this operation. I'm not going to give them a parasecond of help unless we get orders from above. We'll hold the family in custody until this mess is straightened out. If, or when, we find Armathan, his family will be a good bargaining chip to ensure his cooperation."

Dalla was about to defend the Foundation, instead she thought about what she was going to say instead of just speaking her mind. Verkan was right; the Foundation had bungled the Transtemporal Man case from the beginning. If they'd elicited help from the Paratime Police, they'd have found Armathan two decades ago and all the questions they had would have been answered. Now, he was still running around loose and nobody knew where.

XI

Verkan was seated at his desk at his alternate office on Police Terminal waiting for the Transtemporal Man Teams to report in. Over a ten-day had passed since he'd interviewed the family. The teams had already surveyed over half the time-lines in the Gupta Belt; if it turned out Armathan had transposed himself to another sector or belt there was going to be Shpeegar's Own Mouth of feedback on Home Time Line!

There was another ping announcing the arrival of a new message ball at the dispatch desk. Inspector Kostran Garth was manning the desk himself and he knew that any important news would be brought to his desk immediately. Still, that didn't stop Verkan from wanting to go over to Kostran and watch over his shoulder as he opened the mesh-wrapped automatic transposition sphere. But that would be bad for morale, signaling he didn't trust his subordinates to do their jobs—or, even worse, alert them to the fact that their superior was in a dither.

He wished he could be like Dalla, who was still on the Gupta time-line where they'd interviewed Armathan's family. She was collecting data so that she might come up with a better understanding of the cultural matrix from which he'd sprung. It was also true that Dalla had an insatiable curiosity, which on this job was an advantage.

Verkan's problem was he hated inactivity. He was a hands-on type and would have much preferred to be heading one of the search teams.

There were three pings in a row.

Kostran stood up from his desk, after opening the first message ball, saying: "Jackpot! I think you ought to see this."

"What is it?"

"It looks like they've found our quarry, boss."

Verkan looked over Kostran's back at his viewscreen, where he saw a raw-faced man dressed in a faded gray tunic. "This is Field Agent Eldran Kron from Team 447: Two-One-Zero Day, 1145 hours. We made some discreet inquiries regarding our subject and have learned that he arrived on this time-line on approximately One-Seven-Eight Day. He arrived at the central market square and made a commotion speaking in a foreign tongue and attacking a passing youth. He was described as severely agitated, as he broke the boy's wrist and struck out at a member of the local constabulary. He was beaten unconscious and taken to a cell, which is standard operating procedure on this belt.

"The subject was taken into custody, remitted to an infirmary where his wounds were treated. When he was able to travel, he was remanded to the care of the local madhouse, or whatever it is that passes for an insane asylum on this Belt. This facility is maintained by the priestess of the Cult of the Goddess Varnatha, an earth-mother and healer goddess; it appears that our subject has been confined there since his arrival. We are reconnoitering the facility and awaiting further orders. Eldran Kron signing out."

"Excellent! Kostran, send a message ball to Dalla and tell her to meet us here." He rang out the coordinates for the time-line in question. "Next, send Agent Eldran a message ball telling him that he and his team are *not* to approach Armathan personally. Secondly, they are to provide the two of us with local costumes made of material from that time-line, likewise they will also be attired in local garments. I want them to establish credentials for me as a visiting noble and provide me with a purse of local specie more than sufficient to our purpose, which is to take possession of the Transtemporal Man by bribery—with force only as a last resort.

"Thirdly, they are to ensure that they have a safe-room to hold him in until we determine his disposition. Said safe-room will not contain any articles of any sort that are not of local manufacture.

"Fourthly, they are to prepare us a surgery for possible immediate use until we determine the extent of the subject's injuries. They are to find ways to manufacture surgical implements using only ores and metals from said time-line. Finally, arrange a conveyer to transpose us to said time-line; I want to keep this as low key as we can. There will only be the three us—myself, Dalla and Dr. Avron Sorn. If we need any further help, we can request it after our arrival."

XII

Instead of a nightmare, this time Armathan woke up with another blinding headache. They'd taken the wrappings off his skull the day before, but his wound still hadn't healed. Now he had a headache that felt as if someone was pushing a pin through his left eye socket. The attendants had removed the straps while he was sleeping, so he was at least able to wipe the tears from his eyes with his sleeve. They seemed kinder here than at the last asylum he had *jumped* to. There they had beaten him for most of a moon; later he had learned they had thought they were driving the devils from his flesh.

The nice nurse, who still wouldn't look him in the eye, came by every afternoon and gave him language lessons. He was certain she was the one responsible for getting his restraints removed. The dizziness and headaches he suffered from made learning the guttural sounds she spoke more difficult than he'd experienced in the past, but at least he was making progress. Regardless, he was as ignorant of their language as a young child; it would take him another four or five moons to learn enough to speak it with any proficiency.

He was beginning to consider that he might never leave this place alive. And that really wasn't such a bad thing: no more disappearances, showing up unexpectedly or having to convince strangers he wasn't insane or a criminal. After this last *jump*, an eternity of painless, dreamless sleep looked very inviting. He had long ago given up his belief in the gods, who—if they existed at all—were as indifferent to his fate as the very rocks in the ground.

Armathan heard gruff voices outside his door. His heart began to race again and it took all his concentration to slow its irregular beat. The door opened suddenly, illuminating the room with sunlight. He screeched in pain as the bright light speared his eyes.

"Everything is going to be all right," he heard in the tongue of his childhood.

The gods have delivered me! I bow to your greatness, I believe! I just wasn't desperate enough before....

Two big men came in and unfolded a long cot with handles. Another tall hawk-nosed man wearing the signet ring of nobility watched the men carefully. The priestesses treated them as if they were great lords, bowing and shuffling. It only took them a few moments to carefully cradle him onto the cot. He only groaned once.

"Armathan, we'll get you to a healer soon," the noble said. "We are your friends. We will take you to a safe place. Don't leave us."

"No, not at the moment of my deliverance! I praise you Evantos, God of Light!"

One of the men pressed a stick to his upper arm; he felt something cool hit his flesh through the over-garment. Suddenly, he felt at peace. *Now I can sleep....*

XIII

Armathan had been in the temporary surgery room for over four hours. Verkan was beginning to worry, when the Medic came out of the room shaking his head. "It's hard to do good work without the right diagnostic aids and surgical tools. He's got a bad head wound with some bits of bone loose inside the skull; I don't need a machine to tell me that. I got most of the bone splinters out, but he should have been operated on two ten-days ago! We need to get him to First Level for further treatment."

"Will he survive?" Verkan asked.

"Yes, despite his age and poor nutrition, he's got the constitution of an ox. If we can get him some proper care, I'd say he'll make an almost complete recovery. The temporal lobe damage was slight. He may have some residual effects, but it's too early to tell at this time without the proper equipment."

Dalla touched him on the shoulder. "Vall, what are we going to do?"

"We don't have much choice. We'll have to stay here; we can't risk a transtemporal transposition to Home Time Line—"

Kostran barged in suddenly, his face drawn and blanched; behind him were two men in gray uniforms—with a shoulder patch displaying a stylized symbol of a red atom in a yellow field—each holding a long baton-like ultrasonic paralyzer. The paralyzers could either be set on stun or lethal and worked on anything animal or human having a central nervous system. It was a good weapon to use outtime for that reason; even on a civilized timeline, the most elaborate autopsy would reveal no specific cause of death.

Verkan was unfamiliar with the emblem, but recognized the paralyzers as being of First Level manufacture. "Who are—"

"Where is the patient, Chief's Assistant?"

Dalla was rigid, deathly pale.

"I want to see some credentials before I say another word," Verkan answered.

"Here's a note from your Chief," the taller of the two men said, holding out a note between two fingers with the Chief's letterhead.

Verkan carefully took it with his thumb and forefinger. He opened it and read:

Verkan, the Transtemporal Man Case is no longer under our jurisdiction. These men are from the Department of Scientific Oversight. I don't expect you've ever heard of this department, few have other than myself, the Paratime Commissioner and Manager of the Executive Council; if you have heard of them, I want to know how? However, in matters scientific, normal or paranormal, they outrank us, as well as the Rhogom Foundation.

Their authority exceeds my own. I expect you to cooperate fully with the two agents who have been dispatched to remove the subject. After that, we are to purge all files with references to this case and forget it every happened.

Tortha Karf, Chief
Department of Paratime Police

Verkan didn't like this at all; first, he didn't like learning outtime about an organization on Home Time Line that outranked his own. Nor did he like the Chief's order that he cooperate, not after spending over two ten-days locating his elusive subject. However, the writ sounded like the Chief's no-nonsense prose and he suspected it would be in all their best interest to cooperate—no matter how much it rankled!

"I assume you are going to leave with the subject."

"Yes," the tall man said.

"Do you know that he needs medical assistance and quickly?" Verkan asked.

"No, but it's good to know. We have a facility that will take care of him."

"Do you fully understand that we do not completely know why or how the subject transposes from one time-line to another?"

The tall man frowned. "What exactly do you mean?"

"It has been my hypothesis," Verkan stated, "that he transposes when in contact with an item of outtime manufacture, that is, an artifact produced on another time-line that is not from the time-line where he presently resides. Due to Armathan's illness and security issues, we have not been able to put this to the test. However, we have determined once and for all that the mere presence of another human being from another time-line does not trigger his transposition."

"What is all this supposed to mean to us?" the tall man said, with a condescending smirk.

"How do you expect to get him to your 'facility'?" Verkan asked.

"We'll put him on a conveyer and transpose him there—how else?"

"I believe you gentlemen are not as familiar with the subject as you should be. If my hypothesis is correct, anything you have on your person made on another time-line might trigger his transposition. Which means, he might transpose to the Ravartol Equivalent on Home Time Line, if something from First Level triggers his 'talent' first—otherwise, who knows where?"

The shorter agent looked at the taller one. "They didn't tell us anything about this."

The taller one shook his head in disgust. He held out his paralyzer, pointing it at Verkan, Dalla and Kostran. "I want all of you out of here. Go to the conveyer depot downstairs."

As they trudged down the brick stairs, Dalla asked, "You don't think?"

Verkan shrugged. "What else. They didn't come to rescue him."

They heard some shouting from the upper room and looked back. A head was outlined at the top of the stairway: "Get back up here!"

Verkan laughed. "Not our problem anymore. I hope you have fun explaining that one to your boss!"

There were a couple of choice expletives, and then the head moved away and they continued downstairs.

"Do you think he'll get away?" Dalla asked.

"Those paralyzers are made on Fifth Level Industrial, their uniforms are probably from Fourth Level, and who knows what else they were carrying. The moment they hit the trigger range—" He clapped his hands together! "What else? I hope Armathan's far, far away, by now."

XIV

"Hi, Chief," Verkan said, as he entered the Chief's office.

Tortha took the cigar he wasn't smoking out of his mouth. "Verkan, I just got an interesting call from Dalgroth Sorn."

Verkan knew him well. Dalgroth was the Paratime Commissioner of Security. He nodded, "I take it the call was about our Transtemporal Man."

Tortha nodded. "I don't think you're going to like it, old son." Anytime the Chief called him "old son" he knew it was bad news.

"Give it to me, straight."

"The Director of the Department of Scientific Oversight told him to order us to find Armathan, again. I don't believe I need to tell you what my answer was."

"I hope it was no," Verkan said, "because if it wasn't, you're going to need another donkey to pull your load."

Tortha raised his hands up with palms out. "No need to get angry, Verkan. I know you just got back from Ravartol Equivalent, but you're not the only one with tomato all over his face."

"Good, because I've got a bone to pick with you. Why wasn't I ever told about this Scientific Oversight outfit?"

For the first time in their association, Tortha made a sheepish grin. "I didn't learn a thing about it until I was sworn in as Chief—I swear by the Fangs of Fasif! Then I was sworn to complete secrecy. Now, I can talk to you about them because they met with you officially, although I had to pledge my grandchildren and a lot of favors to keep them from giving the three of you a memory obliteration session."

"Thanks for nothing—"

"It wasn't for nothing, old son. Despite all claims to the contrary, you and I know that once you've gone through an obliteration session you lose more than just a few select memories. If you don't believe me, just ask Dalla, she's a qualified Psychist. Sometimes it can take a few more memories, in rare cases even a year or two."

"Well, I thank you for that, but what's it going to cost us?" Verkan asked begrudgingly.

"For one," Tortha said, "you can never tell anyone about the Transtemporal Man Case. All machine and written records have already been wiped. Secondly, you never heard of the Oversight Department. You can never talk about it—to anyone!"

"You mean because they've got us monitored?"

"We're all monitored, all the time. We just pretend we don't know it. Haven't you ever wondered why we don't use all the scientific developments they have on Second and Third Level?"

"Of course. I just put it down to cultural stagnation," Verkan answered.

"That's part of it. The other part is that too much knowledge is as dangerous as not enough. How many civilizations have we watched go down in nuclear flames or die out due to biological warfare?"

Verkan shook his head. "Too many to count."

"Look at Fourth Level Europo-America if you want to see a subsector on the verge of nuclear annihilation. There are whole Sectors on Second and Third Levels that are off-limits even today due to biological and chemical poisoning. What you don't know, is that it's the Department of Oversight's job to find those sectors and belts and keep us Home Time-liners off them. There are sectors thousands of parayears deep that are proscribed—some for the next ten thousand years. Their other job is to see that we don't go down those same roads. . . ."

Verkan sighed. "I've been outtime long enough to know there's some justification for Scientific Oversight. It also answers the question of why a civilization as old as ours is scientifically inferior to those time-lines we frequently harvest. But, damn, I hate it when outsiders and politicians get involved in our police business."

"And I don't?" Tortha cried, jamming his cigar back in his mouth and lighting it. "I was livid when Chief Zarvan told me about the Department just before he retired. Just as my successor"—he paused to look Verkan right in the eyes—"will be when I retire."

"Don't look at me, Chief. I've got other plans."

"Harrumph. We'll see about that. I had to make a few promises to get you off the hook, especially after you refused to help find our missing voyager—"

"Don't even go there, Chief. I've done nothing else for the last two ten-days but look for Armathan. I *even* found him! It wasn't my fault they disregarded my suggestion on how to handle him. . . ."

"Well, lucky for you, that was all recorded and the recordings back you up. They disregarded my advice about outtime artifact contamination, which I got from you. Do you have any idea what happened to Armathan?"

"Dr. Avron Sorn was the only one in the surgery when they busted him. I talked to him back on Police Terminal; he still doesn't know who they were—"

"Don't tell him," Tortha ordered. "By now he won't remember a thing about the whole incident. My blanket wasn't big enough to exclude him from memory obliteration."

"Too bad. Anyway, Dr. Avron told me Armathan was still unconscious from his brain operation, when the two Oversight agents came into the surgery with their paralyzers drawn. He said what happened completely verified my theory; even before they could fire—it appears they had orders to shoot on sight—Armathan flickered a few times and then disappeared, all in blink of an eye!

"Avron's hypothesis is that the flickering was due to all the outtime artifact contaminants the agents brought with them into the room. We'll probably never know which was the overriding 'trigger,' but he did disappear for good."

"Do you think he'll even survive the transposition?" Tortha asked.

"I don't know. Avron thought he might, if he arrived in a secluded area. He said the operation was successful despite the primitive tools; he thinks he was able to remove all the loose skull fragments out of the brain pan. But he lost a lot of blood and it's impossible to guess what might happen when he rematerializes on an unknown time-line unconscious."

Tortha exhaled a cloud of smoke. "Since the triggers the agents brought with them, by their very nature, were from civilized time-lines, it's possible he might receive adequate care as a"—he paused for a moment to use his total recall— "'John Doe,' as they call unknown persons on Europo-American."

Verkan laughed. "If he ends up on that subsector, the officials in charge will never believe a word he says!"

"I know," Tortha chuckled. "Our disinformation broadcasts on 'little green men,' 'flying saucers' and 'Abominable Snowmen' have got them doubting their own senses. Let's hope he transposed there instead of on a really sophisticated time-line such as Second Level Triplanetary."

"We'd better hope so, if we mean to keep the Paratime secret inviolate."

Tortha's face suddenly tightened. "Really, this is no laughing matter. Those agents have jeopardized us all and I'm going to remind Paratime Commissioner Dalgroth of that every time we speak until I retire. From what he told me, those two will be lucky not to be assigned permanently to Second Level Khiftan Sector.

"Now, they've got all their people looking for Armathan. I bowed out when I reminded Commissioner Dalgroth that too many of our troops would have to learn about the Transtemporal Man if we expanded our search to all five levels. He agreed. Now, it's all the Department of Scientific Oversight's problem. Do you think they'll locate him, Vall?"

Verkan shook his head. "I saw those two; they had more gadgets than a paratemporal conveyer tech. Armathan could be anywhere."

"Do you think that might be a problem?"

"I don't think so. He needed medical care, but he's tough. From what I know of him, he doesn't like to talk about his *jumps* as he calls them. Too many people come to the conclusion that he's crazy, as it is. I think the Paratime Secret is safe—for now."

"Good," Tortha said. "I'll pass that one on to the Commission. They'll be glad to hear your summation."

"What about the Rhogom Foundation?" Verkan asked.

"They're out of it, too."

"Armathan's family?"

Tortha paused to relight his cigar with a flick of his everlite. "With Armathan missing, no one's paid much attention to them. Commissioner Dalgroth's worried that the kids may have inherited their father's talent—teletransposing, I believe Dalla calls it. He wants the entire family contained and isolated in a special holding area on an unpopulated time-line on First Level Dwarma Sector. However, I did get one concession out of them; Dalla has an oversight position over the family."

"Well, that's better than nothing. I guess we'll just have to wait and see what happens with the children."

"Meanwhile, thanks to the samples your Medico brought back, the Rhogom Foundation geneticists are going over their father's genes molecule by molecule."

"I hope their search comes up blank."

"Why, Verkan? Bitterness isn't your style."

"Chief, it isn't bitterness; I was just thinking of how complicated *our* job would be if this genetic sport, or whatever it is, became common throughout Paratime. You know your favorite saying—"

Tortha nodded, as he looked up at the Tri-D picture of the beautiful girl being stabbed in the heart by one of the priests of Fasif. In his cups one evening, Tortha had confessed to Verkan that he kept the picture of the beautiful girl being sacrificed by the priests of Fasif on his wall as a reminder to himself that no Paratime Police plan ever survives contact with outtimers.

"Yes, I do," Tortha said, "and it's especially true in this case. I don't even want to think about the chaos of unrestricted transposing, even from our own people!"

Verkan cringed. "Neither, do I."

"As if the force doesn't have enough problems now; and speaking of problems, it's probably time you got back to whatever you were working on before this emergency popped up."

"Gladly, Chief. Gladly."

The End

www.ingramcontent.com/pod-product-compliance
Lightning Source LLC
Chambersburg PA
CBHW060602310726
48982CB00008B/1204/J

* 9 7 8 0 9 3 7 9 1 2 7 4 4 *